VALLEY OF THE SERPENT

ALAN REYNOLDS

Fisher King Publishing

Valley Of The Serpent

Fisher King Publishing Ltd
The Studio, Arthington Lane
Pool-in-Wharfedale
LS21 1JZ
England

www.fisherkingpublishing.co.uk

With gratitude to Rick Armstrong for his
unstinting support, guidance and friendship;
also to Samantha Richardson and
Rachel Topping at Fisher King Publishing.

Dedicated to my family and friends, and to all those
who have supported me in my writing –
your encouragement is greatly appreciated.

Much love, Alan.

Fear is wisdom in the face of danger

Anon

Chapter One

The deafening maelstrom of water raged with unbelievable force, pinning him against the narrow exit to the culvert. The mind-numbing cold, like a million needles, attacked his body; the pain immense from the impact of being thrown against the jagged rock across the only outlet for the torrent. He tried to cling on but the power of the water sapped all his strength... then darkness. His unconscious state took over.

Leeds Central Railway Station, 30th September 2001

Chloe Grainger looked around, all these people. She nervously tugged on her scarf; it wasn't particularly cold and the fabric was irritating her face. Granny Grainger meant well when she sent it to her with a lovely note attached: *'I hope this will come in useful I know how cold it is in Yorkshire. I can't believe my darling granddaughter is going to University. Everyone is so proud. Love, Nan Grainger.'*

It had been a three-hour journey by rail from Bristol and seeing her mum and dad waving to her as the train pulled away from the station was heartbreaking. She missed them already.

"Hi, are you enrolling?" chirped a friendly voice.

Chloe spun around and saw the enquirer.

"Yes... yes, thank you," she replied.

The girl smiled. Her name badge identified her as 'Trina'. She was one of several second-year graduate volunteers acting as welcome guides for the arriving freshers who, like Chloe, were probably experiencing their first time away from home. She was seated behind a makeshift stall littered with schedules and leaflets with maps to the residences and other essential information for new students.

"What course are you taking?" said Trina.

"Geology," said Chloe.

"Ah yes," said Trina after a lengthy scan of her papers. "Here it is, the School of Earth and Environment."

"Hello," said a voice from behind Chloe. "I'm doing Geology as well. Abigail Newton, they call me Abby," said the bright, fair-haired girl, young-looking and fresh-faced.

"Oh, hi, Chloe, Chloe Grainger," and the two girls shook hands.

Trina looked at the newcomer. "Here you are... directions to the halls. They're not far; twenty-minute walk or you can take a bus from just outside the station."

Chloe looked down at her large rucksack and pull-along suitcase. "A bus I think," and started to laugh.

Abby shared the levity. "I'll tag along with you if that's ok?"

"Of course," said Chloe. "It looks as though we might be in the same block."

The two girls thanked their helper and, armed with various pieces of literature, headed for the exit.

"Hey, wait up. Are you for the geology course?"

The girls looked round.

"Yes," said Chloe.

"Can I join you?" said a fit-looking student, pulling a suitcase and carrying a duffle bag over his shoulder. "Harry, Harry Bentham."

"Yes, why not, the more the merrier... Where are you from?"

"Norwich. I just got in. You?" said Harry who had now caught them up.

"I'm Chloe from Bristol. This is Abby from... sorry I don't know where you're from."

"Swindon," said Abby.

"Well, someone has to be," said Harry, and they laughed.

The three made their way to the bus, chatting non-stop.

March 2002

Six months later and well into their first year, the students were having their final briefing for a four-day field trip. The twelve undergraduates on the course had been split into four groups of three.

Chloe and Abby had become almost inseparable since that first day on Leeds station and had opted to go for the caving expedition. Harry had made his own friends and social life but he saw the two girls in lectures regularly and had asked if he could make up their three.

After the initial briefing from the tutor, they sat in the common room discussing their assignment.

Harry was an impressive individual; swarthy looking with a short, stylish haircut. In his sixth form days, he had been a county rugby player. He was also an accomplished rower and had spent many misty mornings lifting his six-foot frame into a rowing eight on the local river. Sport had taken up a great deal of his extra-curricular time. He was naturally competitive and the thought of caving was completely in line with his devil-may-care persona. Both girls rather fancied him but there had been an unwritten rule about fraternising with fellow course-mates so rather than create possible friction they decided to all be friends.

"Do you know anything about caving?" he asked, as they sat at one of the tables drinking cans of coke from the vending machine.

Abby looked at Chloe. "Not a thing. Well, apart from the rock formations, obviously," she said.

"Me neither," said Chloe.

"It'll be great fun," said Harry. "I've done loads of rock climbing; it's why I decided on a geology course in the first place. I've always had a fascination with how they were formed."

"What's that got to do with caving?" said Chloe.

"Well, it's the same thing. You're just going in the opposite direction," he said laughing.

The girls smiled.

"I have to say I wasn't too sure. I'm not good in enclosed spaces, I don't even like going in lifts," said Abby.

"Why did you put your name down, silly? We could have done one of the other field studies," said Chloe.

"Yes, I know but I knew you wanted to and I didn't want to be left out," said Abby.

"I don't mind," said Chloe. "We can do the cliff erosion study in Scarborough if you like?"

"No, I'll be fine. That know-it-all, Dave Chandler, is going on that and I don't think I could stand four days in close proximity with him," said Abby.

"Hmm, there is that," said Chloe laughing.

"Don't worry, there's nothing to it," said Harry. "It's very safe these days and the equipment they use is first class. Plus, it has much better research opportunities. I've been reading up on it; they've been trying to find the entrance to a new chamber down there. It should be really exciting."

"What else have you found out?" said Chloe. "I've not started yet."

"Hey that's cheating, do your own research," said Harry mockingly. "Only joking," he added.

"Go on," said Abby. "Tell us what you've found out."

"Well, limestone, obviously," he said. "The cave system we'll be going to is called Dingwell Cavern, not as big as Gaping Ghyll but not far off."

"Gaping Ghyll? That's up near Ingleborough isn't it?" said Chloe.

"Yes," said Harry. "It was thought to be the deepest cave in the UK until they discovered Titan."

"Ah yes, Titan," said Chloe. "I've always wanted to have a look at that one."

"Well, you can. We'll only be about ten miles away. Our base is in Castleton, it's quite near," said Harry who was clearly up on his knowledge of British caves.

A week later with all preparations complete they packed their rucksacks. Harry had taken charge of the shared laptop, which was an expensive piece of equipment and quite heavy. It was an early start and by seven-thirty the three intrepid explorers were ready for the off. Just a final check before they walked towards the waiting minibus which would take them to their destination.

Just over two hours later the vehicle pulled up outside the Mountaineering and Caving Centre in the middle of the Peak District, an area of Derbyshire world-renowned for its rock climbing and adventure sites.

The approach was along a gravel road through a fir forest. As the trees were left behind a worn white track, reflecting the predominantly limestone countryside, led the way. After ten minutes or so they reached the centre. It was surrounded on three sides by spectacular scenery; steep hills which formed almost a box quarry. In front was an open space which served as a car park. There were numerous vehicles, mostly Jeeps, Land Rovers and other 4x4s parked up. People in serious outdoor clothing were standing in groups waiting for instructions.

The minibus drew up in front of the entrance where they were greeted by Campbell Addison, a wiry Scot with a full brown beard. He looked like he had been hewn from the nearby quarries. He walked towards the minibus and slid open the side door. Chloe exited first, then Abby followed by Harry.

"Och, you must be the Leeds team," he said, spotting the Leeds University logo on the side of the minibus.

Harry assumed the role of leader.

"Hi, yes, I'm Harry Bentham; this is Chloe and Abby." The Scot checked his manifest. "Aye, yes I have you here," he said. "Grab your gear and come with me."

The three collected their rucksacks and followed Campbell into the centre; the minibus drove away.

It was a substantial wooden construction and through the entrance was a large reception area with detailed maps across the sidewalls. There were pictures of the mountain rescue team which also used the base and the helicopter that was available in case of emergencies. Immediately Harry was drawn to the maps and started studying one of them.

There was a line of four people in front of them completing the registration process. While they waited, Campbell explained the set-up. "There's accommodation for twenty people. It's a bit basic but it's clean and comfortable," he said. His Scottish accent was strong and the group had difficulty making sense of his words.

"I'll leave you to settle in and we'll meet outside at ten forty-five; that gives you an hour. There's a small cafe through there," he said, pointing to one of the doors. "It's help yourself but it's fine. There are some pre-packed ready meals and a microwave."

Chloe looked at Abby; as students, they were used to 'roughing' it. The three reached the desk and the receptionist, a ginger-haired girl called Amy, about the same age as Chloe and Abby, welcomed them. She explained while she completed the registration process, that the job was part of her gap year. She gave the three a room key each plus a leaflet describing the layout and emergency evacuation procedures, then pointed them in the direction of their accommodation.

It was through a door to the right of the reception. On the left was the kitchen/cafe which had been pointed out to them by Campbell; it certainly lived up to his description as 'basic'.

Then through another door and down a long corridor which had dormitories on the left, all consecutively numbered.

There were two communal bathrooms, male and female. They included a shower room and looked more like sports hall changing rooms but would suffice for the four days they would be in residence.

"Number seven," said Chloe, as they walked along looking at the numbers on the doors.

"Me too," said Abby. "We must be sharing."

"Here," said Chloe. They opened the room; Harry was behind them with all their gear.

"Bunk beds," said Chloe. "I haven't slept in one of these since I was a kid."

"Bagsy me bottom," said Abby.

"You're welcome to it," said Chloe. "I quite like being on top," and they both laughed at the innuendo.

"Where are you, Harry?" said Chloe.

He looked at his key; "Number eight. Next door," he said.

"Let's see yours," said Abby.

"Don't be cheeky," said Harry.

Abby slapped him playfully on his arm. "You know what I mean," she said.

"Just a sec," said Harry as he opened room eight.

"Same as yours," he said. "Wonder who I'll be sleeping with."

"Probably a seventeen stone rugby player with bulging biceps," said Chloe.

"Now steady on that almost sounds attractive," said Harry. "I've met a few you know."

"I bet you have," said Chloe and the girls laughed.

He looked around at the Spartan quarters. "I'm having the bottom one," he said.

"Well you better hope the top one doesn't belong to a

seventeen stone prop forward," said Chloe.

There were cupboards one beneath the other large enough to keep toiletries and a change of clothing. Behind the door, there was a big picture of a pair of walking boots with a red cross over the top.

"I guess we leave the boots somewhere else," said Harry.

After a few minutes, the group had stowed their stuff and clothed themselves in warm woolly jumpers, thick socks, windcheater jackets, and waterproof trousers. As directed, they carried their walking boots with them. They had rucksacks on their backs which contained their notebooks, snacks and water plus other personal belongings. Harry walked up to the reception desk and handed in the laptop for safe-keeping together with their mobile phones. There was no signal for miles; Campbell had warned them. They would write up their notes when they returned.

They walked back to the kitchen and made themselves a coffee, chatting excitedly about the expedition. "Don't forget to get some chocolate bars, always useful in case of emergencies," said Harry.

"Good idea," said Chloe and the three hovered around the vending machine in the corner and started feeding in coins and selecting their favourite choices.

There were about fifteen other students now milling about and eventually Campbell came into reception and called everyone together. There were introductions as they joined the Leeds group for the briefing. He led them to a large cupboard which was full of climbing equipment, ropes, harnesses, and hard hats. Each helmet had an integral battery-operated flashlight but they were also given hand-held torches. Illumination was almost as important as food and water, Campbell explained. "One wrong turn and you could be lost forever," he said dramatically.

Harry with his mountaineering experience was already

taking charge, rather like a protective elder brother would do, and was soon sorting through the gear and handing the girls what they would need. Chloe and Abby were trying on hard hats finding ones that would fit. Chloe with her thick curly hair was finding it particularly difficult. There were fits of laughter as she tried on various helmets which resembled Christmas party hats.

Eventually, they had all the required equipment and left the centre where three aged but loved Land Rovers were waiting. Campbell split the students into their respective destinations. The Leeds group were the only ones going to the Dingwell Cavern and were introduced to their driver and guide, Paul Forest. He opened the back to enable them to stow all their gear before they got in and they set off.

Paul gave them a running commentary about the Cavern as he drove. It was about three miles away over fairly rough terrain. The white tracks where tyres had worn away the grass continued for a while but gradually faded away and the route was not obvious to the uninitiated. The Land Rover lurched and bounced on the uneven terrain. After a mile or so they dropped down into a small ravine with trees on all sides, bent by the prevailing winds; the narrow track meandered through the arbour. Then in front of them, a fast-flowing stream crossed their path. Paul stopped the Land Rover. The ford had obviously been in regular use and the banks had been eroded leaving a muddy incline on both sides. The girls looked at each other with some alarm; Harry was enjoying every minute.

"Hold tight," Paul said, and gently eased the vehicle down the two feet bank into the water. It jerked unsteadily as it gained its grip on the pebbly bottom and then he accelerated. The Land Rover slid, then gripped, and gradually moved up the other side.

After a few hundred yards, they left the trees and were greeted with spectacular views of the hills in the distance.

To the right, there was a gentle incline before the terrain rose sharply into sheer cliffs. On top, it was green with bushes of all description but completely devoid of any human presence; only the occasional hardy hill sheep gave evidence of any living being.

The excitement continued as interesting rock formations appeared and were discussed; Paul concentrated on the driving. After another ten minutes, the Land Rover pulled up on a bare patch of ground that had been worn by the weight of vehicles.

"Right, we'll park here and continue on foot," said Paul. "Make sure you have everything you need; we won't be coming back for a while."

Paul got out and started rummaging around a holdall in the boot of the car and pulled out some chocolate and his hard hat.

"Wow, it's so deserted," observed Chloe as she got out and started to stretch her legs.

While the students exited the vehicle, Paul went back to the dashboard and picked up his walkie-talkie and called in. "Just a safety measure," he said to the inquisitive looks.

Harry dished out the equipment and the girls strapped on their harnesses and hard hats. The torches were checked to make sure they were working and Paul gave them spare batteries each. The rucksacks were getting heavier.

They congregated at the front of the Land Rover to hear Paul. He was older than Campbell but shared the same rugged features, including what seemed to be the obligatory beard. He was about the same height as Harry. Wearing a neoprene wetsuit and gloves, with knee and elbow protectors; he looked like a deep-sea diver. He detailed his own experience, a product of Snowdonia, where he was part of the mountain rescue team for many years. As he spoke there was only a slight hint of his native Welsh accent, more rural North Wales than the harsh tones of the Gower Peninsular or Cardiff suburbs. He would be good to have around on this trip.

"The entrance is about two hundred yards away and quite narrow; probably why it was only recently discovered. We'll make our way there now and have a final check before we go inside. Everybody ok with that?" he said with some authority.

"Yes," said Harry speaking on behalf of the group.

They followed Paul along a footpath which appeared reasonably well-trodden. Paul explained that since its discovery less than six years ago, there had been a lot of exploration. As the group walked he continued his briefing.

"There are still many areas of the cavern not open yet. Several chambers still need to be researched and we'll be looking at one of these over the next few days so you can start mapping the rock formations. I was told that's what you wanted to do," he said.

There were nods of approval from the followers. "Great, yes, that's what we're here to see," said Harry.

As they turned a corner the wind hit them full on nearly knocking the diminutive Abby off her feet. The group leant forward to reduce the drag. "Good grief," said Chloe. "Where did this come from?"

Paul shouted to be heard. "It's very exposed up here. Wind's veered north-west, we're right in the face of it... straight in from the Irish Sea, nothing to stop it," he said. "Don't worry we're nearly there."

A minute or two later to the right, the cliff face dropped away and seemed to slope backwards. The harsh white limestone was replaced by a large knoll about sixty feet tall. There were huge grey splinters of rock protruding outwards and covered in greenery. In front of them was a giant column of jagged rock, about thirty feet tall and three wide, standing like a sentry guarding the entrance to the cave.

Numerous bushes and creeping plants were growing around

the rock which served to camouflage the cave; no wonder it had taken so long for it to be discovered. A lone tree, bent by years of abuse from gale-force storms, was stationed on the other side of the entrance, further obscuring the cave's presence.

"We're here," said Paul.

The area in front of the cave was again flat from the footfall of cavers and geologists from all over the country and beyond, anxious to discover its secrets. The entrance itself was somewhat of an anti-climax. This was no Aladdin's Cave with an enormous mouth but more an unremarkable gash in the rock, no more than a yard or two wide and around six feet tall.

Paul gathered the group together. "Right guys, this is it. Check your helmets, lights and harnesses. It's a bit of a tight squeeze but you'll be fine. Keep close until we reach the central cavern then you can go to work. If anyone wants the toilet, then you need to go behind that rock. It's not very private but they haven't installed any facilities inside yet."

There was a polite chuckle but it was a point. "I'm fine," said Chloe. "It'll take me a week to get this kit off." More laughter, the mood was upbeat.

"I'm ok," said Abby.

"Me too," said Harry.

Abby wasn't smiling though; looking at the black hole in front of her was making her think that the Scarborough trip might have been a better option. In truth, she was feeling nervous and could probably do with a pee.

"Ok, I'll lead... Harry, you take up the rear. The first part is downhill and slippery, so watch your step. Take it slow and use your hands for balance. I hope you've all remembered your gloves, it's cold down there," said Paul. Chloe lifted her hands in confirmation, Abby and Harry did the same.

"Good... right, let's go," he said and led them towards the entrance.

Paul intuitively bent slightly as he went through, although he might just have made it without hitting his head. It was no problem for the girls but Harry also ducked as they entered the darkness.

The temperature plummeted very quickly and there was a dank feel, the atmosphere damp and clammy, like a freezing cold steam room, if the incongruity was possible.

As they turned their heads, the four beams of light from their helmets bounced around the tunnel sides. Paul had his hand-held torch and shone it into the gloom ahead of him. Abby could feel palpitations in her chest as the sides of the cave seemed to close in on her. She breathed deeply.

The ground underfoot was bare rock and extremely treacherous; luckily the soles of their hiking boots gave them some modicum of traction and they made steady progress downhill. Every so often there was an alcove where rocks had broken off and fallen onto the path which they had to negotiate. They had been walking for about fifteen minutes, the tunnel twisting left and right, when suddenly the narrow path opened up into an enormous cavern.

"Wow," said Chloe. "Look at this."

The three students just stood there for a moment; it was an awesome sight.

Paul turned and briefed them again. "This is the main cavern; they've named it 'The Citadel' because of its size. He turned his flashlight upwards and the beam was lost after about thirty feet. "We've measured it at over fifty metres high," he said. "That's a hundred and fifty feet but there are several tunnels leading away from here. Some are dead-ends, blocked by fallen rock but others go a long way back. He shone his beam to their right and illuminated what looked like the entrance to another cave. "That one over there goes on for at least five kilometres before it branches off. There are several other tunnels leading in different directions but only two have been explored; the others are too dangerous."

The three listened with great interest and stared in wonderment; there was something almost spiritual about the place.

"We'll stop here for a while and you can make some notes," said Paul.

There were boulders all around which made convenient seats. "Ooooh, that's better," said Abby as she removed her rucksack and placed it on the cavern floor next to her. The others did the same. Abby and Chloe were soon discussing the finer points of geological formations of the cavern.

All three had extracted their notebooks and were jotting down points of interest in shorthand. They also had small pointed hammers with them for chipping stone to provide samples which they would take back to the University for a more detailed analysis.

Harry had a different priority and started on one of his chocolate bars. Paul was walking around the floor of the cavern indicating various features that he thought the students might be of significance.

"Look over there," said Abby pointing to three smaller caves to her right with her torch. "It looks like phreatic action. What do you think?"

"Who's been reading up on their speleology?" said Harry.

Paul was intrigued. "What does that mean?" he asked, as he too took on some calories.

Abby was now the authority on cave study. "It means the limestone has been dissolved by water; look you can see by the shape," she said. "They're sort of circular or oval-shaped as opposed to when they're eroded by a stream which cuts through the rock and tends to be narrower." The academic free-flow was lessening her anxiety and she was beginning to relax.

"That's vadose action, by the way." said Chloe, not wishing to lose out in showing off her knowledge of caves.

"Listen to you two," said Harry.

"You learn something every day," said Paul, impressed by his charges' intellect.

"If it's phreatic then we must be below the water table," said Harry.

"Aye, that's true," said Paul, in his Welsh brogue. "Several of the caves are impassable, certainly without diving equipment. We think one of these might join up with Titan but it'll take years to explore all the caves properly. We'll need specialist equipment and unfortunately, it doesn't come cheap."

The team was walking about, examining every aspect of the cavern.

"Wow, look up there," said Chloe, pointing at some blue quartz-like formations.

"Aye, that's Blue John," said Paul. "Not as big as the Blue John Cavern, the one in Castleton but it's early days. We're uncovering all kinds of things all the time."

"They've ruined that place," said Harry.

"What?" said Abby, now on her fourth page of notes.

"The Blue John Cavern; I went there when I was sixteen and it's like Disneyland, illuminated walkways, tour guides, boats. It's just a tourist attraction."

"Aye," said Paul, "but it brings in much-needed money so I can't knock it."

The group had spent over an hour exploring the gigantic Citadel chamber, collecting samples and making notes. Harry had a small camera and was taking pictures, directed by Chloe. They had agreed to share the results. The flash bounced around the walls like lightening.

After the group had taken on some refreshment, Paul addressed them.

"What I wanted to show you is over here," he said shining his torch onto what looked like a hole in the cavern wall to the left. "Bring your rucksacks," he ordered.

The group got up and put on their gear then followed Paul who was speaking as he walked towards the hole in the wall.

"Just a bit of background... the chamber I'm going to show you only got opened up earlier this year. Originally it was thought to be a dead-end but some cavers managed to clear a large rock fall and followed the cavern down for over half a mile."

The students were listening closely. "Don't worry it's quite safe," said Paul, looking at Abby who was showing signs of anxiety again. "There are some amazing stalactites, and we've found some interesting fossils as well. There are loads down there."

"Sounds good to me," said Harry.

"Yeah," said Chloe, "Abby, you alright?"

"Yeah, I'll be fine. Not staying here on my own," she said.

The group lined up behind Paul in the same order as before.

It was at least fifty yards across the cavern floor to the narrow entrance to the tributary cave about six feet above them, a short climb over some large boulders which formed a natural ladder. "Don't worry these have been here for about a thousand years, we think," said Paul. He peered into the darkness; the beam from his headlight bounced down the corridor.

"Right, we'll rope up just to be on the safe side," he said.

Back at base, there was a degree of consternation; Campbell Addison was growing increasingly concerned. He examined the sky again and checked the wind direction.

"It's veered round south-west," he said to Simon Porter, one of the other guides who had returned with his group having noticed the change in weather. He checked his watch, it was just gone two o'clock but you wouldn't have thought it. The lights in the reception area shone brightly as they compensated for the lack of natural daylight. Then the rain came; just a few drops, and then a cascade.

"They didn't forecast this," said Simon who was staring at the sky and sharing Campbell's concern.

"A chance of showers," said Campbell.

Weather variations in this predominantly hilly terrain were not unusual; it almost had its own ecosystem and could be very unpredictable. All the guides were aware of this and always erred on the side of caution when it came to taking parties out climbing or pot-holing. An unexpected downpour or descent of mist could prove fatal to the inexperienced. This time the squall had taken them by surprise; the rain was torrential. A couple of other groups arrived in Land Rovers and dashed inside.

"How many groups are still out?" said Simon.

"Four," said Campbell. "But three of those are climbing; they'll just get a bit wet. It's the cavers I'm worried about."

"No way of contacting them I suppose," said Simon.

"No, they'll be too deep for wireless," said Campbell. "Another hour of this and we could be in trouble. The water table's already high."

"Yes, I'm not surprised with the amount of rain we've had this winter," said Simon.

"We'll just have to sit it out and hope," said Campbell. "I'll put the rescue team on alert just in case."

He went to the communications console and made a call.

Chapter Two

Back in the cave, unaware of the deteriorating weather conditions outside, Paul was leading the group down the pothole which he had selected for their study. It was hard going; the sharp angle of descent pulling on already-tired leg muscles. The passageway narrowed quickly and the group had to stoop for much of the way. It was also littered with boulders which further impeded progress. Abby was third in the line but struggling with the physical demands as well as the psychological stresses of the descent. It was like being in a tomb; the only light source was the light from their helmets. Every few minutes the party stopped to regroup.

The ropes were an important safety precaution but it did mean the speed they could travel was limited by the slowest of the team which was Abby. Harry had to stop himself from crashing into her on several occasions. Chloe, in trying to keep up with Paul at the front, frequently tugged the rope taught almost causing Abby to fall forward. After about twenty minutes the cave opened up into another large chamber. The cavern floor was some way below them but again there were boulders which lay against the cave wall making a convenient ladder and one-by-one the four slid down the slippery rocks to the bottom of the chamber.

It was nowhere near as big as the Citadel, about the size of a large sports hall but rising to about forty feet. At last, they could stand and take a breather.

"Right this is it," said Paul. "We'll stay here for an hour or so and you can get on with some research but be careful this area has not been surveyed in any detail. I've only been here myself a couple of times. Whatever you do, don't enter any side tunnels or shafts without telling me, some drop vertically down and haven't been explored at all yet. Ok, you can go off-rope now."

There was the sound of rustling and clicking as the ropes were unclipped. Abby took off her rucksack and stretched. "Ooooh my back," she said again.

They took out their torches from the rucksacks and scanned the cavern. They could see that the limestone floor was not flat like The Citadel but irregular and pitted. It sloped away about twenty degrees to the left of them for about sixty or seventy metres; it was difficult to tell, the torch beams did not reach the end. There were holes full of water with sharp outcrops of rock dotted around, potential hazards for the unwary.

"Are you ok, Abby?" said Chloe.

"I will be when I get my circulation back. God, it's so cold down here," she said, rubbing her gloves together.

"Be careful where you put your rucksacks, there are puddles everywhere," said Harry as he scoured the cave floor for a dry spot. "Here, over here," he said and walked towards a protruding ledge of rock with a reasonably flat surface. "This will do... dump your stuff on here."

The two girls passed him their rucksacks and he stacked them together. "They'll be fine there," he said and started searching in the front pocket of his haversack for another chocolate bar.

"Keep close and don't wander too far," said Paul. "Remember we're well below the water table here and some of those caves over there are flooded," he said pointing his torch ahead of them. "But I think you will like this," he said, and he shone his torch upwards.

"Wow," said Chloe. "Look at that."

There was no discernible cave ceiling, just rows upon rows of jagged stalactites and shards of what looked like calcite crystals. The light from Paul's torch bounced off them giving a spectacular display of colours glistening in the light like starbursts; every shade of orange, greys and white, reflecting the mineral content of the rock.

"Wow," said Chloe. "That is just unbelievable."

"Now, you have to admit that was worth the hike," said Harry.

Abby looked up in amazement. "Wow, that's just awesome," she said and her earlier anxieties suddenly disappeared.

Harry took out his camera. "Can everyone shine their torches and I'll get some pictures. I'm not sure of the range on this."

There was an excited technical discussion on the geology of the cave, the three had started taking notes again and Harry was chipping away at the cave wall taking samples.

"Hey, look there," shouted Abby waving her torch at a rock formation. It was speckled with crystals that looked like coal.

"Galena," said Paul. "They used to mine it not far from here for years."

"In this state, we call it Anglesite," said Abby moving closer to inspect the crystal.

"Lead Sulphide; one of the lead ores, nasty stuff," said Chloe, not wanting to be outdone by Abby's expertise.

"There's lots of Fluorspar here as well... mind you that's common in this area," said Paul carrying on his role as tour guide, "and keep looking I'm sure you'll find some fossils," he added. "We've had guys from London University down here and they've found some amazing examples."

Chloe was picking up some of the rocks from the cave floor and examining them with her expert eye. Some she discarded but some she put into a cellophane bag and labelled for further investigation. Abby was doing the same but in a different section. This was geology heaven.

"Here, look at this," said Abby showing Chloe a small piece of rock.

"Wow, nice one," said Chloe.

"What have you found?" said Harry.

"A Crinoid," said Abby.

"Yes," said Paul who had heard the call. "They're quite common. Some of the other caves are full of them."

"Didn't know you were an authority," said Chloe.

"I'm not," said Paul. "But you pick up bits and pieces. We've got some up at the centre; in the office. You can take a look at them when we get back. They reckon there was a tropical lagoon around here somewhere."

"Thanks, I will," said Abby and she put the rock into the front pocket of her rucksack.

"Over here," shouted Harry.

"What is it?" said Chloe as she walked towards him.

"An ammonite," said Harry shining his torch on a spiral shape in the rock. He took out his loupe, a small field magnifying glass, from the side pocket of his waterproofs and bent down to examine it closer.

"What do you think?" said Harry, allowing Abby the chance to take a closer look.

"Yeah, nice shape; don't know if you're going to be able to get it out though," she said.

Harry took out a calliper gauge which he laid alongside it. Then took out his camera and took a couple of pictures. The cave was a hive of activity.

They had been working for about half an hour and had stopped for refreshment. The chat was urgent and animated as the students interrupted each other with the excitement of their findings. Paul was sat on a rock and looked on like a protective shepherd guarding his sheep.

Suddenly he stopped chewing on his chocolate bar and listened.

He shouted at the group who were a few feet away. "Hang on guys," he shouted. The chatting continued momentarily;

"Shhhh!"

The group went quiet.

"Quick, grab your stuff... now! We need to get out of here," he shouted. There was urgency in his voice which suggested mandatory compliance.

The three students grabbed their rucksacks and stowed their gear. "What is it?" shouted Harry.

"I don't know but something's not right. Listen," he said as the group approached.

"What's that noise?" said Abby.

"Water," said Paul. "Quick, up there... now!"

The shaft from where they had entered the chamber was behind them about twelve feet off the cavern floor. The three large boulders, one behind the other, which had formed the natural stepping stones for their descent from the entrance had been relatively easy coming down, just a couple of gentle drops but going back up it was a different story; they became obstacles, a shear face of slimy stone.

The first boulder was about four feet in height; Paul gripped the top and with Harry's help managed to pull himself up. The group passed him the rucksacks and he threw them one-by-one into the shaft entrance immediately above him. He grabbed Chloe's arms and lifted her up; she quickly climbed onto the next level just a yard or so, then onto the final rock until she was at the entrance.

"Harry, you go next," shouted Paul. "You can help Abby."

The sound was getting louder and louder; an enormous roar, definitely close. Harry, like Paul, made light work of the first rock but there was no way Abby would make it. She was using all her strength but was unable to pull herself up. Harry stood over her as she raised her arms.

"Grab my hand," he shouted. Paul had dropped back down and joined Harry. Chloe was watching from the shaft. The lads managed to catch her flailing arms and pulled. The momentum of the lift swept her up and she landed in a heap on top of the boulder next to Paul and Harry. It was only three feet or so from the next one and the three quickly made it up with just the final hurdle to go.

"Go on Abby, quick, hurry," said Paul. He pushed her up the last few feet onto the top of the remaining rock and she made a jump into the shaft entrance. Chloe grabbed her.

Then from nowhere, it hit like an express train. The torrent came from an adjacent shaft to their right, the small entrance acting like a hose spraying thousands of gallons of water at immense pressure.

Chloe and Abby were able to duck inside the shaft as the water poured through. The maelstrom splashed against the cave entrance as if trying to find the girls, spraying them with icy water. Paul and Harry were not so lucky, still in the open on the second boulder, they were swept away. For a moment, Chloe could see the lights from their helmets bobbing in the torrent then they just disappeared into the abyss.

They called out but would never be heard over the noise of the water. Chloe grabbed one of the torches and scoured the cavern. The floor, where only moments ago they were walking around, was a raging torrent and was quickly filling with water.

"We can't stay here," said Chloe. "The water could flood the shaft. We need to move."

"What about Harry and Paul?" said Abby.

"There's nothing we can do," Chloe said. "We have to get out. You lead."

"But I don't know which way," Abby said.

"We just keep going up," said Chloe. "Hang on... wait a second, I've got an idea."

Chloe took out a flashlight from one of the rucksacks, placed it on top of the rock at the shaft entrance and turned it on. It shone out across the cavern which was now almost half full with water.

"If they make it they'll know where to come," said Chloe.

The girls turned, picked up their rucksacks and slung them on their backs.

"What about the rope and Harry's rucksack?" said Abby, staring at the baggage in the cave entrance.

"We'll have to leave them... they'll only slow us down. There's just the two of us, we'll be ok," said Chloe.

Abby was on her hands and knees and started to crawl into the darkness but after just a few yards she suddenly stopped. Her body went rigid and she started to shake; she was in shock.

Chloe recognised the signs. "Abby, get yourself together. We have to go... now!"

Chloe gave Abby's backside an almighty shove which propelled Abby forward. Slowly Abby started to move again, their headlamps picking out the way. The sound of rushing water echoed down the damp corridor behind them. Chloe was trying to remember if there were any junctions when they came down but couldn't think. She was on auto-pilot, her survival mechanism kicking in.

It was hard going as they tackled the steep upward gradient and stray boulders were strewn all along the tunnel floor. Abby's hands slithered through the chalky mud, her gloves and knees completely white. Then after about ten minutes, the cave narrowed even further and the roof dropped to around three feet.

"I don't remember this, Chloe. Are you sure we're going the right way?" said Abby.

"We must be; there's no other way... come on, keep going," Chloe replied.

They continued crawling up the slippery slope, their rucksacks scraping the ceiling; Abby slowly shuffling forward, breathing loudly. Chloe was behind trying to encourage her. "Keep going, we're nearly there," she kept saying.

The cave gradually got bigger to almost stooping height but then Abby stopped.

"What's the matter?" said Chloe whose view was obstructed by her colleague.

"I don't know which way to go," she said and pointed her flashlight at the junction ahead. It was their worst nightmare.

"Oh no," said Chloe.

"Come on... think, think," said Chloe to herself. "Do you remember, Abby?" she said.

She shone her torch down each shaft in turn.

"No, they both look the same. Wait... look!" Abby whispered anxiously.

At the entrance to the right-hand shaft, there was a puddle of water. Nothing wrong with that, there were puddles everywhere but this one was getting bigger. Then it started spilling out towards them, slowly but surely.

"Go left..." Chloe said, and the girls went through the dry shaft just as the trickle from the other tunnel was gaining momentum.

The headlights from the girls' helmets continued to bob around the narrow cave. It was mostly a crawl but occasionally they could stoop. Luckily their waterproofs were keeping their legs relatively dry but their windcheaters were soaking wet.

"How far, do you think?" said Abby.

"To the Citadel?" said Chloe.

"Yes," said Abby.

"I don't know but it can't be much further," said Chloe. "We seem to have been climbing forever."

Abby started shivering again, a mix of cold and anxiety.

"I'm so cold," she said.

Some way behind them, the two men were fighting for their lives. The weight of the water was forcing the pair towards a narrow culvert at the end of the chamber. It was Harry that reached it first. He was being propelled backwards at high speed and his head crashed against the limestone rock. Despite his helmet, the force of the collision rendered him unconscious. Luckily the current had moved him to a standing position and his body was now blocking the exit route for thousands and thousands of gallons of water. Had he been lying down he would have been forced through the narrow opening to certain death.

Paul quickly caught up with him but the incredible pressure of the water was forcing him downwards. Their helmet lights bounced hap-hazard beams across the jagged stalactites way above them as Paul tried to negotiate himself alongside his companion.

He grabbed Harry's windcheater by the collar and pulled him to one side where the current was slower waiting its turn to crash through the narrow exit. There was an outcrop to their right and Paul used all his strength to push Harry up and onto a ledge out of the water. As soon as he had moved Harry from the entrance, the water poured through again with incredible power. Paul managed to lift himself onto the rock next to Harry. His wetsuit had proved to be a life-saver and he was still relatively dry. Harry, on the other hand, was soaking wet and Paul knew that hypothermia was going to be the next problem.

In the distance, Paul could see the light that Chloe had left. It was probably sixty metres away but there was a ledge that ran the cavern wall almost to the shaft entrance.

Harry started to come around; he could hear a voice.
"Are you ok?" said Paul.
Harry was groaning incoherently as if he had awoken from

a deep sleep.

"Come on boyo, we've got to get out of here. Can you stand up?" said Paul.

"Yeah, I... think so," said Harry groggily as he started to come to his senses.

Paul looked at the water surging wild and uncontrolled below them. "We need to go now... it's rising fast."

With the narrow culvert entrance providing the only exit route for the raging flood, the water was effectively being dammed and starting to back up; the level was now only inches below the ledge.

Slowly the pair edged their way around the wall of the cavern, the icy water starting to lap at their feet. They could see Chloe's guiding light beckoning them home. Then the ledge ran out with about twenty feet to go. Paul could see the three boulders but only the largest was above the water level. The torch was still perched on the top. He looked at the water it would be over eight feet deep but it was moving slower next to the cave wall.

"We're going to have to swim for it," said Paul. "Do you think you can make the boulder over there, where the light is?" he pointed. "It's not far."

"Yeah, I'll give it a go," said Harry drowsily.

"Ok, we'll drop down, then work our way across. Keep as close to the cave wall as you can, the current's not as strong there. Stay here, I'll go first and test it out," said Paul having to shout above the roar of the deluge.

Harry was now starting to shake with cold and shock.

"Come on boyo, focus... we've got to keep it together," said Paul, sternly.

He eased himself into the icy torrent; it was soon over his head. He bobbed up and shook his head to clear the stinging water from his eyes. He bounced more than swam, to the three boulders guarding the exit and managed to climb onto the second one. It was up to his knees as he stood up, probably ten feet above the cave floor where only minutes earlier the group were comparing fossils. Paul saw the ropes on the next boulder where Chloe's torch was still shining close to the cave entrance; he grabbed one.

"Here, catch," he shouted, throwing an end towards Harry. He missed the first attempt and Paul reeled in the slack and tried again. This time it hit Harry and he was able to grab it.

"Tie it round your waist," shouted Paul and slowly Harry wrapped the rope around him and tied it in a double knot.

"Ok, now jump down, I've got you," said Paul. "Come on Harry, you can do it."

Slowly Harry dropped back into the water and submerged briefly before surfacing and splashing his way to Paul who was pulling the rope towards him. The cold was unbearable and only his survival instincts and extreme fitness were keeping him going.

"Come on Harry, boyo, that's it... to me... come on." Paul continued to encourage him.

Harry gradually reached the boulders. Paul grabbed his arm and with all the strength he could manage lifted him alongside.

"Quick, we can't stay here," said Paul. "I'll give you a hand."

Paul hauled himself onto the top boulder and picked up Chloe's lamp. He grabbed the back of Harry's windcheater and pulled. Half crawling, half standing Harry managed to get enough purchase on the rock to clamber up and reach Paul's vantage point. He stopped and caught his breath; blood was oozing from the side of his head and running down his face. Paul looked at him.

"Come on, we've got you get you some help."

Paul picked up Harry's rucksack and the pair went into

the cave and headed upward with Paul leading. The beams of their headlamps bounced around the narrow tunnel. Paul used Chloe's torch to give them a longer view. He stopped every ten yards or so to make sure Harry was following; it was only supreme fitness and determination that was keeping him going.

Water was cascading downwards but not with sufficient force to do anything more than make it very uncomfortable. They were retracing the steps taken by the two girls and making good time mostly crawling on their hands and knees.

Chloe and Abby had stopped to get a breather and share out a chocolate bar from Abby's rucksack. Suddenly there was a noise coming from behind them.

"What's that?" said Abby. "Sounds like scraping."

"Hello," shouted Chloe instinctively.

"Shhhh," said Abby. "The noise could start a rock-fall."

"Sorry," whispered Chloe.

The sound was getting closer now. Abby's heart was beating faster; she was petrified. Then suddenly they could see the beam from a torch bouncing on the wall behind them.

"Harry? Paul... is that you?" said Chloe.

Abby shuffled back towards Chloe for protection.

"Are you girls ok?" came a familiar voice.

"Paul, is that you?" said Chloe again. Then, he was there, directly behind them.

"Can you give me a hand? I've got Harry. He's in a bad way," said Paul, who was still holding Harry's rucksack.

"Oh, thank goodness! Am I glad to see you?" said Chloe. "I thought we were lost. What's wrong with Harry?"

"Hypothermia and he's hit his head; we need to get him to The Citadel and get him warm. He keeps drifting in and out of consciousness," said Paul.

"Is it straight on?" said Chloe.

"Yes, it's not too far. Abby, can you lead? Chloe, can you move past me and bring up the rear? You can help me with Harry." Chloe squeezed past Paul and started checking Harry.

"Hold on Harry, you'll be ok," said Chloe as she looked at his face. It had turned white

Abby had frozen again. "Abby, we'll soon be out of here... you can do this. Now go," said Paul.

Abby turned around and started crawling unsteadily up the shaft. Paul followed and was now dragging Harry who was making incoherent moaning noises. Chloe was now in charge of his backpack. The gash on his forehead was still bleeding and the side of his face was red. Chloe was talking to him, trying to keep him awake. "Hang on Harry, we're nearly there," she said.

Back at base, concern was growing for the overdue cave party. Campbell was in the reception area pacing around. The weather had not let up and the rain was still pouring down.

"I don't like the look of this," he said, glancing at his watch.

Simon Porter joined him at the window looking at the gloom.

"No, you're right. Have you checked the radio again?" said Simon.

"Yes, just a couple of minutes ago... still no reply," Campbell answered.

"Did Paul log the trip?" said Simon. This was an important safety measure so that in the event of an emergency others would know where they would be.

"Yes. Dingwell Cavern, the Citadel, then one of the other caves," said Campbell.

"They should be ok there; it's not prone to flooding," said Simon.

"No, the Citadel should be fine but some of the other shafts go down a long way and have not been fully mapped yet. If they're in one of those then they could be in trouble," said Campbell.

He looked at his watch for the umpteenth time.

"Right, I'm alerting Cave Rescue. We need to get a team down there," he said.

"How long will it take?" said Simon.

"From Buxton...? It's going to be at least an hour, closer to two, I would think," said Campbell.

Back in the cave after another fifteen minutes of crawling, Abby eventually reached the end of the shaft and the comparative safety of The Citadel.

"Oh, thank goodness, we've made it," said Abby.

She clambered out of the narrow entrance and slowly climbed down to the floor of the giant chamber guided by her headlight. The rocks that had been strategically placed to form a series of steps made the going more straightforward. Paul followed, still half-dragging Harry who continued to drift into unconsciousness. He stopped at the mouth of the shaft.

"We're going to have to help Harry," he said to Chloe. "Can you give me a hand?"

Chloe dropped Harry's rucksack onto the cave floor then took off her own and did the same. Then the pair took an arm each. Harry came around and groaned as they gently supported him down the makeshift stairway to the floor of The Citadel. Abby took out her torch and lit the way.

The floor was wet and the sound of water dripping from the cavern roof was clearly audible.

"Ok," said Paul. "You should be safe here but we have to get Harry to a hospital. I need to go for help."

"You can't leave us," said Abby. "What if it floods?"

"You'll be fine. It'll be safe here," said Paul."

"Why can't we all go out together?" said Chloe.

"It'll take much longer and I know the drill. There'll be search parties out by now. I just need to let them know where we are and I can bring expert help. Stay here and look after Harry. He needs to be kept warm. I'll be as quick as I can."

Without any further debate, Paul disappeared into the cave where they had entered The Citadel.

Harry started groaning again but he was not the only one in trouble. Abby was hyperventilating. Now in comparative safety, she was veering towards shock again and was shivering in convulsions.

"Abby, come on, focus... we need to keep it together. Here, take off your rucksack and help me with Harry."

Abby put her rucksack next to the others then helped drag Harry to a boulder and sit him up. Chloe examined the side of his head with her lamp.

"This is a nasty gash. Pass my rucksack we need to stem the bleeding," said Chloe.

Abby complied.

"Have you any chocolate bars left?" said Chloe.

"I think so," said Abby.

"Good, I've got one Twix and a Mars Bar." Chloe took out the chocolate then continued her search for something to wrap around Harry's head.

"What about this?" said Abby, pulling out an old tee shirt. "I brought a spare in case I got wet," she said, ignoring the irony.

"Yes, that will do... pass it over," said Chloe.

Abby handed it over and Chloe immediately began ripping it into a long strip.

Harry was now conscious but very pale; his lips were turning blue.

Chloe took off Harry's hard hat, wrapped the material twice around his head and tied it tight.

"Come on Harry, stay with us. Here, eat this," she said tearing open the Twix bar and holding one of the chocolate fingers to his mouth.

Harry opened his mouth and chewed slowly as Chloe gradually fed him the chocolate.

"He's absolutely soaking wet," said Abby.

"Have you any dry clothes?" said Chloe.

"Only that tee shirt," said Abby who was starting to shiver again.

Chloe looked at her.

"We need to keep warm. I think a group hug is in order."

Chloe and Abby wrapped their arms together around Harry in attempt share body heat.

Paul, despite his wetsuit, was bitterly cold but his training had kicked in and he ignored his discomfort. He reached the cave entrance in fifteen minutes and raced to the Land Rover. It was pouring with rain.

The keys were still in one of the zip compartments of his leggings. He opened the door and reached for the walkie-talkie.

"Paul to control, over."

"Control here... thank goodness, are you ok?" said the voice on the other end.

"No, we've got a casualty. We'll need the air ambulance and a stretcher team to Dingwell Cavern. I've left them in The Citadel," said Paul.

"Ok that," said Campbell who was manning the communications desk. "Buxton Cave Rescue should be there within the hour. I'll update them with the news and get a chopper up." Paul explained the turn of events to Campbell.

"What's your status?" asked Campbell.

"I'm ok, freezing cold but I've got a change of clothing in the Land Rover and I'll put the heater on while I wait for the medics," he explained.

"Ok, stay put. They'll need you to guide them in," said Campbell. "I'll call as soon as I have an E.T.A. Control out."

Paul turned on the car's engine and put the heater on full blast while he changed into a pair of jeans and a sweatshirt. The Land Rover's windows quickly steamed up.

Back in the cave, the students had no idea what was happening outside and time seemed to drag. They were still huddled together and Chloe kept talking to Abby and Harry to keep their spirits up. Harry's condition was deteriorating; he was losing consciousness again and Chloe was trying to keep him awake.

It was thirty minutes before the walkie-talkie sparked into action in the Land Rover.

"Control to Paul," said the crackly voice.

"Receiving, over," said Paul.

"Cave rescue will be with you very soon. How are you doing?" said Campbell.

"Just about thawed out," said Paul. "I'll be waiting for them. Over"

Paul changed back into his wetsuit which had dried out in the warmth of the car. Within five minutes, another vehicle approached. He could see the logo on the side, "Buxton Cave Rescue".

He got out of the Land Rover and went to greet them. "Am I glad to see you guys," he said as the driver approached him.

Three more men exited the vehicle heavily equipped in what looked like space suits.

"Hi, I'm Dave Chandler, what've we got?" said the driver.

Paul apprised him of the situation.

"Ok, I'll let the Air Ambulance know, it should be here in about ten minutes.

"We'll need to winch," said Paul. "One of them is in a pretty bad way."

"Ok, we'll let them know. Let's get going," said Chandler.

Paul led the way and it took only ten minutes for the experienced rescuers to reach The Citadel.

Chloe heard them coming down the shaft. "Over here," she shouted as the first rescuer emerged from the opening in the cave wall.

"Thank goodness," said Chloe. "I don't think we could have held on for much longer."

Paul joined them. "How's Harry?" his first question.

"Not good, he keeps trying to sleep," said Chloe. "Abby's in shock I think."

One of the rescue team was already with Harry. He had a white armband on with the word "Doctor" printed in black.

He examined Harry's eyes with a pen-torch, then removed Chloe's temporary dressing and checked the gash on the side of his forehead.

"This will need stitching," said the medic as blood started to ooze from the wound. He applied another dressing and taped it up. The others removed some foil heat-retaining blankets from their bags. Abby was just staring at them.

"Come on Abby," said Chloe. "We'll soon be out of here. Put this blanket around you," and she helped one of the rescuers with Abby before wrapping herself.

The rescuers had a portable stretcher and began putting it together as Harry was being wrapped up.

"Concussion," said the medic. "We need to get him to the hospital as soon as possible."

With the three students secure, the group made their way back up the shaft to the exit of the cave. Paul led the way with Abby and Chloe carrying the two rucksacks following close behind. Two rescuers were carrying or, when the roof didn't allow, pulling Harry on the stretcher; as a result, it took nearly twenty minutes to reach the cave entrance. As they got to the surface, they could hear the noise of the helicopter in the distance. Abby hugged Chloe and started to cry with relief.

Dave Chandler, the leader of the rescuers, grabbed the radio from their Land Rover and made contact. Within minutes, the three students were being winched into the helicopter and on their way to a hospital in Leeds.

Chapter Three

Darwin, Northern Territories, Australia, July 13th, 2005

Harry Bentham, a geologist for Helvetia Mining Services Ltd, was looking out of the third-floor window of his hotel and wondering what the next stage of his life would hold. After four years of hard slog at University, he had mixed feelings about the challenges ahead of him.

He sat on the bed, looking at his two suitcases which contained most of his worldly goods, those that he could carry at least. He was likely to be here for some time. Nobody could give him an indication of when the project in Australia would be completed; his work permit was valid for twelve months. It was two days since he'd left the UK and he was starting to feel the effects of the journey.

It had been over three years since the cave incident. Following the accident, he had spent some anxious hours in intensive care before he started his recovery. His fitness level had proved to be the key to his survival. After a short stay in the hospital, he recuperated at his parents' home in Norwich before returning to Leeds four weeks later. His near-death incident affected him mentally and he initially suffered mood swings which took him a few months to overcome. However, the biggest blow came when the doctors advised him to give up playing rugby which had been his passion. Sport had always played an important role in his life and this was a low point for him. Through sheer determination, he overcame this obstacle and became even more determined to make the most of his life.

On his return to university, he was greeted enthusiastically by his fellow students, especially Chloe and Abby. They were none-the-worse for their experience physically but Abby suffered nightmares and her claustrophobia had reached the extent that she could no longer even go in a lift. She made the decision to drop out of geology and switched to the wider geography course. Chloe also changed direction after the first year and changed to a science degree.

It was Harry who turned out to be the real success. He had lost none of his natural drive; if anything, it became even more pronounced. He continued his geology studies, specialising in mining exploration. His thesis on mineral deposits in the Philippines had been widely regarded and had attracted the attention of a prestigious Swiss mining company. He lay back on the bed and reflected on the last few months since his interview.

Helvetia Mining Services Ltd was an international company based in Geneva with offices in London, Rio de Janeiro, Johannesburg, Abu Dhabi and Manila. Some would describe it as a secretive organisation with a unique approach to recruitment. It never advertised but had contacts in most major Universities and was alerted to particularly talented graduates in return for lucrative bursaries. Harry was a case in point.

One afternoon, as he approached the end of his final year, his tutor stopped him in the corridor as he was heading for a lecture. Harry respected the academic who had been an inspiration during his studies.

"Ah Harry, my boy, glad I bumped into you," said the withered professor. "I may have found a job for you."

He went on to explain that the University had been approached by a mining company looking for a geologist. "It sounds just up your street," he added. "I don't have all the details but it's a Swiss company. They want me to email them. What do you think?"

"Yeah, great," said Harry.

"Right I'll drop them a line and ask them to contact you. Do you have a mobile phone number?" said the professor, "just in case."

A few days later Harry was contacted by the head of talent, Lucien de Bruye who had phoned Harry directly from Switzerland. Arrangements were made for Harry to fly out to Geneva a week later.

Harry would never forget the interview, just three months ago, April 2005.

He had travelled abroad several times for field trips sponsored by the university and had managed to save for a trip to the States before he started his degree course. However, he was an infrequent flyer; overseas travel was expensive on a student grant. So there was an air of excitement when he received his tickets through the post the following week and discovered he would be flying business-class. He was told to wait at the airport's executive lounge in Geneva when he arrived and someone would collect him.

It was early when he approached the check-in desk at Manchester Airport dressed in his only suit and carrying an overnight bag. With a light raincoat slung casually over his arm he looked every bit the businessman. He enjoyed the two-hour flight and made the most of the free drinks and canapés. The plane landed at twelve thirty-five local time. With no additional luggage, he avoided the scrum at the baggage carousel and found the lounge on the first floor. He waited as instructed and was drinking a complimentary coffee and reading an American newspaper when a man in a smart uniform approached him.

"Herr Bentham?" the man enquired.

"Yes," said Harry, momentarily startled by the intrusion.

"Please follow me," he said, without any formal introductions, and picked up Harry's bag. He walked purposefully out of the lounge towards the airport exit. Harry followed. There was a reserved parking bay close to the airport arrivals entrance and the chauffeur headed for a black Mercedes Limousine and opened the rear door for Harry to get in.

"Please make yourself comfortable," said the driver in good English with a slight Germanic accent. "We have about forty-five minutes."

From the airport, the car headed away from Geneva city and along the E62 towards Lausanne. It was a glorious spring afternoon, sunny with a scattering of white clouds. The scenery was stunning. To the right, the eponymous Lake Geneva appeared every so often when the topography allowed. Harry took it all in with an air of excitement and apprehension.

After about half an hour, the driver turned off the Autoroute and headed north. The scenery changed and after the small town of Marchissy, they were surrounded by forest. About ten minutes later there was a turning on the right with tall stone gateposts either side of the road. There was a sign, "Privé - Dèfense d'entrer" on the right-hand post. You would not find the road on any map. The car turned down the lane and they were immediately surrounded by fir trees as they headed deeper into the forest.

They eventually came to a large clearing which was ringed by a high fence topped with razor wire. In front of them was a security gate manned by someone in a similar uniform to the chauffeur. The driver opened his window and the guard looked inside at Harry. There was a short conversation in French and the barrier was lifted.

Harry was looking in front of him over the driver's shoulder. The trees had gone, replaced by sweeping lawns and a lake with a fountain spraying water forty feet into the air. In the distance, he could see they were approaching a magnificent Chateau. This was not an exaggeration; it was like something out of Disney and reminded Harry of the structures in the Rhine Valley. Smooth bluish-grey stone walls towered upwards. There was even a drawbridge over a deep moat which the Mercedes navigated with a loud rumble as it traversed the wooden structure. They passed through an archway, complete with a portcullis, and into a courtyard where the car stopped. A man dressed in smart striped waistcoat and evening trousers walked towards the car and opened the back door.

"Monsieur Bentham," he said. "Bienvenu à Chateau Jura."

Harry barely acknowledged him, still trying to take in the surroundings. He got out and walked to the boot of the car where the waistcoat man was retrieving his overnight bag. He lifted it out and said something to the driver which Harry could not translate.

"Suivez-moi," said the man.

"Thank you," said Harry to the driver and followed the Frenchman towards an entrance door in the right-hand corner of the courtyard.

He walked through the wooden outer door into a large lobby where a young woman was attending a desk. The area had a rustic feel to it with high wooden beams, coats of arms and ancient portraits in oil of anonymous people from a by-gone age. There was even a stag's head on the wall over an old disused fireplace. There were other people milling about looking busy; this was a working building. The woman greeted him.

"Harry Bentham?" she said in perfect English.

"Yes," said Harry, trying to acclimatise to his surroundings.

"Welcome to Chateau Jura."

Harry made eye contact. She was bookish with tied back dark hair, wearing a business suit and glasses.

"My name is Lucy and I'm the head of administration here. I'll get someone to show you to your room in a moment. This is your itinerary," she said, handing Harry a piece of paper which was set out as a calendar. He checked his watch it was four-twenty. The first item on the agenda was scheduled for five o'clock; meeting with Head of Talent, Lucien de Bruye.

While Lucy was entering Harry's details into a log, her long fingers and perfect nails pecking at a keyboard, Harry read the remaining timetable.

8.00pm: Dinner with Edward and Madame Duchamp

7.30am: Breakfast with David Leganes, Head of Research

9.30am: Meeting with Geraldine Novik, Head of HR

11.00am Meeting with Edward Duchamp

12.30 Lunch

2.00pm Leave for Geneva Airport

5.00pm Depart for Manchester

Typical Swiss attention to detail, Harry thought. He looked up at Lucy who had finished her administration.

"Mr Bentham, Joseph will take you to your room. Here is your key," she said, handing him a key with a tag showing number 7. The man in the waistcoat was summoned once more to act as bag carrier and guide.

"Suivez-moi," said Joseph and Harry duly followed.

As Harry was escorted through the Chateau, he was amazed at the scale of the place and the number of people working there. He walked past several offices tastefully blended into the castle's interior, including a large room full of hi-tech computer monitors. An enormous screen showing commodity prices from around the world was being scanned by a team of staff who appeared to be speaking into small discreet headsets. Harry was fascinated and would have liked to have found out more about what was happening but he was having difficulty keeping up with Joseph without breaking into a trot. They eventually entered an accommodation block. They reached a stairway, climbed up two floors and came to a series of numbered bedrooms. Joseph led the way to room 7.

"I meet you here at five minutes to five and take you to meet Monsieur de Bruye," said Joseph. This was the first time Harry had heard him speak English.

"Right, ok, thanks," said Harry and he made his way into the room and looked around. It was of a five-star standard he surmised but not having stayed in such luxury before he had no real benchmark. He looked out of the window and from his vantage point could see he was at the back of the Chateau. Below him was the moat and then a gravel car park containing around forty cars. Beyond that, about a hundred metres away was the boundary fence and the forest. Harry decided to freshen up before his meeting with the Head of Talent.

Sure enough, at four fifty-five exactly, there was a knock on the door and Joseph was there waiting to escort Harry to his appointment. He had showered and with a change of shirt and polished shoes, he felt ready. Joseph led Harry back to the ground floor, out of the accommodation block and across the courtyard to an administration centre. This was a newly refurbished wing but had still managed to retain the character of the ancient edifice. Harry was fascinated; there were at least twenty people working at computer terminals.

"This way," said Joseph as he went through a set of doors and climbed two floors again. There was a long corridor with what looked like offices on either side. The doors were all neatly labelled in black script on small wooden plaques; 'Head of Finance', 'Head of Procurement', 'Head of Sales and Marketing', 'Head of Security'. The last but one was the 'Head of Talent' and Joseph knocked. "Come in," said a voice from within.

Although Harry had not met the Head of Talent, he recognised his voice immediately. Joseph opened the door and Harry stepped inside to be greeted by Lucien de Bruye; Joseph shut the door behind him. The office was a good size; bright and airy with a large picture window providing a vista across the grounds.

The man shook hands with Harry. "Lucien de Bruye, we spoke on the phone," he said. "Please take a seat, Harry."

Monsieur de Bruye was an impressive man with dark wavy hair and piercing blue eyes; he would not have looked out of place in a 1950's French movie. He had a slight Gallic accent which added to that assessment. He was immaculately dressed in a slate-grey suit, white shirt, a pink silk tie with matching pocket handkerchief; power-dressing at its very best.

Harry made himself comfortable on one of the leather seats in front of a large hardwood desk. His interviewer was seated behind it in a slightly larger matching executive seat.

"Would you like a coffee, tea or some water perhaps?" said de Bruye.

Harry was in a dilemma. Normal interview protocol would suggest declining such invitations as it leads to rattling chinaware but Harry wanted to give the impression he was at ease with the situation.

"A tea would be fine," he said.

"English Breakfast, Earl Grey, Lapsang Souchong?"

Harry nodded. "English breakfast will be fine, thank you."

"How do you take it?" asked de Bruye.

"Just milk," replied Harry.

Lucien pressed a button on a small box on his desk, an intercom.

"Oui, Monsieur de Bruye," came a voice.

"Can we have some teas please, Veronique? One Earl Grey and one English Breakfast with milk," he said.

"Welcome to our headquarters," said de Bruye turning his attention back to Harry. "I hope your room is comfortable."

"Yes, fine thanks," said Harry.

There was a folder on the desk in front of Lucien which he opened and Harry was curious about what it contained. De Bruye scanned the first sheet.

"I'm here to give you some background of our company, the work we do, and how we would like you to fit into the organisation," he said.

Harry tried to reconcile this statement; he thought it was a selection process but clearly it wasn't.

"Fine," said Harry.

The charm offensive continued. "We are a very successful business with considerable resources. I expect you will have researched the company," said de Bruye.

"Yes," said Harry, "but there's not much information."

"No, there won't be. We publish our statutory accounts here in Switzerland and in London but of course, that is only half the story."

Harry looked at him expectantly but before he could continue, they were interrupted by a knock on the door. Veronique entered, a strikingly attractive young lady with long dark hair which she had tied back in the same style as the receptionist. She was also dressed in a smart business suit, skirt above the knee, and spoke to de Bruye in French. Harry's French was fairly basic but he was able to make out the meaning. She was carrying a silver tray with cups, saucers and two small teapots and jug of milk. There was also a small plate with four biscuits.

Veronique placed the tray on the desk and left. "Merci, Veronique," said de Bruye, and started pouring the tea while continuing his briefing. Harry declined a biscuit.

De Bruye took a sip of his Earl Grey. "Let me give you an overview of our business," he said. Harry was holding his cup and saucer and waited with interest.

"We operate where there are mineral deposits we can viably exploit; anywhere in the world. We have three divisions. Operations, which looks after procurement, administration, security and so on; Finance, which includes our money-market activities; and Prospecting, which is where our geologists are managed. Operations and Finance are based here but our geologists can be anywhere in the world. We control the projects from here, of course but we also have support centres in Rio, Johannesburg, Manila, Abu Dhabi, and London." Harry looked suitably impressed. "Oh, and we've also got an office in Australia. It's fairly new, less than twelve months. The local offices look after our prospecting activities in the respective continents."

Harry knew much of this from his research but it had a new meaning when outlined by the Head of Talent. It was as though he was reading from a brochure but he was expressive and passionate about the organisation.

De Bruye described the extent of the business and Harry was engrossed. The conversation then switched to Harry's background and his work at university.

"You didn't go straight to University from High School, I notice. What did you do?"

"I just tried to make some money. I did all kinds of things; navvying, bar work, anything that would mean I could travel. I did that for two years then I went to the States for nearly twelve months, then to Uni."

From the questions being asked, Harry was amazed how well informed Lucien was. He had emailed his résumé following his phone conversation but it only had outline information. Somehow, they had managed to get copies of his thesis and details of his research which could only have been obtained from the University.

The interview lasted almost two hours before de Bruye called it to a halt. "Any questions, before you meet Monsieur Duchamp?"

"No, thank you. You've covered everything," said Harry, who had quite frankly, been overwhelmed by the whole process.

There was a knock on the door. Joseph appeared and spoke

to de Bruye in French. "Êtes-vous prêt?" He asked if they were ready.

"Oui, merci, Joseph," said de Bruye, who turned to Harry. "I hope you will enjoy your dinner with Monsieur Duchamp. I am sure you will have a good time. He is a fascinating man."

He got up and shook hands with Harry.

"Thank you," said Harry, and he followed Joseph out of the office.

Joseph led Harry back to the administration block where he had arrived only a few hours earlier and instructed him to take a seat. It was seven thirty-five, still twenty-five minutes before his dinner appointment. For the first time, he was beginning to feel slightly nervous. He had managed to find some background on Edward Duchamp, a man with a global reputation. He was not only chairman of a worldwide organisation but an outspoken observer on environmental issues. Harry had watched one of his lectures on the internet; he was an inspirational speaker.

At five to eight Joseph appeared and led Harry to a different part of the Chateau. It was another climb and after two flights they arrived at a door which Joseph opened. It was a magnificent conference centre with views overlooking the lawns and the fountain in the distance. It was set out ready for a board meeting. Harry followed Joseph into an adjoining room. It was half the size of the boardroom and beautifully decorated with several expensive-looking landscape pictures adorning the walls. In the middle of the room, there was a table set for eating with three place settings; silver-service, wine goblets and a pristine white table cloth. There was a vase of freshly cut flowers.

In the corner of the room, on a white leather sofa, sat a middle-aged man and a younger woman. A waiter in a white uniform was attending to them with a bottle of Champagne. The man looked up and saw Harry and Joseph. He got up from the sofa and walked towards them.

"Thank you, Joseph. That will be all," he said and Joseph left the room. The young lady also got up and joined them.

"You must be Harry," said the man. "Welcome to Chateau Jura. I am Edward Duchamp. This is my wife, Monique."

"Pleased to meet you, Mr Duchamp," said Harry.

"Edward," said the man. "Please call me Edward."

Harry was trying to place the accent; American in the main but not originating from there. His biography said he was Swiss. He shook hands with the couple. Edward's handshake was firm and purposeful; Monique's delicate with only the slightest of touches.

"Enchanté de faire votre connaisance," said Monique.

"I'm sorry, my French is not that good," said Harry with some embarrassment.

"Pardon, er, I am sorry... I can speak English," said Monique. "Pleased to meet you," she translated.

Harry looked at her; she was elegant, around five foot five or six, with striking features and dark, auburn hair. She was wearing a short black cocktail dress with a deep cleavage. There was also a significant amount of jewellery; diamond earrings and matching necklace, a gold bangle on her right wrist and a vintage Cartier watch on her left. The ring on her wedding finger must have cost the equivalent G.D.P. of a small country. Harry was trying not to stare but she noticed the interest and smiled. Harry caught the fragrance of her perfume, heady and exotic.

"Champagne, Harry?" offered Edward, handing him a flute.

"Thank you," said Harry. The waiter was duly summoned with the bottle and poured him a measure.

"Beautiful place," said Harry. "Great pictures," he added, looking at the paintings, trying to make small talk and look more confident than he was feeling.

"Thank you," said Edward. "You like art? We have two

by Giovanni Giacometti... those there." Edward pointed to two landscapes in the middle of the opposite wall. He walked towards the pictures and examined them closely.

"I don't know him but they're great," said Harry.

"Yes," said Edward. "We picked them up at auction last year, a good investment, I believe." Edward walked back and continued his introduction.

Harry took another sip of his Champagne wishing he had researched Swiss Impressionists.

"Castle Jura has been our headquarters for just over sixteen years. We moved from Geneva when we started to outgrow our earlier offices," he said.

Harry was trying to weigh up the man; distinguished looking, well-groomed grey hair, immaculate suit but without a tie, in the modern vogue. Everything about him exuded... he was trying to think of the right word... 'class' was as close as he could get but there was something else. One of Harry's favourite old films was 'The French Connection'; he had the DVD and had watched it many times. Edward reminded him of Fernando Rey, the actor who played the villain, Alain Charnier. He even had the goatee beard. Sophisticated menace he would call it; charming but not someone to take lightly. His thoughts were interrupted.

They moved back to the sofa area which was flanked by two matching armchairs with a low walnut coffee table in the middle.

"Please take a seat," said Edward. "We will eat shortly." They waited while Monique sat down; Edward sat next to her, Harry in one of the armchairs.

"You have met Lucien, I think," said Edward. "He will have told you about what we do, I guess."

"Yes," said Harry.

"Well, let me fill in some of the gaps," said Edward, and

he took a sip of his Champagne but did so with exaggerated slurps as though the act of drinking itself was some art form. Harry missed nothing; this clearly was a connoisseur at work. Monique sat attentively holding her glass in her hand but not contributing to the conversation. Harry was trying to keep eye contact with his host but Monique's gaze was starting to unsettle him.

"Our mission statement is quite clear; it's all about stakeholder value."

Harry understood the concept but let Edward explain.

"Our main stakeholders are, of course, our investors, then our clients, and then our people. That's not a hierarchy, I should make that clear; the order's not important. The organisation's fundamental aim is to provide an excellent return for our investors, first-class service for our clients and a great career for those who work for us. That's our philosophy and drives the business direction. Basically, it's about making money."

Harry had finished his drink and the waiter was quick to fill up his glass. Edward and Madame Duchamp were also replenished.

Edward continued his overview. "We make our money firstly by prospecting mineral deposits, then obtaining licences to mine, which, as I'm sure you know, can take a long time."

"Yes, I can imagine," said Harry.

"Then we lease the land for extraction and take a percentage of the mining operation. We also invest in the money markets and in other commodities. You may have seen our dealing room earlier?" He paused and took a drink. "The model is simple and it works very well. It's also very profitable."

"Yes," said Harry, "very impressive."

"Thank you..." said Edward who was looking closely at Harry as if assessing him in some way. He continued. "We also donate a significant amount to charity each year through the Duchamp Foundation, mostly providing educational programmes. We like to give something back to those areas where we have mining interests."

Harry considered this statement; it seemed incongruous to the business objectives which were far from philanthropic.

Harry was trying to ignore the obvious distraction of Madame Duchamp who continued looking at him intensely but he was finding it difficult. She was undoubtedly aware of her allure; her eyes engaging, deep green, more round than oval; she looked a lot younger up close.

"My wife helps me considerably," Edward added, noticing the connection.

Madame Duchamp turned and smiled at her husband but it was a polite smile with no real emotion behind it.

"Oui, I... er... look after some things when Edward is away," she said. She spoke with a strong French accent.

"I couldn't manage without her," said Edward, and he lifted her hand and kissed it. "It's been an amazing six years..." He was still looking at her. "We met at the Joseph Fourier University... in Grenoble. I was lecturing there, Monique was completing her masters."

Despite this background description, there seemed a lack of closeness between them; her body language did not suggest a fondness, more a frostiness Harry detected.

Another man entered the room in a chef's attire.

"Le dejeuner est prêt, madame et monsieurs," he said before Edward could complete the details of their liaison.

"Merci Guillaume," said Edward, and he got up from the sofa. Monique and Harry followed him to the table.

"You sit opposite Monique," said Edward, who was ostensibly sitting at the head of the table.

The waiter stood behind Madame Duchamp, held the seat back then moved it forward so that she could sit; he did the same with Edward and Harry in turn. Another waiter appeared pushing a gold-coloured trolley. There was a tureen with a ladle protruding from it, three dishes and a basket of bread rolls.

"I do hope you like the chef's soup," said Edward. "It's delicious."

"Thank you," said Harry and the soup waiter started serving portions.

The conversation continued during the first course and Harry started to relax in their company. Edward was not quite what Harry was expecting; he was a genial host and appeared genuinely interested in Harry's work at University as well as describing more of the organisation. It became obvious why he was such a charismatic and inspirational character; Harry could almost feel the passion he had for the business. He was still not clear where Madame Duchamp fitted into the organisation but he found her continued stare unsettling; it had an intoxicating effect and he found it difficult to keep his eyes off her.

The soup course was completed and lived up to the host's description. The chef entered with a portable barbecue. The waiter followed with a platter of raw meat and dishes of vegetables on a chauffoir.

"You're in for a treat," said Edward as the chef prepared to cook steaks on the barbecue. There were flames and a sizzle, as the fat from the meat ignited from the heat of the cooker.

Monique was continuing to look in Harry's direction. He was unsure how to respond so he just smiled hoping that it would be a suitable acknowledgement.

The chef delivered the three steaks and placed them on the warming plates. "Help yourself to vegetables," said Edward, and Harry started to spoon suitable portions of carrots, mange tout, and potatoes onto his plate. There had been no attempt to ask Harry for any dietary requirements and he was beginning to wonder if they had researched that too. The waiter reappeared with a bottle of red wine.

"Merci Claude," said Edward. "I have a vineyard in France... in the Loire Valley," he added. "It's a hobby really; a labour of love but we've had some success. Last year we were awarded a Medaille d'or by the CDV." He said, proudly. Edward noticed Harry's disconnect. "Challenge International Du Vin," he clarified. "The oldest and most prestigious competition in wine-making," explained Edward proudly. "It means we can charge premium prices," he added and began to laugh.

Harry smiled; he was not in the least bit surprised. Edward certainly had the Midas touch when it came to business.

"I have chosen a six-year-old vintage which is, I think, our best," said Edward.

The waiter removed the cork in wine-waiter tradition and poured a small measure for him to try. Edward took a sip and rolled it around his mouth.

"Bien, très bien," said Edward, and the waiter poured Monique and Harry a glass before filling Edward's.

The chef, having completed his culinary duties, left the party. Claude had also gone, leaving the guests to their own devices. Another bottle of 1999 was open on the table; left to breathe.

The room was warm and the drink was making the ambience mellow and relaxed. Harry was halfway through his steak, listening to Edward give his opinion on global warming and the implications for the mining industry when he suddenly felt something bump his leg. He realised it was probably accidental but the 'footsie' with Monique certainly had his attention.

Harry instinctively apologised; Monique just smiled. Edward seemed oblivious to Monique's outrageous flirting. Harry's appetite was beginning to wane.

Edward continued his commentary on commodity markets, where the growth areas were, and what were to be avoided.

Harry was trying to concentrate on his host's dialogue but Monique's stare continued to unnerve him. She picked up her wine and took a sip not taking her eyes off Harry; then licked her lips. Harry was getting warm and thought of excusing himself to go to the toilet but manners dictated he would have to finish his main course. Then Edward switched tack and wanted to know Harry's views on a number of issues which Harry tried to answer despite Monique's undivided attention.

Edward asked Harry his thoughts on possible growth areas for expansion for mineral exploration which he was keen to hear. Harry was on familiar ground having studied this very topic. Edward was, of course, aware of this. Harry talked with some authority on some of the more remote areas, Antarctica, the Arctic, Central Africa and the Philippines. Edward listened attentively.

"We will be very interested in looking at some of your studies in more detail, won't we dear?" said Edward.

"Oui, yes," she said. "Hassurément, most definitely."

She continued to look at Harry again and smiled, then started playing with her necklace subconsciously, rolling it between her fingers. She leant forward; out of politeness, Harry quickly turned his head away from the sight of her chest.

The three finished the main course and Claude re-appeared to clear the table; the flirting stopped with the arrival of company. The discussion continued as the chef returned with a selection of desserts in individual containers. He explained the contents to the guests and Monique chose two and Harry did the same. Edward chose one then ordered another bottle of wine to go with the sweet.

"I've selected a nice dessert wine... not from our vineyard this time," he chuckled. "We concentrate on red. This is a nice 2002 Sauterne from Château d'Yquem, quite sweet but excellent with dessert, I think. You will like it, I'm sure," said

Edward which sounded more like an instruction. He continued waxing lyrical about the wine with the same passion he exuded for his business.

"Thank you, I'm sure I'll enjoy it," said Harry and Claude did the honours once more,

The wine, ambience, and the pressure, together with the early start, were beginning to tell on Harry. He was trying desperately to suppress a yawn to the extent his eyes were beginning to water. As he started on his sweet, he caught Monique's gaze. She looked at him with those big eyes and Harry was suddenly wide awake; what was going on?

They finished the desserts and Claude reappeared with a coffee-maker and three brandy glasses. He proceeded to clear the table.

"Café, monsieur?" he asked.

"Thank you," said Harry, "with milk."

While Claude started to prepare the coffees, Monique stood up. "Excusé-moi," she said and walked towards the boardroom where Harry had entered earlier.

"Would you like to freshen up before coffee?" said Edward.

"I wouldn't mind," said Harry.

"It's just through there on the right," he said, pointing to the direction Monique had exited. Edward continued talking to Claude who was clearing the table while Harry got up and headed for the toilets.

He followed the directions and looked right. He could see the male and female signs and he was about to enter the 'gents' as Monique came out of the 'ladies'. She stopped. "Vous faites très bien... er... pardon, you are doing very well," she said. "Edward, he likes you."

"Thank you," said Harry.

"I like you too," she said, and rubbed his arm with her hand, then leant up and kissed him on the cheek.

Harry was taken aback; he had no idea how to handle this situation. He was still unsure whether it was some part of the 'process' or not but recognising Monique's importance decided to do nothing precipitous. He just said "thank you", and hastened into the toilet. Monique walked back to the dining room.

Harry was still feeling the fatigue of the day. He washed his face and applied some sweet-smelling hand lotion in an attempt to wake himself up before making his way back to the dining room. As he entered the room, Edward and Monique seemed to be in deep conversation and broke off as soon as they saw Harry approach.

"Feeling better?" asked Edward.

"Yes, much, thank you," said Harry.

Claude returned with a bottle of Brandy.

"Cognac monsieur?" he said to Harry.

"Small," said Harry, emphasising the amount with his fingers. Claude delivered a measure as indicated by Harry then poured the Duchamps' without reference; he was obviously familiar with their needs.

Edward drank his coffee rather quickly then tipped back the brandy as if it were a shot and stood up.

"If you will excuse me, Harry, I have a breakfast meeting tomorrow at six-thirty and I need to do some preparation." Harry went to stand up.

"No, please, you can stay here. Monique will be happy to entertain you, won't you dear?"

"Mais oui, avec plaisir," she said, and looked at Harry again with those big eyes.

Edward put his left hand on Harry's shoulder in a fatherly way and offered his right hand in farewell. Harry responded.

"It's been good talking to you tonight... I'll see you for lunch tomorrow but I think you'll fit into our organisation extremely well," he said shaking Harry's hand.

"Thank you, Edward. I look forward to seeing you tomorrow," said Harry.

Edward left without a backwards glance and headed back through the boardroom.

"Let's sit over there," said Monique, indicating the sofa. "It will be more... er, comfortable, bring your drink."

Claude entered and removed the coffee cups. "Il y aura quelque chose d'autre?" he said.

"Non, merci," said Monique, and Claude left the room. He could see Harry trying to translate. "I have just told him we don't need anything else. We won't be... how you say... disturbed?"

Chapter Four

Harry followed Monique to the sofa with his glass of brandy and sat on the chair he had vacated earlier. Her cocktail dress rode up as she sat on the sofa and Harry tried not to stare. Her perfume overwhelmed the smell of the earlier cooking and attacked his senses.

"Non, non, asseyez-vous ici," she said, slipping back into French, and patted the seat next to her on the sofa. Harry complied.

"Your husband is an impressive man," said Harry, as he sat down, trying desperately to change the atmosphere.

"Oui, yes, he is. He has done much good," she said. Harry was holding his glass.

"What about you Harry, do you want to do good?" she said.

Harry turned and looked at her; he wasn't sure how to respond to the question.

"Yes, of course," he said.

"You look... nervoux, Harry. Are you?"

"Not really... well, maybe a little," he corrected himself and shuffled in the seat

"It is ok," she said and placed her hand on Harry's thigh. "Edward and I, we have... un arrangement. He is away so much... toujours, so we allow each other... how you say? Une certaine liberté... er, freedom," she translated.

She was confident, clearly at ease with herself and her sexuality. She was older, not much but worldlier than Harry and he found her irresistible; nothing like the girls he had met at the rugby club.

She put her brandy glass down on the table and looked him in the eyes.

"Do you like me, Harry?"

"Yes, of course. You are very... beautiful," he replied, trying desperately to contain his anxiety.

Monique's hand was starting to move upward. Harry was still holding his brandy glass, completely out of his comfort zone.

She moved closer, took his drink from his hand and placed it on the coffee table. She leant forward and kissed him. Harry backed away but she wrapped her arm around his neck and pulled him to her.

"It's ok..." she said.

She took his right hand and placed it on her cleavage.

Harry was in turmoil but he took her lead and slid his hand under the fabric of her dress. She moaned gently as he cupped her right breast and started to play with her nipple. Her hand was rubbing the front of his trousers and she could feel him getting harder. She kissed him again and this time Harry responded, tongues entwining as the passion increased.

Monique broke away. "Attendez... viens avec moi... come with me," she translated, and she stood up, adjusted her dress and took Harry's hand.

They left their brandy glasses on the coffee table and Monique led the way from the dining room, through the boardroom and into the passageway beyond. They walked hand-in-hand to the end of the corridor; there was a door immediately in front of them and Monique keyed numbers into a security pad to the right. The door catch unlocked with a click. She pulled the door towards them and went through. In front of them was a stone stairway heading upwards in a spiral. They started climbing and after about twenty steps they arrived at a landing.

Monique was still holding Harry's hand; she turned left and another door faced them which she opened.

"Ici," she said and led him inside.

It was a magnificent bedroom, dominated by a queen-sized bed to the right. A glass chandelier cascaded from the ceiling, giving off a warm light. Beautiful light-brown drapes, held in place by gold-coloured cords, hung from the two large windows. It was dark outside but arc-lights illuminated the Chateau walls which Harry could see clearly. The carpet was luxurious with a thick pile and at the bottom of the bed, there was a Persian rug. There was another door which was slightly ajar on the left-hand side next to a white dressing-table.

Monique let go of his hand, shut the door behind them and turned the key in the lock. They were not going to be disturbed.

"Attendez ici," she said.

Harry stood there trying to take everything in. She went through the other door and closed it behind her. Harry could hear running water, then a toilet flush, more running water. Monique reappeared, went to the windows in turn and pulled the cords releasing the curtains. Privacy was complete.

She went to Harry, wrapped her arms around his neck and started kissing him again, deep and sensual. Harry responded and pulled down the top of her dress to reveal Monique's breasts. She tilted her head back taking in the sensations as Harry moved down and started kissing them in turn. His tongue weaved around her nipples sending shock waves through her body. Monique wrestled with the zip on her dress; Harry watched as it dropped to the floor and she stood there in just a small pair of French knickers.

She took off Harry's jacket and started undoing his tie, then his shirt. She started rubbing her fingers through his chest hairs then pressed herself against him. Harry responded and moved his hands down her body. She moaned again as he slipped his fingers under the flimsy material tracing the downy hair to her wetness below. Monique broke away momentarily to unzip Harry's trousers and grasp his erection.

He removed the rest of his clothes and Monique led him to the bed. She pulled back the bed covers then went to her bedside cabinet and handed Harry a condom.

"Vous voudrez un de ces... You will need one of these," she translated.

It was gone two o'clock before Monique called time on their passion. They were laid on the bed; Harry kept drifting off to sleep. She leant over and looked at him.

"Vous devez aller, Harry... You have to go," she said.

"Yes... ok," he said, trying to come to his senses.

He got dressed and watched Monique as she got out of bed and put on a robe.

She saw him to the door, kissed him on the cheek. "Au revoir, Harry, goodbye... merci... thank you," she said. There was finality in her statement.

Harry left Monique's apartment and was momentarily disorientated. He walked down a flight of stairs and reached a corridor which stretched left and right. He wandered around totally lost for a few minutes, then spotted a sign for 'Reception'. He followed the signage and eventually found the room where he was greeted on his arrival. The duty night porter was behind the desk and looked at Harry suspiciously as he walked by.

"Goodnight," said Harry. The man acknowledged. Harry recognised where he was and was able to retrace the staircase that led to his bedroom,

Not surprisingly, Harry had difficulty sleeping. Despite being mentally exhausted he was still on a high from his tryst with Monique; he still couldn't rationalise the events. He reviewed the evening in his mind, replaying their love-making and wondering if he had made the right call in succumbing to her advances. He convinced himself that he had no option. Then he thought about the earlier meetings with Lucien and Edward; expectations were undoubtedly going to be high. He took out the piece of paper detailing his itinerary from his jacket pocket and read it again. Breakfast with the head of research was going to be important; he would be Harry's overall boss. Then there was the final meeting with Edward; he had no idea how he was going to face that.

He eventually managed to drift off to sleep and when his alarm woke him at six-thirty he was in a deep slumber. His head felt heavy, the combination of alcohol and lack of sleep. There was a bottle of water and two glasses on a tray on the dressing table. He removed the metal top from one of the bottles and drank it down in one, then headed for the bathroom.

In another part of the Chateau at six a.m., Edward was sitting on an ornate chaise-long, drinking coffee and reading some notes in preparation for his breakfast meeting. He too, had his own living quarters, although that would be doing the description an injustice; it was more a complex really. It covered two floors with a bedroom, large bathroom, lounge, reception area and a state-of-the-art office, essential for his regular global conference calls. Monique walked in, looking immaculate in a dark business suit and white blouse.

He looked up at her and took off his reading glasses. She went over to him and kissed him on the cheek.

"Did you enjoy your evening?" he said.

"Oui, bon... c'était bon," she replied.

He went back to his papers and Monique went into the kitchen to make a coffee. There was no more discussion.

Harry meanwhile, had showered and was preparing himself for his first meeting. There was a knock on his door at seven-twenty. It was Joseph, looking as spick and span as ever in his butler uniform, coming to escort Harry to his meeting with David Leganes. Harry was ready and followed him down through reception, across the courtyard to a canteen area. The glass entrance door had the word 'Refectory' etched in twelve-inch lettering. There were about twenty people having breakfast. Joseph walked through to an area surrounded by temporary screens where a table was set for two people. A man was sat reading a copy of Le Figaro.

He looked up, put his newspaper on an adjoining chair and stood to greet his guest. "Ah, you must be Harry," said the man, extending his hand.

"Yes, pleased to meet you," said Harry.

"Thank you, Joseph," the man said, dismissing the butler. He looked at Harry. "David Leganes, Head of Research. I've been looking forward to meeting you. Please... sit down; someone will be with us in a minute to take our order." His English was impeccable but again with the slightest American accent, not unlike Edward's.

Sure enough, after a couple of minutes, a young lady in a waitress uniform approached their table with a notepad. Harry looked at the man as he ordered a full English breakfast. He was older than Lucien de Bruye but taller, and there was a similarity in his Gallic features even with the spectacles. It seemed the upper stratum of the organisation was cloned. Harry imagined a conveyor belt churning out Helvetia executives.

"Pour vous?" asked the girl.

Harry also asked for a cooked breakfast; he needed the energy.

With breakfast ordered, it was down to business and Leganes described the activity for which he had responsibility. "We have many projects presently ongoing across the world - Brazil, Botswana, Australia, Middle East, the Russian States, and so on. At the moment, there are about forty geologists working for us, some employed and some freelance working on a contract basis."

The breakfast was delivered and duly consumed as Leganes continued to give Harry a résumé of the ongoing geological work. Harry took it all in and then Leganes looked at him. "We were impressed by your thesis, which is why we would like you to join us."

"Thank you," replied Harry.

"What made you think about the Philippines?"

Harry took a drink of his coffee considering his answer carefully. "Well, as I'm sure you know it's largely untapped and there are extensive mineral deposits. I expect you'll have seen my findings from the field trip I did eighteen months ago?"

"Yes, I read your report and as you say, we have looked at the area. We're not totally convinced of the commercial viability yet."

"I think with today's extraction techniques it could well be viable, particularly the gold and nickel. It's all in my report," said Harry.

"Yes, your conclusions were quite comprehensive... and compelling." He paused for a moment as if considering the response. "Hmm, we'll have to discuss this further." He was now on his second cup of coffee.

Harry was feeling more confident now and took the initiative. "How long have you worked for the company?"

"Me...? I graduated in '76; I was based in London, studying at the L.S.E., then on to Harvard, studied Land Management, left there in '78. Been working for the company ever since," replied Leganes who proceeded to give Harry a potted history of his career in the mining industry.

"That's impressive," said Harry on listening to the man's verbal C.V. He was obviously in esteemed company, organisationally speaking.

Leganes switched the discussion again. "We give our graduates a very comprehensive induction, particularly those who'll be working in the field. You are happy with overseas travel I take it? There will be a lot of it."

"Yes, no problem."

"Good, because I think I have just the right project for you." Harry was intrigued.

"What do you know about Kakadu?"

"Northern Territories, Australia, large Uranium deposits. I'm sure I read somewhere recently that UNESCO's World Heritage Committee is going to be voting on whether to designate the area as a World Heritage in danger site," said Harry. "If it goes through it will put pay to any further mining in the region."

"Very good, very good... you are well-informed. Yes, although I wouldn't worry about UNESCO; they will not be a problem," said Leganes cryptically. "Actually, we're prospecting about fifty miles outside the National Park, just aerial surveys at the moment, until we get formal approval."

"Formal approval?" said Harry.

"We're working on that at the moment," replied Leganes.

"But that's all been surveyed, surely?" said Harry.

"Well, yes, other companies have been involved there, some for over twenty years but not where we're interested. We've got a small team out there at the moment and I'd like you to join them when you've finished your course. We need to do some work on the ground to confirm our findings."

Harry was speechless.

Leganes looked at Harry like one of his former school teachers. "I needn't remind you that everything we've discussed is confidential and must not go outside this room." There was something sinister in the way that he gave the warning and it took Harry aback.

"Of course," replied Harry.

"Right, that about covers things unless you have any more questions."

"No, I don't think so," replied Harry.

"Ok, you're meeting Geraldine next I see," said Leganes,

looking at a piece of paper on his desk. "She'll tell you all you need to know about start dates, salary and everything."

He stood up indicating the interview was over and Harry took the hint. "Look forward to a long and fruitful association," said Leganes and shook Harry's hand.

He pressed a button on his intercom. "Joseph...? Monsieur Bentham is ready for his next meeting."

A moment later there was a knock on the door and Joseph entered.

"Thank you," said Harry as he looked back at Leganes who was returning to his seat.

As they walked back through the refectory it was empty with the exception of one or two staff getting another coffee fix. Joseph led Harry back to the admin block and along another passageway with various offices on either side. The last door had a name plaque, 'Geraldine Novik – Head of Human Resources'. Joseph knocked on the door and a voice beckoned them in.

A woman with a distinct Slovak appearance, probably in her mid-forties, with long dark hair flecked with grey, approached and offered her hand in greeting. The handshake was limp and far from welcoming, almost a token gesture. She was dressed in a dark blue business suit, her skirt just above the knee, with a pale blue blouse, open at the neck. Joseph left and closed the door behind him.

"Mr Bentham..? I am Geraldine Novak, Head of H.R. pleased to meet you," she said but there was a tone of formality and matter-of-factness in her voice which suggested she wasn't.

"Pleased to meet you," replied Harry, and she motioned with her hand for him to sit down. The office was similar to Lucian de Bruye's in layout with a tan leather chair in front of the desk. Geraldine was making herself comfortable on her side.

"I hope you have found your visit here of interest," she said.

Harry almost laughed.

"Yes, very," he managed to say.

"I'm here to discuss your contract and tell you about some of the training we will give you before you join your project team." She spoke in perfect English but with a trace of an Eastern European accent. Harry was trying to assess her; definitely lacking in any inter-personal skills, bordering on coldness. Her eyes made contact but were expressionless.

She continued to go over Harry's terms and conditions and the benefits package which was substantial, at least double what he would expect in London; he was flabbergasted. "We pay in Swiss Francs so the tax is much less," she added. "You will need to open a bank account here."

She then produced two documents and described each. "This is your employment contract and this is the standard confidentiality agreement we require all our employees to sign. It is quite straightforward," she clarified seeing Harry's scrutiny.

He took a pen from his pocket and signed both documents; this was his dream job and he had no qualms about committing himself.

"When will you be able to join us?"

"My course finishes end of May, so mid-June, I guess."

Geraldine checked her calendar. "How about the 13th, that's a Monday?"

"Yes, that's great," said Harry, hardly able to contain his excitement. The head of H.R. showed little emotion.

"I will arrange for your two-week induction to start then," she said.

"Where will that be?" said Harry.

"Here," she said and looked at Harry as if it was a daft question. "I thought you knew."

"No, nobody mentioned it."

"Oh ok, well, where possible we try to hold the induction training for our graduates here," she clarified. "It will give you a better opportunity to understand the diversity and complexity of our business. One of my team will email you the details and your flight tickets nearer the time."

The meeting concluded after half an hour; Harry was under the impression she was glad to be rid of him; he felt like an unwelcome interruption to her busy work schedule. The 'goodbyes' seemed forced, with little courtesies, totally at odds with the other meetings he had had. Joseph was duly summoned to escort Harry back to reception and his second meeting with Edward Duchamp. There was almost an hour to kill and Harry filled the time reading some of the magazines on display and drinking coffee which seemed to be on tap.

He was feeling excited about his new job and couldn't wait to start but he was slightly nervous about his next meeting. He wondered if there would be any repercussions following his tryst with Monique.

Just before the allotted time, Joseph arrived to escort Harry. They made their way to Edward's private office and Joseph knocked on the door. Harry was suddenly feeling apprehensive when he heard the "come in" response. Joseph opened the door and he was welcomed warmly by his host. "Harry, come on through to my office; it's good to see you again."

They walked through a lounge area and into the adjoining room where Monique had met her husband earlier. Edward sat at his desk and invited Harry to sit on the chaise-longue.

"Would you like a coffee?" asked Edward.

"I'm fine, thanks," said Harry, who had been drinking coffee almost all morning.

Edward looked at Harry and smiled. "I was pleased to hear you've decided to join us."

"I'm grateful for the opportunity," said Harry.

"I think you'll have an excellent career with us. You've impressed a lot of people here, including me. Monique spoke well of you too."

Harry wasn't sure how to respond. "Thank you," seemed appropriate.

"I understand David's sending you to Australia. That's going to be a great experience for you. I've already spoken to Nate... Nate Gillespie, he's the project manager over there," he clarified. Harry logged the name.

"Did David tell you anything about Kakadu?"

"Not in detail."

"Mmm, it'll be a tough first assignment... a lot of politics, not that you'll be involved in that of course."

Edward did not elaborate.

"And you'll be with us in June, I hear."

"Yes," said Harry. Edward wrote something down on a piece of paper on his desk.

"Right, well, that's great... I look forward to meeting you again then," said Edward. "Now you must excuse me, I know we were supposed to have lunch but something urgent has cropped up which needs my attention. I've asked Lucien to entertain you. Monique has had to go to Lausanne." Harry wasn't sure why this information was relevant but tried to hide any possible sign of disappointment.

"That's fine," said Harry.

Edward stood up and offered his hand. Harry responded; the exchange was warm and cordial.

"See you here in June then... and good luck with your studies, Harry," said Edward and again Joseph was on hand to take Harry to the refectory.

By two o'clock, a convivial lunch with Lucien had been consumed. Harry collected his things from his room and made his farewells; he was waiting for his ride back to the airport in the courtyard. He watched the Mercedes Limousine as it glided through the portico and came to a stop outside reception where he was stood. It was Marcel, the same driver that had picked Harry up from the airport. As the car drove through the archway and over the drawbridge Harry looked back over his shoulder and watched the Chateau gradually disappear into the distance. His mind was all over the place trying to take in the last twenty-four hours; it was an experience he would never forget.

After less than an hour, the limousine pulled up outside the VIP entrance to the departure lounge and a porter in an airline uniform was waiting with a trolley. Harry's luggage was removed from the boot and positioned on the carrier.

"Au revoir, bon voyage," said the driver.

"Merci beaucoup," said Harry, his first attempt at using his schoolboy French. Marcel got back into the car and Harry watched him drive away. The porter pushed the luggage into the airport and to the VIP check in. Future plane journeys would not be like this.

The flight back to the UK was uneventful and Harry tried to get some sleep. The thought of Monique kept haunting him; he had never met anyone like her. He'd had several girlfriends since starting University; mostly girls that frequented the rugby club or the student parties where sex was almost guaranteed. To him it was just fun; he had never felt the urge for any commitment or the inclination to be tied down. His record relationship was three weeks. He kept mulling it over; Monique was different; a class apart, living in a world of fine wine and designer clothes; maybe that was it. Harry was fascinated by her but wondered why she had come on to him. The cynic in him thought it might be some sort of inducement for him to join the company but he quickly discounted that. He would have joined the company without Monique's attention; it was his dream job. He tried to put it out of his mind, it was a one-off; he would just have to accept it.

There were less than two months to go before he would join Helvetia and the next few weeks were an anti-climax after the highs of his trip to Geneva. It was back to the mundane slog of revising for his final exams and he found it difficult to focus on his studies. He couldn't wait to start on his new career and was questioning the relevance of the exams having secured his dream job. His competitive nature, however, meant that any sort of failure was not an option so he kept driving himself on.

During this time, his social calendar suffered considerably, certainly during the week when he would shut himself away to concentrate on his work. This was difficult as he was naturally a social animal and enjoyed the bon-vie. He did allow himself some downtime at the weekends when he would hang around the local rugby club. He liked the crowd there; it's where he felt at home.

After his first year when he was in students' Halls of Residence, Harry had moved into a four bedroomed house with three other students close to the University in Headingly. He was in his room revising when out of the blue he received an unexpected text message. It was Monday 14th May.

"Hello Harry je suis en Londres jusqu'à Vendredi pouvons-nous rencontrer? Monique'.

He re-read the message and worked out the translation. It appeared Monique was in London until Friday and wanted to meet. How did she get his mobile number he wondered; it could only have been from his CV so she must have gone to some trouble but then when you have that much power anything is possible.

It didn't take him long to respond. Harry was happy to be tossed by the waves of the sea of uncertainty, he relished the challenge; in fact, his impulsive tendencies regularly got him into trouble.

'Yes, where? When?'

'Mecredi, Waldorf'.

Harry looked at the reply; "where else?" he said to himself and smiled. He took a moment to consider the timing. He had no lectures, just revision; he would soon catch up he convinced himself.

'Ok, what time?'

'À tout moment'

Harry went online and checked the trains to London. Avoiding peak times which would be prohibitively expensive, he calculated he could be there for around midday.

'I can be in London for midday'

'Parfait, j'attende en hotel x'

Harry noticed the "x"; this did not appear to be a business call.

'Will call you when I arrive in London', he replied

'Très bon, J'attendrai avec impatience à bientot'.

'Impatient?' he thought to himself, not really recognising the nuance in the language.

Any ideas of revision had gone; his mind was in turmoil imagining all kinds of possibilities. He left his room, went to the fridge in the communal kitchen and took out a bottle of beer. It was the last of his stash which he kept on the second shelf. They had an arrangement whereby each resident had a shelf allocated for their own use and the trust between them was such that no-one abused this.

Luke Taylor, one of Harry's house-mates, came into the kitchen to make a coffee.

"Hi Harry, thought you'd hibernated, haven't seen you around in ages," he said as he boiled the kettle.

"What...? Sorry, Luke, I was miles away."

"I said we haven't seen you in ages. You've become quite

the hermit."

"Yeah, sorry just knuckling down, exams next week."

"Well you know what they say; all work and no joy make Harry a dull boy."

"Only another week, then I intend on getting totally wasted," said Harry, taking a slug from his bottle of lager.

"Sounds good, count me in and I'm sure Mike and James will be up for it too. They finish next week as well. Why don't we set something up at the rugby club, we can invite some of the girls too?"

Harry stared at his bottle, his usual enthusiasm for such a suggestion was muted; something not lost on his buddy.

"Yeah, ok."

"You alright Harry, you don't seem to be your usual self?"

"What...? Oh, no. Sorry, just wrestling with a problem... need to clear my head."

"Anything I can help with?" said Luke.

"No, no... Thanks anyway... it's a geology issue. I'll speak to Professor Francis. Yeah, a farewell party sounds great," he said much more enthusiastically.

"That's more like it Harry. I'll speak to the others and ring Brian at the club to set something up. We could have a theme night, 'tarts and vicars' or 'schoolboys and schoolgirls'. What do you think?"

"Yeah, good idea, it'll need to be a week on Saturday," said Harry, entering into the spirit of things.

"Leave it with me, I'll organise it."

Luke was the organiser and was responsible for almost all the debauchery posing as social events, which marked Harry's years as a student. He was going to miss it.

After finishing his beer and catching up with Luke, Harry went back to his room. The issue he was wrestling with had nothing to do with rock formations or tectonic plates; it was, of course, Monique and her unexpected invitation; it had rekindled memories.

Chapter Five

Harry continued the struggle with his course notes for the next day or so; his revision work was behind his self-imposed schedule. By Tuesday afternoon, he'd had enough and caught a bus into town to the railway station to get his tickets to London. His student rail-card entitled him to a twenty percent discount but it was still comparatively expensive and his bank overdraft would feel the effect. When he returned to the house, he checked his emails and there was one with attachments. He opened it and found a copy of his contract and flight tickets to Geneva, economy class. The reality of it all was starting to sink in; time was passing quickly and in less than four weeks his new life would start.

On Wednesday morning at eight forty-five, he was on the platform walking up the side of the train looking for the carriage that contained his reserved seat. He would not be enjoying first class travel this trip. Eventually, he found his seat and made himself comfortable. He had bought some reading material to pass the time but his thoughts kept drifting to his forthcoming meeting with Monique.

The train was on time, arriving into Kings Cross around eleven-thirty. He took out his mobile phone and texted Monique.

'Have arrived at Kings Cross'

A few seconds later his phone rang; it was the unmistakable voice of Monique. "Hello Harry, how are you?"

"Good thanks," replied Harry.

"I have sent for you a car. It is with the taxis, I think."

"That's great, thanks." He was intending to use the Tube.

"I will see you soon, I hope."

"Yes," said Harry, not knowing what else to say.

He ended the call and headed for the taxi rank. Sure enough, a man in a chauffeur's uniform was holding a card saying 'Mr

Harry Bentham'. Harry acknowledged the man and was led to a large BMW. The driver opened the door for him. Harry was travelling light, he had a shoulder bag with some revision notes he had intended to read on the journey but hadn't got around to. He was wearing his business suit but without a tie.

The journey to Aldwych through the crawling traffic took around twenty minutes. The magnificent frontage of the hotel welcomed them as they drew up outside. A porter was quickly at the car and opened the door for Harry to get out. The driver removed Harry's shoulder bag from the boot and handed it to him; Harry looked up at the iconic sign as the car pulled away.

The porter guided Harry to reception. "Harry Bentham for Monique Duchamp," he announced to the girl on the desk.

"Ah, yes... she is expecting you. Please have a seat. I will ring her suite."

Harry sat on one of the comfortable chairs opposite, his shoulder bag on his lap. Five minutes later a thick-set man approached him in a dark suit with a hearing device in his left ear which trailed a curly lead to somewhere beneath his jacket. He looked like a bodyguard.

"Monsieur Bentham?" enquired the heavy.

"Yes," replied Harry.

"Come," he said, and Harry followed the man to the lifts.

He placed a key card against the security pad below the call buttons and they waited for the lift to arrive. It was a matter of seconds before the elevator doors opened; it was empty. They stepped inside and instead of pressing a button the man inserted a key in a security socket and turned it. The lift ascended without stopping and reached a floor that was not indicated on the call buttons. The door opened and another security guard was standing in front of the lift. He eyed Harry with suspicion but noticed his colleague and said something to him in French.

Harry followed the man as he exited the lift and turned left.

Suddenly the nerves returned. There was a door in front of them and the bodyguard knocked. Another man, younger, in casual apparel opened the door and further exchanges took place in French.

"Entrez, monsieur Bentham," and the casual man opened the door leaving the suit men to return to their bodyguard duties.

Harry entered what was a reception room, immaculately presented with classic paintings and traditional furniture in the style of the 1920's. Another door opened to the right, and there she was.

"Hello Harry," she said in a soft voice, the French accent adding a seductive tone to the greeting.

"Merci, ce sera tout, Pierre," she said and the casual man left the room.

Monique walked up to Harry and she kissed him on both cheeks. He could smell her perfume, the same one from the day of the interview and it conjured up memories of their first encounter.

"How are you? You look très bien, er... very well," she translated.

"Fine, thank you... you too," Harry replied nervously.

She took his hand and led him into a magnificent lounge. Harry could hardly believe his eyes. There were two settees, again decorated in the Art-Deco style, wood and gold-covered fabric with red scatter cushions. Several matching wing-back chairs were placed strategically around the room. More paintings in ornate gilded frames hung on the walls, anonymous portraits and unidentified flowers. In the middle, in front of one of the settees, was a low antique wooden coffee table with a coffee pot, a small jug and two china cups and saucers. In the corner of the room, Harry noticed a small dining table with two place settings.

"Please sit," said Monique and he followed her to the coffee sofa. "Café?"

"Thank you," he said and sat next to her with his shoulders slightly turned away, indicating uncertainty in his body language.

Monique began to pour coffee into each cup.

"Du lait?"

"Yes, thank you," said Harry and Monique topped up one of the cups with a dash of milk; the other was black.

She passed the cup to Harry. He took it from her and his hands were shaking which made the cups rattle. She smiled.

There was a silence as they drank their coffee. Harry was waiting for Monique to speak; he didn't know what to say. He looked at her, casually dressed in a pair of figure-hugging denim jeans, black high-heeled shoes and a white blouse with ruffles around the collar down to the first button which was undone revealing the tops of her breasts.

"You were surprised that I make text you, I think," she said.

"Yes, very, I didn't think I would see you again," said Harry.

He took another sip. "Are you happy I did?" she said.

"Well yes, as I said, I didn't think I would see you again."

"Ah oui, I can understand. It is simple... Edward, he came to London on business and I came also but he has to go back to Jura so I stay. I say to him I wanted to... how you say? Faire des achats, les magasins."

"Shopping," said Harry.

"Oui, shopping. Mais vraiment, er... really, I wanted to see you again."

Harry was trying to process this remark and then Monique looked at him with those amazing eyes.

"I have thought about you many times since we met that night. Have you thought about me also?" said Monique.

"Yes, of course, how could I forget?"

She smiled and placed her hand on his. "That night for me it was... formidable, special."

"Me too," said Harry.

Monique let go of Harry's hand and took another sip of coffee. There was a knock on the door.

"Ah, quelque chose à manger? Er, something to eat... I have ordered, er, déjouner for one o'clock .. That is the room service I think."

"Yes, thank you, that would be great," said Harry shuffling in his seat, still feeling uncomfortable; it was a surreal situation.

Monique got up and opened the door. It was the casual man again with a waiter dressed in the hotel livery.

"Your lunch, Madame Duchamp," said the waiter pushing in a hostess trolley, closely watched by the bodyguard.

"Merci," said Monique as the waiter dispensed a plate of sandwiches, savoury biscuits and cheese, two bottles of mineral water and a bowl of fruit on to the table. The waiter and escort left the room.

"Come, ici... we have déjouner."

Harry got up from the sofa and joined Monique. He took off his jacket and wrapped it around the back of the chair.

"You are well protected here," said Harry as Monique poured two glasses of water.

"It is necessary; we are in danger, toujours, always... how you say, er... kidnap, oui, we worry about it all the time but people they want to kill Edward."

"Why on earth would they do that?"

"Edward is a very powerful man, make many enemies." She looked down. "He is not an easy man."

"It must be very hard for you," said Harry not picking up on the nuance.

"Absolutement, of course, I have people all the time with me. I cannot go out on my own. I even have les chaussures... er, the shoes... that say where I am." She laughed.

"They put trackers in your shoes?" said Harry incredulously.

"Oui, yes, it is necessary."

"That must be terrible."

"Oui," said Monique and consumed a sandwich then looked at Harry. "I want to go to les boutiques after we eat. You come with me, oui?"

"Of course," said Harry.

"C'est bon. We will go soon... then we can relax. Do you have to return tonight?" she asked.

Harry wasn't ready for the question and thought for a minute.

"Er, no, I've got an open ticket," he said.

"That is good... Ce soir you sleep here with me, oui?"

Harry looked at her. "Yeah, yes, ok... er... great," he managed to stammer and took a sip of water; his appetite was fading fast.

They finished their lunch having discussed Harry's studies, his family, and his hobbies. Monique was less forthcoming. Apart from the snippet that Edward had mentioned back at the Chateau, he still had little information on her background.

Monique excused herself and went through another door. She did not close it behind her and Harry could see the reflection of a large bed in a wardrobe mirror. The wardrobe opened and he could hear rustling before it closed again. The bed was back. There was a delay for a couple of minutes and then she returned to the lounge wearing a short black leather jacket, the height of chic. Harry caught his breath.

Harry had to ask the question, pressure on his bladder was increasing. "Can I use the toilet?"

"Mais oui... it is there," she said pointing back through the room with the bed.

He walked through the door and could see the bedroom in detail, it was magnificent as you would expect from a hotel of this class. The en-suite was the other side of the room.

He completed his toilet visit and joined Monique in the lounge.

He put on his jacket and Monique held his hand. "Viens, we will go."

She opened the door and immediately casual man, Pierre, was there with the two other heavies flanking him.

There was an exchange in French which appeared to upset Pierre. Monique looked at Harry. "I told him you will protect me. I don't need them everywhere following me. You will protect me won't you Harry?"

"Of course but won't Edward find out? He won't be happy."

Monique considered Harry's comments. "Non, c'est d'accord... it is ok."

She addressed Pierre again and whatever she said seemed to placate him and he pressed the button to call the lift.

"They are going to watch me from far away. We will be very safe," which hadn't concerned Harry until now.

The lift arrived and the five of them entered which made it extremely claustrophobic. In less than thirty seconds, they were on the ground floor. Monique was clutching a handbag and opened it to retrieve a pair of sunglasses. Outside it was bright but not sunny and not many people were wearing shades which, ironically, made her look even more conspicuous.

Harry was beginning to feel more at ease now, despite the presence of the hired heavies. They turned left outside the hotel and headed to Covent Garden. Harry hadn't been there before but it was clear Monique had. The bodyguards had dropped back as they had promised and Monique and Harry walked hand-in-hand like any other couple in the crowded lanes. It felt strange. Monique was someone else's wife and with the bodyguards lurking close by there were witnesses but Harry, in his usual way, decided to go with the flow; it felt good.

It was a two-hour shopathon and Monique and Harry were

loaded with bags; even the bodyguards were drafted into helping with the carrying. As they were passing a boutique specialising in men's clothing, Monique suddenly stopped. "Do you like that, Harry?" she said pointing to a tan-coloured leather jacket.

"Yeah, it's great," he replied.

"I buy it for you."

"No, you can't do that, it costs a fortune," said Harry, seeing the price tag.

"But I want to. You can wear it for me tonight pour le dîner. We go to restaurant, oui?"

Again Harry was in a dilemma. "Ok," he said, rather uneasily.

They went into the shop and Monique was on a roll; she wanted to treat Harry to a complete wardrobe. By the time they had finished, Harry had a new shirt, trousers and shoes, as well as the jacket. He did a quick calculation and worked out the cost of her indulgence, over three thousand pounds. Monique produced a black American Express card.

"Are you sure?" he kept asking. But Monique was adamant and he felt reluctant to decline.

They stopped briefly in a coffee shop for refreshments before making their way back to the hotel. The earlier rather hesitant, uncertain atmosphere had been replaced by one of excitement and jollity even. Monique was giggling like a schoolgirl as they headed for the lift pulling Harry behind her. Pierre was on hand to work the buttons.

Back in the suite, Monique carried her bags into the bedroom followed by Harry.

"Ici, Harry, let me see," and he emptied his purchases on the bed. He took off his suit jacket and put on the new leather one. "Mmm, très bon," said Monique.

He looked into her eyes and it was as though someone had lit a spark; suddenly they were kissing hard, passionately, as though their lives depended on it.

Monique broke away and pushed the carrier bags unceremoniously to one side until they dropped on the floor. She got on the bed. She was kneeling down facing him and undoing her blouse.

Harry joined her and the kissing started again, deep, sensual, and urgent. Monique's blouse was undone and Harry's lifted her bra and started kneading her breasts like they were baker's dough. He started sucking her nipples one after the other and Monique moaned gently.

She broke away and undid her jeans; there was no underwear. Harry quickly stripped off and joined her on the bed.

"Baise-moi, Harry, baise-moi," she whispered softly and handed Harry a condom.

By five-thirty, they were spent and lay under the bed-covers in each other's arms. Monique was staring at the ceiling, Harry was dozing.

"When do you go away?" she said, out of the blue.

Harry tried to focus. "Hmm...? What do you mean?" he said drowsily.

"Australie... you go there, I think."

"That's what I've been told but I've not had any confirmation yet. End of June, early July I expect."

"You must be very careful there; it is très dangereux."

"Dangerous...? What do you mean?"

"People, they try to stop us from, er, working there... many problems. They, how you say? Make protest."

"Protest?"

"Oui."

"But I thought you had only done initial surveys from the air. That's what David Leganes said."

"That is true but there is much, how you say...? Sensibilité."

"Sensitivity," Harry corrected.

"Oui, the Government there, they want more uranium but many they do not. Someone there, they tell the newspapers and now..."

"But that happens everywhere, surely, opposition I mean?" said Harry cutting in.

"Oui, absolutement but in Australie there are people, crazy people, they try to stop us."

"But you have permits from the government?"

"Oui, it is all, how you say...? Above the board." Harry smiled. "It has cost much money."

"What is the problem then?"

"Edward says there are big problems; he says that someone they try to do things to the airplane. It's what I say, they are crazy."

"What do you mean, sabotage?"

"Oui, that is the word he said, sabotage... The people who make protest they er... menaces, er... threaten, the people there."

"What, the Helvetia people?"

"Oui."

"What is Edward doing?"

"Edward has sent some security there to help."

She turned over and held Harry. "You must be careful."

Harry mulled over her comments considering the implications. "Of course... I'll be careful."

She kissed him. "I have a shower and then we go pour le dîner, oui? We can do shower together if you would like."

"Yeah, I'd like," replied Harry.

By seven o'clock Monique and Harry were in the lift, accompanied by the ubiquitous heavies. Harry was in his new outfit. Monique was wearing a beautiful off-white A-line cocktail dress with black trim and waist. She looked stunning and Harry could hardly take his eyes off her.

Outside the hotel, the BMW was waiting for them and the Concierge opened the door for them to get in. An anonymous looking black car was parked behind and the three bodyguards got in; Pierre was driving.

Ten minutes later, the car pulled up outside the restaurant Monique had chosen; it was one of her favourites she said. They went inside and were quickly led upstairs to a private booth overlooking the river. Harry looked around; not a large establishment but everything 'tasteful'. It was on two floors and in their area around twenty covers, all but two taken. He thought he recognised a TV celebrity but couldn't recall her name.

For the next two hours, they continued to enjoy each other's' company. The food lived up to Monique's billing and Harry gained more of an insight into her role in the company. Despite her qualifications, she appeared on the face of it to be little more than a glorified P.A., totally under the control of her husband. She painted a picture of an obsessive need for power; nothing happened without his say so.

As he listened he became more and more intoxicated by her; she was so different to anyone else he had met. With every moment Harry was being drawn to her.

They eventually left the restaurant around ten-thirty and the BMW was waiting for them outside. They made themselves comfortable in the back for the short journey to the hotel and pulled away with the usual entourage in tow.

In the suite, Monique dismissed the bodyguards for the evening. There was a panic button next to her bed directly linked to a central control centre that could have a security team to her within minutes, she explained. Harry considered her comments and wondered for all the wealth she had whether it was worth the restrictions to her freedom.

That night was another to enter in Harry's 'never to be

forgotten' log; the sex was mind-blowing and frequent. Monique had turned tutor and Harry, despite all his previous liaisons, learned new ways of pleasing his partner, ever the eager student. They were now on the second pack of condoms.

There was a great deal of sadness when Harry had to leave the following morning. With a ten o'clock flight back to Switzerland for Monique, it was an early alarm call and room service breakfast.

Harry said his goodbye at six forty-five. With bodyguards around, Monique was restrained and just kissed him on both cheeks as she had when she greeted him. "Au revoir, Harry," was all she said, and he was out of the door being escorted to the exit with his shoulder bag and carriers from his clothes purchases. At least his wardrobe had improved he joked with himself but it was a hollow joke; he felt empty.

He took a taxi to the station, the BMW was unavailable. The fifteen pounds he paid for the fare left him short of cash for the return trip, just enough for a coffee on the train. During the two and a half hour journey he took out his revision notes but concentration eluded him. He thought about the warning Monique gave about Australia and what it meant; he would soon find out. He thought about his induction training and whether Monique would be at the Chateau when he returned in less than three weeks.

Harry resumed university life the following day; he had fended off questions from his housemates on his disappearance. "Doing research," he told them.

The following week he completed his exams and had managed to keep his feelings and thoughts of Monique from interrupting his concentration; he had received no contact from her. He believed he had done as well as he could. Following the final exam on Friday, there was a huge feeling of relief; all those years of study were at an end and he was ready for Luke's party.

Saturday night, Harry, Luke and the other two housemates were in a taxi heading for the venue. Everyone had clubbed together to make sure there would be sufficient alcohol and a disco had been hired to provide the music. Harry was dressed in his London gear; there had been no appetite for fancy dress. He didn't bother with his jacket which was still in his wardrobe; it was early June and a warm summer evening and he didn't want to get it stolen.

The club was on the outskirts of the city, down a long track and well away from any neighbours. The taxi bumped down the dirt road, around the rugby pitch, and pulled up outside the wooden building. The chatter inside was upbeat and full of expectancy of a good night. More friends had arrived at the club; the number of guests had increased considerably once the news of a party had got out and it was packed. It was eight-thirty and the disco was in full swing; the flimsy walls of the building seemed to vibrate with the rhythm of the drum and bass. Harry managed to push his way to the free bar and retrieve a bottle of lager. There were no glasses; the club was rightly concerned about breakages.

Many friends and acquaintances who had shared Harry's university years were there. He spent a lot of time catching up, although the noise from the music made any lengthy discussion impossible. He made his way back to the bar for his first refill and noticed Chloe holding a bottle of lager and dancing frantically with no-one in particular. She had her eyes closed and seemed totally engrossed in the vibe. Harry hadn't spoken to her for ages, there had been the odd campus encounter when they would pass the time of day but that was all. It was good to see her again. He stood next to her trying to decide whether to break her concentration and then the music came to an end.

"Hi," he shouted to be heard. "Do you want a drink? I'm going to the bar."

She opened her eyes as if she had been woken from a dream, looked at him and smiled.

"Oh hi, yeah, thanks... Been carrying this empty bottle around for ages," she replied.

They made their way to the bar and secured refills. The next track from the DJ started and the room was again filled with a cacophony.

"Fancy some fresh air, get away from all this smoke?" she said. The atmosphere in the room had been fogged by a thousand cigarettes.

"Yeah, good idea," said Harry.

"Ah that's better," she said as the warm clear evening air cleansed their senses.

Several others had made the same decision; some were tugging on cigarettes outside. The pair walked away from the clubhouse to the low boundary wall of the car park and sat down.

"So, how did it go?" asked Chloe.

"Yeah, ok I guess, we'll find out in August."

"But you've got something lined up, haven't you?" said Chloe, taking her first slug of the lager.

"Yeah but I still want to pass," replied Harry.

"So what's this mysterious job? You haven't said much about it."

Harry looked at her; she looked different, somehow. Gone were her crazy curls, her hair was shorter and layered; it suited her but that wasn't it. She was more mature, more confident, more at ease with herself. Her tee shirt and distressed jeans were in marked contrast to her usual attire. He hadn't seen her socially before. She was clearly bra-less; the cooler air had made her nipples protrude beneath her top. Harry tried to look away. Chloe noticed the interest but said nothing.

"It's a survey job," he replied.

"Sounds interesting; it was something you wanted to do wasn't it?

"Yeah, looking forward to it," he replied.

"You must be really excited... UK based?"

"No, Switzerland... then going out to Australia next month," said Harry.

"Wow, sounds amazing, makes my job look positively boring. I told you I've been accepted on the graduate training scheme for John Frasers, didn't I?"

"Yeah, can't see you in retail somehow. I had you jumping out of planes or something."

"Yeah, it was a tough decision but I've had enough of science to last a lifetime."

She took another sip of lager. "Do you ever think back to the cave?"

"Yeah, a lot, it nearly killed me."

"Can't believe it was over three years ago. Do you keep in touch with Paul at all?" said Chloe.

"Not really... he came to see me when I was in hospital. My dad sent a donation to the cave rescue charity to say thank you. I got a letter from him to say thanks and wishing me well..."

The conversation tailed momentarily as Harry reminisced. Much of his memory of the incident was hazy now. "What about Abby? How's she doing with her teaching?" he said, breaking the sombre mood.

"Oh, she's fine... she's leaving college this month as well. She got a job as a geography teacher in Swindon or somewhere."

"That's great... it's more like her, she was never cut out to be a geologist."

"No, she still can't go in lifts, she was telling me."

"Really? That's a shame," said Harry.

"She's got a new boyfriend, met him at an arts' fair she was telling me; she seems pretty keen."

"Yeah, I can imagine her with a house and loads of kids," said Harry. "What about you, anyone special?"

"Good God no, enjoying myself too much to have that hassle," she replied and took another drink from her lager bottle. "You?" she enquired.

"No, the same," he replied.

Her nipples became the centre of attention once again; she noticed his gaze. "We ought to celebrate, you know... before we go our separate ways. I don't know about you but I could really do with a good shag. You up for it?"

Harry nearly spilt his drink. It was typical of Chloe, forthright and straight to the point as ever.

"Yeah, why not," he said and they both started laughing.

"Come on," she said, and the two went in search of a suitable place where they could 'celebrate'.

It was almost dark; a red glow over the fields to the west heralded the end of another day.

"Here," said Chloe.

There was an alcove at the back of the club where the rubbish bins were normally kept; it made an ideal spot for privacy.

Chloe leant against the wall and pulled Harry towards her. They kissed hungrily; Harry's hand immediately pushed up her tee shirt and started caressing her breasts. Chloe had unzipped Harry and found his penis and was rubbing it to erection.

"Quick now," she said as she undid the buttons on her jeans and stepped out of them. Harry put his hands between her legs and started stimulating her; she too was ready. He broke away, pushed down his slacks and in a moment he was inside her. She lifted her pelvis forward so he had a better angle and then ecstasy as they consummated their relationship.

"Ohhh, ohhh... I'm coming," Harry said in a whisper.

"It's ok, I'm fixed," she said and then, "yeeeesss."

Chloe's legs nearly gave way as her orgasm waved through her body.

"God, that was good," she said, hanging onto his shoulders. "I can't believe we waited so long."

Harry caught his breath. "Wow, yeah... now that <u>was</u> really good," he replied, still panting from the exertion.

Chloe pulled out a paper tissue from the pocket of her jeans and wiped herself. She dropped the tissue on the floor then put on her pants and jeans.

She put her arms around Harry's neck and kissed him again. "Do you want to come back to the flat later?" she said. "I could do with more of that."

Before Harry could answer, another couple walked around the back of the club with the same intentions; he grabbed Chloe's hand and walked out of the shadows.

"All yours," he said and Chloe started to giggle.

"Yeah, that would be great... I just need to say a few goodbyes," and the two walked back to the club.

After half an hour, Chloe and Harry had made their excuses and were at the front entrance of the club waiting for the taxi they had ordered. They ignored the jocular remarks as they explained their premature departure. "An early start,' Harry said.

The taxi duly arrived and they snuggled together in the back until they arrived at Chloe's bedsit. It was only a few blocks from Harry's flat and of a similar layout. Chloe shared with another girl and two lads but had her own room.

"It's ok, everyone's out," said Chloe as they entered the apartment. They immediately started kissing again.

"Come on," said Chloe and she led Harry to her bedroom. "We have some unfinished business."

The following morning Harry was making coffee in Chloe's

kitchen at eight o'clock. With nobody else in the house, she wore just a pair of knickers and was sat on one of the bar stools watching him. Typical Chloe, Harry thought; he was going to miss her, especially after last night. There wasn't too much conversation, words seemed superfluous somehow. When it was time for him to leave they kissed affectionately but more like a sister and brother.

"Goodbye, Chloe."

"Goodbye, Harry... it's been great knowing you."

He left the apartment with the sight of a semi-naked Chloe waving from the window, outrageous. He waved back and smiled. Then he suddenly thought of Monique and wondered what she was doing on this Sunday morning.

Today was Harry's last time in Leeds; his father was picking him up from his flat at around eleven in a hired Transit to collect his things and take them back to Norwich. He would be staying with his parents until he flew to Switzerland and his induction. It would be the start of an adventure he would never forget.

Chapter Six

June 12th, 2005

Just over a week after saying goodbye to university life and Chloe, Harry was at the local airport waiting for his flight to Geneva. His bag was heavy and he was grateful for the extra allowance the company had paid for so he could bring enough clothing for the two-week stay.

His parents had driven him to the airport at Stanstead. Having just about got used to him being around the house again, there were tears from his mother as she waved him off outside the departure terminal. Harry naturally had some apprehension about what lay ahead. On the plane, his thoughts continually drifted to Monique and he wondered if he would see her again. He hadn't forgotten Chloe; she too was in his mind. That was different; just two very good friends saying goodbye but he did start to wonder what might have been.

The flight was with a budget airline and in marked contrast from his trip in April from Manchester. There would be no champagne and canapés. At the airport in Geneva the driver was waiting for him outside the arrivals terminal, as detailed in his joining instructions; no executive lounges this time either.

They retraced the journey from two months ago and Harry recognised some of the landmarks. In mid-summer, the views were spectacular and the traffic noticeably heavier than on his last visit, no doubt swelled by tourists. He remembered the turn in the forest and the security fencing surrounding the Chateau grounds. His nerves returned as the car crossed the drawbridge, passed through the archway and pulled up in the courtyard immediately outside reception.

There was a different atmosphere about the place now; he couldn't make out whether something had changed or if it was him that had changed. There was a degree of confidence that he didn't have when he arrived in April.

The driver carried his bags through the door to reception; Harry followed.

"Ah, Harry Bentham, welcome back," said Lucy who had greeted him on the first visit. He remembered her straight away; she was wearing the same business suit with a white blouse but different designer spectacles; a fashion statement and testament to the power-dressing culture. There was a name badge on her lapel; 'Lucy Bainbridge, Reception Manager,' it said.

"Thank you, fancy you remembering my name," he said.

"I never forget a face," she replied, staring at a computer screen as she clicked her mouse several times. "Yes, here you are." She thumbed through some papers then produced a room key.

"You're in the same room as you were last time, number seven. I'll get Joseph to escort you and then if you come back here, I'll have your itinerary ready."

"Thank you," replied Harry. Joseph appeared and picked up Harry's baggage.

"Suivez-moi," said Joseph, and once again Harry followed the man to his quarters.

It took half an hour for Harry to hang his clothes and freshen up. He'd travelled in his business suit but would dress more casually whilst he was off-duty.

He returned to reception where Lucy was on her computer and waited for her to make eye contact. "Ah Harry," she said and got up. "Here are your instructions detailing who you'll be working with and when. At the back are the emergency procedures; please read them they're very important."

She handed him a small loose-leaf A4 binder with the words 'Helvetia Mining Services – Induction Pack (English version),' on the front. "Oh, and you'll need this too, your security pass. You must wear it at all times while you are in the Chateau.

There are spot checks," she added, looking at him seriously.

"Thank you," said Harry, placing the pass around his neck. "What about meals and things?"

"Yes, of course... all meals are in the refectory and there's the common room next door. The bar's open till eleven and there's a sports channel TV. It's all in the book."

"What about the gym?" asked Harry.

"The leisure centre's in the corner." She pointed. "You'll see the sign."

Harry thanked her, took his binder and returned to his room to browse through it.

He sat on his bed scanning the pages. It was a comprehensive document with a map of the Chateau showing the position of all the relevant facilities as well as the evacuation procedures. In the back was a loose piece of paper which immediately had Harry's interest; it was his work schedule. It seemed he would be under the wing of David Leganes, the Head of Research, for the bulk of his time there. He was glad of that; it was where the action was. The following morning there were two meetings scheduled. One with someone from H.R, not the ice-maiden from the interview he noticed, then a career planning discussion with Lucien de Bruye. Then he would be based in the research department. A session in the second week with the Head of Security, Leonard Scheck, intrigued him; it was a full day. He wondered why he would need a whole day with him.

An hour later Harry decided to have a look around. It was different not being chaperoned and he felt he had the freedom of the place or at least certain parts of it. There were areas indicated on the map as being 'out of bounds'. He identified the Duchamp's quarters but others he did not recognise.

After settling in, his first port of call was the gym; he intended to make full use of it during his stay. It was in the far corner of the Chateau, the opposite side to the reception area and was clearly marked 'Leisure Centre'. The signage at the Chateau all seemed to be in English. He walked across the cobbled courtyard and through the open entrance door. There was a small dark corridor, about ten feet long and then another door with frosted glass which illuminated the area. He walked through and was confronted by the fitness centre. It wasn't large by any means but there was a quarter-sized swimming pool, a steam room, a couple of cross-trainers, rowing and jogging machines, plus some weights; ideal. It was quiet, there was nobody using the equipment or the pool. To the right of the entrance, there was a reception desk where a bored looking receptionist in a white overall was reading a magazine; she looked up and smiled at Harry.

"Hola, can I help you?" she said. The accent was definitely Hispanic.

"It's ok, I was just looking around... just arrived," replied Harry. The name on her badge was Rosa.

"We are open until nine o'clock," she said.

"That's good, I'll pop back after dinner, I could do with a good workout," replied Harry.

"We are not busy today, as you can see. Where are you from?"

"UK," said Harry. "You?"

"España," she replied, "near Barcelona."

"I like Barcelona, not been for a while," said Harry.

"You know Barcelona?"

"Not really, I was there two years ago with some mates. Muchos alcohol," he said in a mock Spanish accent. Rosa laughed. He looked at her, flowing black hair, dark eyes and slightly olive skin with minimum make-up. Slim, she looked as though she used the facilities regularly. "What about towels and things?" said Harry, getting back to business.

"Si, we have towels here."

"Great, I'll see you later, Rosa," he said, addressing her name badge.

"Si, I will be here," she said.

He left the gym and walked the short distance to the refectory. He had made a friend, he thought.

The refectory was also not too busy, about half a dozen people using the self-service option. It was nearly six-thirty and Harry decided to eat; he was feeling hungry after his journey. There were about thirty tables set for dinner. The area where he'd had his breakfast meeting on his earlier visit had not been cordoned off and the room was airy with a view over the moat to the staff car park. He took a vacant table and a man in a dark suit approached.

"Voulez-vous manger?" asked the man. Harry's French was being tested again.

"Er, yes... please," he replied.

"Ah, it is self-service. You help yourself... do you want to drink? Beer, er, water, fruit juice, we have."

"Just water, thanks," replied Harry.

Harry got up and went to the service area; a man in a chef's outfit was supervising. There were three Oriental looking people queuing in front of him chatting animatedly to each other in what seemed to be Chinese. They chose European cuisine from the food on offer; Harry watched with interest.

His turn and he chose a veal schnitzel with vegetables and a fruit salad for sweet. He was surprised at the number of options, and the quality, as he would attest later. He looked around; the Chinese diners were seated on the opposite side of the room. The waiter brought the water and Harry was just about to start on his veal when a woman walked into the dining room that he recognised. It was Geraldine, the frosty Manager of Human Resources; she was carrying a laptop case. They made eye contact but there was no indication of recognition on her part. He watched her collect her food and walk to a table at the far end of the room. She took out her computer, opened it and stared at the screen while eating her salad. It got Harry considering the work culture; no wonder she was misanthropic. He smiled to himself; here was someone who certainly lived up to that definition.

After his meal, he went back to his room to change into his sports gear. He took a drink of water from one of the complimentary bottles that were available in the room, before heading to the gym.

Rosa was still there reading a Spanish paperback novel. There was a steamy picture on the front cover and she seemed to discard it in a hurry as she saw Harry approach.

"Hola," she said.

"Hi, just come to use the gym," he replied.

"Si, of course... will you need a towel?"

"No, thanks, just going to use the bike and do a bit of jogging," he replied.

"You can shower here. There are changing rooms over there," she said pointing to the far side of the gym.

"Oh right, well ok then, I'll take one."

Rosa got off her chair and bent forward to reach a small supply of white towels below the desk. As she did so, her overall gaped open, giving Harry more than a flash of her chest. He quickly averted his gaze; Rosa appeared oblivious to any sort of allure.

"Here," she said handing him a towel from her stock.

"Thanks," he said and went to the first piece of equipment.

It was a fairly light workout by his standards. He tried out most of the equipment but without his swimming stuff, he skipped the pool. Rosa was sat at her desk reading her book but taking more than a passing interest in Harry's toned physique. After three-quarters of an hour, he went to the changing rooms and showered.

It was just before nine when he returned the wet towel to the waiting Rosa.

"Thanks," he said.

"It's ok... you are very fit I think."

"Thanks," said Harry. "I need to be... I'll be back tomorrow."

"I am here tomorrow," said Rosa, and Harry left the gym leaving her to close up.

As he walked across the courtyard to his room his mind returned to his previous visit for his interview and that first time with Monique; he wondered what she was doing at that moment.

After a good night's sleep, Harry was ready to face the start of his new career. He decided to wear his suit, as he would be meeting some of the executives but without a tie. The geography of the place was becoming more familiar and he was able to find his way about without a chaperone.

The first hour was spent with Zoe Górski, an assistant on the H.R. team according to her name badge. She took his photograph 'for their records' and provided him with his Gold credit card which was to be used for payment of expenses. They gave him details of his new bank account which had been opened with the company's bankers in Zurich. "You will have your bank card before you leave," he was told. There was no sign of the ice-maiden.

Then it was off to see Lucien de Bruye. He was looking forward to seeing him again; they had got on well. He knocked on his office door, there was no escort this time, and Harry presented himself. He was warmly greeted by the Head of Talent.

"Come in, Harry, it's good to see you again." They exchanged pleasantries and then it was down to business. "I understand David Leganes is sending you off to Australia."

"Yes, apparently," replied Harry.

"Hmm, it will be an interesting experience, that's for sure but I'll let him explain all about it."

Lucien started asking Harry questions about his academic background, then his age. Harry wasn't sure why it was all relevant.

There was an open file on the desk which Lucien was trying to scan as he waited for the answer.

"Twenty-seven."

"Yes, of course, I have it here."

He appeared to tap in the information into his computer which dominated the right-hand side of his desk. He reviewed his post then returned his attention to Harry.

"I think you have great potential, Harry, and so does Edward. We will be taking a special interest in your development. I will be getting regular updates on your progress from the field. You're working for Nate Gillespie, that right?"

"Yes," said Harry.

"Hmm, he's not the easiest person to get on with; he's a strong character but he's fair and he'll look after you."

"That's good. I'm looking forward to meeting him."

The meeting lasted for almost another hour and then it was off to spend some time with David Leganes.

Again Harry was greeted with enthusiasm.

"Harry, it's good to see you again. Please take a seat. Would you like coffee?" The slight American twang was evident.

After the introductions and a welcome shot of caffeine, Leganes outline Harry's itinerary for the induction period.

"I'll take you to the office when we've finished. You'll be working there most of your time while you're here in Jura and you can look at some of the projects we're dealing with. Also, I want you to see how we present information for our customers so when you put in your reports you will know how to set them out. Then I want you to concentrate on Kakadu."

"Fine," said Harry. Leganes continued with a stern look on his face.

"There's a lot at stake on this project, we've already invested a great deal of money and I mean a great deal of money. We need to see some return sooner rather than later... which is why I'm sending additional resources." That would be him, Harry quickly recognised. "Between you and me, there's some pressure from our partners to get some results."

"Partners?"

"Oh, nothing to concern you," said Leganes.

"But I'm not sure how I fit in... I'm just a geologist," said Harry.

"Well that's true but let me tell you something, we chose you to join this project because we need a special person on this team. It's not just the geology, you can teach a monkey to find rocks." This was no charm offensive, Leganes was direct and his eyes narrowed as he spoke. "No, it's much more than that. I need leadership and confidence... big time. The team needs a shake up; as I said, it's all taking too long. It won't be easy. You'll have to think for yourself and be prepared for all kinds of resistance. You'll also need tact and diplomacy at times. That's not Nate's forte," he chuckled to himself. "Nothing out there is straightforward. We pretty well know where the uranium is, and the Australian Government is broadly on board but the opposition groups have been difficult and have held things up."

"But I don't know anything about politics," said Harry.

"No, that's ok but we'll need to have someone who knows about the science when we come to meet the various parties and start closing deals. That's where your skills will come in useful..." Harry looked confused.

"Don't worry, that won't be until further down the line, once we're sure there are viable deposits... That will be your first job. We've done some initial aerial surveys and that wasn't easy."

Leganes raised his eyes to indicate the frustration and then continued.

"I want you to lead a team in the field to find the best places to extract the ore, a real prospecting job. Then you'll need to send me a report with your recommendations confirming the viability of the ore and where to start drilling. I can't stress enough the importance of your report, not just for me, or Edward; there are others who have an interest."

"Partners?" said Harry.

"Yes," said Leganes without going into any detail.

Harry was intrigued. Leganes continued. "If all goes to plan, we'll get the licences and then we'll be in negotiation with the mining companies and they'll carry out the extraction. That's where the politics will come in. We'll need you to be in on the negotiation team as a knowledge expert."

Leganes spoke eloquently but directly and with the same passion as Harry had noticed at his interview. He suddenly felt the weight of expectation again.

"What do you know about the situation in Australia?" said Leganes.

"A bit, I've read up about it since I was told I was going."

"Well let me give you some more background which you won't find on any search engines."

Leganes sat back in his chair as if giving a lecture. Harry was in listening mode.

"Ok, well, we've got three parties in play here. The Australian Government, they own the mining rights for the whole country and they're generally in favour of more exploration. They make a great deal of money from it... over two billion dollars in the last five years."

Harry expressed surprise. "Wow."

"There's some opposition from the left in the Senate but generally they can be controlled."

"Controlled?" queried Harry.

"We can limit their impact," Leganes clarified. "Then we have the Greens, the anti-nuclear brigade, who are ideologically against any sort of expansion. They're more than a nuisance at times and can be a real pain in the butt but we've got some guys out there working on that."

Harry was intrigued but again Leganes did not expand. He was taking this all in, trying to absorb the information.

"Then there are the indigenous people, the Aboriginals, who are kind of in the middle. They do very well from the mining but there are problems with ancient burial sites and other sacred areas. The traditionalists, as you can imagine, don't want anything to upset their gods or whatever but that's not the real problem. As you know, the area we're interested in is outside the national park but close to it. We call it the Kakadu Gap. What you may not know is the land is actually owned by an Aboriginal called Miki Rey. He's the last survivor of one of the ancient clans and an Anglican vicar."

"Really?" said Harry.

"Yes, not that's of any real relevance, just information. It's a huge area, over a thousand hectares. We estimate that the reserves there are potentially worth five, maybe six billion dollars, that's what we need to confirm. Then we can strike a deal with him. He's a cute cookie and he's pushing hard on price but we're in discussions with him as we speak to let us do an initial exploration. We're concerned he may have other suitors. The French, we know, are showing an interest but we don't think they've made any firm proposals. As far as we know they've yet to do any proper analysis but we do need to move quickly. We don't really want to get caught in a bidding war. For that reason, everything is very sensitive, you understand. The press are also showing an interest which could make things... difficult. As I said there's a lot of local opposition and we've had one incident... but nothing for you to worry about," added Leganes, seeing Harry's expression.

Harry assumed that this would be the plane sabotage that Monique had mentioned in London but said nothing.

"Quite a challenge," said Harry. "But I don't understand how you're going to make any money if you can't buy the land."

"Simple... as I said, licenses. If we can secure them they're worth a fortune... and strategically we need to have a presence there; mining in Australia is huge. We started on a project last year near Perth but that didn't work out. We need this one to work."

"Ok, I get that," said Harry. "But what about the companies that are there already?"

"The Ranger mine has been open since '81 and was there before the National Park was set up. There's another site at Jabiluka which is also in the park but hasn't been developed yet. Technically they're not part of the park but they are surrounded by it. The mines are owned by a subsidiary of PTZ, Playa Tinto Zinc, they're real big down there. We've worked with them in the past."

"Yeah, I read about the mines but not who owned them. Won't PTZ be interested?"

"They probably would be but they've got enough on their plates at the moment but who knows? That's why we're keen to get this all agreed."

"I can see that," said Harry.

"There's something else you may be interested in... The Australian Government has already paid out five million dollars upfront to the Aboriginals for Jabiluka... the second mine in Kakadu, the one I mentioned earlier."

"Five million, wow?" said Harry.

"Yes... and they've not even started mining yet. That gives you an idea of the money involved..."

Leganes paused for a moment.

"Would you like another coffee?"

"Thanks," said Harry, and Leganes was on the intercom ordering drinks.

The line of discussion continued but was disturbed by a knock on the door as Veronique, who Harry had seen on his last visit, came in with another tray of coffee and cups. She smiled at Harry in recognition.

Veronique took away the empties and left the room.

"I still don't see where I fit in. It looks like all the work's been done," said Harry, picking up the thread again.

"A lot of it has," said Leganes. "But we need a more detailed analysis to put before the Australian Government and then convince the Reverend Rey to let us have the licenses."

"But if this chap Rey owns the land why would he need us?" said Harry.

"Good point... Because he has no idea about mining; we would ostensibly act as his agent on commission so providing we can convince the Australians to grant a license to mine the area, we could then offer the excavation to tender and charge a fee."

"So we need to persuade the government _and_ the Aboriginals?" said Harry.

"Well yes but we do have some good connections there. Edward has already met representatives from the Australian Department of the Environment, and as I said, they're broadly in agreement, it's worth a lot of money to them, and we're pretty confident we can persuade the Reverend Rey to give us the go ahead, for the initial exploration phase anyway. Then, if it proves to have the potential we believe it has, we can start negotiating again."

"That's a lot of "ifs"," said Harry.

"On the face of it, yes but that's why we need to do the on-field analysis. I spoke to Nate yesterday. He's meeting Rey again in a couple of weeks and he's pretty confident he'll sign up; then we can make a start. Once we've got his signature you can do the ground work, send your report and confirm the deposits. Then we can get the licenses from the government, and we're in business."

Leganes became momentarily distracted by the 'ping' of an email arrival on his computer on the right-hand side of his desk. He clicked on his mouse and glanced at the screen, then returned to the discussion.

"There is one other thing. With the opposition around fossil fuels growing... global warming and all that, there's a lot of work going on to... how shall I put it...? Rebrand nuclear as 'clean' energy. As I'm sure you know the new reactors are far safer than those built in the sixties and seventies. This is starting to gain momentum; even some of the environmentalists are wavering, and of course it will push up the price of uranium ore which is why we want to get in now."

"Yes, I can see that," said Harry.

Harry had finished his second coffee and was mulling over the briefing. Leganes continued.

"While you're here I want you to look over all the reconnaissance studies we've carried out and try and identify some of the areas you'll need to visit. Nate will be in overall charge as project manager; your role will be to analyse and recommend optimum drilling sites... those with viable uranium seams, and provide the final report; so you get to advise us on the deposits, possible yields and so on... Oh, did I mention there will be a substantial bonus if we can pull this off?"

Harry smiled but was deep in thought; the idea of a bonus

hadn't crossed his mind. Leganes leant forward to indicate the discussion was coming to a close.

"Any questions?"

"How many people have you got out there?" said Harry, mirroring Leganes' body language.

"Nate's got a team of four including a couple of other geologists who produced the aerial surveys and a couple of support staff. Any labourers he hires locally as and when."

"So you already have geologists?"

"Yes, not with your specialism but you will be working alongside them," said Leganes.

There was a lengthy pause.

"Was there anything else?"

"What about work permits?"

"That won't be a problem. We'll see to everything from here. Anything else?" said Leganes.

"No, no, thank you... you've answered all my questions," said Harry who was now deep in thought.

"In that case then I'll take you down to the office and introduce you to the team. But please don't hesitate to call me if you need anything. I'll put some time in my diary before you leave here so we can go over any last minute stuff."

Leganes got up and escorted Harry down a flight of stairs to a suite of offices. On one of them, there was a sign, 'Research and Prospecting Department' attached to the door. Harry had passed by it before on his initial visit. There was a security keypad and Leganes used his pass to open the door,

"Your pass will open this," said Leganes. "It's a secure area."

They walked into a large room. It was open plan and, despite the number of people working, seemed remarkably quiet. The odd buzz of a telephone and a whispered response intermittently disturbed the silence. The office was segmented into different work areas by six feet high dividers, each working on specific projects, Leganes explained. A lady, probably in her late thirties, approached them. 'Tara Humphries', it said on her name badge.

"Ah Tara, this is Harry, from England. I told you about him. He's going to be with us for a couple of weeks," said Leganes.

Harry shook hands with Tara. "Nice to meet you," he said.

"Same here," said Tara. "Heard a lot about you."

This had Harry thinking... 'A lot?' He hadn't realised there was that much to tell.

"Oh, right," said Harry, unable to think of anything more appropriate.

"Tara's from Australia, not from where you'll be working but she has had some experience of the area and knows the team. She worked with them for a few months. I thought you could work with her for a while," said Leganes.

"Great," said Harry.

"Right, I'll leave you to it but remember what I said Harry... anything, anytime."

"Thanks, I will," said Harry and Leganes left the room.

"Would you like a coffee, Harry?" asked Tara.

"Yeah, thanks," replied Harry, and he followed Tara to a small kitchenette at the back of the office containing a sink, drainer, fridge and a few cupboards. Tara turned on a kettle on the worktop and retrieved a carton of milk from the fridge.

"There are vending machines in the corridor outside but quite frankly it tastes like piss," she said in a broad Australian accent.

Harry smiled. "Yeah, I've had some experience with coffee machines."

As she made the coffee, Harry watched her. In some respects, she reminded him of Chloe but with short fair hair that looked like it had been bleached by extensive exposure to the sun.

She was slim, boyish even, with a tanned complexion which supported that conclusion. She was dressed informally, as was everyone else it seemed in the department, a short-sleeved light blue shirt and smart jeans with flat shoes. She was also wearing jewellery, earrings, necklace and an ornate, gold-plated oura boros bangle, the tail-devouring serpent, on her left wrist.

"Milk?" she said.

"Thanks," said Harry. "No sugar."

"Right, get that down your neck," she said handing Harry a mug.

He took the coffee. "So whereabouts in Australia, do you come from?" asked Harry as he took another hit of caffeine.

"Queensland, down south near Brisbane."

"Ah, the Gold Coast," said Harry.

"Yeah, not far away... you know it?"

"No, not been but I know about the geology," said Harry.

"Yeah, I heard you were a bit of an expert," said Tara.

"Oh, I wouldn't say that," said Harry modestly.

"Well you better be," said Tara. "There's a lot going on there and we need the best people."

This was not a place for false modesty Harry quickly realised.

"Come on, I'll bring you up to speed."

They left the kitchen and went back to one of the pods with Harry tagging on behind.

"This is your desk," she said, indicating a comprehensive workstation in its own area. "I'm just over there," she added, indicating an adjacent pod a few yards away. "I.T. will be down with a laptop for you a bit later. I've dug out a few files on the Kakadu Gap for you and I'll email you the reconnaissance pictures we've got. I'll also give you the heads up on the reporting process as well."

"Thanks," said Harry.

He started to nest-build, laying out the desk and area to his own liking. A few minutes later a bespectacled geeky-looking young man of Asian extraction put his head around the pod entrance.

"You waiting for laptop," he said in a strong Indian accent.

"Yeah, thanks," said Harry.

"I'm Vikrant," he said. "Let me show you the settings and passwords. We have our own encrypted network here."

After almost an hour with Vikrant explaining the intricacies of the company's I.T. system, Harry's head was beginning to spin. It was time for lunch... what a morning. Tara offered to escort him to the refectory as it was his first day and she introduced him to other members of the department.

Over lunch, she outlined her role in more detail. She was director of the Asia/Australia division, reporting directly to David Leganes. The Kakadu project was one of several she was coordinating, she explained. "I helped set up the original team in Darwin before they called me to take over here."

The teams were divided by geographical areas by continents, each with a director. Harry would be introduced to many of them during the course of the day. He was desperately trying to remember their names.

By six o'clock Tara was ready to call it a day and called in at Harry's pod.

"I'm off now," she said. "See you tomorrow." Tara had a flat in Lausanne, about an hour away.

Harry was feeling the effects of an intensive day and decided he would leave and to go to the gym to de-stress. He locked his desk and went back to his room to change. He would make use of the swimming pool in addition to a circuit or two and packed his trunks in his gym bag. He was wearing his tracksuit.

Rosa was on reception again and seemed pleased to see Harry. There were three others using the facilities that Harry didn't recognise. He changed into his swimming gear and padded his way to the side of the pool. Rosa was taking more than an interest in Harry's body as she watched him dive into the water; she bit her bottom lip.

Following a decent workout and shower, Harry returned his towel to reception. He was feeling much more relaxed now. The gym was empty; it was just him and Rosa.

"You swim well," said Rosa, taking the towel from him.

"Thanks," said Harry. "Have a good night," he replied.

"Si, you too," she said and Harry went back to his room to change for dinner.

This set the pattern for the next two weeks. Harry got to grips with the various procedures and the detailed report writing process. More importantly, he had learned more about the Australian project and was looking forward to the challenges that lay ahead. During this time, he had become Rosa's best customer and at the end of each gym session they swapped their news and learned more about each other's background. She seemed glad of the company, there was rarely anyone using the facilities. Harry had no inclination of her feelings for him despite the sometimes outrageous flirting. He had no desire to be distracted from his work, he was totally focussed.

It was the last Wednesday, just two days before the end of his induction and his work schedule indicated the meeting with Leonard Scheck, Head of Security which had triggered Harry's curiosity.

Harry was told to report to the armoury. It was in another area marked 'out of bounds' on his map. He was directed by Lucy on reception to another part of the Chateau away from all the offices and told to go through a small access door and wait in the lobby. She would let Herr Scheck know he was on his way. Harry found the door, only identifiable by a small sign next to it that said 'A2 – Entrée interdite'.

It was an old wooden portal, probably original, with a large black metal ring as a handle. Harry turned it and went in. There were no seats; it was just an empty room with a door opposite which looked like it was made with some sort of re-enforced metal. He looked around at the bare brick walls and cold stone floor; he still wondered what he was doing there. The security door opened and Scheck was stood there, all six foot two of him, in a bodyguard suit.

He was a brute of a man, shaved head, square-jawed; the product of some Special Forces unit of unspecified origin, Harry imagined. Scheck would never be drawn on his background; it was shrouded in mystery. His accent suggested German; Tara said he was Austrian but no-one seemed to know much about him. Harry found his very presence threatening; there was something menacing about him.

"Herr Bentham?" he said, his eyes narrowed as if assessing any potential threat.

"Yes," replied Harry, trying not to feel intimidated.

"Come," he ordered and led Harry down a spiral staircase. They came to another door as heavy as the first and Scheck opened it by tapping a four-digit code into a security pad.

After the heat of the outside, it was significantly cooler in the bowels of the Chateau. Harry followed the man through the door and into a long room. It was stark with just the slate-coloured castle walls, no attempt at decoration. Down the sides, there were wall lights at two-metre intervals providing the only illumination. There was a small desk with two chairs by the entrance door but no other furnishings. "Sit," ordered Scheck as if Harry was a dog, his voice echoing around the room. The Austrian pulled back one of the chairs scraping the stone floor and beckoned Harry. He complied and Scheck sat on the other.

Scheck gave Harry an introduction to the organisation's

security policy and its importance. Then, with the benefit of a video presentation, there was a lesson in kidnap avoidance and cyber safety. Harry was beginning to understand the importance of the session. After a break for coffee at the refectory, Scheck took Harry to the bottom of the room where there was a small firing range. It was brightly lit compared to the rest of the room. Scheck produced some ear defenders and goggles and then left Harry for a moment looking at a target about ten metres away. He returned a few minutes later with a handgun, automatic rifle and two boxes of ammunition. Harry was flabbergasted but said nothing as Scheck proceeded to give Harry a lesson on how to fire the weapons. Why? Harry could only guess.

It was scheduled to last most of the day with only a break for lunch in the refectory and coffee. Herr Scheck declined to join him; he was unsurprisingly not one for fraternisation.

Halfway through the afternoon, a large red button on the wall started flashing on and off. Scheck noticed it. "You wait here," commanded Scheck, leaving through the metal door and closing it. Harry could hear him climb up the spiral staircase, his heavy shoes clumping on the metal steps.

Harry sat there waiting for Scheck to return, looking around the office-cum-rifle-range wondering what was happening. He spotted another door to his right which he hadn't noticed earlier. It wasn't closed properly. As the minutes ticked by, curiosity was getting the better of Harry. After twenty minutes, there was still no sign of the Austrian. Harry slowly got up from his seat and checked again for the returning Scheck but could hear nothing. He walked towards the door and pulled it open slowly so he could see inside.

He couldn't believe his eyes. It was a storage area with row upon row of rifles, grenade launchers, automatic weapons of all shapes and sizes, boxes of ammunition and explosives; enough to equip a small army. At the far end was a heavy security door which stretched to the ceiling; large enough to accommodate a small van or truck. A concealed entrance Harry surmised. He was trying to work out where it would lead; from where he was it would have to be under the moat. Someone had gone to a lot of trouble to secure it, that was for sure. He was speechless; why all this weaponry in rural Switzerland? Harry could only imagine.

He was disturbed by the clanking of heavy footwear coming down the stairs. Harry made a dash back to the seat; Scheck was none-the-wiser.

He entered the room. "We have finished for the day, you can go," said Scheck, and that was the end of the session. It was gone three-thirty and Harry decided to go back to his room; he'd done enough for the day.

Scheck sat at his desk for a moment as if gathering his thoughts, then reached for his briefcase and retrieved a laptop. He filed a report but then noticed the door to the storage area was ajar. He remonstrated with himself for the lapse and went to close it. Then he had a thought, had anyone been inside? He checked around but there was no sign. He closed and locked it and gave it no further thought.

After another visit to the gym, much to the delight of Rosa, Harry caught up on some reading before retiring to bed around ten-thirty. He was ruminating on his visit to the armoury and his encounter with the head of security. He wondered again about the store of weaponry. Then something disturbed him. At first, he couldn't make out what it was, then he realised someone was tapping. Sleepily he got out of bed and went to the door. He opened it a fraction and couldn't believe his eyes.

"Monique!" he said.

Chapter Seven

Harry just stood there; he'd convinced himself that he would not be seeing Monique ever again and for a fraction of a second wondered he if he was dreaming but he wasn't.

He opened the door wider and she quickly entered and closed the door.

"What are you doing here?" said Harry.

"Shhhh," said Monique and she wrapped her arms around his neck and kissed him, deeply, slowly; the intensity almost took his breath away.

Harry was just wearing his boxers and immediately Monique's hands were exploring.

"I have missed you, Harry... so much."

She moved down his body kissing him as she went, his chest, his tummy; she pushed down his shorts and found what she really wanted. She continued the oral stimulation. Harry thought he would explode as Monique traced her tongue around his erect penis and then consumed it hungrily.

Monique was wearing a tracksuit and trainers as though she had been to the gym but it was only to protect her modesty. She stood up and pulled down the zipper of her top; she was naked.

Harry needed no further invitation and in no time they were on the bed. Monique had come prepared and took a condom from her tracksuit bottoms and gave it to Harry. Within seconds he was inside her.

It finished all too soon and they both lay on the bed panting, satiated for the moment.

It was Harry who spoke first. "I thought I would never see you again."

"I have been in New York with Edward. I arrive here only three hours ago."

"Where's Edward?"

"He stays in Genève... He has meeting demain... er... tomorrow. I come back here to see you... you leave soon I think."

"Yes, Saturday, ten o'clock," said Harry, still trying to come to terms with Monique's sudden appearance. There was a few moments silence.

"Why haven't you been in touch?" asked Harry.

"It is not possible, I have been not alone."

"Not even a text?"

"It is for the best, Harry. Edward does not know how I feel. He would be... en colère... er... angry."

"But I don't know how you feel either," said Harry sharply.

"This, I understand. I am sorry. If it was different maybe we will be together but it is how it is."

Harry considered this.

"Are you pleased to see me?" she said.

"What do you think?" said Harry; the sarcasm was not intended.

She leant over and kissed him. "I think you are very pleased to see me," she said and started caressing his penis back to hardness.

She undid another condom and they made love again; this time more slowly. The room was bathed in the low light of the bedside lamp and their movements created shadows on the walls, two people entwined in ecstasy.

Afterwards, it was Monique who spoke first.

"I cannot stay with you tonight, Harry. Nobody here must know."

"No, of course... I understand. Will I see you again?"

"Who knows? Tomorrow I have to go to Genève to meet Edward then we go to Zurich to see some bankers. We will stay there until Saturday. You will be gone I think."

"Yes," said Harry. "Back to England then I'm off to Australia in two weeks, I don't know for how long."

"Oui, I know... one day, peut-être... perhaps," she translated.

They lay together in each other's arms for a while. Harry started to drift off to sleep. Monique heard him starting to snore and nudged him.

"Harry, I need to go." She got out of bed and started putting on her tracksuit. Harry woke from his doze and watched her dress.

She leant over and kissed him.

"Au-revoir Harry... je t'aime."

She left the room before Harry could react and he just lay there feeling very empty.

Sleep did not come easily for Harry, buoyed as he was by Monique's visit. He replayed everything in his mind but it was her parting remark that intrigued him. "Je t'aime", what was that all about?

The next morning, it was back to his pod and some final catching up. It had taken two cups of tea and a large latté to bring his brain into focus; thoughts of Monique had to be dispelled. He had been asked to compile a short report on the findings from the Kakadu Gap aerial shots and present it to David Leganes on Friday. He spent the day analysing hundreds of photographs of the area, detailing possible sites for further investigation. Some of the more remote areas were inaccessible which would preclude them for further study.

Harry managed to narrow the search down to eight possible sites which he graded in levels of importance. He believed these would be the focus of attention when they started prospecting on the ground.

That evening, as he had done every night since his arrival, he went to the gym. He was wondering how on earth the facilities were paying their way with so few users. Rosa complained to him continuously of the sheer boredom she faced day after day and admitted she was looking for a more challenging career. Having said that she was well rewarded for what she did and would find it difficult to find something else that paid the same, she explained.

"Why don't you ask for a transfer?" suggested Harry as he returned his towel after his work out.

"Si, I will do that, I think," she said. She looked at him. "Tomorrow is your last day, Harry?"

"Yes," he replied.

"I will miss you. I will have no-one to talk to," she said. "Will you be coming to the gym?"

"Tomorrow?"

"Si."

"Yes, before dinner, I think they're putting on a special meal for me."

"That will be nice... I will be here," she said and once again provided Harry with a view of her ample breasts as she reached to the lower shelf for a towel.

Friday morning was the last day of Harry's induction, much of the time was spent in meetings and doing last minute preparation for his presentation.

At two o'clock, he met David Leganes and Lucien de Bruye in the conference room and presented his findings. The two men listened with interest.

"Well done, Harry," said Leganes on its conclusion. "I'll email your presentation and recommendations out to Nate, get his thoughts and look at the practicalities. Some of the areas are pretty wild."

"Yes, well done," said Lucien. "It was very interesting," and he shook hands with Harry.

The men left the conference room with copies of Harry's

notes, talking animatedly to each other in French. Harry thought it a bit strange as they normally spoke to each other in English but then thought no more about it. He packed away his laptop and headed back to his pod. When he opened the door to the office he was confronted by the team who broke out in spontaneous applause. Tara, the team leader, approached him with a glass of champagne and a small gift box neatly wrapped with a ribbon and bow. His work area had been decorated with a banner that said "Good luck".

Harry didn't know what to say as he accepted the glass from Tara.

"We just wanted to say thanks and wish you all the best in Oz," she said

Harry put down his laptop and drink and started wrestling with the covering of his present. Inside the decorative wrapping, there was another box which he opened.

"Hey guys, that's great," said Harry as he removed the gift and showed it to the watching audience. It was a beautiful paperweight with specs of different minerals encased in glass. Harry held it up for all to see and it seemed to radiate different colours as the light of the room bounced off it.

"It's for when you eventually get a desk," said Tara to the amusement of the gathering.

"Speech!" they shouted.

"Thank you... that's great," said Harry, overwhelmed by the warmth of his colleagues.

Speeches were not Harry's style and he merely expressed his gratitude for the help he had received and his hope that they would join him in the bar later.

The group dispersed and it was just him and Tara. "You've made quite an impact since you joined us. They don't usually go to this trouble for someone on their induction."

"Thanks, I'm very grateful," said Harry. "Everyone's been

really helpful."

"You're welcome, Harry..."

She looked around to make sure there was nobody within hearing distance. "Listen, off the record, I don't know what you've heard but something's happening down there. You'll need to tread very carefully. I was there a few months back and still keep in touch with a couple of the guys and get the odd snippet. Things are not right, that's what I've heard... Just a heads-up," she added. She checked again for eves-droppers. "Between you and me, mate, I think the whole project's dead in the water anyhow. There's no way we should be mining up there; it'll ruin the place but don't tell anyone I said that or I could be in deep shit."

"No, of course not...what kinds of things are happening?" asked Harry but before she could answer another of the team was approaching to wish Harry well and the moment was lost. This was, however, in line with what Monique had said and got him wondering what to expect.

His farewell dinner was arranged for seven-thirty. The entire department plus David Leganes and Lucien de Bruye would be there. Harry started tidying his desk and shredding unwanted notes and then at five o'clock handed his keys to Tara. He would keep the laptop for use in Australia; it had all his data safely stored and backed up. He took his bits and pieces back to his room and changed into his tracksuit ready for his workout. It was five-thirty as he walked into the leisure centre.

Rosa was waiting for Harry to arrive and welcomed him enthusiastically. The gym, as on many other days, was empty. She had his towel ready.

"Hola, Harry, it is good to see you... your last day, si?"

"Yes," said Harry and he told her of his farewell present and the send-off he had received from his colleagues.

"I am sure they will miss you... I will miss you, Harry."

"I will miss you too, Rosa," he said, which was genuinely meant.

She looked at him and stared into his eyes. Harry couldn't hold the gaze and looked away.

"Thank you," he said holding up the towel and he headed towards the changing room.

Harry had developed his own routine now; a circuit on the machines, a swim, a few minutes in the steam room, and then a shower.

Rosa watched him as he went through his exercise regime. She looked around; the gym was still empty. She went to the front door and locked it.

Harry was relaxing in the steam room in just his swimming trunks. His eyes were closed but he became aware of the door opening and someone walking in. He opened his eyes but all he could see was a thick swirling mist, then moving towards him, a spectral figure dressed in white; it resembled a shroud. His senses were on high alert but then the colour changed, the mantle had been discarded. As he tried desperately to focus through the steam, he soon became aware of the source of this visitation.

"Rosa?" he said, recognising the figure standing in front of him. He sat up.

"What are you doing here?"

"It is ok. I have locked the door, we won't be disturbed... I thought we could say goodbye properly."

She sat down next to him and he could see her very clearly now; she was totally naked. She placed her hand on his thigh and leant forward to kiss him. His first reaction was to pull away but she held the back of his neck and moved him towards her. "It is ok," she said again, and suddenly they were kissing.

Rosa was soon tugging at Harry's swimwear; he stood up and she pushed down his trunks. She held his penis in her hands and closed her eyes. For days she had dreamt of this but never thought it would happen; she never wanted it to end. Water droplets fell from the ceiling, cooler than the ambient temperature and heightened the senses, like needles on the skin. She was on fire.

"You sit," whispered Rosa, trying not to break the spell. The stone seating was not the most comfortable but Harry sat on the edge and Rosa straddled him. The connection was made. The steam swirled around them as they continued their lovemaking. Rosa had never experienced anything like it and screamed as she reached orgasm. Harry soon followed.

They stayed there for a minute or two still joined together, Rosa astride Harry.

"That was maravilloso."

"Yeah," said Harry, "a nice way to say goodbye."

"It is sad I will not see you again."

"Maybe I'll be back one day," he said.

"Si, I hope."

The temperature in the steam room was now uncomfortable. "I'll have to get out of here, I can't breathe," said Harry.

"Si, it is very hot," said Rosa and they uncoupled and started dressing. Rosa's overall was soaking wet.

"I'm going to have a shower," said Harry. "I'll see you in a few minutes."

"You go; I will see you in reception. There are cameras outside, they will see us if we are together," she said.

Harry left the steam room and headed for the changing area. He retrieved his tracksuit from the locker and ran a shower. He stood there in the warm flow, reflecting on the last few minutes. There were soaps and sweet-smelling body lotions in containers next to the shower controls and he applied liberal amounts to his body, reviving and invigorating.

Rosa, meanwhile, had returned to the gym reception and

found a replacement overall; she was waiting for Harry when he went to hand back his wet towel.

"Thank you... for everything," he said.

She leant forward and kissed him on the cheek.

"You also, Harry, and take care in Australia... I will think of you."

Harry left the leisure centre for the last time; he would also remember Rosa.

Harry was in the dining room at seven-thirty and the centre of attention. All but two of the research team was there, child-care issues he had been told, as well as David Leganes and Lucien De Bruye. A special menu had been prepared and the chef had designed a commemorative carte du jour and presented it to Harry as a memento. The wine seemed to be on tap and a great time was had by all. Harry was sat next to Leganes and Tara. As the drink flowed, the ambience mellowed. Tara's Australian accent became broader by the minute and the table was in uproar as she tried to sing 'Waltzing Matilda'. After the meal, people gradually drifted away wishing Harry well. Tara was at the bar on a high stool consuming yet another glass on her own. Leganes and Lucien De Bruye were on the opposite side of the room so Harry went to keep her company and pulled up another stool.

"G'day, Harry," she said as he sat down. "Would ya like me to teach ya some Oz phrases so ya know what they're on about when you get there?"

Her eyes appeared slightly glazed.

"Yeah, why not," he said. He was holding a glass of mineral water.

"Fair dinkum... do ya know that that means?"

"Yeah, that's easy... 'Everything's ok...' Is that right?"

"True blue cobber," she said and laughed loudly. "You've

been swottin' up."

"What about this one, clever bugger?" She whispered something which Harry didn't hear clearly.

"Sorry, didn't catch it," he said and she put her index finger to her lip.

"Shhhh," she said. She repeated the phrase.

"Crack a fat?" said Harry.

"Shhhh," she said again. "It's rude."

"Don't know that one," he said.

She leant closer to him and looked around to see if anyone was listening.

"It means 'get an erection'," and she howled with laughter nearly falling off her stool.

"Well you never know, it might come in handy," said Harry and joined in the levity.

She took another sip of wine and her expression changed.

"Harry, you're a good bloke for a bloody Pom. You make sure ya watch your back while you're down under, ya hear. Just remember, when the shit hits the fan, they'll wanna scapegoat, know what I'm saying? Make sure ya cover all your bases mate."

Harry was trying to make sense of it, she was clearly drunk but the warning seemed sincere. He sipped from his bottle of mineral water.

She shifted on her stool as if trying to get more comfortable then looked around the room. She moved closer to Harry and whispered.

"What I was saying earlier... you know, things happening...? Well, there's been a couple of guys gone missing down there," she said, her words now slurring.

"What do you mean?"

She looked around and put her hand up to her mouth conspiratorially. "I was speaking to Nate a couple of days ago and he said two Abbos working for us down there have gone walkabouts... He said they just left without saying anything which is a bit unusual. The Abbos tend to be very reliable... seems to me like it's all going tits up down there. There are other things too..."

Before she could say any more she noticed David Leganes glancing in her direction.

She finished the remnants of her wine like it was a glass of lager. "Just take care, ya hear."

She put her hand on his shoulder in a blokey sort of way; the kind of demonstration of fondness more associated with one of Harry's rugby chums.

"Yeah, too right," said Harry and Tara laughed at his attempted Aussie accent.

David Leganes, having seen the two in conversation, made his way across the room.

"Tara, your lift is waiting for you," he said as he approached.

"Gee, thanks, David," and she slid off the stool in a most ungainly fashion almost landing in a heap but steadied herself just in time. "Whoa, keep the horse steady," she said.

"Goodnight, Harry, thanks for the party... and good luck Down Under. You're gonna need it," she said and blew Harry a theatrical kiss.

Tara walked unsteadily to the door and Harry saw her get into a waiting car.

"So, how are you Harry?" said Leganes. "Lucien has had to go but he sends his best wishes.

"Thanks," said Harry.

"Look, I hope Tara wasn't speaking out of turn. She can be a bit loud when she's had a drink," said David.

Harry tried to look surprised; he couldn't imagine too many drunken episodes given the corporate culture.

"No... no, not at all, just introducing me to some Australian phrases," he said and laughed.

Leganes seemed satisfied and made his excuse to leave. "Early start tomorrow," he explained. "Off to Warsaw; might see you at the airport."

"Yes, I need to be there for eight," said Harry.

"Right, I'll look out for you," said Leganes. "Goodnight. Thanks for your work here and good luck in Australia. Don't forget you can contact me anytime if you have any problems but I will be keeping a close watch on things."

They shook hands and Harry watched him leave.

There were just a couple of people still left in the bar, none from his team, so Harry decided to get an early night. It was ten o'clock.

He walked back to his room and thought about the day, the generous send-off from the research team, the 'farewell present' from Rosa, and the comments from Tara; he was starting to wonder what lay ahead. Then his mind turned to Monique again; she was never far away from his thoughts these days.

The following day Harry was up early and packing the rest of his things. He had two suitcases and a carry-on; his baggage allowance had been increased to accommodate. Joseph was on hand again to carry the luggage down to reception. Harry had enough time to grab a quick breakfast before the car arrived to take him to the airport. He said his final farewells to Lucy and the reception team and felt a tinge of sadness as he left for the last time. His bags were duly stowed in the boot of the limo by Marcel, the driver. As they left the courtyard Harry caught a glimpse of the entrance to the gym and smiled. He was going to miss his regular workouts and Rosa's company. Then, as they drove under the portcullis, he suddenly thought about the armoury and looked around to see where the concealed entrance might exit but they were soon too far from the building.

It was quarter to eight as the car pulled up outside the departure lounge of Geneva Airport. As he was getting out of the car, there was a 'ping' on his phone alerting him to a text message. Harry was negotiating his baggage onto one of the trolleys with Marcel's help and would read it later; he hoped it might be from Monique wishing him a safe journey.

In the check-in area, he looked around for David Leganes but realised he would be in Business Class and probably in one of the executive lounges. Harry would be on his own. Having safely negotiated check-in and security, he was sat in one of the many coffee shops by the departure gates when he suddenly remembered his text message. He retrieved his phone from his pocket and accessed the texts. He read the message and then read it again.

It was from Robert Tiran, one of the supervisors from the Research Department. Harry had struck up a great rapport with him and had swapped mobile phone numbers.

'Tara killed last night - car accident, Robert'

Harry punched in Robert's number to get more information but the call went straight to voicemail. Harry left a message for him to call back. He thought about Tara, straight-talking and loud but totally dedicated to her job; he had developed a great deal of respect for her. Then he recollected the previous evening and the warning she had given him.

The flight was called and Harry was waiting for the usual queue to board the plane when his phone buzzed. He ushered people to go ahead of him and stood to one side to take the call.

"Hello," he said.

"It's Robert... I can't talk for long; they're watching people... business calls only. The press have been calling wanting to know about Tara."

The connection wasn't good. Robert had a distinctive Slovak accent and with the bustle of the crowd trying to queue to get on the plane, understanding what he was saying was a problem.

"Sorry Robert, can you speak up a bit."

"It's difficult, I am in toilet."

"Ok, what happened to Tara?" said Harry.

"I do not know for sure, police say she was run over when she got out of the car. She was drunk and went into the road. It is terrible... I go now; I will try to call again."

He rang off before Harry could say anything; the queue had gone and a flight attendant urged Harry to board the plane.

It was about two hours before Harry landed at Stanstead Airport, then he got a train to Norwich where his father was waiting at the station. All the while, Harry couldn't get the news out of his head. He wondered if he should make contact with Lucien or David Leganes but something stopped him. Harry was not prone to conspiracy theories but he did wonder if this was too much of a coincidence.

The Benthams lived in a small village on the outskirts of the city and his mother was waiting at the door of their three-bedroomed cottage as the car pulled up in the drive. Naturally, his parents were thrilled to see him back and wanted to know all about his exploits in Switzerland.

"Harry, it's so good to have you back," she said and threw her arms around him in a motherly hug.

Harry's father was carrying the two suitcases as Harry dragged the carry-on into the house.

"The kettle's on, come and tell me all about it," she said and disappeared into the kitchen to finish making the tea.

After a few minutes, she brought a tray with three mugs into the sitting room.

"My Inner Wheel ladies are so excited," said his mother as she passed him a mug of tea. "They can't wait for me to give them a full report."

But Harry was far from excited; Tara's death had cast a cloud over the two weeks and he found it difficult to go into any details.

He eventually excused himself and went to his room to unpack, leaving his parents mystified as to why he wasn't his usual exuberant self.

"Are you all right, dear?" said his mother as he left the room.

"Yeah, just tired from the trip. I'll get my head down for a bit."

Thoughts of Monique returned to him as he set up his laptop on his desk and he wondered if she had heard about Tara. There was no way of finding out.

It was two weeks until his flight to Australia and now, being officially on the payroll, he would be working from home. From Sunday morning emails started arriving at regular intervals with updates and information from the research department. His father had had the Internet installed shortly after Harry had gone to university so keeping updated was not an issue. It would have been a trek to go to the local library and not particularly secure.

On Monday, he tried calling Robert again to see if there was any more news on Tara but again the call was diverted to voicemail. In the end, he phoned the office via the switchboard and was put through to Samuel Fischer, one of the other section heads.

"Samuel? It's Harry. How are you?"

"Harry, it's good to hear from you," he whispered.

"Why are you whispering?" asked Harry.

"It is very quiet here... no-one is talking much," he said, slightly more relaxed. "What can I help with?"

"I was just wondering if there was any more news about Tara, I couldn't get through to Robert."

"Robert is sick, not here," said Samuel again quieter. "Security are here going through Tara's desk. They've taken away her computer... I can't talk about it."

"Ok, Samuel, no worries," he said, realising he had picked up one of Tara's favourite phrases. "Speak soon?"

"Yeah, you take care, Harry."

Harry sat at his desk, unable to concentrate on the papers in front of him wondering what was happening. He clicked on one of the search engines and accessed the local newspaper in Lausanne to see if there was a report. On page two there was a short article, it was in French and there was a picture of Tara in a business suit; she looked much younger.

'Un dirigeant d'entreprise tué dans un accident de voiture', read the headline.

Harry reached for his French-English dictionary and looked up the words he didn't recognise.

'Business leader killed in car accident,' he managed to translate. He read through the rest of the article as best he could, just about ten lines. He checked the words one-by-one but there was no real detail, just the fact that Tara was Australian and was a manager at a local company, not much of an obituary.

He thought about texting Monique; he felt the need to speak to her again but something stopped him. It was best to let bygones be bygones he decided; best he didn't become involved, there was no telling where it would lead.

Later that day, he received an email from David Leganes with a report attached which appeared to come from a government source. *'Can you analyse this and let me have some recommendations on how we might limit the impact of some of the arguments as soon as you can. David.'*

These were Leganes' instructions; there was no mention of Tara which Harry thought strange and disappointing given that she was an important member of his team.

Harry opened the attachment and read it, all fourteen pages. It was signed by an Alex Webber, a researcher in the Department of the Environment in Canberra. He read it again; it was a detailed analysis of the proposals to extend Uranium mining in the Northern Territories. It did not make good reading from the company's perspective. The summary was straight and to the point. It stated that the environmental impact of mining in the area would far outweigh any economic value and that the Government should not grant any new licences.

On closer inspection, most of the conclusions were not new; many had already been made by the Greens and the mining community had successfully defended the arguments at various Government enquiries. There was one paragraph, however, in which Harry took a special interest. It referred to Miki Rey, the Aboriginal landowner. From the narrative it seemed clear that he was under considerable pressure from eco-minded organisations not to allow mining anywhere on his land; that would include the Kakadu Gap. If this were to happen Harry's project would never get off the ground.

Harry spent that evening and half of Tuesday going through the document in fine detail and compiling a suitable response in line with David Leganes' request. In his reply, Harry pointed out he could only comment from a geological perspective, the economic and political implications were outside his remit. He was, of course, savvy to both but he had no intention of getting dragged into murky waters.

Later that afternoon he received a phone call. He didn't recognise the number but with the dialling code 0041, it was from Switzerland.

"Hello... is that Harry?" said the voice after he had accepted the call.

"Yes," he replied.

"It's Robert... Tiran," he clarified.

"Robert...? You ok? Samuel said you were ill."

"No, I'm ok... just needed to get away from the office... I don't know who to trust there anymore."

"What do you mean?" said Harry.

"I think Tara was murdered," he said.

"Murdered? Why on earth would anybody murder Tara?"

"Not sure... but it's got something to do with Australia. She told me that something wasn't right down there. A lot of money was involved. She didn't go into detail; she wanted to get more information. Whether she found something, I don't know."

"Have you told anyone?"

"No, I don't know who to trust. You are new and won't have been... how you say...? Corrupted."

"What about David... Leganes?"

"I do not trust him. He, and Edward also; I needed to tell someone."

"But what can I do? I can't do anything."

"No but you are going there. You might see or hear something. I just wanted to warn you."

"Thanks, I'll bear that in mind. What are you going to do?"

"Nothing, I cannot do anything. I have a family; I don't want any harm for them."

Harry listened in amazement. "When are you going back to work?"

"Tomorrow... I do not want any problem."

"Well you take care, and thanks for letting me know. Don't worry I won't say anything."

"Thank you, Harry, and be careful."

Robert rang off leaving Harry with a range of emotions. His initial reaction was disbelief; Robert was over-reacting but then again...

Chapter Eight

Vine Hotel, Darwin, July 13th, 2005

Harry shook himself from the retrospection and looked around the hotel room. Not the five-star version he'd enjoyed with Monique but functional and totally adequate for his needs. The journey had been arduous; Heathrow to Singapore, Singapore to Sydney, Sydney to Darwin all over two days. His father had driven him to Heathrow; this time his mother tagged along. There was naturally an emotional farewell.

It was two-thirty in the afternoon when Harry landed in Darwin, the state capital of the Northern Territories. Once he had safely negotiated security and passport control, he headed for the taxi rank. It was bright and sunny and Harry rummaged through his carry-on luggage to find his sunglasses. There was a short queue but the turnover was quick and within minutes a white Toyota with 'Darwin Radio Cabs' printed on the side pulled up in front of him.

"Where to, mate?" said the driver who was wearing a company badge with the name 'Richie' on it.

"Vine Hotel, Waterfront," said Harry.

"Yeah, no worries, hop in," said the man.

The driver got out and stowed the luggage safely in the boot while Harry made himself comfortable. It was a relatively short journey compared with most international airports, only about eight miles to the city centre. Harry took a keen interest in the town which was going to be home for the foreseeable future. It was smaller than he had imagined for an administrative centre, just over half the size of his native Norwich. Recognising Harry was new to the town, the driver was keen to fill him in on some of the history.

"Yeah, much of the place was destroyed by Japanese bombing in the war then we had another disaster in '74, a bloody cyclone. Most of what you see here is pretty new," said the amiable Richie. Harry noticed a few high-rise buildings with more under construction but given the propensity for storms, nothing like Sydney or Melbourne. It was mainly single story buildings or the occasional three-story apartment blocks.

As he went past the harbour, boat building seemed, unsurprisingly, to be the main industry, boatyards and yachts everywhere. Harry commented on the activity.

"Yeah, we get the bloody cruise liners quite a bit an' all," said Riche. "Bloody nuisance but we need the money so I guess we can't complain too much."

The driver had his window open; the temperature was similar to when he had left home, a little hotter if anything; it was difficult to imagine this was winter. Richie was on hand again to give him the low-down.

"Yeah, mate... we only get two seasons, the dry and the wet; it's dryer in winter," he said. "You wait till you get the bloody wet."

Harry was aware of what was basically a two-season climate, having researched it; with a minimum temperature across the year of fifty degrees Fahrenheit. He hadn't packed a suit.

It took less than half an hour to reach the hotel on the waterfront and Richie helped Harry carry the luggage to reception. He seemed happy with the five dollar tip.

Harry checked in and found his way to his room, 307 on the top floor. There were three complimentary bottles of water on the dressing table. Harry opened one and drank straight from the bottle. Once he had settled, he opened his briefcase and re-read the instructions he'd received in an email with his flight tickets. He would be lodged at the hotel for the first week and then he would transfer to an apartment which would be provided by the company. Details were still being worked out, he had been told.

Helvetia's office in Darwin was used as a base for the prospecting team in the Northern Territories and had a small support staff. As yet, he had heard nothing from the project manager, Nate Gillespie; no email or note of welcome or any local instructions. Harry had found this rather odd and a bit disappointing if he were honest. He had been instructed to report to the office on Friday which would give him a day to get over the travel. The time difference was nine and a half hours between Darwin and the UK so Harry's body clock was all over the place.

He checked his watch; it was late afternoon local time. He was keen to let his parents know that he had arrived but it would be around six a.m. UK time so he would wait a couple of hours. In the meantime, he would take a nap.

He had no idea how long he had been asleep but a noise woke him; he was momentarily disorientated but recognised the ringtone of his phone. He reached to the bedside cabinet and looked at the screen; it just said 'international'. He pressed the call button.

"Hello," he said drowsily.

"Harry... c'est Monique."

"Monique...?"

"Oui... I am sorry. I could not speak to you... Edward, he take away my phone."

"Why would he do that?"

"I do not know... something has changed with him. I am watched always. I cannot go out without a bodyguard. It is like I am un prisonnier."

"Where are you now?" asked Harry trying to process this information.

"I am at the Chateau... Françoise, my assistant, she let me have her phone... Edward, he is in Genève."

"What are you going to do?"

"Je ne sais pas but I cannot stay like this."

"No, I can see that. Can you get away? Have you anywhere you can go... some family perhaps?"

"Ma soeur, er... my sister, she is in Paris. I will try to get away and stay with her I think but I am watched all the time, it will be très difficile."

"What about when Edward is away?"

"Habituellement, er... usually he takes me with him."

"What about next time he is due to go away? You could pretend to be ill or something and then slip away."

"Oui, I think so. Next week, he goes to Hong Kong... that may be possible. I want to see you again so much."

"Yeah, me too but I am in Australia now, arrived a few hours ago," said Harry, running through possible solutions in his mind.

"Mais oui, I know that. I will try to get to Paris and stay there then maybe I can see you in Australie."

Harry was thinking. "What about the business? I thought you looked after things when Edward was away."

"Non, it is David Leganes; he sees to everything for Edward, I do not have any... er... autorité. It is him that makes all the decisions for Edward...He speaks to him all the time."

"I see," said Harry. "Won't Edward find you? In Paris, I mean. If he knows you have a sister there it will be one of the first places he will look."

"C'est possible but he does not know where my sister lives. We do not see her since I am with Edward."

"Hey, what about your shoes, they will track you?"

"Oui, I have others, it will be ok."

"Can you phone her, your sister?" asked Harry.

"Oui, I will try. Now I must go. Je t'aime, Harry; I will speak soon when I can."

Monique rang-off leaving Harry with all kinds of emotions.

Part of him wanted to fly back to Switzerland and rescue her like some mythical princess but that was not practical. He would stay in Australia for the time being and await events; there was not much more he could do.

At six o'clock, he walked down the three floors to the hotel restaurant determined to get his body into some sort of routine; he was still trying to work out the conversation with Monique. Later he made a call to his anxious parents.

With his metabolism umpteen time zones away, sleeping was difficult and by eight o'clock the following morning he was wide awake and having breakfast in the restaurant overlooking the harbour. It was another clear day and already the temperature was a balmy twenty-one degrees. He decided to have a look around his newly adopted hometown and call in at the office and introduce himself before starting work the next day.

He walked out of the hotel and turned right, away from the harbour. The road was unremarkable, flanked by white single story buildings. Palm trees performed a guard of honour, green and verdant. After about a mile, apartment blocks appeared but no shops or anything of any real interest. He reconsidered his priorities; in the absence of any bus service, he was going to need a car. He headed back to the hotel and asked at reception; they were only too happy to provide the service. It would take about an hour, he was told.

To pass the time, he returned to the restaurant. They were not serving breakfast but were happy to serve Harry a coffee while he basked on the terrace in the sunshine. He was thinking about Monique's call the previous evening and Tara's death. His thoughts were interrupted by the sound of his phone.

"Yeah," he said.

"Harry...? It's Robert."

"Robert, hi, what's the news?"

"I wanted you to know that the police are not investigating about Tara. They say it was an accident. David told us today."

"Hmm, that's interesting and David Leganes told you that," said Harry.

"Yes, he told all of us but I think they are wrong, Harry. I am sure something bad happened," said Robert.

"Well, I don't know what we can do."

"It is true, nothing," said Robert.

"What about there... at the Chateau, what's happening?" asked Harry.

"It is still quiet here. All Tara's things have gone. We think security have her stuff. That's what one of the guys says. Security's examined all our files on the computers, we don't know why. Some of the heads of section have been interviewed but they have been told to say nothing so I do not know what is happening."

"Hmm, it seems someone is worrying about something, that's for sure," said Harry.

"Yeah," said Robert. "So how are things in Australia?"

"So far, so good... I only got here yesterday so it's all new."

"Well, you take care, Harry, I will call you if I get any more news," said Robert.

"Cheers," said Harry, "please keep in touch," and Robert rang off.

Harry sat in the mid-morning sunshine considering the latest news; not that he could do anything about it, he was just a geologist investigating possible uranium deposits. He would stick to his job and let others worry about possible conspiracy theories.

His thoughts were interrupted by one of the porters from reception telling him that his car had arrived. He finished his coffee and followed the man back through reception to complete the paperwork. A white Suzuki 4x4; ideal for running about town and going further afield if necessary, although it's off-road credentials would not cope with the harsh terrain outside the city limits. The representative from the car-rental company explained the controls and took the credit card payment. Harry would claim it back from expenses in due course. The man left Harry with a map of the town which would come in very handy.

It took Harry only a few minutes to familiarise himself with the internal layout of the Suzuki. Driving on the same side of the road in Australia as in the UK, meant it was very similar to his car back home. He started the engine and set off to see more of the town.

Darwin is divided into four Wards which are further divided into suburbs. His first port of call was a shopping mall. He needed to buy a few bits and pieces that he couldn't carry in his luggage; a sturdy pair of boots was a priority, he was going to need them. The receptionist had directed him to the Mall in Casuarina, a suburb of Chan Ward about ten miles away on the other side of the city. It is the largest shopping centre in Darwin and would take around half an hour to reach he was told. He wound down the window which provided a welcome breather and took in the scenery. Being a tropical climate, it was remarkably green; Palms and Coolabahs were predominant and the smells were fresh with a wood-like aroma. Harry found himself singing 'Waltzing Matilda' as he drove along; he chuckled at the connection. Every now and then he would catch glimpses of the sea to his left. Red open-topped double-decker buses, like the ones in London, passed him going in the opposite direction with tourists and their cameras peering out looking for interesting images to capture. After more countryside, the scenery became more urbanised as he entered the suburb. He eventually reached the four-story car park and headed for the shops.

After an hour or so he'd acquired the necessary purchases

and returned to his car. He consulted his map and decided to leave the shopping area and visit the coast before returning to the city centre. After a short stop for a sandwich in one of the beachside bars, he drove back into town to find the office.

The Central Business District, as the name suggests, is the commercial quarter of Darwin and includes the local Government Headquarters and Supreme Court. Harry checked his directions; it was only a couple of miles from the hotel but inland. Within twenty minutes, he was sitting outside the Darwin office of Helvetia Mining Services Ltd. It was another of the three-story buildings in the heart of the commercial district with a small car park outside. He looked up at the drab building; it was nothing like he was expecting, not lavish or flash, anonymous almost. Some spaces had been allocated to other occupants of the building but there was a section with about ten spaces marked out with the initials HMS stencilled on the tarmac. Several were taken by a variety of vehicles including two mini-buses bearing the name 'The Duchamp Foundation'. He parked next to one of those.

As he got out of the car and looked at the entrance, he felt a strange déjà-vous, a sense of foreboding almost; a premonition that all was not well. Since the cave incident, he'd had similar sensations but nothing as strong as this. He would generally give little away emotionally; he was always objective, in control, it was one of his strengths but this was different. He had no idea what he was really getting involved in and it bothered him.

Putting his reservations to one side, he walked up to the main entrance and through the swing doors. The interior matched the exterior for drabness. The decor was stark; bare walls colour-washed in off-white, looking like something from a 1950's East German communist building. There were no pictures or welcoming potted palms; in fact, there was nothing to suggest the company's presence, just a reception counter.

On the wall behind the desk, there was a black notice board with names of businesses in white plastic lettering, the sort that you press into grooves to make up words. He could see the name 'Helvetia Mining Services Ltd', about a third of the way down the list of names. This was just a leased office; there was nothing permanent about this location.

Behind the reception desk sat a young lady of Aboriginal origin, dark skinned with corkscrew hair, who was operating a computer. Harry approached and she looked up from her keyboard.

"Hello, can I help you?" she said. Her eyes seemed to be too large for her face but communicative and interested. Her badge hung on a cord around her neck and gave her name as 'Tallara'.

"Hi, yes my name is Harry Bentham, I work for Helvetia, I'd like to see someone please," he said.

"Just one moment," said Tallara.

There was a telephone on a shelf below the top of the desk next to her keyboard and she picked up the receiver and dialled two numbers.

"Oh, hi, it's Tallara on reception. I have a Harry Bentham here... wants to see someone," she said.

There was a pause while she listened to the response.

"Someone's coming down," she said. "They won't be a moment."

There were no seats so Harry stood at the desk feeling a bit self-conscious as Tallara got on with whatever she was doing.

To the right of the desk, there were two lifts and next to them a set of doors which would lead to the staircase, controlled by a security pad on the adjacent wall. After a few minutes, a shape appeared behind the small frosted glass window of the security door. Harry watched the door open and a young woman walked towards him. She was in her late twenties/early thirties, of Asian appearance, short, with long black hair. She was wearing a bright flower-print shift dress, similar to those seen on summer picnics in the UK.

"Hello, you must be Harry," she said. "I'm Winda, please come with me."

There were no handshakes. Harry thanked Tallara and followed the diminutive Winda through the security door and up a flight of stairs.

"We are on the first floor," she said as she walked.

At the top of the steps, there was a corridor which ran the length of the building with doors leading off at intervals; other offices Harry assumed. Again there was no decor, just stark white emulsion. Spiders' webs adorned the ceiling littered with dead insects, emphasising the neglect. Immediately in front of them was the entrance to Helvetia's Headquarters controlled by another security door. A small nameplate with the words Helvetia Mining Services in black Times New Roman font was the only indication of the occupants. The staircase continued upwards and to the left; further along the corridor, on the right, were the toilets.

Winda tapped in a four digit code on the security pad and the door clicked open. Harry followed her inside. The floor space was split into eight pods, each with its own workstation resembling those in Switzerland but that was the only similarity; it appeared functional, little else. Four people seemed to be occupied, concentrating on their monitors, oblivious to their surroundings. There were no pictures or anything to make the office homely. Winda explained the layout. On the right-hand side there were three rooms; at the far end, the kitchen, in the middle, the manager's office and nearest them a small conference room.

It was eerily quiet and Harry followed Winda to the first pod where a woman was working. She was staring intently at her computer screen. She looked up but didn't appear to appreciate the disturbance; there was a scowl on her face.

"Marci, this is Harry," said Winda.

"So you're Harry are you?" said the interrupted Marci. There was an Australian accent but with an American edge; like someone who had been in the country for some time but not originating from there.

"Yeah," said Harry, underwhelmed by the indifference.

"We weren't expecting you until tomorrow."

"Well, I was in the area," said Harry.

"You better come with me. Do you want a coffee?"

"Yeah, cheers," said Harry.

"Can you get two coffees, Winda? How do you take it?"

Harry looked at Winda. "White, no sugar thanks," he said, and Winda walked away towards the kitchen.

Harry followed Marci to the middle room.

"We can use Nate's office; he's out today."

Marci opened the door and the office looked as though one of the seasonal hurricanes had hit it. Maps, pictures and paper were scattered around the room. Filing cabinets surrounded the floor space and there was a small safe on the floor in the corner. The desk surface was hidden by more paper and the in-tray and out-tray baskets on either side of the desk were overflowing.

"Excuse the mess, Nate's not an organised guy," she said. "Grab a seat."

There were two standard office chairs in front of the desk and Harry chose the far one; Marci sat on the other, close to the door. As they were getting comfortable, Winda appeared with two mugs of coffee.

She passed one to Harry. "Thanks," he said.

He moved a magazine out of the way of where it had been gathering dust for goodness knows how long and placed the mug on the desk. Marci took hers from Winda without acknowledgement.

"Shut the door on the way out, Winda," she said. Harry was beginning to wonder about the rudeness and started to make judgements about his new colleague.

She sipped her coffee and looked at him. "So you're the whiz-kid they've sent to sort us out," she said.

"Eh?" exclaimed Harry. "Don't know where you got that from. I'm just here to help with the prospecting."

Marci seemed to be viewing Harry with more than a hint of suspicion. "So you're not a spy then?"

"A spy?" said Harry. "I have no idea what you mean."

"Something Nate said. They were sending down some smart-ass kid from the UK to sort things out down here... something about reporting back to Leganes and Edward."

Harry took a sip of his coffee; there was clearly some misunderstanding here.

"Don't know where he got that from. I'm not a smart-ass or a whiz-kid, just a geologist. They've asked me to make recommendations on possible mining sites in the Kakadu Gap, that's all."

Marci digested this information. "Hmm," she said and sipped her coffee. She looked at Harry. He noticed she looked pale as if she had not been sleeping too well. She wore little makeup and dressed casually in a black tee shirt and black jeans. Her hair was in need of a wash and style. He might move the age estimation up a few years.

She took a sip from her mug and looked at Harry. "Look, sorry if you weren't given the red carpet treatment but things are a bit shitty around here."

Rather than play his hand, he wanted to explore this comment. "What do you mean?" he said.

"Oh, nothing for you to worry about."

"Well, I'm going to be working here for the foreseeable future, so if there is stuff I need to know, I need you to tell me," said Harry assertively.

"Do you know what's going on here?"

"Only what I've heard," he said.

"And what's that?"

"Local opposition... that sort of thing."

"Local opposition, ha! You can say that again," said Marci. "You don't know the half of it."

"Well, tell me then," said Harry.

"Did you hear about the plane being sabotaged?"

Harry wasn't sure how much he wanted to give away.

"What was that?" he said.

"A few weeks back...we were onboard waiting to leave on another fly-by and the pilot told us someone had messed with the wiring on the fuel tanks. Luckily, he spotted it or we'd have been stuck in some creek somewhere fighting off the crocs... or dead."

Harry raised his eyebrows in fake surprise. "Do they know who did it?"

"There's a bunch of 'em, fucking eco-warriors they call themselves, not local, come from all over... After the plane incident, Nate got security down here and it's been a bit better since. We've had protesters outside the office, threatening emails, phone calls, the lot."

She sat there with folded arms not looking at him directly; Harry could detect the high level of frustration. He wanted to move on to more neutral ground. He took another sip of his coffee.

"So, how long have you been here?"

She looked at him but only a glance, as if eye contact was uncomfortable.

"We came out here about six months ago; we were asked to look at possible uranium deposits outside Kakadu but we haven't been able to get proper access to the area so we've just been using aerial research."

"Yeah, I saw the reports and the pictures," said Harry. "Did you get my recommendations?"

"Yeah, they make sense but I don't know what we can do about them at the moment," said Marci. "Things were going fine until the press found out we were intending to start prospecting. It stirred up a hornet's nest. It was front page news here. That's when all the trouble started."

"What the eco lot?"

"Yeah, we don't know who leaked it, we keep things pretty tight but since then we've had the demos, rallies at the University, all sorts... then the plane... then two of the Abbos disappeared. Someone said they'd been threatened."

"Threatened?"

"Yeah, that was the rumour. They just didn't turn up one day and no-one knows where they've gone."

Harry looked down; there was a short silence.

"So, what's Nate doing about it?"

"As I said, he called in security straight away and they sent some guys down. They turned up about three weeks ago just after the demos started. Things seem to have gone a bit quiet over the last week or so, thank goodness. The protestors have all gone at least."

Harry took another sip of coffee which was starting to go cold. "What's he like?"

"Nate...? He's ok, blunt as hell, typical Aussie but he's a good bloke... been getting plenty of pressure from Leganes... and Edward too. They're desperate for us to come up with some results so they can start talking to the politicians and getting a deal done on the mining but until we can get on with some prospecting and get the data, we're fucked. We're still waiting to get permission to start from the owner," said Marci.

"Miki Rey?" said Harry.

"Yeah, you heard about him?" said Marci.

"Yeah," said Harry. "But I thought it'd all been agreed, that's what Leganes said."

"It has, verbally; it's taken ages but there's no contract yet. Winda's drawn up papers to make sure everything's watertight. He's a slippery bastard our Miki."

"Yeah, I heard that," said Harry. "Where is he...? Nate?" he added.

"Nate...? He's gone across to Jabiru to speak to Miki to sort out the details and, hopefully, get the contract signed so we can get started. He's also looking for a couple of guys to replace the ones that left."

"Hmm," said Harry. "Jabiru? That's the mining town, isn't it? What's it like?"

"Yeah, it's ok, a bit grim, not much there but growing fast... got its own airstrip. That's where we had the problem with the plane," said Marci.

"Is it far?" said Harry.

"About two-fifty k's... three hours by truck."

"When will he be back?" said Harry.

"Not till Monday. We may get some more news then," said Marci.

"Let's hope so, I don't want to be sat on my hands," said Harry.

"Oh, I'm sure we'll find you plenty to do," said Marci.

She finished her drink and got up. "Tell you what; let me introduce you to the rest of the team while you're here."

"Yeah ok, great," said Harry but he had another question he wanted to ask.

He stood up. "Did you know Tara, Tara Humphries at all?"

Marci was almost at the door but stopped in her tracks and looked at Harry intently, her eyes narrowed. "Yeah, I knew Tara. She worked here until a few months ago, a great mate, shared many a bottle with her."

"Know her long?" asked Harry.

"Yeah, a while. We were exploring a potential project out near Perth about nine months ago which didn't come off. Then they switched their interest to Kakadu. That's when they put this group together and we were asked to join it. Well, I say 'asked'… 'told' would be more accurate. They closed that one down and we came here but Tara got called back to Switzerland to coordinate things from there. Why do you ask?"

"You heard she was killed?" said Harry.

"Yeah, I heard. Someone sent us an email; apparently, she got pissed and got herself run over. That's all we were told, bloody typical. Mind you, she could down a drink or two that's for sure... very sad. We were all choked at the time."

Harry decided to say nothing about Tara's warning. "Yes, terrible."

"So you knew her too?" said Marci.

"Not knew her exactly," replied Harry. "I worked with her for a short time on my induction. We got on really well. In fact, it was after my leaving do that she got killed... desperately sad, as you say."

Marci turned away and Harry thought there was more to be said but felt unable to push it.

"Come on, I'll introduce you to the team," she said and Harry followed her to the pods.

"We've got two other geologists then there's Winda who you've met and we had the two Abbos; they help with the kit and stuff. Useful as well when we're talking to the locals," Marci was talking as they walked towards the first occupied pod.

"So you manage the office when Nate's not about?" said Harry.

"Yeah, and see to all the transport, equipment and logistics," replied Marci. "Winda looks after all the admin and legal stuff."

They reached the pod. "This is Ying Tao, one of the other geologists; she's from Thailand," said Marci. "Ying, this is Harry."

Harry looked at her. She would be about the same age as him, painfully slim, with black hair like Winda's, which was tied back. Her complexion was pale, white and almost ghostly; she was wearing jeans and a white tee shirt with a logo in Chinese characters.

"Hello," said Harry.

"Hi," said Ying and looked at Harry with big eyes. She turned and went back to her screen.

"Harry starts with us tomorrow," said Marci.

"Yes," said Ying, not turning from her screen. "I know."

She had an oriental accent but not distinctly Thai; more Chinese.

Harry couldn't understand the coldness. Marci led him away from Ying's pod.

"Let me introduce you to Den, he's in today," said Marci.

"Right," said Harry as they walked to the next pod.

"Don't worry about Ying; she doesn't do people," said Marci. "Actually, her parents were killed in the tsunami last Christmas so we need to cut her some slack."

"Right, yes, I can understand that," said Harry, who was now feeling guilty at being offended by her rudeness.

The next pod was separated from Ying's by a clear space of about six feet allowing people to move easily from one side of the office to the other.

"Hi Den, this is Harry. He's joining us tomorrow," said Marci as they arrived at the adjacent workstation.

Harry was greeted by a man in his forties with a beard and thinning lank hair which hung to his collar at the back. Dressed in a ragged looking tee shirt and khaki shorts, his office attire was completed by a pair of flip-flops. He looked more like a roadie from a rock band.

"G'day... Den Travis," he said and smiled. He got up from his desk and shook hands with Harry.

"Harry Bentham." Harry returned the greeting.

"So you're the guy they've sent?" said Den.

"I guess so," said Harry.

"Well, it's good to see another bloke around here. You've come to sort things out I hear."

"Not exactly," said Harry. "I'm not sure where people got that idea from. I'm just here to help find Uranium."

"Right, ok. Marci's told you 'bout all the problems, I guess."

Harry looked at Marci. "Some," he said.

"Yeah, well you watch yourself. There're some pretty screwed up idiots amongst 'em. You heard about the plane?"

"Yeah," said Harry. "Marci told me."

"I think Nate's got it all under control now, been no bother since he got the security guys down here."

"Pleased to hear it," said Harry. "The sooner we get started the sooner we get home."

"How long you out here for?" asked Den.

"As long as it takes, I guess. They never gave me a finish date," replied Harry.

Marci was looking on at the banter. "Well if you guys don't mind I've got work to be getting on with."

"Yes, of course. Well, good talking to you Den. We can catch up properly tomorrow," said Harry.

"Sure thing," said Den and Harry followed Marci towards the exit door.

"Right then, we'll see you tomorrow," said Marci.

"What time?" said Harry.

"It's pretty flexible. I'm usually in about eight-thirty, leave around four-thirty. No-one's got the clock on you."

"Ok," said Harry. "I'll see you then. Thanks for showing me around."

"Yeah, see you tomorrow," said Marci and opened the security door.

"There's a lift if you like but we tend to take the stairs it's only one floor," said Marci.

"Cheers," said Harry, and left the office with a head full of thoughts.

It was three-thirty and Harry decided to drive back to the hotel. He was starting to feel the effects of the jetlag.

As he came out of the building he noticed that one of the Duchamp Foundation mini-buses had gone, leaving an empty space next to the Suzuki. Two men were standing in front of the other one; they took little notice of Harry as he got into his car. He avoided any eye contact but was desperately trying to hear what they were saying. He glanced across for a moment pretending to make a call on his phone. They were hard looking; almost gangster-like. One was tall with a clean-shaven head, wearing a dark jacket with a white shirt; the other was probably a foot shorter but was broad shouldered with thinning fair hair. They were talking animatedly. The men continued arguing for a couple of minutes and then one got into the driver's seat and backed the minibus out of the parking lot leaving the other shouting what appeared to be abuse; they were speaking in German.

Chapter Nine

Harry eased the Suzuki out of the car park and into the late afternoon traffic. He was considering the day; the mixed reception in the office and the arguing Germans, what was that all about? As he made his way back to the hotel, his thoughts drifted back to Monique momentarily and he wondered how she was. Given their circumstances, he had tried to blank her from his mind but not for the first time he wished he could contact her; was she in danger, he wondered. Was he in danger for that matter?

Within ten minutes, he had arrived back at the hotel and parked behind the building in an area reserved for residents. As he was getting out, he noticed one of the Duchamp Foundation mini-buses was parked in a bay allocated for disabled users close to the wall of the hotel. A fellow resident, it would seem.

That evening Harry was restless; a mixture of jetlag, reflections about the new job and concern about Monique. These thoughts rattled around his head like balls on a pool table after a break-off. He phoned his parents around ten o'clock which gave him a few minutes of welcome respite; a connection with a different world, a world where he felt secure and comfortable. Right now, he felt none of these things.

At midnight, there was another call which woke him from a deep slumber.

"Hello... Harry, c'est moi."

"Monique?!" said Harry, trying to regain his senses.

"Oui, I am in the apartment... in Jura. Edward... he goes to Frankfurt. I did not know this. He says it was inattendu... not expect."

"Not expected?" said Harry.

"Oui, he says he does not want me to go to the office so I cannot do work. I do not know what is happening."

"Why would he do that?" asked Harry.

"I do not know but there are things he does not want me to see, I am sure."

"But you must know what's going on, you're married to him."

"Oui, c'est vrai... er, true but he says nothing. There is much money er... how you say... impliqué."

"Involved, much money involved," said Harry trying to clarify.

"Oui... much money... some money he takes from the business; I am sure of this, I have seen things. When I ask him, he says it is not for me to... er... worry."

"Why would he do that?" asked Harry, trying to take in this revelation.

"I do not know. Recently he is how you say... dissimulé."

Harry had to think about this word; it was beyond his basic French.

"Wait," said Harry as he rummaged around in his bedside cabinet for his dictionary. It had come in very handy since his association with Monique. He flicked through the well-thumbed pages.

"Dissimulé...? Wait... ah, here it is... secretive?"

"Oui... secret. He tells me nothing now. It is not the same. I was always there with him, even at the board meetings but now no, I am not er... permis... permitted. He takes my phone and says I must stay at the Chateau when he is away. I have the men... er securité, always they watch."

Harry was listening to Monique and felt the need to protect her in some way. "I wish I could help but I'm stuck here the other side of the world."

"I know that also. I wish you were here now. I want to hold you like in London and I feel er... safe."

"Yes, a special time," said Harry, he paused in thought for a moment. "How have you managed to phone?"

"C'est Françoise, again... she does not believe this is happening so she helps me but we have to be er... careful."

"Yes, I can see that. I don't know what to suggest. Have you thought any more about your sister in Paris?"

"Mais oui but how will I get away? He has my passport and money, all my cards... everything."

"Maybe Françoise could help."

"Oui, but it is dangerous, I think."

"Do you think Edward might harm you?"

"Harm...? I do not understand," said Monique.

"Just a minute," said Harry. There was more frantic page flicking. "Ah, here it is... nuire."

"Mais oui, I think so. C'est possible."

"Is it about us? You and me," said Harry.

"Non, I do not think so..."

"What are you going to do? Have you any ideas?"

"Oui, I will try to go to Paris and then er... maybe I will come to Australie."

"But how? You don't have your passport."

"I will find a way. I must get away from here."

Harry could hear a noise in the background. "I must go, someone is coming. I will phone again soon."

There was a discordant sound as the call dropped. Harry was trying to take in the information. Sleep would be elusive tonight.

The following morning at ten past eight, Harry walked around the back of the hotel to his car. It was another warm and glorious morning with the temperature already over twenty degrees. His body clock was starting to adjust to the time difference but with a lack of sleep the previous night he was not feeling particularly alert. He did, however, notice the minibus had gone. He got in the Suzuki and headed for the commercial district. It was only a fifteen-minute drive and he had the window open, allowing a cooling breeze to waft around the car. He was wearing a short-sleeved shirt, trainers and a pair of light coloured chinos he had bought in Norwich before he left home.

It was his first official day at work in his new role and he pondered on his earlier welcome; there were some trust issues to work on.

Tallara was on reception and remembered him from the previous day. "Helvetia?" she said with a smile.

"Thanks," replied Harry.

Tallara called through. It was Winda who met him again and they retraced the steps from the previous day up to the first floor. "Hello, please come," was her greeting when she entered the lobby and Harry wasn't optimistic that feelings had changed at all.

As they entered the office area, Marci was already at her workstation and Harry could see the top of Den's head in his pod but there was no sign of the Thai girl, Ying.

Harry walked across to where Marci was answering emails. With the time delay, most of the emails from Switzerland had come in overnight and first priority was to clear them. Again Marci was not happy with the interruption.

"Be with you in a minute. Get yourself a coffee. Winda will show you," she said without taking her eyes off the screen.

Harry followed Winda into the kitchen area in the corner. It wasn't a large room but contained a sink, fridge and a worktop where several mugs were positioned. There was a small table with various magazines on top; two chairs were at the table, two more against the wall. He watched as she switched on a kettle.

"How long have you worked here?" asked Harry trying to

make conversation.

"Not long," was the reply, which seemed to kill off that line of enquiry.

"No sugar, right?" said Winda, as she took out a carton of milk from the fridge.

"Yes, you have a good memory," said Harry still attempting to thaw the iciness.

The kettle boiled and Winda spooned a measure of instant coffee into a mug and poured in the water. She passed the mug to Harry with the carton of milk. "Help yourself to milk."

"Thanks," said Harry and added the milk to his preference.

"So what do you do here?" said Harry continuing the charm offensive.

"Whatever I'm told," said Winda. "Like making people coffee." Her tone was on the aggressive side.

"Ok... I get it," said Harry. "Look, I'm a long way from home and this is my first day. I don't know the protocols or office politics."

Winda looked at him with her arms folded. "You soon will."

The exchange was interrupted by Marci who had finished her earlier task. Winda left the room.

"Not sure what her problem is," said Harry.

"Winda can be a moody bitch sometimes. I wouldn't worry about it... keeps telling everyone that menial jobs are beneath her just because she's got a law degree."

"What's she doing here?" asked Harry.

"Basically, she looks after the admin but she's quite useful at sorting out some of the land-law stuff, and contracts. She just happens to be the youngest," said Marci and smiled for what was, in Harry's recollection, the first time since their first meeting. This morning she seemed less stressed and appeared to have made more of an effort with her appearance; her jeans and tee shirt looked new and she'd washed her hair.

"Come on, let's get you fixed up with one of the workstations and get you logged onto the computer system and Intranet. We have a pretty secure system here, as you can imagine. Den's in, I'll get him to look after you and show you the ropes. We can't do a great deal till Nate gets back on Monday but there are some emails you need to read. There's one from David Leganes, just come through, and it seems we could be going native next week."

Harry looked at her blankly. "A field mission," she clarified. "It seems Miki Rey's signed up to a preliminary exploration. Nate must have called Leganes, looks like he's managed to tie things up."

This was more like it; it was what Harry had been sent out to do. "That's great," he said.

Friday passed quickly and any issues Harry had with fatigue had disappeared with the sixth mug of coffee and the intense concentration required to follow Den's tutelage. Even Winda had thawed her frostiness by the time she had to leave. It was Ying's day off so he had not had to face her again. Harry had had his laptop configured, security pass printed and was able to access the internal web pages that had been set up to support the Darwin project. Everything was channelled through this medium to ensure all communication was secure. He had even received a personal email from David Leganes, wishing him well and offering support whenever he needed it. In the circumstances, Harry thought it was a nice touch, despite questions voiced about his integrity.

As he was packing up his things, Marci walked by. Den and Winda had already left; it was just the two of them.

"Marci, there was something I wanted to ask," he shouted to her.

She stopped in her tracks and went back to his pod.

"There were two Germans outside the office last night,

driving Duchamp minibuses. They were having a bit of an argument. Do you know about them?"

"Yeah... they're part of Scheck's crowd."

"Leonard Scheck?" asked Harry. "I met him in Switzerland."

"Yeah, Head of Security, he paid us a visit after the plane problem. Right evil-looking bastard he is, I can tell you."

"Yeah, I got that," said Harry, remembering his intimidating features from the armoury visit.

"It's him that's sent in the security team to sort out the eco-mob. Like the fucking Gestapo. Luckily they've not been in the office too much. There's a couple more gone over to Jabiru with Nate... looking after him, apparently."

"So there're four of them?"

"I think there's a couple more as well but we don't get to see them... shadowy guys. They give me the creeps."

Harry decided to share his observation. "Well, the two that I saw were having a right go yesterday. I don't speak German so I had no idea what they were saying."

"Don't know what it could be about; they weren't in the office. I think they've been keeping tabs on one or two people who were causing trouble," replied Marci.

"But why are they driving around in the minibuses? I thought they were for the charity projects."

"They are. We've presented a couple to some school over in Jabiru; the ones you've seen are just cover."

Harry looked bemused.

"Yeah, I told you they were shady," said Marci.

She walked back to her pod and started closing down her laptop and collecting the bits and pieces she would need to take with her. Harry did the same and they left the office together a few minutes later.

Driving back to the hotel, Harry felt better; early days but he believed he was starting to become accepted in the office.

He had got on well with Den and even Marci was far more amenable than the previous day. Winda and Ying he would have to work on but they would come round, he was sure.

It was yet another glorious late afternoon and he decided to take a drive down to the harbour before returning to the hotel. He stopped at one of the waterfront bars for a beer. He was sat at a table watching the yachts bobbing up and down at their moorings below him; the sun glistening on the top of the ocean reflecting radiant colours. It was a perfect setting. His mind flipped back to Monique; he had been thinking about her off and on for most of the day. He hoped she was ok but was desperate to hear from her.

His reflections were disturbed when he noticed an approaching minibus which he thought he recognised. It was coming up the coast road towards him in a small queue of traffic to a roundabout directly in front of the bar. Turning right, the road was a dead end and went towards the yacht club and marina; left, where nearly all the traffic headed, would be back into town from where Harry had just come. The minibus reached the interchange and turned right. Harry saw the sign on the side of the vehicle; 'Duchamp Foundation'.

Without thinking, Harry downed the rest of his beer and left a couple of dollars on the table to cover the cost and then some. The Suzuki was parked in a cul-de-sac at the back of the bar and he quickly spun it around and headed after the minibus.

About two hundred yards along, the road came to an end and in front of Harry was a barrier. There was a white wooden sign arched across the track; 'Darwin Marina, No unauthorised vehicles', it said. Beyond the barrier, Harry could see a white picket fencing lining the road which had become a causeway; there was sea on both sides with rows of yachts bobbing at their berths.

Harry decided to park up and go in on foot; the barrier wasn't manned. The fencing stopped after a short distance replaced by buildings on the right and left, predominantly wooden; repair shops, shipwrights, a chandlery and then it opened up to the waterfront and docking area. The gravel/dirt roadway which serviced the berths stopped about fifty yards further on and Harry could see the minibus at the end of the track, adjacent to a small vessel. The engine was still running; there was exhaust coming from the pipe at the back. He stood close to the wall of the last building, a boat sales office and watched from out of sight.

He could see two men carrying cargo of some sort to a Sas Adriana 44; a six-berth cabin cruiser popular for short charters. It was a boat Harry knew well; back home in Norfolk, sailing The Broads was a favourite pastime before his university days. He couldn't make out clearly what was going on but he saw them make a couple of journeys. The last load looked particularly heavy and it took the two of them to carry. Then one of the men got into the minibus and reversed it back down the track. Harry turned his back to the approaching vehicle and pretended to be looking in the window of the sales office where there was a list of boats for sale. The driver was still reversing and would not have noticed him. The road widened just before the Marina entrance and the driver made a three-point turn. The barrier rose automatically and the minibus headed back to the main road. Harry was trying to make out the man. He thought it might be one of the arguing Germans from the previous day but couldn't be certain.

Harry turned towards the boat to see it chugging slowly out of the harbour towards the Marina entrance and open water. He had no idea what was going on or how he might use this information; it was merely curiosity so, with little option, he walked back to the car and returned to the hotel. With the weekend ahead of him, he had some free time to catch up on his sleep and he was looking forward to enjoying some of the facilities available. He parked the Suzuki; there was no sign of the Duchamp minibus. He walked through the hotel reception and was hit by the reviving coolness of the air-conditioning.

That evening he received an email from H.R. in Switzerland giving details of his apartment which he would move into the following Thursday. It was in the City suburb, not far from the hotel and about the same distance to the office. He would do a drive by tomorrow and check it out.

Around two a.m. Harry was again in a deep sleep when he was awakened by his phone. He managed to find the light switch and the call answer button. "Hello," he said, croakily.

"Harry, c'est moi."

"Monique... Are you ok?"

"Oui, I am ok, I just wanted to speak with you. I really need you."

"But what's happening?"

"Le meme, it is the same. Françoise she give me her phone so I can talk to you."

"What about Edward?"

"He is still in Frankfurt."

"When does he come back?"

"Dimanche... er Sunday, and then en Mercredi, he goes to Hong Kong."

"So, Wednesday he goes to Hong Kong. Can you get away before he gets back from Frankfurt?"

"Not possible, the bodyguards they are outside. If I want to go anywhere, les magasins... or the salon de coiffeur, they come also."

"That's terrible."

"Mais oui... but it is how it is."

"What about when he goes to Hong Kong. How long will he be away?"

"Dix jours...er, ten days, I think."

"I don't know what to say. What about Françoise, did you ask her if she could help, maybe when he is in Hong Kong?"

"Non, I do not want her to be in trouble."

"Do you know where your passport and things are?"

"I think maybe they will be in Edward's appartement."

"Can you get in there?"

"Non, it is not possible."

"What about when Edward returns? You'll be seeing him. I mean you are his wife."

"I do not know," replied Monique.

"But he can't hold you against your will, that's illegal. You could go to the police. Why don't you call them while you have a phone?"

"The police? They will not believe me. Edward, he is a very powerful man; he will say I am... er fou... er crazy."

"Mmm... What about people at work?"

"Edward say to them that I am sick."

"What about Françoise? Surely she could tell people what is going on?"

"But then Edward will find out and she will be in trouble."

"But he seems to be controlling you," replied Harry.

"Oui that is what is happening. I wish I could see you, Harry. I miss you so much."

"I miss you too. I don't know what to say. I think you will just have to wait for the right moment. Something will happen and you will be able to get away."

"Oui... I hope so," said Monique.

They continued chatting for a few more minutes before she was disturbed and had to break off. Harry felt incredibly frustrated at not being able to help; he was a problem solver by nature. Monique said she would try to phone again the following day.

Saturday morning and Harry had a lie-in and it was almost nine-thirty before he went down to the restaurant for breakfast. He checked his phone for messages, hoping he might get a text from Monique and then he caught up on the news from the CNN website. As he walked in he had picked up one of the complimentary local newspapers from the rack to read while he enjoyed his full-English breakfast.

He flicked the pages as he tucked into his fried bread, mushrooms and bacon; nothing of real interest unless you lived in Darwin, and then a headline on page five grabbed his attention. *Eco-campaigner missing.*

He read the narrative. '*Professor James Harvey (46) from Queensland University, a prominent campaigner against further mining in the Kakadu region has been reported missing according to police. He has not been seen since Thursday evening after addressing a rally at Darwin University. Police are appealing for information.*'

The article went on to describe his role in the various protest factions, including his involvement in holding up the Jabiluka Uranium mine project. He was a member of the Green Party, Greenpeace and a significant figure in the eco movement; clearly a thorn in the side for the mining industry. Harry could think of several agencies who would want him off the scene. He finished his breakfast and went to his room, his mind processing all kinds of scenarios.

Today would be a relaxing day he had decided but there were things a work away geologist needed to do and his first port of call would be a launderette. Unfortunately, his expenses would not stretch to the hotel's laundry service. Having enquired at reception, the nearest facility was back in town, not far from the office and close to his new apartment. It would give him a chance to have look at his soon-to-be residence and check out the area. He piled up his dirty washing and put it in one of the hotel laundry bags, before locking up and heading to the car.

It was another warm morning, some high cloud but white, like floating pieces of cotton wool; rain was not due for another three months.

It took about fifteen minutes to find the launderette which, he discovered, was opposite the Darwin Entertainment Centre where they hold concerts and plays. As he viewed the stark 1960's building, which was seemingly untouched by the '74 typhoon, he made a mental note to find out what entertainment was available. It could come in handy if he was ever at a loose end. He parked in the small car park at the rear of the launderette which also serviced a Motel on the opposite side of the parking lot. He took out his washing bag from the boot of the Suzuki and slung it over his back like a sailor returning from his ship. Inside, it was quite small with only ten washing machines and three big rotating drum-dryers. There was a vending machine selling chocolate snacks and crisps. In the middle of the room, there was a table with six chairs surrounding it; they were not expecting many customers. It was mercifully cool thanks to the air-conditioning. He was pleased he had the foresight to get some change from reception; he was going to need plenty. One thing he didn't have, though, was washing powder but fortunately, this was provided in a self-serve machine next to the confectionery.

Within a few minutes, his washing was brewing nicely in the machine and he watched his clothes rotating in the suds. He hadn't bothered to separate them out; it would be fine. The process was going to take forty-five minutes so he decided to have a walk around the area. As he left the building, he could see a large block of flats behind the motel and realised that this was where his new apartment would be. It was much taller than most of the surrounding buildings, probably fourteen floors. He decided to explore further. He walked by the motel in the direction of the flats along an adjacent road lined with Eucalyptus trees which gave a welcome respite from the heat of the sun. There was a petrol station on the corner and on the opposite side of the road, the building towered upwards dwarfing everything in the vicinity.

Having surveyed the immediate area, Harry made his way back to the launderette to see to his washing. The machine was just finishing the final spin when he got there and he waited the five minutes for it to finish the cycle. He removed his clean washing and was transporting it into one of the dryers when the door opened and a young lady entered carrying a basket of washing. Harry looked up but she made no eye contact and went to the opposite side of the room and started filling one of the machines.

Harry loaded the dryer and fed in the coins; it would take another forty minutes. He groaned at the thought but there was a coffee shop over the road from the launderette and he would decamp there until it was finished. He stopped for a moment and noticed the woman. She looked like a student, early to mid-twenties, shoulder length dark hair, wearing a tee shirt and jeans. She turned around and he saw the tee shirt logo; it was the all-too-familiar CND emblem. Harry was suddenly on his guard; he didn't know why but he thought she might pose a threat. He decided to make for the coffee shop to avoid any possible conversation.

He crossed over the road and into the cafe. It was fairly quiet with only two of the thirty or so covers taken. Harry found a seat next to the window and a man walked across to take his order.

"A medium coffee and a pastry," said Harry on enquiry.

He took out his mobile phone. With a free Wi-Fi connection, Harry logged on and started to check his emails. These would be personal ones; he would be unable to access work communication for security reasons. He was not unhappy about that. He had been in the cafe about twenty minutes enjoying the revitalising Brazilian Blend; he had eaten half his pastry when he noticed a minibus go by. He recognised the colour and then the logo on the side; 'Duchamp Foundation'. It pulled up outside the cafe; there were two occupants, the driver and a passenger. The passenger got out and the minibus pulled away. The man crossed over the road and stood in front of the Entertainment Centre; he appeared to be taking more than a passing interest in the launderette. Harry had a ring-side view.

After about five minutes, he noticed the girl with the tee shirt leave the building and walk along the road which Harry had used earlier, towards the flats. The man from the minibus who hadn't moved from his post outside the Centre suddenly crossed over the road and gave pursuit.

Harry drank the rest of the coffee and paid for his refreshments. He put on his sunglasses and turned right to see if he could see anything. The man was walking down the road about fifty yards from the garage; he couldn't see the girl.

He started following, out of curiosity more than anything. He kept the man in sight and watched as he reached the petrol station. Harry thought he could see the girl in the distance entering the tower block but he couldn't be certain. He could see the man quite clearly and watched him cross the road and disappear into the building.

Harry was in a dilemma but common sense dictated it was time to return to the launderette; his washing would be ready. He had no idea what was going on but the reality was he could do little about it in any case.

The tumble dryer had finished its cycle and his washing was in a heap on the bottom. He took out his shirts, folded them and paired his socks before recycling the hotel laundry bag to transport his, now clean, washing. With his clean laundry safely stowed in the boot of the Suzuki, he drove out of the car park and decided to head to the shopping mall in Casuarina which he had visited on Thursday.

It was late afternoon before Harry returned to the hotel with two more tee shirts and a pair of khaki shorts. Back in the room, he hung his shirts in the wardrobe and put his underclothes and socks in one of the drawers. The hotel had reasonable facilities including an outdoor pool so Harry decided it was time for a swim.

That evening after dinner in the hotel restaurant he spent some time catching up on emails and speaking to his parents before watching some TV.

Sunday morning and again Harry decided to have a lie-in but despite the restful atmosphere, he was far from relaxed. His sleep pattern had been interrupted, not by any midnight phone calls but by a nightmare. Following the incident in the cave, he regularly had dreams involving water and being trapped. They gradually lessened in frequency but recurred when he was under pressure; last night they started again following a similar pattern. He woke several times covered in sweat and at four a.m. he took a shower. The air-conditioning was not at fault, it was cool in the room but as he dozed he kept thinking about Monique and wondered if she was ok; he hoped she would call.

At breakfast, he went through the local newspaper looking for any further information on the missing professor. Sure enough, there was another article, this time on the front page; his disappearance locally was big news and Harry read it with interest. There was a brief biography, a list of books he had written and some messages from fellow activists; it seemed more like an obituary. There was not a great deal more on police activity; just a brief note that investigations were continuing and a further appeal for information from the public. There were several photographs including a recent one where he was addressing a meeting in Darwin. Harry stared at the picture; sitting just behind him was a young woman in a CND tee shirt. "No, it couldn't be," thought Harry but despite the less-than-clear image; he was sure it was the girl from the launderette; what a coincidence, or was it?

Chapter Ten

Sunday had been a boring day in many ways and Harry was keen to get back to work; he was beginning to miss company. The hotel was very comfortable and the guests pleasant but there had been no-one with whom to enjoy a conversation. Although he still had some reservations, he felt more prepared following Friday and was ready to meet Nate for the first time. So, it was with a different mindset that Harry made his way to the office. It had been another interrupted night but again it was a nightmare; he'd heard nothing from Monique.

He parked the Suzuki in one of the designated bays and noticed that one of the minibuses was back. Harry was able to access the door to the office with his new pass and on entering he could see Marci was at her desk and Winda was walking around holding a piece of paper.

"Morning," he said to Marci as he walked past her pod. "Good weekend?"

"Hi Harry, yeah, good thanks," she said without turning her head from her monitor. "You?"

"Yeah, fine," said Harry, recognising this was not a time for small-talk.

He sat down at his desk and fired up his computer. He was waiting for it to boot up when Winda appeared holding a mug of coffee.

"White, no sugar... right?" she said.

"Yeah, that's great, thanks. How was your weekend?" he replied, receiving the mug.

"Yeah, it was ok," she said. Harry watched her walk away towards her workstation. This was completely different from Friday.

Harry scrolled down the myriad of emails that had come in over the weekend. It was clear work didn't stop on Saturday and Sunday for those in the Chateau. Den arrived just before nine and again Harry engaged in some social banter before Den said, "best get on." Ying followed shortly after but went straight to her workstation without acknowledging anyone.

After about half an hour, there was a commotion at the office door and Marci went over to see what the problem was. Five people were stood there led by a bearded man in khaki shorts, sandals, woollen socks and a yellowish shirt which looked like it had been slept in.

"Morning, Nate. Forgot your pass again?" said Marci.

Nate proffered a response which Harry didn't hear properly but it wasn't complimentary. He barged in with a bluster that reflected his position as leader of the pack.

"Winda, get me a bloody coffee," he bawled across the room to the lawyer/admin assistant who was at the photocopier. He led the four accompanying men into his office.

Harry watched the goings on with interest but decided against introducing himself just yet.

He noticed that two of the men following Nate were Aboriginal, the other two were white. Winda delivered the coffee but was then ordered to bring three more and a glass of water. Her body language as she walked to the kitchen reflected her annoyance. Harry made a note to stay clear of her for a while.

After about fifteen minutes, Marci was summoned and a little later Harry was called. The four men who had arrived with Nate left his office and went into the adjoining conference room. Harry walked in; Nate was sat at his desk with Marci in front on one of the seats. The room was no tidier than on his last visit.

"Take a pew," said Nate, nodding to the spare chair next to Marci. "So you're the bloody trainee they've sent us, that right?"

Harry was trying to remember a worse introduction but he couldn't. Nor could he immediately think of a suitable reply. "No," said Harry. "I'm fully qualified and I know what I'm doing," was the best he could manage. He waited for Nate's response.

"Well, I fuckin' hope so for all our sakes or we're up the fuckin' creek without a fuckin' paddle."

"Mind your language Nate, eh?" said Marci. "He's only just arrived. Don't want to scare him off, do we?"

Nate started laughing. "Sensitive ears have we? You fuckin' Poms are all the same... arrogant bastards the lot of ya."

He looked at Marci, then at Harry. "Yeah, ok, I get it. Harry... right?"

"Yes," said Harry.

"Ok, you better listen up we've got a lot to do. Do ya want to get a coffee before we crack on? We maybe some time."

"Yeah, ok, thanks," said Harry.

"You can get Marci one as well. Mine's black, two spoons," and he passed his empty cup. Harry was concerned he might be taking over from Winda in the coffee making duties but for the moment he would play the game.

Five minutes later, Harry returned with the coffees and Marci closed the door behind him.

"Right, we've had a productive few days over in the shit-hole..." Harry looked at Marci.

"Jabiru," Nate clarified.

"The good news is, I met with the Reverend and he's finally agreed to let us start prospecting. Signed the papers on Friday; just a preliminary exploration, mind, so we can assess the feasibility. Leganes' pleased, I can't tell you. Perhaps he'll get off our backs now and let us do our job. Mind you, it's cost us a bob or two. Edward's stumped up six million to get the ball rolling. The Reverend is Miki Rey, the guy who owns the land we want to mine," clarified Nate, looking at Harry.

"Yeah, I know about him," said Harry.

"Good, glad you've been doing your homework," said Nate. "I've brought a couple of his blokes back with me. They're gonna be our tour guides when we make a start."

"When are you thinking of leaving?" said Marci.

"Later this week, Friday probably. It'll take us that to get everything in place," said Nate. "Thought we could check out a couple of sites old wonder boy here selected," he added, looking at Harry.

Marci looked at Harry. "Don't mind him; he's a bit pissed. What's got your back up, Nate?"

"Oh nothing, just those bloody Krauts... driving me nuts. Can't go to the fuckin' dunny without one of them stood outside," said Nate. "They're out of control; don't know what they're up to half the time. Reckon one of 'em's got a kangaroo loose in the top paddock. Still, on the bright side, we've not heard any more from those fuckin' eco bastards."

"Nate," Marci admonished.

"Yeah, you're right, sorry Harry," said Nate and he took a slug of coffee from his mug.

Harry looked at him; piercing blue eyes, bushy beard, and shoulder-length bleached hair that looked like it hadn't seen a comb in a few years. He seemed to be the very epitome of the 1980's bushman personified by Paul Hogan's Crocodile Dundee.

"Right, listen up," continued Nate. "Marci, you know the drill. Harry here's choosing the sites, so he goes, you and one other. Who do you think...? Den or the Chink?"

Harry stifled a laugh.

"Well, we'll need to have someone here who knows what they're doing to co-ordinate everything and feedback to the Chateau," said Marci.

"Yeah, ya could be right. Ying's communication skills are about as good as Skippy's."

"Knows her stuff, though," said Marci, "and not afraid of hard work."

"Right, the Chink goes, Den can be co-ordinator with Winda. We'll have some company with us, the Abbos, they'll keep us on track and we need to take a couple of the Krauts in case we run into any trouble while we're out there. Leganes's insisting on it... Spoke to him last night, to give him the latest."

"What's he think?" asked Marci.

"Yeah, ripper, happy as a dingo on a road-kill," replied Nate.

Harry looked at Marci who raised her eyebrows.

"How long do you think we're gonna need?" asked Marci.

"Right, if we leave Friday, it'll take us a day or two to get over there. Then we need to find the place and make camp... then it's in the hands of you, golden-boy here, and the Chink."

"What do you reckon, Harry?" said Marci.

"Depends on the area, I guess. We'll need to do some mapping and collect soil samples, the usual stuff. A couple of days; maybe three if it's just a preliminary survey. We can drill down and get some deeper samples once we've analysed the core findings. We'll need bigger equipment for that," replied Harry.

"Yeah, a thirty-foot drilling rig. It's gonna cost big bikkies... and we need to be able to get one out there. So I'd wanna make sure we were in the right place before we started down that road," said Nate.

"So basically we're just going to have a look round a couple of spots from the aerial surveys and find the most suitable, get some samples, then bring in the big stuff later," said Harry summarising.

"Sounds like a plan," said Nate. "I need you to work on location, sort out possible access routes... don't wanna go traipsing through the bush too much; we'll never get the trucks in." Nate turned to Marci.

"Marci, you see to the logistics, sort out with Harry what you're gonna need. Don't forget tents, tucker, you know the stuff."

"Yeah," said Marci.

"Right, I'll get back to Leganes and let him know what we're doing. Then we need to speak to the Krauts and the Abbos and let them know. Right, meeting adjourned. Speak again at four for an update."

Marci and Harry got up.

"Not you Harry; need a natter," said Nate.

Marci left the room; Nate sat there and looked Harry up and down.

"So what's your story, Harry? Why are you here?" said Nate.

"I'm not sure what you mean?" replied Harry. "I'm just here to find uranium; that's all I've been told."

"Well, there was a bit of a furphy going round that you've been sent here on a spying mission."

"Sorry, what's a furphy?" said Harry.

"Shit, I forgot you Poms don't speak English. A fuckin' rumour, gossip... you know."

"I've got no idea where you got that idea from. I've only been with the company a month."

"Yeah, but well in with Duchamp, I hear."

"No, I just met him on my interview, that's all. I don't know why there's all this suspicion. Why would anyone want to spy on you anyway?" Harry was sat up quite assertive; he was not going to be intimidated by Crocodile Dundee.

"No reason... everyone's been a little on edge here that's all, especially since the plane incident. You heard about that?" Nate seemed to be backing down.

"Yeah," said Harry.

"Then we've got the fuckin' Krauts everywhere. Christ knows what they're up to."

Nate picked up his coffee, looked into the empty mug then put it back on the table. Harry was waiting to be called to make another coffee run. Instead, Nate looked at him with those piercing blue eyes.

"Someone tipped us off that they might pull the budget like they did in Perth, you know."

"Who tipped you off?" said Harry.

"Doesn't matter... she's dead now anyway."

"Tara?"

"Of course, you knew her," said Nate.

"Yeah, I worked with her for a while. We got on really well."

"Yeah, I remember now; she said you were a bright bloke." Nate looked down. "Worked here, helped me set up the office... great girl; one of the few Sheilas who could drink me under the table. Then goes and gets herself bloody run over."

"That's what they say," said Harry.

Nate didn't pick up on the innuendo; he was looking at his desk with a faraway look for a moment before continuing. He looked at him with a stare that Harry found difficult to maintain.

"Well, I'll tell you something, Harry. There's a lot of money at stake here. They've already put in a shit-load and there're some people in Frankfurt who've got an interest an' all... according to Leganes; so, as you can see, the pressure's on to sell those mining licences. Personally, I can't see 'em pulling out with what they've put in."

"Yeah, makes sense," said Harry.

"I'll tell ya something else too. Did you know the bloody Abbos get four per cent of uranium sales from Ranger?"

"No, I didn't know that," said Harry.

"Yeah, Miki Rey told me. Anyway, that's a lot of dollars but if we're gonna make any moolah we need to find the right place to drill, right?"

"Yeah," said Harry. "But what I don't understand is if the locals are getting all that money, why's Miki Rey been playing hardball?"

Harry looked at Nate who didn't appear entirely comfortable with this scrutiny.

"Fair point, I'll tell you this much, he's as cunning as a dunny rat, is our Miki. Between you and me, I think he's been waiting to see if any other players come into the game. Then he'd play us off for the best deal but the demos and all the politics have put people off. My guess is the Reverend's stock was beginning to fall so he's taken Edward's money that was on the table."

"Yeah, I can see that," said Harry.

"All these delays have been a right pain in the backside but with the eco-idiots out the way and the Abbos onside, we should be able to make some progress. So are you up for it?"

"Yeah," said Harry. "That's why I'm here."

"Good man. Get us another coffee, mate, on the way out," said Nate, and handed Harry his mug. "Black, no sugar," he shouted as Harry left the room.

Marci was also in the kitchen making a coffee and took over the duties for the three of them.

"So, how did you get on?" she said.

"With Nate...? It was ok, I think. Still have no idea why he thought I was a spy."

"Don't worry about it; he's always suspicious of new people. He'll come round." Marci handed him Nate's mug of black coffee.

"Just one thing," said Harry.

"What's that?" said Marci.

"What was that about Kangaroos loose in the paddock?"

said Harry.

"Ha, ha... it's an Aussie thing. It means, not all there. You know, got a screw loose."

"Thanks, I get it now," said Harry.

Marci finished making the drinks and handed another mug to Harry. "Thanks..." said Harry. "He mentioned Tara."

"Nate? Yeah, they were close for a while; we thought they were probably having a fling. It hit him hard, I think, when she went back but then he just seemed to move on. Typical Aussie bloke; shows no feelings... except when he's mad." She smiled.

Harry thought carefully about what he was going to say next. "Don't know if you've heard but there's a rumour that Tara's death wasn't an accident."

He waited for the reaction.

"What do you mean?" said Marci, looking at him with some surprise.

"Nothing, just something I heard."

"But why would anyone think that? Who told you?"

"Just one of the guys in the project team," said Harry, deciding not to disclose too much or his own views.

"Hmm," said Marci and seemed to be in deep thought as she walked past him to her pod. Harry left the kitchen with the two mugs, delivered Nate's to his office and then returned to his workstation.

Back at the desk Harry was feeling motivated following his meeting with Nate and wasted no time in starting his planning. At last, he could show them what he could do. He turned on his laptop, found the reconnaissance pictures and opened the ones that he felt were the most promising. He started examining them in more detail; the terrain, access and estimated level of uranium oxide from the mineral analysis taken via the aeromagnetic survey.

The two sites he had highlighted as having special interest

ticked all the boxes and these would be the recommended areas for the ground study; they were about fifty miles apart. It was a question of doing last minute checks and mapping out the terrain. He had the GPS coordinates which would allow the team to find the location to within a metre but in this remote area there would be no phones or internet connection; any communication would have to be made by radio. Harry checked the distance, over four hundred miles much over dirt tracks; the tarmac disappeared after Gunbalanya which was a settlement north of Jabiru and on their route. It would be hard going and he might have to adjust his timeline for getting to the site.

The whole office was a hive of activity; after an hour or so, Marci appeared at his pod for an update which Harry provided.

"You need to share that with Ying when you've got a minute," she said.

"Yeah, will do," said Harry.

A little later Harry decided to confront Ying with his information. He approached her pod.

"Hi Ying, have you got a minute?"

"I'm a bit busy... what is it?" was her response.

"I want to go over the area with you and discuss what we're going to need."

"You better sit down then," she said.

Harry looked at her; she was dressed in a black tee shirt and black jeans with flat shoes. She had a boyish frame with no definition of a figure; she resembled an adolescent youth who needed a decent meal.

Harry explained all the technical specifications and outlined the terrain he was proposing to survey in more detail but Ying wasn't as forthcoming as he had hoped. If anything, she appeared disinterested. "Whatever you say," she replied when he outlined his ideas and strategy and went back to her laptop. He was disappointed but not surprised at her response. Harry was ready to present the information to Nate.

Lunchtime and Harry had to get some fresh air and clear his head. There was a general provisions shop which sold sandwiches about fifty yards down the road and he joined the short queue for his refreshment. There was a rack of newspapers and he picked up a copy of the Darwin Gazette and started to read it while he waited his turn. He searched the pages for any more news on the missing professor. There was a short paragraph with the headline; *'Missing Professor's Gambling Shame'*. Reading the article, it appeared the eminent eco-activist had a dark secret. Harry read the narrative; according to 'sources' he had racked up several thousand dollars in gambling debts and the police were using this information as a line of enquiry. Given the size of the article, it seemed the press interest in his whereabouts had waned. Harry decided against buying it and put the paper back on display before getting served. He still wondered if there was something more to the professor's disappearance.

Around four o'clock, Nate called a full team meeting in the conference room. As they congregated, Harry could see the two Aboriginals and the Germans had also been invited. Harry set up his laptop with the projector and they sat waiting for Nate. He walked in about ten minutes later.

"Right, listen up," he said, as he bounded in armed with yet more papers, charts and maps.

He pinned a large map of the area onto one of the white boards.

"Ok Harry, talk us through it," he said, without any warning.

Harry was slightly taken aback. "Ok, I've got it on my laptop."

"Never mind the bloody computer. Show us on here," replied Nate.

"Right," said Harry regaining his composure.

He outlined the sites and the proposed routes, described the terrain, water courses, villages, and the estimated time it would take, based on the likely speed the team were going to manage. He made particular reference to the latter part of the journey which would be mainly dirt tracks.

Suddenly one of the Aboriginals stood up.

"Can I speak?" he said.

"Yeah, sorry folks," said Nate. "Forgot some introductions. This is Amaraga, calls himself Banjo and his sidekick here," he pointed to the second Aboriginal, "is Charrah... known as Charlie... yeah?" The second man nodded. "They're gonna be with us on the trip."

Harry looked at them. They were dressed smartly in white shirts, the sort you would buy from a discount store, trousers and trainers; both were wearing lightweight, dark sports jackets which were open.

"While I'm about it, these two guys, who look like the bloody Mafia, are Heinz and Pieter. They're part of the security team Herr Scheck has sent us. They'll be on the trip as well, in case we bump into a bloody rogue croc." There were some smiles from the team.

The two men who seemed unsure of the introduction nodded in acknowledgement.

"Sorry Banjo... you were saying."

"The second site you are showing," said Banjo.

"What about it?" said Nate.

"It is a valley, yes?" Nate looked at Harry.

"Yes," said Harry.

"This place is known to our people. We call it the Valley of the Lost Souls. It is a place of the Witij, the Rainbow Serpent. It is a place where evil spirits gather."

"Bollocks," said Nate.

"It is what we believe. We will take you there as Miki has

agreed but we will not enter the valley."

Banjo looked at his buddy who nodded in agreement.

Nate looked at him in astonishment. "I don't want to hear any of your mumbo-jumbo sh..."

Harry cut him off before he could finish. "It's ok Banjo, we understand. That's fine... if you can help us get there we will go in on our own."

Nate threw his arms in the air in frustration. "That's bloody great. That's all we need, a couple of belligerent Abbos."

"No, it's fine, Nate. We can manage," said Harry again. "We can't afford any more delays."

The others, including Marci, didn't want to get involved but Nate recognised Harry was right.

"Marci, what do you lot think?" said Nate.

"If Harry can get us to the spot then I think we should go for it. After all, we've paid Miki enough, and as Harry says, we don't have many options," said Marci.

Nate was not one for losing an argument but was coming around to the logic. "Maybe I can get a discount from Miki. You bastards are costing us an arm and a leg." It went quiet for a moment.

"Yeah, ok Banjo; you help get us there and then you can wait for us to come out. That right by you?"

Banjo sat down with just the briefest of nods in acknowledgement.

"Right, Marci, what have you got for us?"

Marci gave an update on the logistics. "I've got us a Scania off-road truck and a ten-metre drilling rig which will be big enough for a prelim. What do you think, Harry?"

"Yeah, that should be enough. The deposits look pretty shallow from the pictures. Will you get it on the back of a truck ok?"

"Oh yeah, we've used them before. Nate can drive it, can't

you Nate?"

"What...? Oh yeah, piece of piss," said Nate, who was trying to read an email he had printed off. He looked up. "What about wheels?"

"Yeah, a Toyota FJ Cruiser; got a good rate for a week."

"Ripper," said Nate. "Car's a beaut... may need it for ten days, though, just in case we meet any problems. When do we pick it up?"

"They'll deliver it and the Scania on Thursday with the drill. I'll get them for ten days."

"Yeah... Ripper," said Nate.

Harry was still stood in front of the group and several discussions seemed to be taking place at the same time. The Germans had said nothing and Harry wasn't sure if it was deliberate or they just couldn't understand English. Ying hadn't spoken either. Nate eventually called the group to order.

"Right, that's about it... Marci, what about tents and stuff?"

"Yeah, I'm on it... I'll get the food and camping gear arranged tomorrow."

"And Harry... anything else from you?" said Nate.

"No... Everything's in hand."

"Hope so," said Nate. "We're relying on you and the Abbos to get us there. Right, class dismissed," and everyone left the conference room.

It had just turned five o' clock and everyone started to pack up for the day. Ying had already gone a good half an hour before the others; an appointment she said. Winda and Den shouted "goodnight" as they left. Harry was discussing logistics with Marci; there was still a lot to do.

After another twenty minutes, Harry and Marci called it a day; Nate was still in the office. There was no sign of the Aboriginals or Germans. Harry had his empty laptop case over his shoulder containing some work that he wanted to do later.

He locked his computer in his desk drawer, then went over to Nate's office and put his head around the door.

"Night, Nate... see you tomorrow."

Nate seemed surprised at Harry's courtesy but acknowledged him with what seemed to be a grunt, and Harry left.

Marci was chatting to Tallara in reception and joined Harry as he walked outside to the car park. The minibus had gone but there was an open-top Jeep which Harry assumed was Nate's; it certainly suited his persona. Marci walked towards her car and opened the boot to stow a couple of bags and Harry opened the door of the Suzuki, threw the laptop case onto the back seat and got in.

He was about to put on his seat belt when he became aware of movement in the foot-well. Suddenly he felt a searing pain in his ankle just above his trainers.

"Shit," he shouted. There was no mistaking the brown shape as it slithered over into the passenger side,

He opened the door and got out and shouted to Marci who was about to start her car.

"Marci... help me... I've been bitten by a snake."

Marci immediately got out of her car and ran towards him.

"Right, don't panic... keep very still," said Marci. "Did you see what snake it was?"

"It's still in there," said Harry.

Marci peered through the passenger window and the snake was coiled on the seat waiting to pounce again.

"Jesus... it's a Brown." She saw the two Aboriginal's waiting at the bus stop on the main road just outside the car park.

She ran down towards them and called out; "Hey guys... can we get some help here? Harry's been bitten by a Brown."

The two men responded and ran back to the car park. Harry was still standing against the car.

"Where...? Show me," said Banjo. "You better call an

ambulance," he added, looking at Marci.

"Harry slowly lifted up the trousers and there were two small puncture marks on the back of his ankle, above his heel.

"Keep standing up, if there's venom inside it will slow down the speed of it reaching your heart," said Banjo.

He stooped down and examined the wound very closely.

"Harry, you are a lucky man... it's a dry bite. You will be ok but you should go to the hospital just in case and get checked over. Where's the snake?"

"On the passenger seat... in Harry's car," Marci replied.

Harry was starting to go pale. "Are you sure he's ok? He's gone very pale," said Marci.

"That's the shock," said Banjo. "I have seen it many times. The Browns are very bad. The area around the bite goes black if there is poison. Is the car door open?"

"Yes," said Harry in a frail voice.

Banjo went to the car and rolled down the sleeve of his jacket so it covered his hand. He gently opened the passenger side door and pulled it very slowly towards him but hid behind it. The snake was still sat coiled on the seat but started moving as it saw the door open. In a flash Banjo grabbed the snake by the back of the neck and pulled it from the vehicle, then slammed the reptile's head onto the tarmac, killing it instantly. He lifted up the lifeless animal.

"We need to show this to the medics; it's a male about two years old. They can kill you in about half an hour."

"Jesus," said Marci.

Harry started retching and brought up his lunchtime sandwich.

Five minutes later, the ambulance arrived and two medics rushed to Harry.

"Right, what have we got?" said the first guy.

"He's been bitten," said Marci.

"Right, we need to get you in fast," said the medic. "What's your name?"

"Harry," said Marci. "He's in shock, I think."

"It's ok," said Banjo. "He's been very lucky. It's a dry bite, I think."

"Right... that's good. Where's the snake?"

Banjo held it up and shook it.

"Christ, mate, don't do that, eh?" The medic examined the snake. "Yeah, it's an Eastern Brown alright. You <u>have</u> been a very lucky boy, Harry, mate."

The other medic brought a stretcher from the ambulance and they laid Harry down.

"Don't worry, I'll look after your car," said Marci. "I'll follow the ambulance."

The Royal Darwin Hospital is in Tiwi in the Northern Suburbs, the opposite side of the city and about half an hour away. Marci took Harry's car keys and locked the door; she noticed that the driver's side window was open by a couple of inches. She turned on the ignition and closed it. Banjo and Charlie left to get their bus.

"Thanks, guys," Marci shouted to them as she pulled away from the car park in pursuit of the ambulance. Banjo waved in acknowledgement.

Once at the hospital, Harry was placed in a special unit set up to deal with snake bites. The ambulance had called ahead and a consultant was waiting. He was of Asian origin but spoke with an Australian accent. After a detailed examination, the doctor confirmed Banjo's assessment.

"It looks like your jeans have saved you... it's punctured your skin but it was not able to inject any venom. You should be ok with some antiseptic and a course of antibiotics just to be on the safe side. We'll keep you in overnight, just observation but you should be right as rain in a day or so... mostly shock I think."

"Thanks," said Harry.

"It's ok... we get a lot of snake bites here, as I said you were very lucky. About half of Brown snake attacks are dry but if you do get envenomed then it's really serious." He looked at Harry; his eyes narrowed reflecting the seriousness of the situation. "They cause more deaths in Australia than any other snake. We had a little girl in here last week, airlifted from the outback; she's still in a coma."

"That's bad," said Harry.

"Yeah, for sure..."

He picked up a clipboard and started writing some notes. "So, how did it happen...? Only it's rare to find one of these snakes in town, they tend to stick to the bush."

"I don't know. It was in my car," said Harry. The consultant made a gesture of surprise.

Just then Marci came in and walked to where Harry was being treated.

"How is he?" she said as she approached the bed.

"He'll be ok... You his girlfriend?" asked the consultant.

Marci laughed; "No, just a work colleague."

"I was just asking Harry how he got bitten; only it's very unusual to see a Brown in the city."

"It was in the car," said Harry to Marci.

"But how did it get there?" asked Marci.

"I have no idea," said Harry.

"Well, we're gonna keep him in overnight but if there's no infection he can go home tomorrow morning," said the consultant.

"Thanks," said Marci.

The doctor left and a porter came in to transfer Harry to a ward.

Marci looked at him. The colour had returned to his cheeks.

"Well, all I can say is that if we're going to the Valley of the Serpent, then I'm glad you're going to be about."

"Thanks," said Harry and he smiled. "Hey, just had a thought... what about medical insurance?"

"It's ok; the company will pick up the tab. I'll sort it out when I leave."

Harry had another restless night; apart from being in an uncomfortable, unfamiliar bed his mind raced all over the place; his mind turned to the snake. How did it get into the car?

Chapter Eleven

Chateau Jura, Sunday, the day before the snake incident in Darwin

Monique was awake in bed in her private quarters, frustrated at not being able to contact Harry. She was desperate to be able to speak to him again but with no phone that was going to be impossible. Françoise was not at work today.

She looked at the clock on the bedside table, six twenty-nine. She exhaled sharply, still early; she was going mad at being imprisoned. She had been confined to her private apartment since Wednesday; there had been no explanation. Edward just waltzed into her room announced he was going to Frankfurt on urgent business matters and she was to stay at the Chateau. She thought nothing of it; it was not unusual, she had stayed behind whilst her husband was on business trips many times. Normally, she would answer calls and field enquiries then pass them on as a personal assistant might do but not this time.

On overseas visits when she accompanied Edward, her position seemed more that of an attractive fashion accessory rather than for any significant business reasons. She was no bimbo; she had a good grasp of business affairs and with an executive role in the organisation she was present at most board meetings. Recently, however, things had changed; just small things; secret meetings, hurriedly hiding papers when she walked in the room, that kind of thing. "What's that?" she would say. "Oh, nothing to concern you, my dear," Edward would reply.

Edward was ruthless when it came to business matters and Monique knew the game. He encouraged her to flirt with clients, particularly the Arabs who had propositioned her on more than one occasion but she was never tempted to take it further. Edward, on the other hand, was quite open about the 'escort girls' he would encounter on his business trips. For Monique, this was the price she had to pay for the lifestyle she enjoyed. It was the 'arrangement' Monique had described to Harry at his interview dinner. Meeting Harry had changed things, however. She was attracted to him immediately but what started as a bit of harmless fun had turned into something much deeper. Monique thought maybe Edward had discovered her true feelings for Harry and perhaps this was the reason for his behaviour. She couldn't make it out.

After Edward had left for the airport for his trip to Frankfurt, Monique decided to leave her apartment to go and advise the heads of department of Edward's movements. She was surprised to see one of Scheck's 'goons', as she called them, stationed outside her door.

"What's going on? Why are you here?" she said to him.

"Please stay inside," said the man.

"I will not!" she said and went to walk passed but the man grabbed her arm. Just then the lift opposite Monique's apartment opened and Leonard Scheck was stood there. He remonstrated with the bodyguard in German who immediately let go of her arm.

"I am sorry about that, Frau Duchamp. I was coming to explain. Can I talk to you in private please?"

She went back inside her room and Scheck followed. He shut the door and Monique was stood in front of him with her arms folded. She spoke in English.

"What is going on? Why cannot I go out?"

"We have our orders," said the Austrian. "It is your husband; you are to stay in your apartment until he returns from Frankfurt."

"But you cannot do this."

"I am sorry."

"Attendez... er... wait I will call him," and she picked up her mobile phone from her bedside cabinet. As she began to dial, Scheck grabbed the phone from her and put it in his pocket.

"I am sorry. He said he was not to be disturbed."

"Give me my phone. I am his wife. You cannot do this. You wait until he hears about this."

"I am sorry. It is his orders we are following," said Scheck. "You are to stay in your apartment until he returns."

"But my work, I need my computer."

"I am sorry, that is not permitted. We will say you are unwell. If you need to go out, you can but Kurt will go with you. That is what Herr Duchamp has said."

"You cannot do this," said Monique again.

"I am sorry," said Scheck for the umpteenth time. He bowed his head and left the apartment.

Monique was in a state of shock; she sat on her bed with her head in her hands not knowing what to do.

At one o'clock, there was a knock on the door. Monique opened it; it was Françoise Fouvert, her assistant. They spoke in French.

"Madame Duchamp, what is happening? First, they tell me I cannot see you and then Monsieur Scheck says it is ok," said Françoise.

"It is Edward. He says I must stay in my room."

"But why? That is crazy."

"I do not know. They have taken away my phone. They say I cannot go out without a man with me."

"But what will you do?" said Françoise.

"I do not know," said Monique.

"But when is he back, Monsieur Duchamp?"

"Sunday," replied Monique.

"But what will you do until then? You cannot stay locked in your room."

"No, I will not."

"Do you want me to bring you anything, your computer, files, or anything?"

"Scheck says I cannot have my computer." She paused for a moment and looked at her assistant. "Can I have your phone, just for a moment? I need to make a call. I will pay you for the charge."

"But of course... anything else? What about food?"

"Scheck said they will bring me what I want from the kitchen."

"I will come back in one hour," said Françoise. "You can make your call in private."

"Thank you. I will let you have your phone back."

Françoise kissed Monique on the cheek and left the room.

It was two-thirty in Switzerland, around midnight in Darwin but Monique was dying to speak to Harry and let him know what was happening. She made the call but as she was talking to him, there was a noise outside the door and she watched it open. She quickly dropped the phone onto the bed and covered it with the sheet. It was Kurt, the goon. He looked around the room. "Who were you talking to? I heard voices."

"No, no-one is here. I was watching the TV." It was all she could think of but it seemed to satisfy the German and he left the room. Monique hid the phone under the pillow and waited for Françoise to return.

Monique was able to make further calls to Harry on Thursday and later on Saturday but today Françoise was not working; it was going to be a long boring day. The contact with Australia had kept her going; she had spent the rest of her time either reading or watching TV. She had managed to go to the local town for some cosmetics on Thursday and to her hairdressers on Friday but each time Kurt was a constant shadow. She detested him; to someone used to being active and involved, it was torture. She had, of course, remonstrated with

Scheck and her guards, cursed, and pleaded with them but to no avail. They remained loyal to her husband.

She got out of bed and put on her dressing gown. Was there anyone outside her door at this time of day, she wondered and decided to check.

She turned the handle on the door and pulled. It was locked. She banged on the door with both fists. "Let me out, let me out," she shouted.

The lock turned and Kurt, the goon, was stood there. "Can I help you, Frau Duchamp?"

"Yes, I want to leave."

"I'm sorry," said Kurt. "That is not possible. Can I get you some breakfast, coffee or anything?"

"Merde!" she exclaimed at the top of her voice. "This is not happening."

"I am sorry," said the German which was becoming a cliché. "Herr Duchamp returns today, I think. You should speak to him."

"Oh, I will... I will." She shut the door and she heard the lock turn.

During her confinement, she had spent hours contemplating the reasons behind Edward's behaviour. She couldn't understand why he would do this to her. She knew his moods; he could be cold and calculating one minute, then generous and accommodating the next. He would sometimes get very angry and, on a couple of occasions, he had hit her but he was always remorseful and showered her with gifts to apologise. These events had become more frequent in recent months; Monique put it down to the pressure of work. Those who were inspired by his speaking, the people who were prepared to pay a great deal of money to hear him, had no idea what it was like to live with him. Whatever love she had had for him was being severely tested.

There was a knock on the door.

"Entrez," she shouted.

Keys rattled and one of the kitchen porters entered with a breakfast tray and a coffee pot.

"I hope you are feeling better," said Albert, the porter.

"Oui, très bien, merci," she replied and the man put the tray down on the table by the window and left.

As she ate her croissants, she was running events through her mind trying to gauge when things with Edward had changed. Was it Australia? She was aware of some of the problems. First, there was the failure of the Perth venture; that had proved very expensive. Then the local opposition to the Kakadu project which had caused delay after frustrating delay. It had played heavily on Edward's mind; he had spoken about it. The money, substantial amounts, paid to the politicians in Canberra appeared to have produced little return so far. She had dealt with some of the payments; 'commissions' was how they had been described but they were bribes in all but name.

There was other money which Edward had tried to hide from her; offshore transfers, which she had queried. "Nothing for you to worry about," he had said. Over recent weeks Edward had also been in regular contact with some people in Frankfurt; 'new partners', he told her.

Suddenly, a thought occurred to her. There had been an email from Tara Humphries just two days before she died. If only she could get to her laptop she could open it and read it again. "What did it say? What did it say?" She remembered it was after she had come back from New York, the last time she had been with Harry. It was one of the emails that she had waiting for her when she returned; one of around three hundred. She'd only skimmed through it, something to do with problems in Australia but it was the tone of the email. She remembered it said something about not knowing who to trust but thought she could trust Monique.

Monique tried hard to recall more of the message but it was about three weeks ago and she had filed it in one of her folders without taking that much notice at the time. There were so many emails that day; she had become distracted and had completely forgotten to go back to it. She would check it again as soon as she could get her laptop returned.

It was early evening when the door opened and Edward walked in. Monique had become engrossed in a movie on the TV and had lost track of time. She was laid on the bed and the interruption had made her jump.

She had been rehearsing what she was going to say but was caught off-guard.

"Monique, darling... I am so sorry. I don't know what has happened. There has been a complete misunderstanding."

"Edward, what is happening? Why have I been kept like a prisoner?"

"It is Scheck. He misunderstood my instructions."

"But why have I been kept in my room, only allowed out with the bodyguard?"

"That was for your own safety. There have been threats on my life, your life too. I wanted to protect you. I knew you would be safe here until I returned."

Monique was lost for words; the sting had gone out of her anger.

"Here, I have bought you something; I hope you like it."

Edward produced a jewellery box from his trouser pocket and gave it to her.

She read the label, '*Cartier*' and carefully opened the case. She gasped as she looked at the content; a bracelet in pink gold, encrusted with diamonds and amethysts. She had seen a similar one in Paris, almost a hundred thousand Euros.

"Here, let me help you put it on," said Edward before Monique could say anything, and he removed the bracelet from the box and placed it around her wrist.

"Just to say sorry; please understand I was just trying to protect you."

Monique looked at it, his words not registering. "It is beautiful," said Monique. "But why was I not allowed a phone... or my computer? They would not let me speak to you."

"Yes, I am sorry. As I said, Scheck misunderstood my instructions. That is all."

His face was stern as if he was doing business, not the look of a devoted husband.

He lifted her hand and kissed it. "I have arranged a special surprise for you. Tonight we are dining out. We are going into Lausanne, I have booked dinner at the St George, and I have reserved the suite that overlooks the lake."

Monique was speechless; this is not what she was expecting.

Edward made to leave. "I need to finish off some business; can you be ready for seven? I have ordered the car for then. Wear something glamorous."

Monique didn't respond. Edward turned and left the room.

Monique looked at the bracelet on her wrist and tried to take in the conversation, she needed to know more.

She showered and changed. She knew the restaurant well, three Michelin stars; it was one of her favourites. She had been there several times before with Edward. Her mind was in a whirl of confusion. Why had he treated her this way? She didn't believe the 'misunderstanding' explanation; it didn't make sense.

Edward called back at her apartment just before seven wearing an evening suit and black tie, carrying an overnight bag. This time he knocked on the door before walking in.

Monique was just finishing her make-up in the bathroom;

her overnight bag was next to the bed.

She turned out the light and walked into the bedroom wearing a beautiful Dior cocktail dress, her jewellery, and black stilettos.

"You look wonderful, my dear," he said as she picked up her valise.

"Thank you," she replied and followed Edward out of the room.

The journey to Lausanne was made with little in the way of conversation; the traffic was light and they made the hotel in little over forty-five minutes. The black limo parked up outside the lobby and the chauffeur opened the door for the couple to get out, then went and fetched their baggage from the boot. Edward was already at reception checking in when the driver delivered their luggage.

"Can you be here for eight o'clock tomorrow morning, Wilhelm?"

"Ja, na sicher...er, of course, Herr Duchamp; Gute Nacht," said the driver and he left the couple to complete the registration.

It was a strange evening. The resentment Monique felt for Edward following his treatment of her the previous week had not gone despite his effort of reconciliation. She was also missing Harry; thinking of him had given her some respite during her incarceration. The hotel suite was beautiful and the meal exquisite but it had been eaten in silence for the most part. She asked about the business trip to Frankfurt but the response was general and not informative so Monique did not pursue the matter. Then later, Edward started paying more attention to her, clearly wanting sex. Monique acquiesced but was no more than a passive participant.

The following morning Edward was at reception settling the bill when Monique came down the sweeping staircase to join him. Edward had gone ahead while she finished her makeup.

Their two cases had been collected by one of the porters. Monique was wearing Boss casual trousers, a Lacoste yellow polo shirt, flat shoes and short Italian leather jacket. Her new bracelet was on her wrist. She placed the room key on the reception desk as Edward completed the formalities.

Wilhelm, the chauffeur, entered the lobby

"Guten Morgen, Herr Duchamp... Frau," he said, and nodded reverentially to the couple.

Edward acknowledged, and the driver took the luggage and headed through the swing doors to the waiting limousine. As he got outside the concierge took one of the cases from the driver and followed Wilhelm to the rear of the car for stowing. It was a fine morning and the early rush-hour was in full swing with queuing traffic snaking past the hotel and on towards the lakeside road.

Edward and Monique followed moments later through the swing doors and were walking towards the car when suddenly there was a disturbance. Edward turned to see Wilhelm wrestling with someone on the pavement just metres away from the limo. There was a gun in the man's hand.

"Quick, inside," said the concierge.

Edward pushed Monique back through the swing doors and into the hotel lobby.

"This way," shouted the concierge and they followed him into an office behind reception. There was a gunshot, followed by another.

Edward looked out from the office and saw Wilhelm stagger through reception and collapse on the marble floor of the lobby. Blood started oozing from the chauffeur.

A bystander rushed into the hotel. "Quick phone an ambulance, someone has been shot," he said.

There was pandemonium as hotel staff rushed backwards and forwards. A first-aider was helping the stricken chauffeur while others were outside attending to a man lying on the pavement that had also been shot.

Edward left the shelter of the office despite protestations from Monique.

"How is he?" he said as he approached Wilhelm who was being attended to by a medic.

He was now sat up and Edward could see blood coming from a shoulder wound. "He will be ok, I think," said the medic. "It is a flesh wound, nothing more."

"What happened?" said Edward, who was looking at the driver with some concern.

"I saw the man..." rasped Wilhelm. "He had a gun, he was waiting for you."

"But how did he know we were here?" said Edward.

"I do not know... maybe we were followed last night. I do not know... it is possible but I did not see anyone," Wilhelm replied.

"Ok, don't worry; There's an ambulance on its way," said Edward.

Against his better judgement, he went through the swing doors to see what was happening outside. To the right of the entrance was a man on the ground, surrounded by a number of people including a policeman.

Edward approached the officer. "How is he?"

"He's dead I'm afraid. Do you know anything about what happened?" said the officer.

"No," replied Edward and went back inside.

He went through to the office where Monique was waiting.

"Come on, we need to get out of here, now," he said.

Monique followed him. She saw Wilhelm sitting up being attended by the first-aider. Edward walked across the lobby and said something to the stricken driver.

"Come on," said Edward.

Edward led Monique back to the limo. The door was still open with the ignition keys in the dashboard. "Get in, quickly," said Edward. "I'll drive."

They set off and were soon enveloped in the flow of traffic. Edward passed Monique his mobile phone. "Here, call the Chateau, tell them what has happened. We should be back in an hour or so."

Monique phoned reception. "Hello, this is Monique Duchamp. There has been an incident at the hotel in Lausanne. Can you tell Monsieur Scheck to call Edward quickly?"

A few minutes later a call came through to Edward's phone.

"Edward, it is Scheck. I have just heard. What has happened?"

Edward brought Scheck up-to-date with events. "Wilhelm has been injured but I think he will be ok. We need to keep this quiet. Can you see to everything?"

"Ja... leave everything to me," said the Austrian and he rang off.

"Why is this happening?" said Monique after Edward had finished the call from Scheck.

"Nothing for you to worry about, my dear," replied Edward.

"But someone has tried to kill us. That is what you said, to Scheck."

"That is why I did not want to leave you on your own while I was in Frankfurt."

"But why? You must tell me."

There was a silence for a few moments; the limo was now out of Lausanne and on the road to Jura. Edward was not going to be as forthcoming as Monique wanted.

"It is just a problem with one of the projects that is all; we are dealing with it."

"Which project?" asked Monique.

"It doesn't concern you, my dear," replied Edward.

"Of course it does if my life is in danger."

"We are dealing with it," said Edward. "It won't happen again."

Monique decided not to pursue it further at this time; it was clear Edward was not going to say anything more. It did get her thinking about her own safety and importantly her future. Her desire to escape had been heightened; the sooner she could get away the better. He was due to fly to Hong Kong in three days so there may be opportunities then. She would work on it as a matter of priority.

It was mid-morning by the time they reached the Chateau. Edward parked the limo in the courtyard and handed the keys in at the reception.

"Get Joseph to see to it," he said brusquely to Lucy Bainbridge who was manning the desk.

Edward turned to Monique. "I am going to the office; I will be along shortly," he said. Monique acknowledged and walked off to her apartment.

Monique was still trying to come to terms with their narrow escape; if it hadn't been for Wilhelm, who knows what might have happened. Then a thought went through her mind: if Edward had been killed, her troubles would be over.

She was in the bedroom sorting out her things from her overnight bag when there was a knock on the door. It was Françoise. Naturally, she wanted to know all about what was happening and Monique told her what Edward had said. They spoke in French.

"Have you heard? Edward and I, we were attacked today at the hotel in Lausanne."

"What?!" said Françoise. Monique explained the course of events in Lausanne and the bodyguard's bravery.

"I have to get away, Françoise, I have to."

"I will help, of course, if I can," replied Françoise.

"Thank you... I do not know what I will do yet but Edward, he goes to Hong Kong on Wednesday. I will think what I can do."

Monique was playing with her bracelet on her wrist. Françoise noticed. "Is that new?"

"Yes, he bought me this, from Frankfurt," and she passed the bracelet to Françoise to see.

"Wow, that is amazing," said Françoise, holding it on her wrist to see what it would look like before returning it to Monique.

They continued talking over a coffee then, after about half an hour, Edward walked in carrying Monique's laptop and mobile phone. Françoise got up to leave.

"No, it's ok," said Edward. "I'm not staying. I'll see you later, my dear," and he put down the items on the table and walked out. Monique looked at Françoise and shrugged her shoulders.

Monique looked at the laptop. "Here, pass me the computer."

Françoise obliged and a few minutes later Monique had logged onto the internet and opened her email account.

"No, this cannot be right," said Monique. "My files, they are gone."

Monique went through her documents; all her personal files were there but any that were business related had been removed.

"But why...? Why would they do that?" said Françoise.

"I do not know but I need to find out." Monique got up, closed her laptop and put it under her arm.

"Where are you going?" said Françoise.

"To see him... Please, wait here."

Monique left her apartment and went down the stairs. There were one or two looks, then whispers, as she walked through reception; across the courtyard. The private residence of her husband was out of bounds to staff and was protected by a security pad. Monique was, of course, privy to the code and keyed in the number.

She decided to take the spiral staircase to the first floor rather than the lift and as she reached the top of the stairs she could hear voices. She stopped and listened, out of sight. She could hear Edward and Scheck, and another voice; David Leganes, she soon recognised. They seemed to be talking about the morning's assassination attempt. They were speaking in English. Monique stepped back down a couple of stairs so she could not be seen,

"So the police in Lausanne don't know this man." It was Edward's voice.

"No, my contact there said they have not been able to make any identification." It was Scheck who spoke.

"What about the police, have they linked it to me?"

"I think they suspect that you were the target. The hotel would have said something."

"But they will come here, the police," said Edward. "We have a delivery scheduled."

Monique heard that but couldn't understand... delivery, what delivery?

"Don't worry; I explained you were there as a last-minute celebration and no-one knew you would be there. No-one could have planned a hit even if you were a target."

"And they believed you?" said Edward.

"I think so; I explained you were going away on business shortly but if they needed to speak to you it would be when you returned," said Scheck.

"But it is a good point; how did they know we were there?" said Edward. "Wilhelm thought we might have been followed."

"That is the only way, I think," said Scheck.

"What's the latest on the Australian problem?" said Edward.

Hearing the reference to Australia, Monique moved to the next step to hear more clearly.

It was the third voice that answered. "Much better, the security team down there seem to have things under control. It looks like most of the opposition has been neutralised and with the payment to the Aboriginals, they are now on board."

Monique was desperately trying to make the translation but they were speaking quickly.

"We are starting prospecting this weekend and we're hopeful of having a full report in a couple of weeks. Nate is pulling out all the stops," said Leganes.

Monique was lost; she didn't understand the colloquialism.

"That is good news; at least it will keep our friends in Frankfurt happy. Do you think the hit was connected, Leonard?" asked Edward.

"Quite possibly, these people have connections across the world. The Green Party is very big in Germany and France. It is also, of course, active here in Switzerland," said Scheck.

"Yes but they are just a political party and they are not <u>that</u> influential. I've had several meetings with them over the years, as you know," said Edward.

"Yes but they do attract a certain fringe element that is not as liberal as the mainstream," said Scheck.

"Do you have any ideas?"

"We are working on it," said Scheck

"What about Frankfurt? How did the meetings go?" said Leganes.

"The meeting with our Middle East agents went very well. I told them we can provide another shipment in two weeks. We will have payment on delivery, as last time. You can meet that I take it, Leonard?"

"Of course," said Scheck. "We have plenty of stock and we will have more arriving tonight."

"You will need to make sure security is absolutely watertight. If we are being watched we do not want to alert anyone," said Edward.

"It will be, no-one will know anything," assured Scheck.

"Good," said Edward.

Monique couldn't understand the conversation, what stock? They didn't hold any stock.

Leganes spoke. "What about the consortium?"

"Ah yes, that was more... difficult," replied Edward. "The consortium is still anxious about the Australian project but I managed to persuade them to stick with it. They have already invested a lot of money and to back out now would be foolish. But I did have to give them some assurances."

"What assurances?" asked Leganes.

"That there would be no further delays," said Edward.

"Well, we have a good team down there," said Leganes. "I spoke to Nate yesterday. That new graduate seems to be settling in ok."

Monique's ears pricked up.

"Oh yes... Harry isn't it?" said Edward.

"Yes," said Leganes. "He should help move things along."

"Hmm, let's hope he doesn't meet any problems out there," said Edward.

Monique was worried. Problems...? What did he mean?

She decided to go back to her apartment before she was discovered; she would pursue the laptop issue with Edward later. She quietly retraced her steps and left Edward's quarters. She was running through what she had heard in her mind, that which she had understood. Was she in danger? She sensed she might be, and possibly Harry too. She needed to speak to him and she needed to get away, of that she was certain.

Back in her room, Françoise had ordered more coffee and

some pastries which were waiting for Monique on her return.

"How was it?" asked Françoise.

"Ah, he was not there. I will speak to him later," said Monique, and put the laptop back on the table; she had other concerns. "I need to make a phone call."

"Of course, do you want me to go?"

"No, it is fine," said Monique and picked up her mobile.

"Merde! The battery, it is flat. Edward, he has the charger I think."

"Borrow mine," said Françoise. She rummaged into her handbag and passed Monique her phone.

Monique looked at the clock. It would be around eleven in the evening in Darwin. She dialled Harry's number and the phone rang out for about thirty seconds before diverting to the answer phone. She decided against leaving a message. Monique passed the phone back to Françoise. "I will try later," she said, deep in thought.

That afternoon she continued trying Harry but there was no reply. At five o'clock, Françoise had to go to pick up her children from Kindergarten and as she was packing her things away, Monique asked her a question. "Do you have any sleeping tablets?"

"No, I don't use them," said Françoise. "Why, do you have a problem with your sleep?"

"Hmm," said Monique. "Sometimes."

"Maybe the pharmacy will help."

"No, it is fine. I will manage," said Monique.

"Wait, my mother uses them. I can get some from her," said Françoise.

"Can you...? That will be great. Just a few, till I get to the village."

"I will call in on the way home," said Françoise.

"Thank you. I will see you tomorrow."

Françoise left and Monique realised how much she had come to depend on her, not just her assistance at work but her friendship. She was the only friend Monique had.

Just after Françoise left there was a knock on the door and Kurt, the goon, was back with a message from Edward. It was like a royal summons; would she join him for dinner this evening? This method of communication was not unusual; in fact, lately, it was becoming more frequent. Despite her initial instinct to decline, she decided there were matters she wanted to discuss; she was starting to formulate a plan in her mind, so at seven o'clock Monique went over to his quarters.

She opened the door to the apartment and Edward was waiting for her. He kissed her on the cheek quite formally, business-like even.

"Hello, my dear, how are you?" he said but he could tell straight away that she was not happy. "I'm sorry for not being able to spend time with you today but after the incident this morning, as you can imagine, I have had things to attend to. At least you are here now."

Monique was not going to be placated that easily.

"I thought you would have been to see me; to see how I was at least."

"Yes, I'm sorry it has been a confusing day. Did Françoise stay with you?"

"Yes," said Monique.

"That is good; at least you were not on your own. Dinner is ready."

They walked to the table which was set out for two. There were platters of food heating on hot trays.

Monique sat down and Edward began to serve. She helped herself to a glass of wine.

With the meal on the plates, Monique started her inquisition.

"Why have my files on my computer been deleted?"

"What files?" replied Edward.

"My files, my business files."

"I have no idea; Scheck has been reviewing everyone's files. I will speak to him."

She had nowhere to go with this discussion and she changed tack.

"Can I have my charger for my phone? You have it I think."

"Of course, my dear, I'll give it to you before you leave."

"And my passport?"

"Why would you want that?" said Edward.

"When you are away in Hong Kong, what happens if something is wrong?"

"Scheck will see to everything," replied Edward.

"But I need it. You cannot keep me here as a prisoner."

"But you are not a prisoner; you can do anything you want," said Edward.

"So why can't I have my passport?"

"I will speak to Scheck. It is for your own safety," he replied.

Monique didn't pursue it further and the rest of the meal was eaten without any meaningful conversation.

Chapter Twelve

Chateau Jura, Tuesday morning, the day after the snake incident in Darwin

Monique was up early; with a lot on her mind, she had not slept particularly well. She thought of Harry and wondered why he had not answered his phone; she hoped he was ok. Edward had returned her charger the previous evening and it had been on all night; she would call Harry later. The plan to get away was taking shape but success would depend on a lot of events; if they didn't come together then she had no idea what would happen. The thought had occurred to her that she might even be killed.

She had her laptop open and checked Edward's diary; at least that hadn't been removed. She was aware that he was in a meeting this morning in Geneva and he would be leaving early; he had mentioned it the previous evening but it was tomorrow that warranted her attention. He was due to fly out to Hong Kong but she needed to be certain of the time he would be leaving. She looked at the screen; the flight departure was ten-thirty, even the great Edward Duchamp would need to be there two hours earlier. To do that, he would need to leave the Chateau at about seven-thirty. He was an early riser, normally at his desk by six-thirty, which did cause Monique some difficulty. For her plan to work she would have to leave before he was awake. Edward may well have her locked in her room again; she couldn't risk that.

Everything, however, depended on Monique finding her passport; without it, the escape would be pointless. Almost certainly it would be in the safe in his office; she couldn't think of anywhere else. Monique was the only other person who knew the combination; if he hadn't changed it.

At eight o'clock, Monique decided to visit Edward's office

to see if she could find it. Access to his quarters would not be a problem, she had the codes and, as his wife, the authority. She walked across the courtyard, entered the passcode in the security pad adjacent to the entrance door and retraced her steps from the previous day. As she reached the top of the stairs, a figure appeared which made her jump. She spoke in French.

"Monsieur Scheck, que faites-vous ici?"

"Herr Duchamp has asked me to work here today while he is in Geneva. Can I help you?" he replied in English

"Non... I need to get something from le bureau... er office."

"Herr Duchamp said no-one was to go into the office until he returned."

"Mais je suis sa femme er... I need to get something... c'est urgent," said Monique.

"I am sorry Herr Duchamp was quite insistent... and specific."

"Même moi?"

"I am sorry... Yes, including you, Frau Duchamp. He will return at two o'clock; you can speak to him then. I am sure whatever it is can wait."

There was a look of resignation on her face. "Oh, d'accord, oui, I wait."

Monique could see there was an impasse and decided not to press it. She didn't want to draw attention to the fact that she had been visiting Edward's quarters; he might realise that she was after her passport. It would have to be plan B.

Her assistant arrived at eight-thirty; she would be another important factor in her plan. After the normal greetings, Françoise went to her handbag and pulled out a small medicine bottle.

"I have these. I hope it will be enough for what you need," she said, handing the bottle to Monique.

Monique looked at them and shook the bottle. "Yes, thank

you; that will be fine."

It was time to discuss her escape with Françoise and Monique outlined her plan.

"But I may not see you again," said Françoise.

"No, I know, that is possible... and you will not be able to work here. It would be best for you to stay away; I am not sure how they will react."

Monique could see the concern on her face. "Do not worry. I will pay you for three months which I hope will give you enough time to find something else. I will let you know where I am but you must tell no-one."

"Yes, I understand," said Françoise.

"I will need you here very early tomorrow."

"That is not a problem, my husband can look after the children," said Françoise.

"How is Patrick?" asked Monique.

"He is well, thank you."

"I need to make some calls, can you get us coffees and some pastries please?" asked Monique.

"Of course," said Françoise and she left the apartment to collect the refreshments from the refectory.

Monique took out her diary, looked up a Zurich number and made a call. She spoke in French.

"Nicolas Arthaud... It is Monique Duchamp."

She was put on hold while the operator connected the call.

"Arthaud," said the voice.

"Nicolas, it is Monique Duchamp."

"Madame Duchamp, how are you? It is good to speak to you," replied Arthaud.

"I am fine but I need to speak to you in confidence."

"But of course," said the man. "Our service is strictly private."

"That includes my husband," asserted Monique.

"Of course, yes, that is so," said Arthaud.

"Ok, you will not know this but yesterday there was an assassination attempt on me and my husband in Lausanne."

"No, no, that is terrible," said Arthaud.

"It is for this reason that I have to leave Switzerland. Edward is leaving for Hong Kong tomorrow but I am making my own arrangements."

"Yes, I see," said Arthaud. "How can I help?"

"I will need to raise some money from my investments."

"That is fine... How much will you need?"

"Can you access my portfolio?"

"Of course, just one minute." There was a clicking sound as the banker tapped at his keyboard.

"The short-term stocks... how much are they worth today?"

The man checked the records. "About five hundred thousand Swiss Francs, just over."

"What is that in Euros?"

"Let me see, at today's rate, about four hundred and seventy thousand."

"And I could get the cash for those now?" asked Monique.

"In two hours I can have the money into your account."

"Yes, please go ahead. What about the other stock?"

"Well, they are worth around three million. That's not including your Helvetia shares," said Arthaud.

"And how much are they worth?"

There was a delay as the banker made some calculations. "At today's price about eight million two hundred thousand francs."

Selling these would give Monique a problem. The share price would fall dramatically if she were to sell all of them in one go which could alert Edward. Certainly, the finance department would be interested. It was ironic that Edward had transferred a significant number of shares to Monique on his accountant's advice to avoid paying tax.

"How many can you sell without it causing a problem with the share price?" asked Monique.

"That is difficult to say. The market is quite bullish at the moment; there are buyers out there. The shares were trading twenty cents up earlier this morning."

Monique was thinking. "What are they now?"

"Ten francs eighty," replied the banker.

"Sell ten thousand... that should be safe," said Monique.

Arthaud made a note of the transactions. "The money will be here from the Helvetia shares in five working days," he explained.

"That is fine. There is one other thing," said Monique. "People may try to do things with my accounts either by computer or by telephone call. I need to make sure that my money is safe and I can move it if I have to."

"Your money is quite safe here, Madame Duchamp," said Arthaud.

"I need to be certain."

"We could set up a password for you."

"Yes... let's do that. How will it work?" asked Monique.

"You give me a password which only you and the bank know and there will be no transactions without that."

"Yes, ok. Let me see, how about... hmm... I know, "The Courtesan"... It's a book I used to read at college. No-one will know that." Not even Edward, she thought to herself.

"'The Courtesan' it is," said the banker and typed it into his records.

"So no-one will get to my account without that password... whoever it is?" said Monique, by way of clarification.

"That is correct," said Arthaud.

He summarised the transactions and the code word and Monique hung up; a major hurdle had been crossed.

After the call to her banker, she made another. The call just rang out before the voice message came on. Why wasn't he answering? She needed to let him know what was happening.

She was writing out a cheque when Françoise returned with two coffees and a plate of pastries.

"I have spoken to my bank and I have made the arrangements. I have written you a cheque to cover your wages and some more for the telephone calls."

Françoise looked at it. "Are you sure?" she said, looking at the amount. "That is much more than my three months wages."

"Yes, it is to say thank you for helping me," replied Monique.

"I need you to book my usual hair appointment in the village for tomorrow morning at eight o'clock."

Françoise raised her eyebrows.

"It is ok. I will not be going. You will."

"You want me to pretend to be you?" said Françoise.

"No, but I am hoping that if anyone asks they will have a note of the booking in my name. Maybe they will say it was me if you gave them a big tip." Monique smiled and took out a hundred franc note from her purse. "That should do it," she said as she handed it to Françoise.

"Before then, I will need you to take me to the station in Lausanne. Can you book me on the eight-twenty train to Paris?" said Monique. "One-way."

"Of course," replied Françoise.

"I will pick up the tickets from the station.

"Anything else?" asked Françoise.

"Yes, I will need some help with my clothes. Can you help me pack? I cannot take too much, two suitcases only. I will need you to take them and put them in your car today."

"But how...? People will see."

"Yes, they will see but they will not notice," said Monique.

"I don't understand," said Françoise.

"If you go at lunchtime just walk through the corridor and through the back entrance to the car park. There shouldn't be many people about and I don't think they will take any notice of you."

"Ok, I can do that."

"Then if you take my other case when you leave tonight, that should be the same. What time will you need to leave?"

"About five but I can stay later."

"No, that will be fine," said Monique.

"Is your husband here today?" asked Françoise.

"He is in Geneva this morning but he will be back later."

"Will you see him before he goes to Hong Kong?"

"Yes, I will stay with him tonight..."

Françoise looked surprised.

"It's alright, it's what I need to do," said Monique.

By lunchtime, Monique had packed her two cases and Françoise was able to take one of them to her car as arranged.

"How did it go?" asked Monique on her return.

"Oh, it was fine. I did not see anyone," said Françoise.

"Good," said Monique.

"What about all your jewellery?" said Françoise.

"I will wear some and carry the rest in my overnight bag," replied Monique.

"But how will you manage with all of your luggage?"

"I will be ok; I can get porters to help me at the station."

The rest of the afternoon Monique made sure she had all she needed. She would have to leave a great deal behind but she could always replace clothes. "Help yourself to anything that is left. I will have no need for them."

Françoise looked at Monique. "Are you sure?"

"Yes, Edward will probably have them thrown away."

Monique and Françoise were about the same size and she wasted no time in choosing two outfits and three pairs of shoes from Monique's collection.

"Thank you," said Françoise. "I will take them to my car."

While Françoise was gone, Monique tried the Australian number again. Still the same, no reply but this time she did leave a message. "Harry, c'est Monique... I am worried I cannot speak to you. I hope everything is ok. I wanted you to know I am leaving Edward tomorrow. I will go to my, er, sister, en Paris. I will call you again when I get there."

Later in the afternoon, she called her husband on the internal phone.

"Edward, what is happening tonight? I will need to see you before you leave tomorrow. I will join you for dinner, yes?"

"Hello, my dear... Yes, sorry I didn't call you when I got back earlier but I have been so busy. Yes, please come over, I need to explain the new security arrangements I have made to keep you safe while I am away. I will ask the chef to bring the food at eight o'clock."

"Yes, ok I will come over at eight o'clock."

Edward was in discussion with Scheck concerning security following yesterday's assassination attempt.

"While I am away I need you to make sure my wife is looked after and under no circumstances must she be allowed out on her own."

"What about her computer and phone?" asked Scheck.

Edward thought for a moment. "Yes... that will be fine. I don't think she can cause us any problems. It was good that your team found that email from the Humphries girl. I don't know why Monique ignored it."

"Yes," replied Scheck. "It is deleted now and in the circumstances, it was right to eliminate her. She could have caused a great deal of problems for us in Australia if her warnings had been taken seriously."

"Yes, quite so... How is Wilhelm, by the way?"

"He is much better today. I am taking him from the hospital in Lausanne and moving him to the medical centre here in Jura. It will be more secure."

"And the police...?"

"It is not a problem. They know what happened and are not pursuing it. It is in the national interest. The press has been informed it was a mental patient with a grudge."

Later that afternoon, Françoise left the apartment with Monique's second suitcase and made the same journey as at lunchtime. She was fully briefed on the escape plan and would help her employer in any way she could; she despised Edward for the way he had treated Monique.

Monique had plenty to do. Her small overnight bag was open on her dressing table and she was adding her jewellery and cosmetics until there was no room for anything else.

Having completed her packing she took the bottle of sleeping pills that Françoise had provided from her handbag and went into the bathroom. She read the label; *'Nitrazepam: two tablets to be taken at night. Do not take with other medicines, do not exceed maximum dosage'.*

She needed Edward to be sound asleep for around eight hours and despite the warning, decided to increase the dose just to make sure. Five should be enough, she thought. If she was careful maybe Edward would just think he'd had a particularly restful night and not been drugged.

She tipped out five tablets onto the glass top of the vanity unit next to the sink. She needed to break them down into fine particles small enough to dissolve in a drink. She thought for a moment, and then went to her closet and picked out a pair of black stilettos and went back to the bathroom. The sharp point of the heel made an ideal pestle and she ground each one into a white dust. The result looked like a line of cocaine but this was not for inhaling. Monique took a small polythene bag that contained two of her lipsticks and cut off a corner with a pair of nail scissors. She gently pushed the powder off the worktop into the resultant cone with the blade of the scissors and sealed it with a hair-grip. Desperate circumstances beget desperate measures.

She checked her watch; six-thirty. She would shower and change ready for her meal with Edward.

Monique chose an outfit that Edward particularly liked, short, low-cut and deliberately provocative; she needed him to be distracted. She wore nothing else except a pair of three-inch heels.

Tonight her life would change irrevocably.

At ten to eight, she walked across to Edward's quarters with a light jacket over her shoulders. He was waiting for her in his lounge reading some notes. As she walked in he took off his reading glasses and looked at her.

"Monique, my dear, how are you? I'm sorry I was not able to join you this afternoon but with me going away it has been hectic as you can imagine." He got up and kissed her on her cheek.

"It's ok, I understand," said Monique.

"The dinner will be here very soon. Would you like a glass of champagne?" said Edward handing her a half-full flute.

"Thank you," replied Monique as she took off her jacket. She took the glass from him.

"You look very nice, my dear. How was your day?" said Edward.

"Thank you... it was fine, thank you," replied Monique. Lengthy conversation seemed in short supply.

Just then the buzzer to the apartment sounded and Edward pressed the access button to allow the chef to enter; he would use the lift. Moments later there was a knock on the door and the chef wheeled in a hostess trolley with plates and eating utensils. He went to the dining table and set out the two placings.

"If you would like to take your seat I will serve, Monsieur Duchamp," said the chef.

"Thank you, Charles... Shall we, my dear?" said Edward and escorted Monique to the table.

The chef produced various trays of food and served the couple their meal before leaving.

"Pan-fried scallops and fresh salmon, I know how you like fish," said Edward.

"Thank you," said Monique and started eating. There was an atmosphere she could detect which could lead to conflict and she didn't want that; she had no idea how he might react.

"So how is work? You have not said much lately," asked Monique in an attempt to get on neutral ground.

"It is going well, I am pleased to say. We have resolved a number of problems."

"What about Australia?" asked Monique.

"Why do you ask? Ah... of course, you have an interest there, don't you?"

"No," said Monique, more defensively than she had intended. "I have no interest there."

"But your friend... Harry isn't it?" replied Edward.

"He is not my friend." Her voice was raised.

"Well, from what I hear he is more than a friend." Edward looked down at his meal, stuck his serrated knife into his salmon steak and cut vigorously. "No matter, everything is ok there now," he said, then changed the subject. "What about you, my dear? What have you been doing?"

"Without my files, I cannot do much."

"No, no, I can see that. Maybe I can rearrange things differently while I'm away. I will speak to Herr Scheck in the morning and make sure he gives you what you need. I don't want you to feel... how can I put it? Unproductive."

Unproductive seemed a strange term to use but Monique said nothing. There was a silence as they finished their food. Edward poured out more champagne.

"Am I going to be locked away again while you are away?" said Monique.

"No, that is not necessary but Kurt or one of the others will be with you if you need to leave the Chateau. It is for your own safety. You understand that, don't you? I mean after Monday. It is only for ten days or so, fourteen at the most."

"No, it's fine. I understand. It is ok if I can keep my phone and laptop?" said Monique.

"Of course, my dear, of course... as I said, it was a misunderstanding before... that is all."

Monique considered his response but knew that was not true. She needed to ask another question.

"What time are you leaving tomorrow?" asked Monique.

"Early, I need to be at the airport for eight-thirty." That was a bit vague for Monique.

"Well, I might not see you then. I have an appointment at the hairdresser tomorrow morning."

"But how will you get there?" asked Edward, seemingly surprised.

"Françoise will take me."

"No, no, I cannot allow that. Kurt will drive you and I will have another car to escort you. I insist."

Monique was in a quandary; her plan was beginning to unravel.

"No, Edward, that is not necessary. I do not want to live my life as a prisoner."

"But you are not a prisoner, I explained. You must not think that, dear; your safety, that is all that matters," said Edward. "What time will you need to leave for the salon?"

"Early," said Monique.

"And Madame Fouvert will be here?"

"Yes, she takes me all the time."

"I will think about it," said Edward.

"It will be ok," said Monique.

"But you will stay here tonight, surely?" said Edward.

"For a while but I am very tired and you will need your sleep as well with your trip," replied Monique.

Edward looked at her with some disappointment.

"Don't worry we will make the most of the time," she said. She unzipped the front of her dress and pulled down the sleeves. She stood up and let the dress fall to the floor revealing his surprise.

Edward almost spilt his drink; suddenly his wife's security was the last thing on his mind.

"Why don't you go to the bathroom? I'll be waiting for you," she said.

Edward couldn't keep his eyes off her and made a move towards her.

"In a minute... you go to the bathroom. I will be in the bedroom. Go on, I will bring the drinks."

"Ok... I won't be long," he said and left the room.

This was it; now or never. She opened her handbag, retrieved the crushed up sleeping tablets and poured the powder into his glass and then topped up the Champagne. She swished it around with her finger helping it to dissolve.

She went into the bedroom and got into bed. Edward returned from the bathroom dressed in a robe and saw Monique in bed. She removed the bedclothes revealing her nakedness; she was holding the two glasses of champagne. As Edward approached she handed him his glass.

"No, no more... I need a clear head tomorrow."

"But you must," she said. "I am not drinking alone," and

started pouring a small dribble from her glass down her body. Edward grabbed his glass and started to drink while Monique poured some more over her breasts.

"And when you have finished that there is more here for you to drink," said Monique.

There was a sense of urgency as Edward tipped back the glass until it was all gone; he did not notice the traces of white sediment at the bottom. He removed his robe, then leant over her and started licking the champagne off her body. Monique lay back and hoped the drug would take effect quickly.

It was not quick enough and Monique had to endure his lovemaking for what she hoped would be the final time. After he had climaxed Edward lay on the bed recovering but within minutes he was in a deep slumber. Monique wrapped the covers around him and tucked him in like a child.

She put on her dress and went to Edward's safe. It was in his office on the wall behind a picture of a cavalry charge battle scene overlooking his desk. It was hinged and she pulled it back to reveal the safe; then entered the code. There was a click as it unlocked. She breathed a sigh of relief; thank goodness he hadn't changed the code. She pulled open the small but heavy door and looked inside. It was not a large safe; no more than eighteen inches but inside there were rolled up wads of money, high-value notes, together with several computer discs in protective covers.

She took out the items one by one. Yes! She exclaimed to herself as she picked up a passport but then realised it was Edward's. Her heart sunk; there was no sign of her passport. She was getting desperate, her hands were starting to shake as she rummaged further but then right at the back she saw it, the unmistakable shape. She removed it from its hiding place and put back the contents, rearranging them in the hope they would conceal the removal of her document. She was about to shut the safe when she had a thought. She took out the discs and put them in her handbag along with her passport. She had no idea what they contained but they just might prove useful in some way in the future. She locked the safe and pushed the picture back in its place.

Monique was breathing heavily; her whole future depended on these few minutes. Her hands were still shaking as she went back in the bedroom. She took Edward's empty glass from the bedside table and washed it out under the tap in the bathroom. Then she poured in the remaining dregs from the bottle of champagne. She could do no more. She checked around the bedroom, turned out the light and left the apartment.

She looked at her watch; it was eleven-thirty and there would still be people around so she decided not to take the lift in case the noise was heard. She reached the bottom of the stairs and slowly opened the external door to Edward's quarters; no-one about. She quickly left the block and made her way back to her room in the shadow of the walls of the Chateau.

Everything so far had gone to plan; she just needed Françoise to play her part in the morning.

Monique changed out of her dress and got into bed but sleep was impossible. Thoughts ran through her head; what if the drug didn't work and he woke up before she had left. She wanted to leave now but that would be impossible, the security guard at the gate would almost certainly alert someone and an investigation would result.

She had no idea what time she had drifted off but the alarm on her phone woke her at five-thirty. The adrenaline kicked in straight away. She showered and changed into her smart casual gear then applied her makeup. She had one last look around the apartment... six-fifteen; time to go.

She collected her handbag and went to her own safe at the

back of her wardrobe. It was where she kept her most expensive jewellery and cash for her shopping trips. She took out the bracelet that Edward had bought her and put it on, then took out the cash, about seven thousand francs and put it in her handbag. She checked again, the safe was empty. She closed it, and then picked up her things from the bed; her phone, charger, purse and passport. She put them in her handbag with her money. The overnight bag containing her jewellery was on the dresser. She picked it up and had a final last minute check; she was done. She had no intention of coming back.

She went downstairs and opened the outer door. Françoise was there in the far corner waiting next to her Fiat with the engine running. Monique held her breath as she crossed the courtyard towards the car carrying her two bags. She felt conspicuous and could only hope that Scheck or any of his goons were not around. The sun was already illuminating part of the building and Monique stopped at the car and put on her sunglasses. She handed the bags to Françoise who opened the car door and put them on the back seat; Monique got in.

"Thank you Françoise, you have saved my life, I think. Did you have any problem?"

"It is ok, I think. The guards at the gate asked why I was working at this time but I told them you had an early appointment at the salon before a meeting."

"And it was ok?"

"I think so; they let me through no problem."

Françoise drove out of the Chateau building, across the drawbridge, past the fountain and along the gravel drive into the outer grounds. She slowed to a walking pace as she approached the external gate. This was it.

Monique watched as the barrier rose from its frame and Françoise drove through; she breathed a sigh of relief.

"So, to the station in Lausanne, yes?" said Françoise.

"Yes, thank you. You have ordered my ticket?"

"Yes, you can pick it up at the ticket office. I have used my mother's name, in case anyone asked." She looked across at Monique and smiled.

"What name is that?" asked Monique.

"Of course... Alette Brenôt."

"Alette Brenôt," Monique repeated.

Traffic was light until they reached the city boundary when rush hour traffic impeded their progress but they made the station in about fifty minutes. Françoise parked at the drop-off point, got out and opened the boot of the car. Monique went to find a luggage trolley. She returned moments later and Françoise helped her retrieve the two suitcases from the trunk and put them on the transport. There was a poignant farewell. "I hope you are ok, please you will let me know," said Françoise. A tear fell from her eye and ran down her cheek. Monique too was caught up in the emotion of it.

"Yes, of course. I will send you a message when I arrive. Now go to the salon and enjoy your haircut." Monique smiled, kissed her colleague on the cheek and gave her a final hug.

"Au revoir, Françoise... Thank you for everything."

Françoise got back into the Fiat and Monique watched as it pulled away and was swallowed up by the rush-hour traffic.

Lausanne Station is a beautiful ochre-stone building; the external façade is square-shaped and resembles a pagoda with three arches at the base. She pushed her luggage through the middle one and found her way to the ticket office. Monique had been to the station many times before on shopping expeditions to Geneva in different times. The ticket office was open and she paid for the reserved first-class ticket in cash. She had a wait until her train left at eight-twenty.

There was, though, one final thing she needed to do. Across

the station plaza from the main entrance was a phone shop; she pushed her luggage inside. She explained what she wanted and the assistant was very helpful. On his advice, she bought a cheap pay-as-you-go phone and added a generous credit which she thought would last her some time. Then she swapped the SIM card. Now it could not be traced.

She looked for a coffee shop.

Back at the Chateau by six-forty-five concern was growing when Edward had not appeared for an early morning team briefing; six-thirty meetings were not uncommon. As they waited in the conference room, there was a great deal of clock-watching as the time ticked by.

"Something's not right," said David Leganes, one of the five divisional heads who were waiting. Leonard Scheck was the only one in the group who had access to his apartment and he was dispatched to find out what was happening. He keyed in the code and ran up the spiral staircase to Edward's quarters. The curtains were still drawn and there was no sign of him.

Scheck started calling. "Herr Duchamp, Herr Duchamp... are you there?" He walked through the office suite and into Edward's private quarters. He called again; still no response. He reached the bedroom door and knocked sharply. "Herr Duchamp, are you ok?"

He could hear a groaning noise coming from inside. He knocked again and entered the room. It was in darkness and Leonard walked past the bed to the window and opened the curtains.

Edward was trying to sit up but was having great difficulty. "Herr Duchamp, are you ok?"

Edward tried to focus his eyes. He couldn't remember a hangover like it. "My head... Can you get me some water?" he groaned.

Leonard went to the bathroom and filled a tumbler with water and handed it to Edward. Edward gulped it down in one. "What time is it?" he asked.

"Ten to seven," replied Scheck.

"What? How can that be?"

"You have overslept. That is all."

Leonard picked up the champagne bottle and looked at it with some disdain. Edward noticed. "I didn't drink that much. Monique was here... Monique...? Where is she?"

"I believe she is at the salon, Herr Duchamp."

Edward sat on the bed with his head in his hands. "Yes, she said, I remember now. Did Kurt go with her?"

"No, it was Frau Fouvert. Do you want me to do something, Herr Duchamp? I can send him to the salon."

"What...? Yes... No... Wait, I can't think. Can you get me some black coffee? I'll get in the shower."

After a cold shower and two cups of strong coffee, Edward was gradually becoming more coherent. Caffeine neutralises the effects of Nitrazepam.

He started getting dressed, Scheck was still with him. "What about the team meeting?" said Scheck.

"You'll have to cancel it; it wasn't urgent. I need to be at the airport for eight-thirty. When did my wife say she will be back?"

"I do not know, I have not seen her. Did she not tell you?"

"No," said Edward, still trying to regain his motor senses. His mind was all over the place; it was like his brain was immersed in cotton wool, a psychedelic experience. "Can you get Joseph up here? He can help me pack."

"Of course," said Scheck and he phoned reception on the internal phone to summon Joseph. Then he called Leganes to let them know Edward had cancelled the team meeting. There was a collective sigh of relief. The group dispersed and Leganes went check on Edward. He'd agreed to accompany him to the airport for a last minute briefing; he would be looking after things at the chateau in Edward's absence.

Within twenty minutes, some sort of order had descended. Edward had showered and dressed and Joseph had packed his clothes and accessories he would need for the trip. Scheck returned to the courtyard to supervise the loading of the limo that would take Edward to the airport.

Edward was trying desperately to get his head together and concentrate on his business affairs. His meeting in Hong Kong was important; it had taken several months to arrange and could lead the way to future projects in China. Still trying to focus, he had one final check.

"Wait," he said to Joseph. "I need my money... oh, and passport."

He moved unsteadily to the picture on the wall and pulled it back. The keypad seemed to mock him as his fingers tried to press the correct numbers. "Here, you do it, Joseph," he said. "My fingers won't work... 2-6-3-4." Joseph joined Edward at the safe and pressed the numbers and there was a click as the safe unlocked. Joseph opened the door for Edward and moved back. Edward took out the nearest rolled-up wad of money and put it in his briefcase, then picked up his passport and shut the safe. Joseph returned the painting to its rightful position. In his stupefied state Edward had not noticed the missing discs or Monique's passport. He put the money and his passport in his jacket pocket. Joseph picked up the cases as Leganes entered the apartment. "What's happened? Are you ok, Edward?" he said.

Despite the caffeine, Edward found any level of concentration hard; he was unable to string a sentence together and didn't respond. He began hallucinating as Leganes and Joseph helped him down the stairs. Two bodyguards were also travelling with

Edward to Hong Kong and they were waiting by the limo as Leganes and Joseph emerged from Edward's apartment almost carrying their boss towards the awaiting vehicle. "It's ok, I will see to it," said Leganes, helping Edward into the car. Scheck stood watching, clearly concerned and trying to make sense of what was happening. Joseph stowed Edward's luggage in the boot and the car pulled away, leaving Scheck and Joseph bemused at Edward's condition; they had never seen him lose control before.

As the car made its way to the airport in Geneva, David Leganes could get little sense out of Edward who was lay on the back seat in a stupor. He suggested the trip be cancelled but Edward insisted it went ahead; he was slurring as if he were drunk and then he promptly fell asleep again.

At the airport, Stephan Morin, the head of sales and product development was waiting for the car outside the Arrivals terminal. He would be accompanying Edward to Hong Kong as part of the small delegation. Edward also had his two bodyguards for the trip. Between them, they managed to get Edward on the plane. He and Stephan were travelling club-class while the bodyguards went economy for the thirteen and a half hour flight.

Back at the Chateau, around midday, Lucy Bainbridge, the reception manager, was heard calling. "Has anyone seen Madame Duchamp?" Leonard Scheck took an interest.

Chapter Thirteen

The Royal Darwin Hospital, Tuesday morning, the day after the snake incident

Harry was sat up in his hospital bed in the private ward waiting for the doctor to discharge him. His puncture wounds were red but not unduly swollen and he felt no ill effects from his snake bite; he was anxious to get back to work. Although in a private ward, sleeping had not been easy; he spent a long time racking his brain trying to work out how the snake could have got into the car. He discounted the idea of it crawling in of its own accord; the Eastern Browns were rarely seen in the city. Someone had deliberately tried to kill him; it was the only conclusion. It was a scary thought and he wondered if they would try again.

Like most people in Darwin, he had kept the driver's window of his vehicle open a couple of inches to keep it cool. Someone putting the snake through the window was the only logical way it could have happened unless someone had a key. There was no sign of anyone tampering with the lock but it would have been dangerous trying to push a venomous snake through that small space; so many questions. Where would the perpetrators even get an Eastern Brown?

A few minutes later, a welcome face appeared around the door.

"Come on, Harry let's get you out of here, we need you at work."

"Hi Marci, good to see you," said Harry, as his work colleague approached his bed. She was smartly dressed in a pair of light trousers and a blouse.

"How are you?"

"I'm fine, they're letting me out."

"Yeah, I know I've come to give you a lift," said Marci.

"Didn't bother with the grapes."

Harry smiled. "Great, give me a minute to change."

"I'll wait outside," said Marci.

Just then the doctor walked in and saw Harry starting to get dressed.

"It is ok to go isn't it?" said Harry.

"Yes, that's why I'm here. There's no sign of poison in your system and everything looks fine; you can go. Just stay clear of Eastern Browns in the future. Next time you might not be so lucky," said the doctor. "Oh, and you will need these." He handed Harry a small paper bag. "Painkillers, anti-septic cream and antibiotics," he explained. "If the wound gets painful or swollen take the antibiotics straight away."

"Yes, will do, doctor. Thanks for everything," said Harry and he left the ward accompanied by Marci.

It took them over half an hour to reach the office and Harry and Marci spent the journey chatting about the attack.

"What about the police?" asked Harry. "Do we need to talk to them?"

"I would wait until you've spoken to Nate. I phoned him last night and told him what had happened. He thinks it might be the same idiots that messed with the plane. He's got the security guys working on it."

"They pulled into the car park. Harry's Suzuki was still parked where he had left it and Nate's jeep was parked next to it. One of the minibuses was also parked up next to the office entrance in the disabled bay.

As he entered the office, Harry became the centre of attention; first Den, then Winda, welcomed him, showing concern for his well-being. Ying was not due in until later; she said she needed to collect some equipment from one of the mining stores.

Nate came out of his office and called to Harry.

"Ya got a minute, Harry, mate?"

Harry left his workstation and joined Nate; one of the security guys was stood in front of the desk.

"Come in... you remember Heinz?"

There were nods of acknowledgement.

"How ya feeling today? Have ya spoken to your folks?"

"I'm ok, thanks. No, not spoken to them yet. Didn't want to worry them."

"Yeah, too bloody right," said Nate. "Look, I've been chatting to Heinz here trying to work out what the hell happened."

"Yeah, I need to know that too," said Harry.

"Well, we reckon it's those eco-bastards again, the same ones who fucked up the plane." Heinz nodded although whether he understood or not was a moot point.

"We're gonna take a look at the CCTV tapes and see if that shows up anything. Do ya want to join us?"

"You bet," said Harry. "I want to know who was trying to kill me. What do the police think?"

Nate looked at the German.

"Actually, mate. We're not going to involve the police."

Harry looked surprised. "Why's that?"

"It's all a bit sensitive at the moment, you know. There's a lot resting on this project and we don't want any hold ups. I mean the cops could be here for days once they get their teeth into something."

Harry looked at Nate, then Heinz. "Yeah, I can see that."

"What about the Chateau?" said Harry; the team tended to use the term when referring to the Swiss HQ.

"Yeah, right, I've spoken to Scheck; wants me to keep him up to speed. He said he'll send another couple of blokes if we need it. Told him we would manage it, for the time being, see how it goes."

"What if they try again?" asked Harry.

"We'll be ready for 'em," said Nate.

"Right," said Harry.

"Right, that's settled then. Let's go check out those tapes, see what we can see, eh?" said Nate, and he led Harry and Heinz out of his office and down to the ground floor.

Tallara was on the desk as usual. Nate walked up to her.

"Tallara, love, we need to see the CCTV footage from last night. You heard we had a bit of a problem?"

"Yeah, Marci told me, sounded dreadful. Are you ok, Harry?" said Tallara.

"Yeah, thanks, I was lucky," said Harry.

The CCTV system, including the recordings, was owned by the building's landlord who employed Tallara. She had the responsibility of making sure the tapes were replaced each day and the old ones stored. The tapes were kept for a month before being recycled. She led the three into a back office where there were monitors showing activity at the front of the building and the parking area at the back.

"These were yesterday's," said Tallara, pointing to three tapes next to the recording equipment.

"Right," said Nate. "Let's see what we've got."

Tallara inserted the first cassette into the video machine which was linked to a monitor and pressed 'play'.

The recording was time-stamped and it started at seven a.m. Nate flicked the 'fast-forward' button. They watched the comings and goings in the car park.

"Here's Harry arriving," said Nate as the Suzuki drove up. "We just need to keep an eye on that and see what happens."

The tape continued at double speed, the images moving about like a silent movie.

"Wait, what's that?" said Nate. Tallara stopped the recorder; the time was four twenty-three and forty-eight seconds. She pressed 'play' and the tape moved at normal speed.

They watched as a figure in a dark tee shirt, jeans and a baseball cap, wearing gloves, carrying a brown canvas bag walked up to Harry's car. The individual was the other side of the car and clearly looking around to see if anyone was about. The person then stooped down out of sight presumably rummaging in the bag. Then, as bold as you like, they held the snake in one hand and guided it headfirst through the open window. The person disappeared from sight again for a moment, then could be seen quickly walking away.

"Did you recognise him?" said Harry.

"No chance from that tape. Looked like a kid," said Nate. "What did you think, Heinz?"

"Yes, I think so also," he said. It was the first time Harry had heard the German speak English. "Let us watch again."
The footage was re-run at half speed. Tallara paused the tape at various intervals to view it freeze-frame but there was no clear image which would help them identify the perpetrator. It was not even possible to ascertain whether it was male or female; the general consensus was still that it was a youth.

"Definitely white, so it wasn't an Abbo," said Nate. Heinz nodded in agreement. "Whoever did it has got some balls, I'll say that," said Nate. "You wouldn't get me messing around with an Eastern Brown, that's for sure."

"Do you want to see anymore?" asked Tallara.

"Yeah, we need to see everything you've got," replied Nate.

Tallara handed them the remaining two tapes and went back to her reception duties.

The group tediously viewed the other tapes but again the results were inconclusive. After half an hour they left the office and thanked Tallara.

"Do you need anything else?" she said.

"No, thanks anyway; we'll let you get on," said Nate.

They headed back to the office. "Well that's been about as

useful as an ashtray on a motorbike," said Nate as they climbed the stairs to the first floor.

Harry went back to his workstation, leaving Nate and the German in deep conversation. Marci joined Harry in his cubicle.

"Any luck?"

"No," said Harry. "It was too grainy to see anything. Looked like it might be a young lad, small, about fourteen maybe, black tee shirt, and baseball cap... anyone you know?"

Marci looked at Harry. "Do I look like someone who hangs around with young boys? Prefer real men," she said and laughed.

Harry tried to push his troubles out of his mind; he needed to resume the preparation for the trek on Friday; there was still much to do. From the geoscientific surveys carried out earlier, he'd worked out the routes and areas within the two sites that he felt would yield the best results. This would be where they would do their test drilling. The biggest challenge was finding an access which would enable them to get the trucks and equipment to the sites; the terrain was very rugged.

Despite the work pressures, however, his mind kept drifting back to Monique; he wondered how she was and hoped he would hear from her.

Later, around lunch-time, Ying appeared.

"Hi Ying, did you get what you needed?" said Marci as she walked through the office.

"Yes, everything is ready, it will be delivered on Thursday," she said and stopped in her tracks when she saw Harry at his workstation

"Harry what are you doing here? I heard you had been bitten by a snake," she said.

"Yes, I was lucky, it was a dry bite."

"Yes, you were," Ying replied, and walked on to her pod.

Harry's ankle had been dressed by the nurse at the hospital

and he hadn't thought about his bite. The effects of the antiseptic cream she had applied were wearing off and the wound was suddenly irritating, not painful, just a need to scratch. He rubbed it through the covering gauze to relieve the itching. He would need to apply more cream soon.

Mid-afternoon, Nate called the team together to announce new security arrangements. The four staff ambled into the conference room where Nate was sat on the desk waiting; Heinz was sat on one of the chairs. Nate called the group to order.

"Right, listen up. As you know we've had another incident following the problem with the bloody plane. Luckily, Harry's ok but we can't take any chances so from now on you will have company to and from your homes. Either Heinz here or one of the other security guys will follow you from a discrete distance; you won't even know they're there."

There were looks at each other. "Well I don't want to be followed," said Ying.

"I'm sorry Ying but we're in this together. We'll have another look at things when we get back from the trek. Anyone else want to bloody moan?"

There were looks at each other and shakes of heads; compliance seemed to be a requirement. There were looks of concern as the team went back to work.

By five o'clock Harry was feeling the effects of his sleep deprivation from the previous night and decided to call it a day.

"Make sure you check your car," shouted Marci as he made his way out of the office.

"Yeah, will do," said Harry with a wry smile.

This time there were no dramas facing Harry and he drove back to the hotel without incident. He noticed one of the minibuses following about three cars behind. He wasn't sure if he felt safer with their presence or not.

As he walked through reception, there were about twenty

copies of the local newspaper on the desk which were provided free for guests. He picked one up before going to his room.

He changed and freshened up before settling down with a glass of water and reading the paper. His attention was drawn to a picture on the front page which he recognised instantly. He read the headline; *'Missing student found dead on Myilly Point beach'.*

He checked the picture again; it was the same girl he had seen in the launderette, the one with the CND tee shirt, no doubt about it. There was a lengthy narrative; she was named as Sophie Darling, a third-year politics student at Charles Darwin University, originally from Melbourne. Parents had reported her missing on Monday morning but no-one had seen her since Saturday. A walker had found her body washed up on the foreshore. Although they were waiting for the results of a post-mortem, it appeared she had drowned. Police were trying to track her last movements.

Harry started thinking; he would be a witness and might even have been one of the last people to see her alive. He thought about the security guys; he was sure one of them was following her into the flats. Something was definitely not right. He was in a dilemma but going to the police was not an option. He read the article to the end. There was no mention of the professor; in fact, that story had been quiet for a couple of days since the revelation about his gambling debts. He wondered if the police would make the connection. The fact that two prominent objectors to the Kakadu Gap project had ostensibly been silenced was not lost on Harry. Then there were the two Aboriginals; were they harmed in any way? He felt the need to speak to someone but wasn't sure who to trust.

He decided to go for a swim to relax and get his thoughts in order.

After twenty lengths, Harry exited the pool. He felt much

better. He had covered his snake bite but the chlorine in the water had irritated it and he applied more cream to the wound when he returned to his room. After the traumas of yesterday, he didn't feel like venturing far so he ate his evening meal in the hotel restaurant. As he was eating, he became conscious that he was being observed. The hotel restaurant was an annexe to the bar. Harry noticed a woman sat on one of the high stools chatting to the barman. Every so often, she would turn and look at him; well not so much a look, more of a lingering stare. She looked to be in her thirties; auburn hair tied back in plaits and dressed in a pair of beige-coloured shorts with a white blouse and sandals. In a different time, Harry might have returned the gaze but following the snake incident he had suddenly become very wary and decided to ignore the apparent attention.

He finished his dinner and signed for his food. He checked the bar area and saw the woman had gone. Harry felt a sense of relief and left the restaurant, walked through the bar, into reception and towards the lift. Suddenly, there was a voice behind him. "You're not leaving me to drink on my own, I hope."

He turned around; it was the woman from the bar coming out of the ladies toilet.

"Well, I was about to turn in," said Harry. "It's been a long day."

"That's a shame; I could do with a bit of company right now. Just one drink, that's all?"

Harry looked at her; his initial instinct was to walk away but something changed his mind.

"Go on then, just one drink," he said, and he went back into the bar followed by the woman.

"What can I get you?" said the barman.

"Half of Fosters, please Jack, and a...?"

"Dry white wine," said the woman.

"Take a pew, I'll bring 'em over," said the barman.

The woman walked towards the window which overlooked the harbour and chose a seat. "I love the view here, don't you? Sorry I don't know your name."

"Harry," he said and sat opposite her.

"I'm Rebecca Connolly but everybody calls me Becs?" said the woman. She spoke with no more than a hint of an Australian accent, like a news presenter on TV.

Jack brought the drinks to the table and Harry signed the tab.

"Cheers," said Becs and raised her glass.

Harry raised his glass in acknowledgement.

"So what's a Pom doing all the way out here?" said Becs.

"Just working," replied Harry, deliberately being vague.

"You?" said Harry.

"Yeah, here on business, work for a law firm in Adelaide."

"So, what's your line of work?" said Becs.

"Commodities," replied Harry. Given his recent experience, he didn't want to be too specific; he was trying to weigh her up.

She seemed surprised at his answer. "What, buying and selling you mean?"

"Yeah, something like that," said Harry.

She looked at her glass for a moment, analysing the response.

"Whereabouts?" she fired back.

"CBD," Harry replied.

"Really? Me too. They've given me an office on Mitchell Street. Anywhere close?"

"Yes, not far away," said Harry. It was the next block but he was still reticent about any disclosure.

"So what about back home?" said Becs, trying a different tack.

"I'm from Norwich, England, in the East."

"Yeah, I know it... never been; a big cathedral there, right?"

"Yes," said Harry.

"How long have you been in Oz?"

"A couple of weeks, not long," replied Harry.

"So what company do you work for?" asked Becs.

He looked at her closely. She was not 'girly' pretty but still very attractive, she certainly looked the part of a business woman. She oozed confidence; her face was stern one moment, a mask of professionalism but then softened as she spoke. Her blouse was tight-fitting and emphasised her full figure; she was clearly aware of its allure. It would not be the first time she had used her natural assets to good effect.

"You won't have heard of it," he said after a pause while he drank his beer.

Becs decided to raise the stakes. "Try me," she said.

Harry didn't feel ready to divulge that information.

"Helvetia, by any chance?" said Becs.

Harry nearly spilt his beer. "How did you know that?"

"I've seen your car around."

"You've been following me?" said Harry.

"No, no, of course not," replied Becs. "I know the company. We did some work for them last year. They want to prospect for Uranium in Kakadu... that them?"

"Yes," said Harry.

"The offices are just up the road from me. Thought I recognised your car, there's not too many white Suzuki's about; it was parked in their car park."

The thoughts of snakes flashed through Harry's mind.

She could tell Harry was not comfortable in discussing this topic. "It's ok... no big deal. Just trying to make conversation, it does seem we have some common ground."

She took a sip of her drink. "So how long have you worked for them?"

"Not long," said Harry.

"No, I guess not. It was a guy called Leganes I used to deal with... oh and some bloke called Nate... thinks he's bloody Crocodile Dundee."

Harry started to laugh. "Yes, I know him."

"Yeah, interesting character," said Becs.

There was a pause as Harry took another drink.

"So what do you do? For Helvetia," she clarified.

"I'm a geologist," replied Harry.

"In commodities?" said Becs and smiled. "It's ok; I understand. There's a lot of opposition to the Kakadu project; I've been reading about it."

"Yes, you could say that," said Harry.

For some reason, Harry found a release in being able to talk to someone outside the organisation. He had not had any proper social interaction since he landed in Australia, apart from the odd chat with Jack the barman. It was a solitary existence up until now.

"Would you like another beer?" said Becs.

Harry looked at his empty glass. "Yeah, ok, go on, thanks."

Becs went to the bar and returned with refills.

"So how long are you staying here, in the hotel?" said Becs, as she handed Harry his drink.

"Tomorrow's my last day," said Harry. "They've got me a flat on Smith Street."

"What, Launceston Towers?"

"Yes," said Harry. "Do you know it?"

"No, I don't know it, not been there but you can't miss it. Hope you're not on the fourteenth floor," she said and smiled.

"What about you?" said Harry.

"I'm staying here in the hotel. It's a nice enough place and they're picking up the tab," said Becs.

"Who are 'they'?" asked Harry.

"The firm I'm working for," said Becs. It was her turn to be evasive but Harry didn't pursue it.

They carried on talking until well after eleven-thirty and another round of drinks. Harry had overcome his earlier weariness; his chat with Becs had been invigorating.

It was Becs who made the move. "Right, I'm for bed. I've enjoyed our chat, Harry."

"Yeah, me too." replied Harry.

"What about tomorrow night; do you want to meet up again?" said Becs.

"Yeah, ok, that would be good." said Harry.

"You could join me for dinner if you like. It's a shame to eat on your own," said Becs. "About seven?"

"Yeah, ok," said Harry.

They left the bar. Harry made his farewells to Jack and followed Becs to the lift.

"What floor?" said Harry, who was next to the buttons.

"Two, please." Harry pressed two and three.

The door opened on two and Becs leant across and kissed Harry on the cheek.

"See you tomorrow, Harry."

"Yeah, look forward to it," replied Harry.

Back in his room, Harry was trying to make sense of his evening. She seemed to know quite a bit about him and, given recent events, this was concerning. Despite that, he had enjoyed her company and was looking forward to seeing her again.

Wednesday morning and Harry was awake around seven. He checked his phone and saw there was a missed call and a voice message timed at twelve-thirty a.m. Harry hadn't heard it. He played the message.

'Harry, c'est Monique... I am worried I cannot speak to you. I hope everything is ok. I wanted you to know I am leaving Edward tomorrow. I will go to my, er, sister, en Paris. I will call

you again when I get there. '

Harry replayed it and his thoughts returned to Monique. He was trying to gauge his feelings for her. She had affected him, for sure, more than anyone else had done. He found himself thinking about her when his mind was in downtime. He'd not experienced that level of emotion with someone before but he didn't want to become embroiled in her marital troubles; it could cause no end of problems. What would she do if she did leave Edward as she said? More importantly, what would Edward do about it? He couldn't see him taking that sort of rejection kindly. For all his uncertainty, Harry wanted to hear she was safe and hoped she would make contact again.

Wednesday morning in the office and everything was on full throttle preparing for the trek on Friday. Harry was finalising the details of the two sites. He had split the areas into smaller, manageable plots which they could excavate, then do an initial analysis of the soil samples on site. These would then be sent to the Chateau where they had their own laboratory facilities with more sophisticated equipment. This second analysis would provide them with the data they would need to take the prospecting process to the next stage; or not, depending on what they found.

With everything that was going on, the security issue had not been on his mind. The missing professor and the dead student were no longer a concern; it was none of his business. His focus had been fixed on the job in hand. He did, however, find himself strangely buoyed at the prospect of meeting Becs that evening.

He left the office around five; his trek preparation was almost complete and he would finish before the final briefing on Thursday. Back at the hotel, he showered and changed and read the paper before his dinner date. There was more on the missing student and the police were now treating her death as murder following the post-mortem which found she had suffered head injuries. Speculation was that she had been beaten to unconsciousness, dumped in the sea and had subsequently drowned. Harry thought back again to the laundrette and wondered if he should report his observations to the police. Given Nate's comments earlier, he would do nothing but it still bothered him.

By six fifty-five, Harry was in the bar chatting to Jack and enjoying half a lager. He was dressed casually but smart, shirt and jeans; he was feeling slightly apprehensive about the evening ahead, like a first date. Becs appeared just after seven; her hair was down, almost shoulder length. She was wearing a smart pair of skinny jeans, high heels and a pale blue blouse buttoned at the front about half way, displaying a considerable amount of bra and cleavage. She looked stunning; Harry caught his breath.

"Hi, what are you having?" said Harry as she approached. He kissed her on the cheek.

"Gin and tonic, please," said Becs.

He made the order. "You look nice," said Harry as he passed her the drink.

"Thank you."

"How was your day?" said Harry.

"Oh, so-so. What about you?" replied Becs.

"Yeah, not bad... busy." He took a sip of his beer and, for a moment, he couldn't think of anything else to say.

He played safe. "Shall we go through?" he said and led Becs to the dining room.

They were shown to a table by the window overlooking the bay by a waiter who presented them with two menus. Harry chose a steak, Becs, pasta and they continued with the small talk, bouncing around meaningless questions like a ping-pong ball. It was that period of uncertainty when you first meet someone. That guarded time when you don't really know what to say in case you give the wrong impression or offend them in some way by saying the wrong thing.

The wine waiter appeared and Harry ordered a bottle of red.

The meals arrived and the wine was opened. After the first glass, it was Becs who fired the first tricky question.

"So when do you start prospecting? I take it that's why you're here... a geologist I mean."

Harry was a bit taken aback. Given the security and the issues, he wasn't going to give much away.

"There's still a lot to do," said Harry.

"But you must have an idea?" said Becs.

"Yeah, but it's all a bit sensitive as you know."

"Don't worry, I won't say anything," said Becs.

"It's ok. We're still preparing but it won't be too long," replied Harry, which he thought would answer the enquiry but still be vague enough.

Becs picked up the wine bottle and refilled their glasses.

"Did you read about that student that was murdered?" she said. Harry had a mouth full of wine and almost choked.

"Sorry, went down the wrong way," he said as he regained his composure from the coughing fit.

"Yes, I read about it in the Gazette, sounded dreadful."

"She lived in Launceston Towers," said Becs.

"Really? I had no idea," said Harry.

"Terrible business," she said. She took another sip of her drink and changed the subject.

"Have you been to the beach here?"

"No, not yet, haven't had the time."

"Oh, you should it's fabulous. Maybe we could go down there together sometime. What do you think?"

He looked at her eyes, her expression had changed. She leant forward again. Harry couldn't avert his gaze; she noticed and smiled.

"Yes, that would be great. What about the crocs?"

"They won't be a problem; they fence off a section so it's safe enough."

"Yeah, ok, yes, let me know when you're free," said Harry.

"I will," she said and finished her glass. The bottle was empty. "Fancy a refill?"

Harry finished his glass. "Yeah, go on, why not?" he said.

"We could take it upstairs," she said.

Harry looked at her; he felt a sensation in the pit of his stomach. "Ok, sounds good to me," he said.

The waiter was summoned and a bottle duly ordered. Becs made a move for Harry's hand and held it. She started rubbing her fingers across the back of his wrist. Her eyes locked on his. It had been unexpected. Harry thought she had been friendly but slightly distant; he hadn't found conversation easy. Perhaps it was the wine: she had consumed three glasses and a gin and tonic.

Harry signed for the meal and drinks and Becs held his hand as they walked out of the restaurant towards the lift. Becs pressed the call button; Harry was holding the bottle of wine. The lift opened and they got in.

"Your place or mine?" said Becs and started laughing.

"I think all the rooms are pretty much the same," said Harry.

Becs pressed two. "Mine it is then."

There was a silence as the elevator trundled upwards before jolting to a halt on the second floor.

"Two one eight," she said as she walked down the corridor.

She opened the door. As Harry had guessed, the room was the same layout and decor as his. He put the bottle of wine on the dressing table opposite the bed. Becs went over to him and suddenly they became consumed, their lips locked together, tongues exploring, hungrily. Harry started to unbutton Becs' blouse. She was reciprocating with Harry's shirt. Both were discarded to the floor. Becs unclipped her bra and Harry feasted on the pleasures before him. Becs started moaning softly as he gently kissed and teased her nipples. She started negotiating the zip on his jeans and pushed them down to his ankles. She could feel the hardness of his penis in her hands. Their lips met again, deeper and deeper, the carnal need rising to a crescendo.

She broke away momentarily and took off her jeans and pants. "Let's get into bed; it will be more comfortable," she said.

Harry stripped off and got in beside her; the kissing continued, becoming more and more urgent. Then he moved on top and she gently guided him into her. There was a frenzied coupling, building to an incredible crescendo; Becs couldn't hold back and screamed as she reached orgasm... then the release. They both lay there staring at the ceiling, bedclothes on the floor. Harry was panting from the exertion.

It was Becs who broke the silence. "That was good."

"You can say that again," said Harry.

She turned over and kissed Harry. "Thank you," she said.

"My pleasure," he said and started to laugh.

She cuddled up to Harry and lay in his arms. She looked up at him. "You will be careful, Harry, won't you."

"Yes, of course, why wouldn't I be?"

There was a pause. "Because I think you're one of the good guys, and you may be in trouble."

Harry looked at her. "What do you mean?"

"Let's just say I have an interest in what goes on in Helvetia."

Harry sat up in bed. "I think there are a lot of things you're not telling me."

"But can I trust you Harry?" she said.

Chapter Fourteen

Harry looked at her. The confident businesswoman looked different, soft and warm. Trust was two-way.

"I could say the same?" said Harry.

"Yes, that's true. Ok, a trade, I'll tell you something then you answer me a question."

"Ok," said Harry.

Becs sat up. "I'll pour us a drink," she said and went over to the dressing table and dispensed two glasses of red wine. Harry watched her naked body walking towards him. She handed him a glass and got into bed.

She took a large sip of wine and looked at Harry. She was sat with her legs folded, knees to her chest, pondering what to say. "There are things I could tell you which may be dangerous. It could even get me killed so you could say I'm trusting you with my life."

"Yes, I can identify with that; you can trust me," said Harry.

"Ok... let me tell you one or two things about Helvetia." She took another gulp of wine. "They are ruthless and totally driven by the need to make money."

"Aren't most businesses? We do live in a capitalist society," countered Harry.

"Not like this; bribery, corruption and murder are part of the company's mission statement."

Harry considered this remark. "Go on."

"I told you that I worked on the Helvetia portfolio in Adelaide. That's true; it was when they were just starting to consider prospecting for Uranium up here, about eight or nine months ago."

Harry looked at her. "Yeah, you said."

"Well, there were things I saw which made my flesh crawl; huge sums of money being passed to politicians and

Aboriginals, local people being threatened and intimidated, all sorts of things. I was so appalled I left the law firm and joined a national newspaper as an investigative reporter. I used to be a journalist till I switched careers. I knew the editor quite well and told her that I wanted to expose what was happening, said I could get them an exclusive story and they gave me a twelve-month contract."

"Who are 'they'?" said Harry.

"The Tribune," said Becs.

"You work for The Tribune? The Sydney Tribune?" Harry was aware of this prestigious newspaper, renowned for its tenacious journalism.

"Yeah, joined them six months ago."

"And you need my help?" said Harry.

"No, well not really, I probably know more about the business than you do but I do think you need to know what you're caught up in."

"But I'm just a geologist," said Harry. "I've had no involvement in, or knowledge of, any of the things you're talking about."

"So you say, but it's only a matter of time."

"What do you mean?" said Harry.

"You are not incorruptible, despite what you think. You're working on this project which means you are endorsing the organisation."

"Hmm... not really, I don't see it like that. I just study rocks and minerals; it's what I do, it's what I've trained for."

There was a silence as Harry considered her words. "Ok, what do you want from me?"

"I'm not sure yet but you could let me know what's going on," replied Becs.

"But as I said, I don't know what's going on. I just do what I'm told."

Becs took another sip of wine. Harry was deep in thought; he looked at her.

"There is one thing. Someone did try to kill me on Monday," said Harry.

"What?!" said Becs.

"Yes, someone put a snake in my car. Nate thinks it was one of the eco lot that are trying to disrupt the project."

"Well, they're certainly capable," said Becs.

"You know them?" said Harry.

"I know some of them; that girl who got killed, the one in the paper."

"What about her?" said Harry.

"I interviewed her a few times, Sophie Darling, a lovely girl but a little misguided. She was with Jimmy Harvey." Harry looked blank. "The professor... the one that's missing."

"Really," said Harry. "I thought I read he had a family."

"He has but she had been with him for some time. They were always at rallies together. That's how I got to meet them. I attended one of the rallies here in Darwin at the University. I could understand why she was attracted to him; old enough to be her father but he did have a certain... charisma."

"How did you get involved?" asked Harry.

"I pretended to be sympathetic to their cause. Then I got to hear certain things... two Aboriginals went missing a few weeks ago."

"Yeah, I heard about that. They said they just jacked it in. Nate's recruited another couple of guys."

"From Miki Rey?"

"Yes... you know him?" said Harry.

"Only by reputation... smart cookie, almost as hungry for money as Helvetia, it gives him power. He was playing hardball with the company on mining rights, screwed them for a wad of cash I heard. Has he signed anything yet?"

"Last week," replied Harry.

"Yeah, but my guess is it'll be for preliminary exploration only. Am I right? He'll be back for more if you find anything. That's what he's like."

"Yeah, preliminary exploration... you could be right... but how do you know all this?" asked Harry.

"I've got some good connections in the Aboriginal community; that's all I can say."

She took another sip of her wine; her glass was almost empty. "Then there's the bloody politicians, crooks the lot of them. To my reckoning, they've taken at least ten million dollars in back-handers."

"That's crazy," said Harry.

"Yeah, as I said, my former employers were involved in the transactions. Don't worry; it will all seem above board, you know, consultancy fees, that sort of thing. Nothing on the face of it to indicate anything shady or illegal; they covered their tracks pretty well."

Harry was deep in thought. "You were saying... about the Aboriginals."

"Yeah, the two that went missing; I heard about them from Sophie. She said they were at one of the rallies and after the speeches went up to her and said they had some problems in their village and didn't know what to do. She never saw them again."

Harry was listening intently; Becs was staring at the ceiling as she spoke.

"What problems? The village?"

"They told Sophie some of their people were getting sick; they thought it was because of the mining over at Ranger. After she told me this story, I went out there to speak to the men myself but the villagers told me they had just disappeared. While I was there I took some samples of their water supply and sent them away for analysis. We found that it contained dangerously high traces of uranium oxide."

"What?!" exclaimed Harry.

"Yeah, the village cancer rates are off the scale, around seventy-five percent higher than the national average."

"But surely other agencies will have discovered this."

"Yeah, you would think so but the mining industry is very powerful up here and it earns a great deal of money for the Australian and local economy. The Aboriginals get a good whack of all mining royalties too so no-one's doing much rocking of the boat or, should I say, cash cow? That's the problem; there's no appetite to do anything, and with the new exploration looking like it's going ahead, it'll only get worse."

Becs turned over and put her arms around Harry.

"Now you understand."

"Yes, I think so," said Harry. He held her close.

"One other thing," continued Becs. "Don't be fooled by the Duchamp Foundation. It's just a front."

Harry said nothing about Marci's description.

"A front for what?" said Harry.

"Just about anything they can get away with. They present the minibuses to the community which is great but the so-called charity also funds their security operation."

"That makes sense; the buses here are being driven by the security guys," said Harry.

Becs continued. "Well, I can tell you a bit about them. They're recruited by a guy called Leonard Scheck."

"Scheck...? I met him on my induction," said Harry.

"Hmm, Herr Scheck... now he's a guy you should really stay away from. Ex-Stasi, the East German Secret Police," she clarified. "Recruited by Helvetia about three years ago with a hideous reputation but he certainly gets results. I checked and, since he joined them, there have been very few problems with the organisation getting mining licenses. Any opposition is... how can I put this delicately? Discouraged. It's only here that they've run into difficulties," said Becs.

"I'm not surprised. He's a really scary guy." Harry paused for a moment. "There is something I can tell you," he continued. "One of my colleagues back in Switzerland I worked with on my induction tried to warn me about things out here... she said it was dangerous."

"What was her name?" asked Becs.

"Tara," said Harry.

"Tara...? Tara Humphries?" said Becs.

"Yes," said Harry. "Do you know her?"

"Yeah," said Becs. "I met her when I was doing the prelim work and we kept in touch, you know, texts, the odd phone call... great girl."

"Yeah, she was... Did you hear she died...?" said Harry.

"What?!" said Becs. "How?"

"In a car crash, they said it was an accident but another guy in the department phoned me after it had happened and said he thought she'd been murdered."

"Fuck.... I had no idea... I wondered why I hadn't heard from her. I left a couple of messages. I just thought she was busy. Yes, that's entirely possible... murder, I mean."

"Jesus," said Harry. Becs was quiet for a moment.

"So where do you get all this information?" said Harry, breaking the silence.

"Can't say," replied Becs. She paused for a moment. "Well, actually, I suppose I can; it doesn't really matter now she's dead."

"Tara?" said Harry.

"Yeah, I told her I'd left the law and that I was working on a possible story and she fed me the odd snippet. She was very worried about what was happening... I had no idea she was dead; they must have found out?"

"Who?" said Harry.

"Duchamp, Scheck, Leganes... I don't know; they're all crooks," said Becs.

"Leganes? David Leganes?" said Harry.

"Yeah, he was just being driven by Duchamp but according to Tara it was him who was using Scheck."

"How did she find all this out?" asked Harry.

"She did a bit of snooping for me; you know the odd file, conversation."

Harry was very reflective following these revelations; it had put the whole project into context and suddenly things started to make sense. It also explained Tara's warning.

It was Harry who spoke again. "I just wish I knew who tried to kill me. I don't think it was anyone from the company; they've been pretty supportive overall. Apart from Ying, now she's a strange one."

"Ying..? What does she look like?" asked Becs, sitting up on one elbow and looking at Harry.

"Short, tiny almost, long black hair, Chinese background, comes from Thailand I think... parents died in the Tsunami apparently."

"Hmm, don't recognise her at all but I'll ask around," said Becs.

They lay in each other's arms and Harry could feel himself drifting off to sleep.

"Do you want to stay with me tonight?" said Becs.

"Yes, that would be good," said Harry. "Just one thing."

"Yeah," said Becs.

"Friday," said Harry.

"What about Friday?"

"The trek... our initial exploration."

She kissed him. "How long will you be away?"

"Ten days, maybe less if all goes well," said Harry.

"Will I see you when you get back?" said Becs.

"I hope so. You can see me tomorrow night if you like, in my new flat. I have no idea what it's like so you'll have to excuse any mess."

"Yeah, ok. I'll give you my mobile number and you can text me the address."

She wrote it down on one of the hotel's complimentary notepads.

Harry stopped the night with Becs but as the sun dawned, casting a bright light above the curtains, he woke up thinking about the project and her revelations. He had no idea what he was going to do but he was committed to his present task. He would consider his options when it was completed. He quietly got out of bed so as not to disturb Becs and went to the bathroom. He needed to get back to his room as he had not packed and he would need to vacate the hotel. He checked his watch; it was five forty-five. He went over to Becs.

"Hi, I've got to go back to my room and pack. I'll call you later."

"What time is it?" said Becs as she tried to clear her head.

"Quarter to six... I need to pack my things," he repeated.

"Yeah, ok, you've got my number. Text me later," she said drowsily.

"Yeah, will do... bye," said Harry and he got dressed leaving Becs sleeping soundly.

Harry went back to his room and started getting his things together. He now had two suitcases and hand luggage, enough to hold his clothes and bits and pieces. He packed with no real enthusiasm; his motivation for the trek had waned since his chat with Becs.

He was starting to think about the security team and the

missing Aboriginals and the Professor, not forgetting the deaths of Sophie Darling and Tara of course. With Herr Scheck as their mentor, they were capable of anything. Then a recollection... the boat, the two security guys with the baggage... a body? It was a possibility but he had no idea what he would do with this information, in the wrong hands it could get him killed.

He went to breakfast and then signed out of his room and in two trips he had loaded the Suzuki and left for the office. He wasn't sure if the security team were following him on the way in but he hadn't seen them.

Tallara was on duty in reception once again.

"How are you, Harry? How's your leg?"

"Fine, thanks, much better," replied Harry and headed for the office. Actually, he realised, he'd completely forgotten all about the snake bite; he was feeling back to normal.

By eight o'clock, everybody was in including Nate, the two bodyguards and the two Aboriginals. There was going to be a briefing that would last all afternoon. Nate had warned. Then, they would leave for the depot to load the trucks up ready for the morning.

Harry's motivation gradually returned as the morning progressed. There was an incredible buzz which he hadn't experienced before as everybody strived to finish their part of the project.

Nate called everyone into the conference room at one o'clock and handed around sandwiches and pastries which Winda had been consigned to collect.

"As you're not coming with us, ya might as well make yourself useful," Nate had said to her.

Needless to say, his comments didn't go down well and Harry chuckled as he watched her reaction. She slammed the office door as she left to fetch the lunches. "Stroppy bitch," said Nate. Harry couldn't help laughing.

"Right, listen up," said Nate, bringing the group to order. Bits of sandwich flew from his mouth as he started to speak and he stopped for a moment to finish eating before continuing.

"Everything's ready for tomorrow. Harry's going to fill us in on the route again and the area we're gonna cover. Marci will tell us about the equipment and stuff we'll be taking. Our priority is to get the samples we need and get them back to the lab for analysis then our bit's done for the moment."

Nate stopped and took another bite from his sandwich. "Some health and safety stuff ya need to hear about. The terrain's gonna be ok for the first site but the valley may give us a bit of a problem, particularly as old Banjo and Charlie here refuse to come with us."

Nate scowled in their direction and they avoided eye contact and just looked at the floor.

"You're gonna need a good pair of boots, and strides... trousers," he said, looking at Harry. "Remember it's not the crocs that are the problem, it's the bloody mozzies. We'll be taking some medicine just in case but, as me old mum used to say, prevention is better than the cure. Then there are the wasps, they'll sting ya, and hairy caterpillars... if you see any of them don't touch 'em, you'll be out in a rash in seconds and the itching will drive you mad. We've got nets, sleeping bags, bunks to keep you off the floor. Don't forget your 'Rid-Off' or any other tropical bug spray you may want to bring. You'll need it. While you're out there don't pick up rocks or logs unless you have to and stand well back. There are Jumping Spiders." There were looks from the team. "The clue's in the title... then there's red backs and mouse spiders... oh yeah, and scorpions, not deadly but will lay you low for a week or two. Heinz and Pieter will have rifles in case of emergencies. Just don't go bathing in any of the creeks; bloody crocs everywhere. It means you might smell a bit when you get back but it's better than being a croc's lunch. Any questions?"

"What about medical evacuation, in case of emergencies?" said Marci.

"Yeah, good question; there's no mobile phone signal out there or internet but we'll have a radio phone and will be in contact with Den here on a regular basis."

Den nodded and took over.

"Yeah, I've alerted the National Park Authorities and explained our expedition. Although our dig is officially outside their jurisdiction, they've agreed to cover us in an emergency... subject to an appropriate fee I might add. They'll have a helicopter on standby."

"Too right... not bloody cheap either. I'll let Harry go over the route," said Nate.

Harry produced a large map of the area and pinned it to the wall along with smaller more detailed plans of where they would be drilling. "These are the most likely places we'll find uranium based on the geoscientific surveys you did," he explained to the group. It was only a short presentation but an important part of the overall briefing.

After Harry had finished, Nate looked at Ying. "What about you, Ying, anything more to add?" She just replied "no". Harry wondered what she was doing there.

After another half an hour of briefings from Marci and Den, who would be monitoring the whole exercise from the office, Nate dismissed the group. "We leave at three for the depot," he reminded everyone.

Harry remembered to text Becs with the address of the flat. Winda had collected the key from the letting agents earlier and it was safely in Harry's pocket. At two-thirty he received a reply from Becs; *'Look forward to seeing you later Becs x'*

By ten to three, everyone was packing their stuff away. Marci had packed the various pieces of scientific equipment they were going to need into two large leather cases; space was going to be at a premium. Banjo and Charlie were summoned to carry them to the cars. Harry would need to take his laptop which had all the information they were going to need; he wouldn't need an internet connection to access it. Luckily, he didn't have much to take from the office as his boot was full of his personal belongings. He would put the rest of the office gear on the back seat.

Everyone started to make their way to the car park; the lift was used to transport the heavy gear. Once loaded, Nate, accompanied by the two Germans looking like characters from 'Men in Black' with their suits and sunglasses, led the way to the depot. It was a small convoy with Harry following Nate and Marci bringing up the rear in her Fiat. Ying was sat next to her and the two Aboriginals were in the back. With limited boot space, they had the two leather cases on their laps.

The 'depot' was a warehouse adjoining a mining supplies company. Nate went into the adjacent office and collected the key while Harry and Marci parked up. Nate opened the roll-over doors and everyone filed inside. It was a comfortable size with plenty of room to move around. The two vehicles were lined up; the red Toyota FJ Cruiser looked brand new and the Scania was equally impressive. On the back was the ten-metre drilling rig which Nate had ordered. Nate looked at it with pride.

"Right, let's get loaded up," said Nate. "The tucker and water are next door. Banjo, you and ya mate nip and get it will ya and stick it on the back of the Toyota."

"There should be a portable refrigerator somewhere for the water and stuff we need to keep cool," said Marci.

Harry was looking around the Toyota. "Yeah, it's on the back," he shouted to Marci.

It took until almost four-thirty for everything to be loaded onto the two vehicles. Despite everything, Harry felt a degree of satisfaction and was looking forward to his first 'real' field trip; it was a chance to shine and show off his expertise. That was not vanity, just his competitive streak which was never too far away.

Nate dismissed the team and locked up. "Right, you need to be here bright and early; we leave at seven. Now go and get some kip, you're gonna need it."

There were shouts of goodbyes among the team. Harry noticed the two Aboriginals walking back up the road and he got in the Suzuki and caught them up. "Hey guys, hop in, I'll give you a lift."

"Thanks," said Banjo and he and Charlie got in the back.

"Where're you heading?" said Harry.

"If you can take us to the bus station that will be fine; we live in the north."

"Yes, I can do that. I'd give you a ride home but I'm moving into my flat today and I'm running short of time."

"It's fine, thank you," said Banjo.

In ten minutes Harry had reached the bus station, dropped off the Aboriginals and headed for his apartment. He was looking forward to having a more permanent base but he would miss the hotel comforts.

It was another ten minutes before he passed the Entertainments Centre and the laundrette, he turned left following the same route as the student had done the previous Saturday. He reflected on the turn of events and made up his mind to tell Becs what had happened.

He pulled up to the entrance of the tower block; there was a passcode for the underground car park and he consulted the piece of paper Winda had given him with the details on. He drove into the basement; it was a large area with spaces for about forty cars, all numbered. Harry checked for his allocated spot and parked up. He took his luggage out of the boot and with his laptop slung over his shoulder, managed to struggle to the lift. Within a few minutes, he was riding to the twelfth floor and his new apartment.

He took his stuff out of the lift and left it while he went to find his flat, 1203, which was just along the corridor. He unlocked the door, dropped off his first suitcase and laptop then went back for the rest.

Once in, he did a quick scan of his new home. The lounge was small but comfortable; there was a nearly-new settee in the middle of the room, a TV, one armchair, a small dining table with two chairs. There was a door at the far end of the room. Harry opened it and he was in the kitchen which had all the necessary appliances, fridge, cooker, store cupboards but no washing machine. The laundrette would have to do. Thankfully, the air-conditioning was working.

Off the lounge was a corridor with the bathroom on the left; just a toilet, basin and shower; then into the bedroom. It was smaller than the lounge but there was a double bed, cabinets either side, a dressing table and a reasonably sized wardrobe.

Harry was very happy with his new abode; he would be comfortable. It was almost six o'clock by the time he had sorted out the room to his liking and hung up his clothes. His first priority was to get some supplies. Given he would be away for possibly ten days, it was not worth getting much, but cereals, milk, coffee and tea would be essential.

He locked up and took the lift to the ground floor. The petrol station over the road also had a mini-market attached to it and he would be able to stock up from there; he would do a larger shop on his return.

Within ten minutes, he returned to his apartment with the shopping and a bottle of wine. He checked his watch again and had just enough time to shower before Becs arrived. The landlord had also supplied some towels and bed-linen, paid for by the office.

Harry changed and was ready for his guest just before seven. He looked out from his window; it faced the petrol station, the motel, launderette and the Entertainment Centre beyond that. He was looking for Becs' car but realised he didn't know what she drove. Outside the front of the building, there were about twenty spaces for guests and deliveries and after a few minutes, Harry noticed a white Audi pulling into one of the spaces. Although it was some distance Harry recognised Becs, straightaway. He called her on the phone.

"Hi, just seen you pull up. Go through the main doors and take the lift to the twelfth floor, I'll be here."

"Great, see you in a minute," she said.

Harry was dressed in jeans and a short-sleeved shirt and felt a twinge of excitement as he walked down the corridor to greet his guest.

A couple of minutes later, the lift opened and there she was. She was wearing a short summer dress, white, with a yellow pattern and light brown sandals. Her hair was down and makeup just right.

"Hi," said Harry as she exited the lift. "You look great."

"Hi, thanks," she said and they kissed, longer than a customary greeting, slow and sensual.

"Any more of those and we won't get any food," she said and laughed. "Here, I've bought you this... house-warming present," and she handed Harry a bottle of sparkling white wine. "Not champagne but as good as."

"Thanks, that's great, you didn't have to," he said and led Becs back down the corridor. "Just down here."

He opened the door. "Hey, this is ok," she said as she followed him inside and scanned the room.

"Yes, you'll have to excuse any mess, I've only been in an hour."

"Busy day then?" said Becs.

"You could say that; getting everything ready for tomorrow."

"Your trek…you will look after yourself won't you?"

Harry took hold of her hand and drew her to him. "Yes, I will," he said and the kissing started again.

Becs drew away. "I think we better get some food, don't you?"

"Yes, good idea. Do you know anywhere good around here?" said Harry.

"Not really," said Becs.

"There's a bar just down from the Entertainment Centre which sells food but I haven't eaten there."

"Sounds good to me, let's check it out," said Becs.

Harry took his wallet from the table and put it in one of his trouser pockets; he put his keys in the other.

"Let's go, then," he said.

As they waited for the lift the corridor was empty and Harry again engaged Becs in some serious kissing, which continued all the way to the ground floor. Becs was looking flushed as they exited the lift.

"Good grief Harry, you've made me wet," she said and exhaled.

"Plenty more where that came from," said Harry.

"Pleased to hear it," said Becs and they walked out of the complex and retraced the steps Harry had taken earlier.

It was another beautiful evening, warm but with a dry heat, little humidity. There was a smell of Eucalyptus in the air from the many trees that lined the road as they walked along towards the bar.

"I need to tell you something," said Harry and he related his laundrette experience on Saturday and seeing the student.

"You saw this guy follow her?" said Becs.

"Yeah, well that's what it looked like. She left the laundrette and then one of the guys got out of the minibus and appeared to be following her. I saw her cross the road by the garage but I didn't see her go into the flats, she was too far away but the guy went in. I didn't think any more about it until I read in the paper that she'd been killed; I recognised her picture."

"Have you been to the police?" said Becs.

"No, I just haven't had the time what with all the preparation that's going on and to be honest, given the situation, I didn't really want to get involved."

"Yeah, I can understand that," said Becs.

"Do you think I should go to the police?"

"No, not at the moment; I've got a contact in the Headquarters on Smith Street. I'll give him the nod and see what he says. He may need a description."

"Well, as I said it was definitely one of the Duchamp minibuses, that's why I noticed it but I've not seen either of the men before, or since. They weren't any of the usual guys. There was another thing," and Harry described the incident at the Yacht Club. "I've not told anybody," he added.

"Yeah, probably wise. Leave it with me," said Becs.

"Do you think they've murdered the professor as well?" asked Harry.

"Could well have but he didn't make many friends up here; certainly not in the mining quarter... could've been any one of them. Of course, now the press have got hold of this gambling story, which I'm sure is not true, he's being slurred by all and sundry."

"Yes, I noticed the papers had gone quiet about his disappearance," said Harry.

"Yeah, no-one's bothered anymore. Someone's done a good job in dampening the story," said Becs.

They turned the corner and the bar was on the left. There

was a menu under glass outside on a dais and they inspected the food on offer.

"This looks ok," said Harry. "Not sure about Kangaroo steak, though."

"No, I think I'll give that a miss," said Becs.

They went inside; it was quite busy. The clientele was mainly young, many students it seemed, and the noise level resonated with the sound of urgent chatter. There was a long bar on the left with several staff members serving waiting customers. At the back, Harry could hear the clacking of balls on a pool table and could see a large screen TV with a scattering of lads watching a soccer match. There was a seating area to the right which was cordoned off for diners and Harry and Becs walked over to be greeted by a young lady in a waitress uniform.

"Table for two?" said Harry and the girl escorted them to a table in the corner which was comparatively quiet and handed them two menus.

"Can I get you any drinks?" she said and Harry ordered half a lager, Becs a large red wine.

"So how was your day?" said Harry.

"Yeah, it was ok," she said. The waitress returned with the drinks and took their food order, they both opted for a chicken dish.

"I've been doing a bit of digging around about your Thai girl. I haven't found anyone called Ying but there is a Chinese girl involved with one of the groups. I tried to get a name but no-one seems to know."

"Thanks for that," said Harry and took a sip of his beer. "So when are you going to run the story?"

Becs thought for a moment. "Not until I get more information. I can't go in with half the tale."

"Yeah, I can see that. I've been thinking about what you told me and I will help if I can," said Harry. "I would love to see

Tara get some justice."

"Thanks," said Becs.

They continued chatting over dinner. Harry learned about Becs' family; her father was a lawyer, her mother an administrator. She had two sisters, one still at university, the other in Corporate Entertainment which was ironic. He told Becs about his time at university and for the first time in a long while described his near death experience in the cave. It was a comfortable discussion, as close friends might have.

They left the bar around nine-thirty and walked arm-in-arm back to the flat. It was quite dark by this time and the street lighting not that efficient. Neither of them would have noticed two men in the shadows of the buildings on the right-hand side of the road who were watching them as they went by, and then followed.

The couple reached the flats. "Are you coming up for a night-cap?" said Harry as they reached the front of the building.

"I hope it'll be more than a night-cap," said Becs and kissed him passionately.

"You're very welcome to stay but I do have to be out by half-six."

"Ouch," said Becs. "That's early."

"Yes, it's Nate's idea; he wants us on the road for seven."

The two men watched and noted, then disappeared.

Back in the flat, as soon as they were through the door, they became engrossed in each other. Becs removed Harry's shirt and then revealed another surprise for him. She lifted up her dress and took it off. She was totally naked.

Harry gasped. "Wow, have you been like that all evening?"

"Yes," she said. Harry was lost for words.

The new apartment was well and truly christened. Becs decided to accept Harry's offer to stay the night.

The alarm clock woke them both at six a.m. to groans of

disapproval.

"Bad timing," said Harry,

"You can say that again," said Becs and Harry went to the bathroom while Becs made the coffee.

By six-thirty, Harry was ready to leave and Becs was collecting her bits together.

"Thanks for everything, I hope I'll see you when I get back?" said Harry.

"Yeah, hope so, too," said Becs.

"I'll call you if I can but there won't be any signal once we leave Jabiru."

"I know that, don't worry, just look after yourself," said Becs.

They kissed again. Harry had managed to pack the clothes he would need into a hold all together with his toiletries. He picked up his laptop, wallet and luggage and escorted Becs to the lift. She was still wearing her sundress but with underwear this time.

They said their goodbyes and Harry watched the Audi drive away before descending to the basement to collect his car. It was another hot day, the temperature was already in the twenties and he had the window down as he drove to the depot. He couldn't remember the journey, a mixture of tiredness and lack of concentration; his mind was elsewhere.

He reached the warehouse and he could see Nate's jeep and Marci's Fiat. It was a couple of minutes before seven o'clock.

Just as he was getting out of the car, his phone rang. Thinking it might be Becs, he pressed the green button.

"Hi?" he said.

"Harry is that you. C'est Monique."

"Monique...? How are you? Are you ok?"

"I am in Paris but I'm effrayé... er, scared... Edward's security men, they might find me here... Samedi, Saturday, I will come to Australie. Harry... je t'aime............"

"Monique... Monique are you ok?"

The phone went dead.

Chapter Fifteen

Monique was sat on the Paris-bound train, waiting anxiously for it to leave Lausanne station. It had been half an hour since Francoise had dropped her off following her escape from the Chateau; so far, so good.

She nervously watched the Wednesday morning commuters coming and going from the carriage window half-expecting to see Scheck's security men searching for her at any minute. She pulled the curtain forward to obscure the view of her from outside. Every passenger that entered the first-class compartment was a potential threat and she avoided eye contact in the hope it would somehow make her invisible.

She checked her watch again; five past eight. The second hand sweeping around her Cartier watch showed no sign of stopping but she wished it would move more quickly. She picked up her newly-adapted mobile phone and tried the Paris number again. If she couldn't reach her sister, she would need a hotel tonight. It kept ringing out. She tried again, the same.

She looked once more along the platform; a few last-minute stragglers were rushing to get the train. Then, with a jolt, she detected movement. The station concourse and coffee shops appeared to move backwards slowly; an optical illusion as the train departed the station. It quickly gathered speed and Monique breathed a sigh of relief. She felt more confident now and looked around the first-class compartment at some of her travelling companions; mostly businessmen.

She started to relax; her plan had gone better than she had hoped. Much of it, she knew, was down to Françoise; she could never have managed it without her and would be eternally grateful for her loyalty. She would always be in her debt. There was a sense of relief at escaping the clutches of her domineering husband but the sense of frustration at being kept a virtual prisoner had been replaced by fear. She had no idea what Edward's reaction would be but given his track record, it was likely to be extreme.

She dozed for much of the journey having not had much sleep, interrupted only by the ticket collector and the 'executive' attendant who seemed intent on supplying a continuous stream of coffee and pastries.

The train reached the outskirts of Paris just after eleven-thirty and weaved its way through the east of the city. Monique stared out of the window at the graffiti-strewn buildings, neglected and defiled, as it snaked through the outer suburbs towards its destination. Neglected and defiled; she could identify with that.

It was just before midday as they entered the Gare de Lyon, a major transport hub and the terminus for rail passengers from much of Eastern Europe. The train attendant helped Monique collect her luggage and escorted her from the compartment carrying her two suitcases; she was clutching her smaller valise and handbag. The man called for a porter and within moments a uniformed man arrived pushing a baggage trolley. Monique tipped the attendant with ten Euros. "Merci beaucoup," he acknowledged and doffed his company hat in respect.

As Monique exited the train, the heat of the day was noticeable after the controlled temperature of the carriage.

Despite many attempts, she still hadn't managed to contact her sister. A hotel seemed her only option. As she walked down the platform towards the main concourse, she decided to try one more time. Then on the third ring; "Oui, hello."

"Bernice, it's me, Monique."

"Monique! Oh my God, how are you?"

"I am ok. I am in Paris. I need a favour; can you put me up for a couple of days? I will explain when I see you."

"Of course; do you know how to find us?"

"I think so, are you still in Passy?"

"Yes, same place, Rue Raynouard."

"Ok, I will get a taxi; I am at Gare de Lyon. See you soon."

"Yes ok, take care."

Monique rang off and turned to the porter.

"Taxi, please," and they walked across the magnificent concourse towards the taxi rank. There was a short queue but within a couple of minutes she was overseeing the loading of her luggage into a taxi and tipping the porter.

"Sixty-eight, Rue Raynouard, please," she said to the driver.

As they set off, she remembered her promise and sent a text to Françoise; *'I have arrived in Paris. Thank you. I will never forget your kindness. Love Monique.'*

Monique prayed that Françoise would not be caught up in the ensuing investigation into her escape; a naive hope, as it would turn out.

It was a cloudy day but very warm and the driver was using the blower on the air-conditioning to keep the temperature cool. The noise precluded any discussion, not that one was likely to be forthcoming; Parisian taxi drivers are renowned for their gruffness.

Monique watched the buildings go by. There was a familiarity; it was her home town and it was good to be back. They drove down the Avenue de New York towards the Eiffel Tower. The Rue de Passy is in the sixteenth Arrondissement area, on the Trocadèro side of the river, and is lined with shops and boutiques. It is a busy one-way thoroughfare; Rue Raynouard is a side road flanked with apartments, two schools and offices.

The taxi ambled down the narrow street, mindful of wing-mirror collisions with cars parked on both sides. A couple of times it had to stop and pull to the side to allow oncoming cars to pass, the delays doing nothing to relieve Monique's anxiety. Around every corner, she imagined Scheck and his goons waiting in ambush.

Number sixty-eight was two hundred metres down on the left-hand side; a line of bushes fronting the block. The taxi stopped and the driver got out and helped Monique with her luggage and carried it to the entrance of the apartments. Bernice had seen the taxi pull up and was waiting for her sister.

She was two years older than Monique but shared the family traits, similar height, build, and hair colour, although Bernice had a more traditional styling than Monique. She was dressed in a pair of slacks and a patterned blouse.

Monique paid the taxi and there was an emotional greeting as the sisters hugged each other. Bernice was in tears at seeing her sister for the first time in six years. They managed to carry the suitcases between them to the apartment on the second floor.

"Where is Victor?" said Monique as she entered the flat.

"In Brussels for three days on business; went this morning."

"Is he still working for that economics organisation?" asked Monique.

"Yes, divisional director now so he is always away. Leave your cases in the hall, we can sort out your room later," said Bernice.

They walked into the living room. Monique looked around; it was elegant, a good size with a traditional high ceiling and tastefully decorated. There was a large sofa with three scatter cushions, TV, gas fire, two armchairs, dining table which had a vase of fresh flowers on top and four chairs around it. There was a box of children's toys in the corner.

"Sorry, I haven't had time to tidy up you must excuse the mess."

"Don't worry; I am just so pleased to see you... and grateful you could put me up at such short notice," replied Monique.

"Sit down, I will make a coffee and you must tell me what has happened," said Bernice.

"Thank you. Where are Sophie and Guy?" asked Monique. She had never met her niece and nephew and was looking forward to seeing them.

"Both at kindergarten, I will pick them up at three o'clock. They will be so pleased to see you. They think you are a fairy princess, living in a castle."

"It has been no fairytale I'm afraid," said Monique.

A few minutes later Bernice returned with two mugs of coffee and some biscuits.

"I will do some lunch later, these will keep us going," she said.

"Thank you," said Monique. She was sat at the dining table and Bernice sat opposite. She picked up Monique's hand and squeezed it.

"It is so good to see you. I have really missed you."

"Yes, I've missed you too. It has been a difficult time."

Monique explained how Edward had changed from when they were first married and had become more and more controlling. "I had to do many things I did not want to do," she said without elaborating. "Then a few days ago someone tried to kill us outside a hotel."

"What?!" exclaimed Bernice. Monique explained the circumstances.

"Yes, it was terrible. Then he would not let me leave the Chateau alone and the last time he went away to Frankfurt, last week, he had me locked in my room... no phone, no Internet. I was a prisoner. I just had to get away."

"How did you manage to escape?" asked Bernice.

"My assistant, Françoise, she helped me. I could not have done it without her."

"But what will you do? Long term I mean."

"I will get divorced, I cannot live like this. I am planning to go to Australia as soon as I can get a ticket. I am worried he might find me here."

"Australia...? That's a long way... why there?"

"I have a friend there..." replied Monique.

"Do you think you are in danger?"

"No, I don't think so, I hope not, no but I just don't know how Edward will be when he finds out. He is obsessed with money... and power. He treats me like one of his possessions. This will be a blow for him, to his ego, I mean. He never likes to lose."

"Won't he look here?" asked Bernice, who was listening to her sister with concern.

"I do not think so. He does not know where you live... and I hope I will be away by the weekend."

They continued to catch up; their closeness as sisters had returned.

Over recent years, the pair had become estranged. Bernice thought it was because Monique had become a high-powered business executive and had no time for her family. Communication had drifted to the extent it had become just an exchange of Christmas cards.

"I had no idea things were so bad," said Bernice as Monique described some of Edward's more extreme behaviours.

"He even wanted me to sleep with men to secure business deals."

"What?!" exclaimed Bernice.

"Yes, they were mostly Arabs but I refused," said Monique.

At just before three o'clock, Bernice announced she would need to pick up the children. "You could come too."

"I will need to change," said Monique. "Just one minute."

"Of course, I will show you."

Like many in this wealthier part of Paris, the apartment had three bedrooms; the two children shared a room and the third had been used as a guest room. Bernice helped Monique with her bags and led her to her room.

"Please help yourself; use the wardrobe and cupboards if you like. I will text Victor and let him know you are here."

"He won't mind will he?" asked Monique as she started emptying her suitcases and putting her clothes on the bed; she would sort them later.

"No, no of course not, you are my sister."

Bernice left Monique to change and freshen up. A few minutes later the pair left the apartment to collect the children from kindergarten.

"They will be so pleased to see you," said Bernice.

"I will be pleased to see them also," said Monique.

The school was very close, just a couple of blocks away and the two children ran excitedly to their mother when Bernice appeared at the gate. She hugged them each in turn.

"You see this lady here?" said Bernice to the children. "She is your Auntie Monique; the one who lives in the castle."

Their eyes widened. "You are a princess," said Sophie, the elder sibling.

"No, but I do live in a castle," said Monique. She picked Sophie up and hugged her.

"You are so big. How old are you?"

"I am four," said Sophie. "Guy is three."

"Hello Guy," said Monique, and picked him up too.

Guy did not seem so sure about his Auntie and stretched out his hands for his mother.

The four walked back to the apartment, Monique holding hands with Sophie, Bernice with Guy; the children chatting animatedly about their day.

It was midday back at the Chateau and concern had started to grow about Madame Duchamp's whereabouts. Reception had tried to pass on telephone messages but there was no reply from her extension.

Lucy Bainbridge was on reception. "Has anyone seen Madame Duchamp?" she called as Leonard Scheck walked past. There was no reply from those around her. She looked up at the security chief.

"Herr Scheck, have you seen Madame Duchamp? No-one seems to know where she is. Her diary said she had a hairdressing appointment but that was much earlier. She should have returned by now."

"No, I have not seen her," he said sternly to the reception manager.

He called Kurt; they spoke in German.

"Kurt, it is Scheck; meet me at Madame Duchamp's quarters. We may have a problem."

Scheck had access to Monique's rooms and tapped in the passcode. He knocked on the apartment door. "Madame Duchamp, are you there?"

There was no reply.

Scheck used his key and went inside, calling as he went through the rooms. He checked the wardrobes.

"Her clothes have gone," he shouted to Kurt. He opened the drawers to the dressing table, "and her jewellery. Have a look around; see if there is anything that might tell us where she might have gone."

The two rummaged through the apartment. Kurt came into the bedroom where Scheck was going through the pockets of the clothes that Monique had been unable to take with her.

"I've found this," he said and showed Scheck the brown medicine bottle. There were two tablets inside. Scheck shook the bottle producing a sharp rattle. He read the label. "Where did you find this?"

"In the trash bin," replied Kurt. "What are they?"

"Sleeping tablets," said Scheck.

"Perhaps she was taking them," said Kurt.

"Possibly, but I don't think so. There are two left in the bottle; why would she throw it away?" There was a pause. "Do you remember Herr Duchamp this morning?"

"Yes, he was not himself."

"No, and I think I know why," said Scheck. "Come, we have work to do."

They left the apartment and went back to reception. "Can you speak to Madame Duchamp's salon and see what time she left," said Scheck to Lucy Bainbridge.

Lucy went to the office and came back a few minutes later. Scheck was on his mobile phone; he dropped the call. "Well?" he said.

"They said she left about ten o'clock," replied Lucy.

Scheck was thinking. "What about Frau Fouvert? Where is she?"

Kurt cut in. "I have spoken to the gate. She was here this morning, very early about half past six, then left to take Madame Duchamp to the salon. She has not returned."

"That is early for a haircut, I think. What time does it open?"

"About eight-thirty, I think," said Lucy. "I use the same one."

Scheck was getting angry; Kurt recognised the signs. "Something is not right; something is not right; we need to pay a call to Frau Fouvert, I think. Where does she live? Get me her address," barked Scheck to the reception manager.

Lucy opened up the personnel files on the computer and wrote it down on a piece of paper.

The address was in Denges, a picturesque village just outside Lausanne; about forty minutes away by car.

Kurt and Scheck headed out of the Chateau in a company Mercedes. As they approached the village, Scheck was reading the instructions provided by the receptionist who knew the area.

"Route du Lac," said Scheck. "Go right at the white house with the clock on top."

About three-quarters of a mile, they reached a row of cottages, typical Swiss chalet-style architecture.

Françoise's Fiat was parked outside the last one. "Here I think," said Scheck.

Kurt parked the car behind the Fiat and the pair got out and looked around. It was almost two o'clock and the area was deserted. Scheck scanned the terrain; it was verdant, and flat, although the ever-present mountains loomed large in the distance like sleeping giants. It was, unsurprisingly, a farming community with fields of crops; a tractor could be heard in the distance.

Scheck walked up to the front door; he could hear the sound of a young child shouting playfully. There was a bell push and Scheck pressed it; a chime resonated inside. The door opened and straight away Françoise recognised Scheck. He pushed the door open and barged in. Kurt followed.

"Get out, what do you want? I'm calling the police," she shouted.

They pushed her into the living room and onto a three-seater sofa. A small boy was on the floor playing with a toy car. The sight of his mother being pushed around frightened him and he started to cry.

"Shut him up or I will," shouted Scheck to be heard over the boy's wailing.

Françoise picked up the boy. "Shhh, it's ok, it's ok," she said. The boy went quiet and looked at the two men in turn.

Scheck sat alongside Françoise on the settee; she could smell body odour.

"I want to know where Madame Duchamp is," said Scheck. Françoise said nothing.

Kurt was looking around the room and took an interest in a

photo frame with a picture of a family group taken on holiday.

"Nice family," said Kurt, picking up the picture and showing it to Scheck.

"Yes," said Scheck. "It would be a shame to upset it in any way."

"What do you want?" said Françoise.

"I just told you. I want to know where your boss is," said Scheck.

"I do not know where she is. I took her to the salon this morning; that is all I know."

"But why so early? They don't open till eight-thirty," said Scheck. Kurt was in the kitchen looking around.

"She had a meeting. They said they would open early for her. She is an important client."

It seemed plausible but Scheck was not convinced. Kurt returned from the kitchen with a small paring knife. He picked up an apple from the fruit bowl and started to peel it.

"I do not believe you," Scheck bawled at Françoise; his nostrils seemed to flare like some wild stallion. "Kurt; cut off one of the boy's fingers; any, it doesn't matter which,"

Kurt made a move towards the boy. Françoise was hysterical. "No, no don't hurt him, don't hurt him. I will tell you what I know. Don't hurt him. She is in Paris, she has a sister there. That is all I know. She told me to take her to the station in Lausanne."

"But why say she was at the salon?" said Scheck.

"She told me she wanted to get away from her husband; that is all I know."

Scheck looked at Kurt, then back at Françoise. "Is there is anything else you are not telling me?"

"No, no, I swear; that is all. I took her to the station in Lausanne." Françoise was holding onto her son tightly, tears flowing down her cheeks.

"Where does this sister live in Paris?" said Scheck.

"I do not know. I swear I do not know." Françoise was almost convulsing with fright; her son was also crying again seeing his mother's distress.

"If I find out you have not told me everything I will be back and I will be cutting off more than his finger," he said, nodding in the child's direction.

They left the cottage and headed back to the Chateau leaving Françoise traumatised.

It was almost three-thirty before they returned to base. Scheck and Kurt were discussing what they should do. "What time does Herr Duchamp arrive in Hong Kong?" asked Kurt.

"Not until midnight; we can't do much until then but get one of the cars ready. We may have a long trip ahead of us."

The flight from Geneva landed on time at Hong Kong International airport, just before midnight, Swiss time; it was seven a.m. locally. The four men teamed up in the arrivals hall and made their way to passport control, before collecting their luggage. Edward was still feeling the effects of the drug and had slept for most of the journey. Stephan Morin was concerned for his boss. They negotiated security checks and were at the carousel waiting for their baggage when Edward's mobile phone rang. He listened intently to the call.

"Herr Duchamp, it is Scheck, I have some news."

Scheck described what had happened and he believed that Monique was now at her sister's in Paris. He also mentioned the bottle of sleeping pills. "I think she drugged you," said Scheck.

"What?!" said Edward. "Yes, that would make sense."

"What do you want us to do?"

"Well, I assume she'll want a divorce but that cannot happen; there's too much at stake. We need to think of a different, more permanent solution. Can you do that, Scheck?"

"Of course, you're the boss. But how will we find her?"

"Have you still got the files that were on her computer?" said Edward.

"Yes," replied Scheck.

"It will be there, her name is Bernice. I don't know her other name."

"Ok, we will go to Paris first thing."

"Yes, as soon as you can. She may try to get to Australia."

"Australia? Why Australia?" said Scheck.

"Just a hunch; she knows someone out there," said Edward.

"Leave it to me," said Scheck.

"Update me as soon as you have news," replied Edward and rang off.

Scheck moved quickly. He accessed his computer and the files he had downloaded from Monique's laptop. He opened the 'contacts' file and sure enough just five names down the list, 'Bernice'.

He jotted down the address then called Kurt.

"Get in touch with Helmut, we leave for Paris at six tomorrow. Be here at the Chateau for then."

The following morning at six a.m., Scheck and his two cohorts were on the road. It was just over five hundred kilometres, about three hundred and ten miles to the French capital. It would take them well over five hours to get to the outskirts and then they were in the lap of the gods. Traffic locally was a nightmare, particularly the Boulevard Périphérique. Entering it from the south would mean about eight miles on the notorious Paris inner ring-road before they could turn off at the Bois de Boulogne.

As it happened, having made better time on the autoroute, traffic was reasonably light and they arrived at the Rue de Passy by one o'clock. Helmut was driving the last leg as he had driven in Paris many times before. They decided to park in one of the underground car parks and check out the area by foot after they had had some lunch.

Earlier that morning Monique was up around seven o'clock having heard the children calling for her. They were keen to see their Auntie before they went to school. After not too much persuading, Monique agreed to accompany them. It had been a wonderful evening playing with them and she was only now coming to terms with how much she had missed her family.

It was a cloudy but warm morning, and she dressed comfortably, jeans and tee shirt with her hair pinned back, hidden by a scarf. She would not be easily recognised by any casual observer.

Once the school run had been completed, Bernice suggested a look around the shops; it had been a long time since they had spent any time doing 'girly' things together.

"Yes," said Monique. "I would like that very much but I must find a travel agent and book my flight. I also need to find somewhere to change some money."

"Why don't you stay longer? It seems a pity that you arrive and then leave again in such a short time; the children would love it and I know Victor wouldn't mind," said Bernice.

"I would love to but I do not know what will happen when Edward finds out I have left."

"But I thought you said he was in Hong Kong."

"He is but he has a security team in Jura and they are evil. I will tell you this, I am sure that they have murdered people to get what they want. I think the sooner I leave, the safer I will be."

"But that is terrible," replied Bernice.

It was around ten-thirty by the time the sisters left the apartment and headed for the shops along the Rue de Passy. There was a travel agent next to a store selling exclusive leather goods and Monique went inside while Bernice explored the handbags.

It was a modern travel agent with pictures of exotic destinations on every wall. There were two seating positions with a computer monitor at each one. A young lady was sat behind the nearest.

"Can I help you?"

Monique explained to the agent her requirement. "I need a flight to Australia, as soon as possible, please."

"Whereabouts?" said the agent.

"Darwin... I need to go to Darwin; one-way only."

There was a great deal of tapping on the computer keyboard but eventually, the agent had found a flight leaving Charles de Gaul Airport at ten a.m. on Saturday morning.

"You will need to fly to Sydney and then connect to Darwin. It will be two days. You will need a visitor's visa as well but I can look after that for you."

"Thank you," said Monique. "Is there nothing tomorrow?"

"No, I'm afraid not," said the girl.

It was not ideal, Monique was desperate to leave Paris but there was no option. She was so concerned that she might be putting Bernice and her family in danger; she just couldn't risk that. She decided she would check-in at a hotel Friday afternoon, close to the airport. With Edward in Hong Kong, she hoped she would be safe until then.

She paid for the first-class ticket on her credit card; check in, eight-thirty.

"Oh, nearly forgot, do you exchange money?" she asked.

"Of course, we have a bureau de change," said the agent.

Monique handed over her Swiss Francs. "Can you change this into Euros please?"

"One minute," said the agent and she went into a small secure area which had a teller's position. Monique watched her make some calculation and return a few minutes later with her Euros.

Monique left the travel agent and went next door to meet Bernice. She was eying up a beautiful designer bag costing fifteen hundred Euros.

"Hi, how did it go?" asked Bernice.

"Fine, I can fly out on Saturday morning. They have seen to my papers, everything is arranged."

"Oh, I wish you could stay longer," said Bernice.

"I know but when everything is settled I will come back here to live. That is my plan. What have you seen... anything nice?" she said, changing the subject.

"It's all nice but that one there is beautiful," she said pointing at the one she had her eye on.

"I will buy it for you," said Monique.

"But you can't. It is too much."

"Yes, I can. It will be my gift to you to say thank you for looking after me."

"But you don't have to, you know that. You are my sister."

"Yes, I know but I want to," said Monique.

"Well, in that case, thank you," said Bernice.

So, with the bag purchased they looked for a coffee shop. "Come on, there's one in the Passy Plaza," said Bernice. She felt like a kid again reunited with her sister.

Passy Plaza is a small shopping mall about halfway along the Rue de Passy, containing some boutique shops and a supermarket. It is a favourite place for people to stop and people watch over a coffee. Monique and Bernice found a seat in the open cafe and while Monique went to get the drinks Bernice was quick to open her purchase and do a more detailed inspection. Monique returned with two coffees.

"Thank you for my present, Monique; I will treasure it forever."

"I'm happy that you like it," said Monique, and they continued chatting until it was time for lunch.

As the sisters walked out of the Mall, three men were on the escalator surfacing from the lower floor where they had visited the supermarket to get some supplies and cigarettes. They turned left into the coffee shop and sat at the table recently vacated by Monique and Bernice; such is fate.

Back at the apartment, Bernice served soup and bread rolls for lunch. After they had eaten, Monique went to her handbag and gave her sister an envelope, A5 size. It was quite bulky and Bernice could feel the square shapes of the plastic CD covers. Her time on the train had not been wasted. "I want you to look after this but please do not open it unless anything happens to me. There are some instructions inside. When I come back you can return it to me."

"Yes, of course, but it all seems very dramatic," said Bernice.

"I hope you will never have to open it," said Monique.

Bernice went over to Monique and hugged her sister. "Please keep safe, always," she said.

As they had done the previous day, at just after three o'clock, the sisters walked to the kindergarten to pick up the children. There was a great deal of excitement as Sophie and Guy saw the pair waiting at the gates. They excitedly discharged all their news in urgent chatter and walked hand in hand down the road to the apartment. In the thrill of the moment, Monique did not notice three men crouched behind a parked car opposite the apartment. The men waited for them to go inside.

"It's her," said Scheck. "Ok, we need a plan. Helmut, you collect the car and park it down here. We can stay undercover for a while and then make our move."

It took almost twenty minutes before they saw Helmut approaching them in the Mercedes. There was a parking space about fifty yards down the road from the apartment on the opposite side of the street.

"Perfect," said Scheck, as they got in. "Now we sit and wait."

"How long for?" said Kurt.

"As long as it takes... until it's dark," said Scheck.

"But that will be ages."

"But safer," said Scheck. "We don't know who else is in there. We will wait and watch and see if anyone goes in, then we will move."

"And in the meantime?" said Kurt, not really in tune with his boss's demands.

"You and Helmut can go for a meal. I will keep watch and call you if there is any news. Be back in two hours and then you can take over."

There was a reluctant acquiescence and Kurt and Helmut got out of the car and walked back towards the Rue de Passy. Scheck lit up a cigarette and considered the next move.

Monique and Bernice played with the children, oblivious to events elsewhere. Outside in the car, time passed slowly but Scheck's concentration did not waver. He had spent many hours in the Stasi on stake-outs.

Helmut and Kurt returned just after six o'clock and Scheck took his turn to eat. The three men were reunited by eight o'clock. The car, by this time, was full of smoke from the many cigarettes that had been consumed and Scheck held the door open for a while to clear the air. Helmut and Kurt got out to stretch their legs. It was still too light to make any moves.

With the children asleep, Monique had decided to have an early night. The bedroom matched the lounge; again there was a high ceiling with chandelier lighting and white wooden panelling around the walls. The room was completed by a very comfortable brass double bed. She had hung most of her clothes up in the closet and her jewellery case, which included Edward's gift, was on the dressing table. Monique was sat on her bed in her night attire, a sloppy top and pyjama bottoms; she checked the time, almost nine-thirty, seven o'clock in Darwin; he should be up and about by now.

She made the call.

"Harry is that you. C'est Monique."

"Monique...? How are you? Are you ok?"

"I am in Paris but I'm effrayé... er, scared... Edward's security men, they might find me here... Samedi, Saturday, I will come to Australie. Harry... je t'aime............"

Monique was distracted by a noise coming from the lounge. She switched off the phone and went to investigate.

"Ah, Monique, there you are. Edward was worried that you might have left without saying goodbye. He wants you to come back to the Chateau with us and he will discuss everything with you when he returns."

Monique exhaled nervously. It was the unmistakeable form of Scheck, standing there, a menacing presence.

Monique was petrified; Bernice was sat on the settee holding a cushion against herself.

"I am not going back... ever!"

"Well, I think you should reconsider," said Scheck. Helmut and Kurt were stood next to him looking equally as menacing.

"This is your sister, I think... so like you... and the children, we saw them earlier, delightful. I am sure you would want to see them growing up." The threat was obvious.

"Kurt go and fetch one of them, the boy perhaps."

"No, no wait. I will go with you. Do not hurt them. They have done nothing," said Monique.

"No, that is true but sometimes life is not fair," said Scheck.

"It is ok. I will come." Monique glanced at her sister with

a look of resignation. Bernice was still clutching the cushion in a vain attempt to protect herself.

"I need to change," said Monique.

"Yes," said Scheck. "That would be wise... Kurt, go with her."

Monique went back to the room wondering if there was any way of escape. She couldn't think of any. Then she rationalised; she had escaped once, she could do it again. He couldn't keep her a prisoner forever.

Kurt watched as Monique stripped off and changed into a pair of jeans and a tee shirt. She grabbed her jacket from the wardrobe.

They returned to the living room.

"That is better. We go now," said Scheck. He turned to Bernice. "And you, sister, if you want to see your children go to the big school then you will say nothing, understand?" There was no reply.

"I said, do you understand?" repeated Scheck. Bernice nodded.

"Good that is settled, we go now."

"What about my things?" said Monique.

"Leave them," said Scheck. "You have plenty more at the Chateau, I think."

Kurt opened the door to the apartment and Scheck pushed Monique through. Helmut closed the door behind them.

"What about the sister?" said Kurt as they walked through the main door and out onto the street.

"She will not be a problem," said Scheck. "In any case, we know where she lives."

Scheck sat in the back with Monique as the car started, Helmut was driving.

"You know where to go?" said Scheck.

"Yes," replied Helmut.

Scheck turned to Monique. "You know Edward is not happy with you since he found out you drugged him."

"I did not drug him, just helped him sleep," replied Monique.

"Well, whatever. We can do better than that."

Scheck pulled out a syringe from his pocket, took the protective cap off the needle and tapped the stem with his index finger to make sure it was primed. In one movement, he had grabbed Monique's wrist and turned it around.

"No, no," she cried as Scheck stuck the needle in her arm and pressed the plunger.

Within seconds, Monique was asleep.

Scheck checked her pockets. "There is nothing," he said to Kurt. "Let's get this done and get back."

After twenty-five minutes the Mercedes was heading down the Quai Marcel Boyer which runs parallel to the Seine on the left-hand side. Lights shone in the riverside bars on the opposite bank but this side it was completely dark, just commercial property, much of it derelict, or wharfs where boats carrying cement or other building material would dock.

The car turned off the main road into a deserted yard and stopped. Helmut killed the lights and turned off the engine. The three men got out of the car and between them dragged the sleeping Monique to the edge of the wharf, then pushed her into the murky, fast-flowing water, twenty feet below them.

"Ok, let's go home," said Scheck and they got back in the car and headed south.

Chapter Sixteen

Darwin, Northern Territories, Friday Morning

Harry got out of the Suzuki and collected his gear from the boot. He'd tried again to call Monique but the phone just went to voicemail. He was concerned for her safety given everything that he had heard over recent days but he was at a loss at what he could do.

"G'day Harry," said Nate as he approached the warehouse.

"Hi Harry," said Marci.

Harry exchanged greetings.

"We're all here except the bloody Chink," said Nate. "She'd be late for her own bloody funeral."

Harry stowed his gear in the Toyota. "Here, you'll need these," said Nate, tossing him the keys.

The Aboriginals and security guards were doing last minute checks when a ten-year-old rusting Nissan Sunny pulled up. It was driven by a scruffy looking young man in his early twenties with long unkempt hair, wearing an old tee shirt. Ying was next to him in the passenger seat. She got out and picked up her gear from the back then said something to the driver who blew her a kiss and drove away.

Harry looked at Marci who had also seen the exchange. "Didn't know she had a bloke," said Marci.

"Poor sod," whispered Nate to Marci. "About bloody time," he bellowed to the approaching Ying. "Don't they have alarm clocks in your dommo?" he added.

Ying ignored the comment and went to the Toyota and put her stuff on the back seat.

"Right, now we're all here," Nate glared at Ying. "Listen up; Harry's driving the Toyota and he'll be leading the way. Marci, Ying and Heinz, you ride with him; Banjo, Charlie and Pieter, You're with me in the truck. We'll drive out and you can park your cars in here."

Harry drove the Toyota out of the compound and stopped; Nate did the same with the Scania and then those who had cars parked in the warehouse; Nate locked up.

With everything ready, Harry led the small convoy towards the main road. Both vehicles were fully laden and it took some time to get up any speed but soon they were driving out of Darwin and down the A1. Once through Palmerston, there was only a spattering of dwellings; the odd ranch, a roadside diner. Having been brought up around a city, it was nothing like Harry had experienced before. The sheer vastness of the terrain was difficult to take in; that and the isolation.

The A1, Stuart Highway, is the main road leading to Alice Springs, over fifteen hundred kilometres away. It's a dual carriageway and driving conditions were good. The temperature outside the vehicles was approaching thirty degrees and the air-conditioning was on full blast. Traffic was light, just the occasional truck heading into town in the opposite direction. The glare of the sun meant sunglasses were essential. Through tiredness of the early start or anxiety, there was little in the way of conversation, everyone seemed to be locked in their own thoughts.

Around thirty miles later, the Toyota reached Bees Creek. Harry checked his rear-view mirror to make sure the Scania was with him. He turned left onto the Arnhem Highway which stretches over three hundred miles to Jabiru; mile upon mile of nothingness. The terrain was flat and totally interest-free. Shrubs, mango trees, palms, gum trees and Eucalyptus lined the road in various concentrations, from small copses to more dense areas; just the odd sign or bridge broke the monotony.

Harry was fascinated at the first town they passed through. It was called Humpty Doo. The word 'town' was an exaggeration; more a scattering of properties including the odd guest house.

Harry had noticed the unusually named place when he was planning the trip and was interested to see what it looked like; he'd enquired about it at the hotel. It was on the tourist map and a good place to view the Kakadu National Park he was told. There was not much else to see and the highway continued onward relentlessly.

Harry kept the speed down, mindful of the capability of the Scania following behind but they made good time gradually rolling back the miles. Then Harry noticed a sign for a truck stop ahead; they had been on the road for over two hours.

"Hey, there's a stop ahead; Marci, why don't you test out the radio and see if the others want to stop."

"Yeah, good idea," replied Marci.

She picked up the microphone which was attached to the dashboard with a plastic clip.

"Hey you guys... come in; we're stopping at this truck-stop. You ready for a break?

There was a static crackle then Nate's voice.

"Yeah, good call; me throat's as dry as a Nun's naughty," said Nate.

The Toyota reached the entrance to the truck stop just before the Mary River crossing, about halfway to Jabiru, and pulled into the large gravel parking area. The Scania followed a few seconds later and pulled up alongside it. Everyone got out of the vehicles; it was scorching hot in the direct sun. Harry stretched his back then went to see Nate.

"Everything ok?" said Harry as Nate approached.

"Yeah, no worries, mind you this is a doddle compared with what's ahead," said Nate.

"Twenty minutes, people," shouted Nate to the team who were starting to disperse. "And make sure you've got ya mozzie cream on; they'll have ya for breakfast out here."

Harry and Marci went to get a coffee, the Aboriginals and

Germans grouped together; Ying wandered off and was trying to make a call on her mobile phone.

"You won't get a signal out here," shouted Nate seeing her frustrated attempt. Ying gave a big huff and walked into the cafe to get some water.

Nate joined Marci and Harry who were drinking their coffee outside. "We'll stop for lunch in Jabiru and top-up the diesel; fill the jerry cans too. Don't want to run out of gas when we start going wild," said Nate. He went back to the Scania and checked the drill-digger to make sure it had not shifted in transit.

After the allotted twenty minutes everyone filed back to their transport; Harry got into the Toyota, opened a snack bar and started eating it. It was much cooler inside the car with the air conditioning and he had avoided the mess of melted chocolate on his khaki shorts.

"Everybody ok?" said Harry.

"Yes," said Marci. There was a nod from the German; Ying just stared out of the window.

It took another two hours to reach Jabiru at a steady fifty miles an hour. It was a small town, around fifteen hundred people, and was built to service the nearby Ranger Uranium mine which was vital for its economy. It was where Nate had met Miki Rey the previous weekend. The journey continued in relative silence although Marci and Harry did manage a conversation which helped to pass the time. As they entered the town, Harry pulled into another transport stop; this time with a small supermarket and other shops adjoining. He dropped off the passengers and then went to the filling station and topped up the diesel, then filled three large jerry cans. It would be enough for at least six hundred miles, certainly sufficient for the journey and a margin. Nate drove up in the Scania and did the same.

"Good journey, so far," said Harry as Nate came out of the pay kiosk.

"Yeah, it'll get a bit interesting from here, mind."

"Have you been around this area before?" asked Harry.

"Not where you're taking us but I've been in the Park loads of time," replied Nate.

The team were inside the cafeteria and Nate shouted to them. "Make sure ya get some food inside ya. It'll be the last chance to get some proper tucker for a bit."

Harry went outside and tried his phone; he had a 'one-bar' signal and called Monique again. It would be about three a.m. in Paris, and unsurprisingly there was no reply but it was worth a try. Then he noticed a number of missed calls; it was Becs' number.

He called her number and it was answered on the fourth ring.

"Harry, Harry, is that you? Thank goodness... I've been trying to contact you. I'm sure I'm being followed."

"Who by?" asked Harry

"I don't know but I'm worried it might be the same people who were following the student; the ones in the minibus you saw."

"Have you seen the minibus about?"

"No," replied Becs.

"Where are you now?"

"I'm in a cafe; I think I've shaken them off."

"What about the hotel? Do they know where you're staying?"

"I don't know."

"It might be worth moving just in case."

"Yeah, I might just do that," she said.

"I wish I could do more but I'm going to be out of range any minute and we might not be able to speak. I've got a radio phone but it's only two-way with the office."

"No worries. Look, I'll keep my head down until you get

back," said Becs. "I do have some other news, though. I've been making some more enquiries. That Chinese girl on the protest group?" she said. "Her name's Li Chun Zhi; they call her Lucy. They said she's a real radical, a fanatic, wants more direct action; a bit of a loose cannon apparently, that's what I heard. She's also mates with the Professor who's missing and Sophie, the student that was killed."

"Right, ok, thanks. Any news on the professor?" asked Harry.

"No, nothing, he's still missing. Oh, there was one other thing; that Lucy girl hangs out with some hippy fellow called Davey, drives around in an old..."

"Becs, Becs... are you there?"

Harry checked his phone; 'no service' it said. "Shit," he whispered under his breath.

He looked around and saw Ying was also on the phone. She seemed to keep looking around to see if she was being watched and was talking quite animatedly. Harry paid little attention and walked back into the cafe.

An hour later, the convoy was back on the road. It was just after one o'clock and the sun was blazing. Harry was still wearing his sunglasses and covered in cream of all descriptions. Marci was now navigating and had Harry's detailed notes of the journey on her lap. Ying and the German were in the back; neither had said a word since they'd left Darwin. Harry was trying to make sense of Becs' message. He hoped she would keep safe until he got back; there was little he could do at the moment.

Once outside Jabiru, the tarmac road became rougher and narrower, barely the width of the Scania as they headed north towards Gunbalanya, an Aboriginal settlement. They were now out of the National Park and in an area even more desolate if that were possible. Harry had to brake on more than one occasion to avoid a kangaroo that had strayed onto the road. "Now there's a sight you don't see in Norfolk too often," he said to Marci.

With no rain for three months, the scrub vegetation on both sides of the road was brown but the roadside trees still seemed able to survive in this inhospitable landscape. Harry pressed on.

Just outside Gunbalanya, he called Nate and they agreed to stop in the settlement for a break and refresh, the first sign of civilisation for an hour. Then it was back in the vehicles for the final leg, about fifty miles according to Harry's estimate.

Once out of the village, the tarmac ended and they were on dirt tracks. In the wet season, some of the route would have been underwater with crocodiles being a major threat. Although not officially a 'road', the track was well-worn and clear of obstruction, apart from the odd road kill that Harry negotiated. It would be mostly used by local Aboriginals and the odd tourist. Marci was in charge of navigation which was by no means straightforward. Every so often the track crisscrossed or joined other trails and it took all her powers of concentration to keep on the right path to reach the first drill site.

Harry kept the Scania in his rear-view mirror; it seemed to be keeping up with the pace he was setting. Marci called them a couple of times to check. After an hour or so, the terrain changed from flat and featureless to rocks and hills. Abandoned termite nests, some nearly three metres tall, littered the landscape. The hills were not soft and undulating like you might normally see in England, but sharp and jagged with cliffs which rose several hundred metres. It was like a moonscape. The terrain reminded Harry of his traumatic field trip to Derbyshire and the cave but hotter, much hotter. He shuddered at the thought. He was vigilantly negotiating the Toyota as the track took them down steep slopes to dry creek beds, then up the other side. For the loaded Scania, the journey was even more hazardous. This was the most difficult part of the journey.

It took almost another two hours before the GPS coordinates of the proposed site matched their position.

"We're here," shouted Marci as she looked up from the map, "Warren Creek."

Harry stopped the Toyota and everyone got out. It was almost as he had pictured it. There were features he recognised from the aerial reconnaissance photographs but that did not reflect the scale of the place. The immediate landscape was flat but about two hundred yards away the ground rose into a plateau about three hundred feet tall. The escarpment was peppered with rocky outcrops and tufts of vegetation. A bird of prey circled which Harry could not identify but it was big.

The Scania pulled up and stopped. "Jesus, Harry, that was some bloody magical mystery tour you took us on," said Nate as he climbed down from the cab.

The two Aboriginals and the German followed Nate and there was a buzz from the group as they examined their surroundings. Immediately they were attacked by flies desperately trying to reach their skin and drink the salt from their sweat. Swishing them away became an involuntary action.

Marci scanned the vista. "It's beautiful," she announced to no-one in particular.

"Yes it is," said Ying, which was her first effort at conversation since they had left Darwin.

"Well, we're not doing any drilling today. So I suggest we make camp and get some rest," said Nate. It was five p.m. and the group had been on the road for the best part of ten hours.

In his excitement, Harry was already picking up small rocks and examining them. He picked up a larger example and a monitor lizard darted out from underneath and skittered across the arid ground; Harry almost jumped out of his skin.

Nate saw him. "Careful Harry what ya picking up, ya never

know what's underneath 'em. If ya staying outside ya might wanna change ya strides as well."

Harry was still wearing his shorts which were comfortable for driving but inappropriate as protection from insects.

"Yeah, thanks, Nate, you're right."

Harry went back to the Toyota and retrieved the small case which contained his change of clothing. He took out his walking boots, thick socks and long khaki jeans; he put his jeans on over his shorts, tucked them inside his socks and applied more insect repellent.

"That goes for all of ya," said Nate, and the rest of the party took his advice and changed, except the Aboriginals who appeared amused at the antics of the others. It seemed they were immune from predatory insects.

Harry put on his 'mozzie-proof' hat, resembling a beekeeper's, with thin gauze attached which came down to his shoulders. Marci and Ying had done the same. It looked like an apiarist's convention.

There was a shout. "Hey fellas, can ya rig us up a fire of some description so we can get some tucker going." It was Nate giving instructions to the Aboriginals.

Fire was a real issue. In the middle of the dry season, a stray spark could prove catastrophic. Living at one with nature Banjo and Charlie were adept at building campfires; it was in their DNA. They examined the area carefully before deciding on an appropriate spot. Banjo grabbed a spade from the back of the Scania and started digging a trench, surrounding the spot with the excavated earth. Collecting fuel was going to be a problem; trees were few and far between. They would be restricted to using wood from the ground; chopping trees for the purposes of making a fire was illegal.

Harry surveyed the scene. The area looked like it had never been troubled by man's intervention, no sign of human life, litter, tyre tracks, nothing; it really was nature in the raw. After half an hour, Charlie had managed to collect some kindling and larger pieces of wood and within a few minutes, they had a fire going.

"If anyone wants any bush tucker you can catch your own witchetty grubs," shouted Nate to anyone who was listening.

Heinz and Pieter took out their rifles from the back of the Scania cab and walked around looking menacing.

"Not sure why those guys are here," said Harry, looking across at the bodyguards. Nate was taking out various pieces of camping equipment from the back of the truck. Harry was stood next to him.

"Me neither, mate. It was Leganes' idea, insisted they come along. Can't see we'll get many bloody eco-idiots out here. Still, they can help lug some equipment about, make them earn their beer."

"Here Heinz, set up these portable dunnies will ya," said Nate, lifting the chemical toilets off the truck.

There was a look of defiance on the German's face but he complied after expressing his reluctance.

It took a further hour but in that time the place was beginning to look like a campsite. The collapsible beds had been set up between the two vehicles with the fire in the middle. The bed legs were placed in metal containers, like drinking mugs without handles, in which Nate poured a small measure of diesel. "So the creepy-crawlies can't climb up," he explained. There was a sleeping bag then a mosquito net over each one. Food had been distributed and there were primer-stoves for heating. Nate placed some potatoes in the embers of the fire.

"There we are, just like the barbie back home," said Nate.

Banjo and Charlie sat away from the rest of the group and seemed to have their own food. Harry noticed and went to join them after he had eaten. He'd already thanked them for helping him after the snake bite incident but wanted to know more about the area, purely from a geological perspective. As they talked he became more and more interested in their culture and spiritualism.

"Why are you here if you believe that what we're doing is wrong?" he asked at one point.

Banjo looked at him; his white eyes against his dark skin seemed to penetrate Harry. He twisted his curls in his fingers; his hands were rough and gnarled from years of heavy labour. His voice was low, bass-baritone, and gravelly.

"Miki Rey, he tells us," said Banjo. "He is our elder, it is something we must do but we will not enter the valley."

"The lost souls?" said Harry.

"Yes but more," said Banjo. "I said before, it is the land of the Rainbow Serpent."

Harry was intrigued. "Tell me more."

Banjo looked at him, looking for sincerity, a serious interest, not just well-meaning or patronising curiosity. He was content.

"There are many tales about the Witij... it is what we call the Rainbow Serpent, which have been passed down for generations. It protects us and punishes evil; it is the giver of life... and taker. Always our people are careful not to disturb it; it is one of the Dreamtime creatures that shaped the land. To us, it is like your God."

Banjo looked at Charlie. "We are both Yolgnu. We were born in Arnhem Land; these traditions are important to us." He looked at Harry. "You need to be careful, my friend, not to disturb the Rainbow Serpent."

Harry reflected on this and thought he understood. Not for the first time he was starting to question the mission.

The team settled down to sleep about ten o'clock. They all had sleeping bags except the Aboriginals who just lay on blankets and Nate who decided to sleep in the cab of the Scania.

Harry found sleep difficult; not just because of the noise of insects and animals but because of thoughts of Monique, Becs and Banjo's warning. Eventually, he drifted off but was haunted by a dream; it was one he had had before, the one about the cave. He dreamt he was being swept away by a torrent of water of immeasurable force. He kept dropping below the surface, and then he would bob up and gasp for air. He could see the sides of the cave; there was no way out. He couldn't breathe; suddenly a hand grasped his shoulder and he woke up.

"You ok, mate?" It was Nate. "Only you were making a bit of a noise."

"Yeah, a dream, sorry."

"No worries, you try to get some sleep, we've got a lot to do tomorrow," said Nate.

"Yeah, will do, thanks."

Harry watched Nate walk back to the Scania, and then scanned the rest of the group. Everyone else seemed to be asleep.

Harry was covered in sweat. Through the mesh of the mosquito net he could see the stars as bright as he had ever seen them; a thing of beauty and wonder. Then he thought about the Rainbow Serpent and wondered if it would protect them or harm them.

It was first light when Nate called the group together.

"Come on ya lazy bastards, get ya backsides in gear; there's work to do," was his greeting.

The Aboriginals were already walking about; the Germans had taken it in shifts to keep guard. Heinz was splashing water on his face to freshen up. Washing was a problem; there was only bottled water and given the need to conserve it, only a limited amount was available. Harry decided not to shave for the duration of the trip.

By eight o'clock, Nate was starting to reverse the digger off the back of the Scania down the metal ramps with Harry on navigation duty. It wasn't easy but Nate showed great dexterity in manoeuvring the ungainly machine off the truck; they were ready to start drilling. Harry checked his GPS coordinates again and selected the first spot about fifty metres away from the camp. Marci had already taken some soil samples and was able to analyse them using a very expensive hand-held spectrometer. This would only give an indication of the soil content; the main work would be done back in the laboratory at the Chateau but the initial findings suggested they were in the right area.

They watched as Nate drilled deeper; Harry was stood next to Banjo who seemed less than happy with the activity.

"You alright Banjo?" said Harry.

"No, not really... this is not right."

The words came straight from the heart and Harry felt like a trespasser, an interloper.

"Yes, I understand," said Harry.

"No you don't," said Banjo and he walked away into the shade of the Scania.

There was a whoop as the first pile of earth was raised by Nate's drill. Marci moved in with her trowel. Ying just watched. "Come on Harry, give us a hand," shouted Marci.

A selection of samples was taken and stored in special metal cylinders, like small thermos flasks, about six inches tall, two inches in diameter. They had labels on the side and Marci wrote the GPS co-ordinates on each in a felt-tipped pen.

That continued for most of the day. Banjo and Charlie were required to fill in the holes from the drilling once samples had been taken but otherwise stayed well clear of the work. The Germans seemed to spend most of the time chatting and walking around with their rifles. "Ya won't get no crocs around here till the wet," Nate shouted at one stage.

Around four o'clock Nate called a halt. They were all happy that they had enough samples and would camp tonight and move to the second site in the morning. "If it goes as well as this tomorrow we'll be home early," said Nate portentously.

Marci had been in touch with Den in Darwin from time to time to let him know what was going on and that everyone was safe apart from the odd insect bite.

Later that evening Marci, who had been examining a selection of the day's samples on a laptop, announced her findings to the group. There was an air of excitement in her voice. The spectrometers had indicated a high yield of Uranium oxide.

"That's great," said Harry.

"Ripper," said Nate.

Marci looked at Ying who was laid on her bed staring at the sky. "What about you, Ying, aren't you interested?"

"Not really, I'm trying to sleep," she replied. Marci looked at Harry and shrugged her shoulders.

It was another night under the stars and despite the basic conditions Harry, tucked up in his sleeping bag, slept quite well; this time the bad dreams stayed away.

Sunday, day three, and at first light, the team broke camp. Banjo and Charlie were in charge of the fire to ensure it was properly extinguished, covering the area with earth. With everything packed away, there was nothing to suggest that there had been any trace of human interference. Banjo and Charlie seemed placated by the efforts of the team to leave things as they had found it; it was at Harry's insistence.

Getting the drill-digger back on the truck was another tricky exercise; Nate showed great skill in manoeuvring it up the ramps and back on board the Scania. It took about ten minutes but eventually, it was safely secured.

As Harry started up the Toyota, a bandicoot scurried from beneath the vehicle to find another hiding place. Harry watched it with interest scooting into the sparse undergrowth. He pulled forward and slowed for the Scania to catch up. It was after nine o'clock.

It took over two hours to travel the fifty miles to the second site. The group had kept the same travelling teams and Harry and Marci were talking enthusiastically about the quality of the soil they had excavated.

"What do you think, Ying?" asked Harry, trying to engage her.

"About what?" she said, having not been involved with the conversation.

"Uranium Oxide... the concentration," clarified Harry.

"Yes, it would seem so," she replied but with a degree of apathy.

This was hardly the excitement of a gold-rush, but in economic terms what they had discovered could be just as valuable to the company.

Nearing the second site, the convoy came to a plateau; Harry remembered it from his studies. They were close now. The red dirt track suddenly veered ninety degrees right just before the land ran out. Harry stopped the Toyota and Marci, Ying and Heinz got out. The area was barren apart from the ubiquitous clumps of scrub and scattered rocks. It was about a hundred yards to the end of the plateau and nothingness; it was like walking off the end of the world.

Marci, Harry and Heinz walked towards the end of the plateau and stared at the view. Ying had stayed behind and was standing next to the Toyota.

"Look at that," said Marci, as they reached the cliff edge. The valley in front of them dropped down probably six or seven hundred feet, maybe more; it reminded Harry of the Grand Canyon. It was vast, probably five miles across, and stretched as far as the eye could see in both directions. It was breathtaking in its size and beauty; the only word Harry could think of was 'awesome' but even that hardly did it justice. He looked up at the sun and shaded his eyes with his hand; the temperature was topping forty as it shimmered across the landscape creating the illusion of water. He wiped the sweat from his brow.

Moments later, the Scania stopped behind the Toyota and Nate and the other German got out and walked towards the group who were still surveying the scene.

"Jeez, now that's what you call a view," said Nate as he approached Harry and the others. "Hope you're gonna tell us how we're gonna get down there."

Harry pointed to the track. "Yes, the track follows the side of the cliff; it's steep but should be manageable. It is used, I checked," said Harry, seeing Nate's reaction. You could just make out signs of old wheel marks.

Banjo and Charlie also left the Scania and retrieved their belongings from the back.

Banjo walked up to Nate. "This is where we get off. We will stay around here and wait for you to return."

"What about tucker and water?" said Nate.

"We'll take what we need," Banjo replied and unloaded two rucksacks from the back of the truck. Charlie took a two-litre bottle of water.

"Ok, it's up to you guys. If all goes well, we'll be back in two days, I reckon," said Nate.

Banjo acknowledged. "Ok, we will be here tomorrow, same time... and the day after if you're not here."

The pair turned and walked off; Harry watched in sadness as their silhouettes got smaller and smaller. He had no idea where they would go or find shade; there was none visible, just mile after mile of plateau and scrub.

Nate turned and went back to the others who were still taking in the Valley of the Serpent in all its glory. He stood next to Marci and Harry who were pointing out various features and rock formations, commenting on suitable places where they could make camp. The two Germans had now joined them.

Nate proffered his thoughts. "I reckon if we head down the track and make our way over in that direction it may be cooler by that large rock... May even be some shade when the sun drops a bit."

"Yeah, that seems good and it won't be far from where we need to drill," said Harry.

There was one member of the group not interested in the view; she had another mission and now was the chance she had been waiting for. While attention was drawn away from the vehicles, Ying walked back towards the Scania and ducked behind it.

She was disappointed that her efforts with the plane had not produced the results she had hoped, and the snake had also proved a let-down but this time...She looked at the wheels which almost dwarfed her.

Chapter Seventeen

Davey and Ying had been together since February. He was the real fanatic, having been involved with many protests across Australia but this particular project was now an obsession; it had to be stopped at all costs. He had proved to be a significant influence on Ying.

It had been just over six months since the Boxing Day Tsunami that had taken the lives of her parents. Her brother had survived and it was he who had called Ying with the devastating news a few days later. Ying had studied geology at Adelaide University and was inspired by a lecture that Edward Duchamp gave as a visiting speaker in her final semester. He seemed to endorse her own views on ecology. She joined the company after she graduated in September 2006 and instead of the normal induction in Switzerland, she was attached to the Darwin team later that year under Marci's mentorship.

The deaths of her beloved parents, unsurprisingly, rested heavily on her and she was unable to shake the feelings of guilt at not being home at the time. As the project gained momentum, she gradually became more and more disillusioned with what the company was doing believing that in some way it was upsetting the balance of nature. She also felt let down by Edward Duchamp; she was beginning to realise his eco-friendly messages and apparent philanthropy were just propaganda to appease possible opposition to his organisation. This belief led her to start secretly attending the protest rallies against Uranium mining in Kakadu, being held locally.

There was already a strong eco-movement in Darwin; opposition to the Jabiluka project had been ongoing for several years and rallies in the locality, particularly at the university were frequent. They had been successful in delaying any new drilling there. As a result, Helvetia's arrival in the area was not broadcast and much of the company's early preparatory work was done covertly.

The company at this time was still at the initial stages of seeking the permissions from the Australian Government that they would need to start exploratory drilling. Most of the action was happening in Canberra. Edward Duchamp and his team spent a great deal of time and money lobbying politicians. The Darwin office had been put together to manage logistics in the area in preparation for the eventual dig. It was just Nate, Marci, Winda, Tara and Ying at this time. Den replaced Tara after she was transferred to Switzerland.

Ying had met Davey at one of the meetings and was quickly caught up with his enthusiastic opposition to Helvetia's activities in the area. This led to an uncomfortable conflict of interest for her but Davey persuaded her to continue her work and support the opposition from the inside. She was able to feed him with regular information on Helvetia's progress.

The friendship developed into a closer relationship and within weeks of their meeting, Ying moved in with his family. Davey's father owned a small cattle station just outside Palmerston about fifteen miles from the office in Darwin.

As the government lobbying started to bear fruit, it became clear that it was only a matter of time before Helvetia would be given the go-ahead to start prospecting. Once the Government's decision was confirmed in early May, Ying told Davey and he contacted a local reporter who was covering the Uranium mining expansion story. Much to the consternation of the company, who continued to maintain a level of secrecy, it soon became headline news and attention was immediately focused on Helvetia. Jubiluka was now a secondary consideration.

Ying attended several of Professor Harvey's meetings and he had proved inspirational. She had met him on a number of occasions and news of his disappearance had worried her. She also knew Sophie Darling and news of her death had increased this concern. She was in no doubt about the potential danger she was in. There were already rumours among the movement that the professor had been silenced. Unfortunately, without him, the rallies seemed to lose impetus.

Ying had been anxious about the prospecting trek from the start, recognising that she would be expected to contribute in some way, thus appearing to directly endorse the project. Davey, however, had convinced her that this was the chance to finally scupper the project for good. "Just go along with it and wait your chance," he had said.

The earlier attempt to sabotage the research plane was a disappointment. Ying had been part of the small team tasked with surveying for possible sites. The group also included Marci and Nate. Nate, with his good knowledge of the area, took charge of surveying and directing the pilot; Marci and Ying were there to help the information gathering. They had carried out several earlier sorties; Den, and Tara before him, would normally go but Nate thought Ying could do with the experience. This was the first time she had been out of the office on a field trip.

She was understandably reluctant to participate but again Davey encouraged her to go along and discussed with her the possibilities of sabotage. They had researched the workings of light aircraft on the Internet particularly the Cessna 172, which the team were using, and came up with the semblance of a plan.

She told Nate she would not go on the flight claiming a phobia of flying but as the aircraft was a four seater; this was not really an issue. Ying's primary purpose would be to help with the analysis on the ground once the surveying was done.

At the airstrip, there was a wooden building where flights were monitored. It included an office and a small accommodation block where pilots and the occasional passenger could rest while waiting for their flights. There was no discernible security. Tourists were invariably the main customers who would pay good money to be flown over the rugged scenery; dawn and sunset were popular times for photography. Nate booked the room for one night so they could have more time surveying; two, maybe three trips, he reckoned.

The aircraft was parked on the apron of the short grass runway and, while the team were asleep, Ying managed to sneak out. With the knowledge she had gained, she was able to access the engine casing and cut the wires to the aircraft's fuel line.

In reality, it had been a naive attempt. As soon as the pilot did his pre-flight checks, he quickly discovered a problem with the fuel tanks and the trip was aborted. A quick investigation revealed the damage. Nate persuaded the pilot not to inform the police; they could not afford any adverse publicity. The owner was suitably recompensed by Helvetia.

Back at the Chateau, this development had caused a great deal of consternation. There had already been protests outside the Darwin office following the press exposure. The team regularly had to endure a phalanx of chanting eco 'idiots', as Nate called them, to get into work. The attempted sabotage on the plane was seen as an escalation. David Leganes, with Edward's backing, instructed Scheck and his team to fly to Australia to 'take care of things'.

Ying and Davey had discussed other options of disrupting the research but here was a real opportunity. He had already shown her what she would need to do and she was prepared; she had even practised it with him on his father's truck. It was just a question of timing; waiting for the right moment. She was trying to remember Davey's instructions. "There will probably be five wheel nuts but you won't need to undo all of them if you don't have the time; three should do it," he told her.

She checked the group again; they were still surveying the area from the cliff edge. Then, seeing the coast was clear, she pulled out an adjustable spanner from her haversack and placed it over the first wheel nut like Davey had instructed. The spanner was ratchet driven which meant it didn't require a great deal of leverage. She also had a small piece of small-bore scaffolding pipe, no more than nine inches long. It was what Davey's father used. She put the pipe over the spanner and pulled as hard as she could until she felt it give. Being a relatively new vehicle meant the nuts were still well-lubricated, making them easier to loosen. There was a noticeable squeak, however, as the first nut started to give way. She stopped for a moment to see if anyone had heard but they were still engrossed in conversation. She loosened the nut until it was almost off the thread. She checked the group again and then went to work on the second; then two more. She was about to undo the final nut when she saw the team was starting to disperse and head back to the vehicles; she thought quickly. She swiftly put her tools back in the haversack, then pulled down her jeans and pants and started to pee. Nate turned the corner to be confronted by Ying in full flow.

"Do you mind?" she said.

"Jeez, Ying, ya might have said something," he said as he quickly turned away.

Ying finished, pulled up her pants and trousers and picked up her bag.

"Right, let's get the show on the road. Pieter, you can join ya mate in the truck if ya like. There's plenty of room," said Nate. Avoiding the small pool left by Ying, he climbed up into the cab and fired up the Scania.

Harry got in the Toyota with Marci sat next to him; Ying was in the back. They pulled away and slowly started their descent down the side of the cliff. Nate agreed to keep the Scania fifty yards back, in case of problems. Harry had insisted, although Nate said he was confident in the Scania's automatic braking system. It was very steep for the first hundred yards and not much wider than the Scania; it reminded Harry of a ski-jump. To the right was the cliff wall, to the left a sheer drop to the valley floor several hundred feet down.

"Good grief, Harry, I wish you could've found another way in; this is giving me the willies," said Marci, who was on the side of the drop. She looked out of her window and there was nothing between them and oblivion. Harry kept the car in low gear; as an off-road vehicle, it was built for this terrain. Small and, not-so-small, rocks from the cliff littered the track and the car bounced every time it hit one; it did nothing for Marci's nerves. Ying just sat there in a dream.

Suddenly, Harry sensed something was wrong. The Scania seemed to be gaining speed; it was catching up with them. He checked his mirror again; definitely, no mistake. He could see Nate struggling with the steering wheel. Harry accelerated to avoid a possible collision.

"What's happening?" shouted Marci.

"I don't know," replied Harry. "Something's wrong, Nate's in trouble."

Then, without warning, the Scania veered right, crashed into the cliff wall and bounced off. The shock dislodged the digger which immediately toppled over, the momentum taking the Scania with it. Harry saw everything in his mirror and stopped the car. He watched in horror, totally helpless, as the truck cart-wheeled down the cliff face. Over and over it went; there was sickening thud as it hit the ground some five hundred feet below.

Harry started the Toyota and floored it. Marci was in shock and had her hand to her mouth. Ying just sat there but she knew she had accomplished one of her objectives.

It took several minutes to reach the stricken truck. It was on its side, smashed almost beyond recognition. There was a strong smell of diesel fumes and steam was spurting from what was left of the radiator. Debris was scattered everywhere; the drill-digger was lay on its side twenty metres away, forlorn and broken.

Harry pulled up as close to the wreckage as he dared and leapt out of the Toyota. "Quick, we've got to get them out; it could catch fire," he shouted to Marci.

He ran across to the Scania, clambered up and looked inside through the cab window. The three occupants had been tossed around like rag dolls in a tumble dryer. With the truck lying on its side, getting to the occupants was going to be a real problem. Harry stood on top of the cab to be able to get the leverage to manoeuvre the door open; gravity was working against him and it was heavy. With a huge effort, Harry managed to raise it towards him and look inside. Nate was slumped with his leg trapped by the steering wheel; the two Germans were in the back; there was no sign of life. Nate made a groan.

"Come on mate, we've got to get you out, quick," said Harry. "Marci, here, climb up; give me a hand."

Harry jumped inside the cab and was able to get behind Nate and free his leg. He started to lift him up.

"He's unconscious," he shouted to Marci who was waiting at the cab entrance trying to grab Nate's flaccid arms.

"Pull him up; I'll push," said Harry and between them, they managed to get Nate out and on the edge of the cab. He was slumped with his head on his chest; arms hanging limply by his side. Marci was sat behind him with her arms around his waist to prevent him falling. He was just wearing a pair of shorts and a tee shirt and he was barefoot; his trainers had been removed during the impact of the crash.

Harry got out of the cab and dropped to the ground. "Ok

Marci, pass him to me."

Nate was a dead weight and, although possibly risking further injury, Marci eased him over the edge of the truck and into Harry's arms.

Marci jumped down and helped Harry lay Nate out on the ground. "Quick, grab a sleeping bag and the medical kit from the car," shouted Harry. "Where's Ying?" he said, noticing she was not in the Toyota.

Marci looked around. "I don't know," she said. "She's gone."

"Never mind, we need to sort Nate out; he's in a bad way," said Harry.

Marci ran to the Toyota and grabbed a sleeping bag and the medical chest which was in the back, then went back to Harry who was checking Nate over.

"Broken leg, by the look of it and a bang on the head... difficult to see anything else; he may be bleeding internally," said Harry.

"What about the bodyguards?" said Marci.

"I'll check in a second but I think they're both dead."

They were concentrating on tending to Nate and didn't hear footsteps behind them.

"I'll take the car keys," said a voice.

Harry turned around and saw Ying pointing one of the bodyguards' rifles at them.

"Don't be silly," said Harry. "We've got to see to Nate. If you want to make yourself useful call Den and let him know we need help."

Ying fired a shot. The bullet ricocheted off the ground just by Harry's feet. "I mean it," she said.

Harry jumped back, startled.

"What are you doing Ying? We're your mates," said Marci.

"You are no mate of mine," said Ying. "I said this project

was wrong, I told you."

She raised the rifle. "I mean it; I will shoot you," said Ying.

Harry put his hands in his pocket and pulled out the keys.

"Throw them to me," she said.

Harry complied and tossed them in her direction; she bent down and picked them up not taking her eyes off Harry and Marci.

"Now you, Harry, lie on the floor."

Harry lay on his back. "No, on your front; hands behind your back... Marci, tie his hands together."

Ying took out a black plastic zip cord from her pocket and threw it to her. Marci threaded the garden tie around Harry's wrists and pulled it tight.

"And the feet," ordered Ying, and Marci put another tie around Harry's legs and fastened it.

"Now you Marci, on the floor... hands behind your back, the same, like Harry."

Ying still had the rifle pointing at Marci. "Here, put this on... both hands," she shouted. She handed another zip chord to Marci. She placed her hands in the loop as instructed and before Marci could move, Ying bent down and pulled the chord tight; then she wrapped another around Marci's legs until she too had been immobilised.

"Why are you doing this?" said Marci.

Ying didn't answer and walked away leaving Harry and Marci helpless. Nate was on the ground drifting in and out of unconsciousness.

"Ying... Ying," shouted Marci.

Ying ignored the pleas, got into the Toyota with the rifle and started it up. She turned the car around and went back up the track. Harry and Marci watched helplessly as the trail of red dust gradually disappeared from view.

"Quick, see if you can move your wrists. If we twist the ties they should break," said Harry. They both tried but the plastic cord was just too strong.

Harry, on the ground, had inadvertently disturbed an ants' nest and he could feel the insects starting to crawl over his body, biting and stinging. He was wriggling in an attempt to crush them with his weight as he tried desperately to break the bonds. He shook his head violently as they attacked his ears and eyes and spat as they reached his mouth.

"Can you get up?" asked Harry who was still rolling around struggling to defeat the insects.

"I'll try," she said and managed to manoeuvre herself onto her back and sit up. Her legs were not as tightly bound as her hands and rather clumsily, like a new foal taking its first steps, Marci managed to stand up.

"We need something sharp," said Harry. "See if there's anything on the truck."

With her legs still tied together, it was impossible for Marci to walk, so she jumped forward with a two-footed hop. The momentum immediately upset her balance and she fell forward. Without her hands to protect her, she hit the ground. She groaned in pain as her head made contact with a small boulder. Blood started trickling from her forehead. She staggered to her feet again and tried a second time. She was about twenty feet from the truck. This time she kept her balance and reached the stricken Scania with a few ungainly leaps. It would have been comical if it wasn't so serious.

Meanwhile, Harry's writhing had moved a small rotting log. It was only perhaps a foot long but happened to be the home of one of the area's most vicious predators, a scorpion. It was not big, probably half the size of its recent home. Harry watched in horror as it arched its back and raised its stinging tail. It seemed to shake its two pincers, challenging Harry to take it on. Harry momentarily froze. Nothing would normally faze him but scorpions were his worst nightmare. He wriggled backwards trying to put some distance between him and the arachnid. The scorpion didn't move, seemingly satisfied that it had seen off the danger. Harry was still moving away; the ants were now in his hair.

Marci was looking around the truck, unaware of Harry's predicament. The front of the cab had been completely pushed in by the force of the impact and part of the metalwork had sheared off. She spotted the silvery shard of shiny metal where it had fractured and started rubbing the ties on her wrists up and down along the jagged edge. After a few seconds, the chord snapped. There was blood oozing from a deep scratch to her wrist where she had caught it on the metal. She leant down and managed to release the cord around her legs. She quickly returned to the first aid box lying next to Nate; she grabbed the scissors then went over to Harry, who was still squirming and cut the ties.

Harry jumped to his feet and started frantically brushing off the ants from his face, hair and clothing.

"Are you alright?" said Marci.

"I feel like I've been eaten alive," he replied as he took off his tee shirt and shook it vigorously. One or two insects were still crawling down his torso and he crushed them against his skin. He took off his shorts and repeated the process, killing the remaining ants still on his body. He put his shorts back on as Marci walked up to him. She looked at his face and chest with concern. "You're covered in bites," she said. "I'll get you some cream."

"In a minute, we need to see to Nate; how is he?"

"Not good," said Marci.

Harry could still see the scorpion which had moved back towards its misplaced former home. He left it well alone and went across to Nate who was making strange whimpering noises in his delirium.

Harry looked at Marci as he put his tee shirt back on.

"Hey, you've got a nasty gash on your head; you need to clean that up."

He walked over to take a closer look.

"Just a bruise I think. It's not deep. I'll see to it in a sec... I'll have a look around and see what we've got... Keep an eye on Nate. You need to put a plaster on that as well," he said pointing to the wound on her wrist. Marci looked at it. "Yeah, thanks, will do," she said and raided the first-aid box.

With the debris of the crash scattered over a wide area, it took a while for Harry to do an inventory. He returned to Marci holding a two-litre bottle of water. "Found this but the others must've burst open in the fall. The rest of the water's on the Toyota. There're some packs of food in the cab which will keep us going for a bit but we need a plan to get us out of here and get help for Nate. I've found these as well; we need to make a splint for his leg," he said, holding up two pieces of wood.

"What about the radio?" asked Marci.

"Smashed up; not sure if it was the crash or Ying. It looks like the wheel nuts on the truck have been messed with, three of them are missing."

Harry pulled his phone from his pocket and switched it on. 'No service', it said. Marci was watching. "Check yours, Marci, just in case."

She also had her phone in her pocket but again, the same result; it was a forlorn hope. There was a look of despair.

"Why would she do this?" said Marci.

"Don't know but I bet she's the one who tampered with the plane... probably put the snake in my car as well. You know the more I think about it, the more I think it could have been her on the CCTV."

"Jesus," said Marci.

Harry's first-aid training for the Derbyshire field trip was now bearing fruit. He washed Marci's face with some of the water, then cleaned and bound her head-wound. It had stopped bleeding, more a deep graze. A bruise was beginning to form. Once he had made sure she was ok, he went over to Nate and checked his left leg. The bone was definitely broken mid-shin; the bottom half of his leg was bent at a strange angle. Luckily it hadn't cut through the skin. A compound fracture would have been beyond Harry's rudimentary knowledge. He straightened the leg as best he could. Despite being semi-conscious, Nate screamed in pain as Harry manipulated his tibia. Harry then put the two pieces of wood either side. "Can you wrap some plaster around that... as tight as you can?" said Harry and Marci took out a roll of Elastoplast and between them, within a few minutes, they had Nate's leg bound.

With Marci bandaged up and Nate made comfortable, Harry had a semblance of a plan.

"I need to get some help," he said. "No-one's going to come looking, especially if Ying's calling in."

"But we should stay together," replied Marci.

"Ideally, yes, but there's no way we can carry Nate, certainly not in this heat, and I'll be quicker on my own.

"But where will you go?"

"I've spent a week studying this area; there are Aboriginal settlements around. I expect that's where Banjo and Charlie have gone."

"But how will you find them?"

"I'll head back along the track until I do," said Harry.

Marci wasn't happy at being separated but couldn't think of a better idea.

"We need to get him in some shade, I'll give you a hand," said Harry and gently they lifted Nate onto the sleeping bag and dragged it next to the Scania. "It should be safe here now; just don't go lighting any fires."

"What about the Germans?" said Marci.

"I'll check again," said Harry. He jumped back inside the cab and after a couple of minutes re-joined Marci.

"Pieter's dead, Heinz may have a pulse, I'm not sure but I think it's best to leave them where they are, for the time being, they're not in any danger."

"You'll need some water," said Marci.

"There's nothing to carry it in, and you and Nate will need it more," said Harry, taking a large swig from the container. "That'll have to keep me going," he said. "I'll take a couple of energy bars, there's some in the truck." Harry collected three and put them in his pockets, then went back to Marci.

"What about your clothes? The mosquitoes will have a field day with you in those shorts," said Marci.

"There's nothing I can do about that. I'll be ok," said Harry.

Marci looked at him; he was covered in small red blotches from the biting ants. His sweat was making them sting but he couldn't afford to use any water. He would have to put up with it.

"Well at least put some cream on. It may stop them from itching and it'll keep away the mozzies for a while. There's some here, it should help," said Marci and passed him a tube from the medical kit.

"Thanks."

Harry took the tube from Marci and squeezed a dollop into his hands then rubbed it on his arms, legs and neck, then his face.

"Ok, I'll get going. Keep an eye on Nate and give him some water when he wakes up."

"Yeah, will do... Good luck, Harry," said Marci, and he set off up the track.

He checked his watch; it was nearly one-thirty, the hottest part of the day.

Harry started at a brisk pace up the steep track at the side of the cliff but the gradient was against him and it took over fifteen minutes to get to the top of the plateau. He stopped for a moment and looked back at the valley to get his breath back; then he remembered Banjo's warning. Maybe he was right; the Rainbow Serpent had been violated and was fighting back.

He could see the tyre tracks, the large ones from the Scania and two smaller sets from the Toyota. It was clear that Ying had headed back the way they had come. There were also the footprints of the Aboriginals going in the same direction.

Harry followed the tracks; the heat now approaching forty degrees and, with no shade, totally draining. After another fifteen minutes or so, he started eating the first of the energy bars but, having finished it, he was left feeling very thirsty. He tried to put the thoughts out of his mind. Flies were starting to become a real problem. The sweat had washed away much of the cream he had put on his face and there was a constant buzzing. He swished them away with his hands.

Every so often, he broke into a gentle trot to break up the monotony and quicken the pace. There was no shade of any kind here, just tufts of bush. He recalled from the journey there were copses of trees which would provide some respite from the sun but they would be some distance away. He stopped for a rest and checked his watch, ten to three; he was trying to estimate the distance he'd travelled, four or five miles, maybe more; it was difficult to gauge. He wondered how far he was behind Banjo and Charlie; he was still following their footsteps. Then, a few minutes later he came to a large empty termite nest. It was a solid structure and taller than him; nothing unusual, there were hundreds around but in front of it Harry noticed the track split in two. When the convoy was coming in the other direction, he hadn't noticed the junction. One set of tracks made by the Toyota had gone left, whereas the footprints and the earlier tyre tracks from the Scania and Toyota were to the right. He looked at each path; a vast emptiness in both directions; pools of waters shimmered like ghostly apparitions, thirst-quenching mirages teasing Harry. The serpent was having its fun.

He was desperately trying to remember the route; he thought he knew it by heart; he hadn't had to call on Marci's navigation too often. He couldn't understand why Ying would have gone left. From memory, that route went south and well away from any civilisation until it crossed the A1 at least three hundred and fifty miles away. There was no tarmac, just dirt, rocks and dried creeks; that's if you didn't get lost.

He went right, following the footprints which were still fresh.

Marathon runners often focus their minds on mundane things to take their minds off the arduousness of their task. Harry was trying to do the same and his thoughts turned to Monique. After her last message, Harry was really concerned about her. He made up his mind to try to make contact as soon as he returned to Darwin. Then there was Becs and her message. Why was she being followed? Was she in danger? He continued to wrestle with these thoughts; it was keeping him going.

He was beginning to feel the sun on the back of his neck, despite the cream; his calves ached and he was now desperately thirsty. He noticed the big bird of prey again and hoped it wasn't a vulture. Then, up ahead, he spotted a grove of trees; it lifted his spirits. He would stop and take a breather in the shade he decided.

As he got closer, he saw a sight which would live with him for a long time. Under one of the trees close to the track, sat two familiar faces. He jogged up to them.

"Oh guys, am I glad to see you."

He leant forward and put his hands on his knees then collapsed on the floor in front of them. Banjo went to him and lifted his head.

"Harry, Harry, my friend, what are you doing here?"

The man passed Harry a water container and he drank and drank. Harry was breathing in gasps, panting heavily.

"There's... been... an accident," he managed to stammer.

"What sort of accident?" asked Banjo.

Harry explained the circumstances. "The two bodyguards are dead I think, and Nate is in a real bad way. We need to get help to them as soon as we can."

"The nearest place is about four miles away. It's where we're going," said Banjo. Charlie passed the water to Harry again. "There's a radio there I think, and maybe we can get someone to drive back to the valley. How do you feel now? Do you think you can make it?"

"Yeah, yeah, I just needed a drink and a rest," Harry replied.

Harry struggled to his feet; his muscles had stiffened up but he was soon back on the track keeping pace with Banjo and Charlie.

It was another hour of brisk walking before Harry noticed a building in the far distance on the right-hand side. It looked like a giant barn and beside it a small house. He couldn't remember seeing it on the journey in, probably just off the main track but he was mighty glad to see it now.

As they got nearer Harry could see an old Ford pick-up truck. Various farming implements and machinery littered the yard outside. There was a chugging sound of a generator coming from the barn. An Aboriginal was sat on the porch of the house whittling wood; a pile of shavings lay on the floor at his feet. He saw the three men walking towards them.

"Yow, Jarrah," said Banjo.

"Yow, Banjo... Charlie."

The man got up from his labours and walked towards them. He seemed pleased to see his fellow tribesmen and shook hands with them with a broad, white smile.

Banjo talked to the man in the local dialect which Harry couldn't understand. Every now and then, the man would look at Harry.

"He said you can use the radio and he will drive us back to the valley," said Banjo.

"Thank you, thank you," said Harry and shook the man's hands. He smiled again with a big toothy grin which seemed to light up the porch.

Harry went inside. After the glare of the sun, it was dark and cool. The house was small and built of wood; through the porch door was the kitchen. There was a large white sink, a refrigerator and an ancient looking cooker which looked like it hadn't been cleaned for some time. There were several shelves fixed to the walls by metal brackets holding cups, saucers, plates, and other kitchen utensils. The two windows were covered with dust, grime and dead insects; discoloured net curtains hung from wooden rails above; one of them was torn allowing more light through. In the middle of the room, was an old wooden table with four chairs placed around it. Jarrah was chatting away to Banjo and Charlie nineteen to the dozen clearly pleased to have company. A dog ran in and stood next to the Aboriginal wagging its tail. Jarrah spoke to it and patted its head.

"There," said Jarrah, pointing to an old radio with a black Bakelite headset in the corner on a small stand. Its brown cord had started to fray and was twisted around itself.

"Do you know how to contact Darwin?" asked Banjo.

"I think so, I know the frequency but you may have to help me with these controls," said Harry.

Harry had called Den a couple of times and was familiar with using the radio. Jarrah showed him how to tune the dial. There was a great deal of crackling then Harry started talking.

"This is Harry Bentham... Are you there Den?"

No reply; Harry moved the dial slowly, a fraction to the left and repeated the call. Then a crackly voice returned.

"Hi Harry, mate, this is Den. Wasn't expecting a call until later."

"Den, mate, listen, we've got trouble; we need help fast,"

Harry described what had happened. "It was sabotage, Ying messed with the truck."

"Ying?!" said Den.

"Yes, be very careful if you get any messages from her."

"She called in about half-one and said everything was going to plan," said Den.

"Well, you'll need to call the police but in the meantime, can you get a chopper out for a medivac. We'll need a doctor on board. Nate's in a bad way and I think the two guards are dead." Harry gave Den the GPS coordinates which he knew by heart.

Harry closed the call. "Thanks, Jarrah," said Harry and shook the man's hand.

There was more talking between the Aboriginals. "Would you like some tea or something to eat?" asked Banjo.

"I really think we should get back if that's ok. I don't know how long it will take the helicopter to get there."

More talking. "Jarrah says he will drive us there," said Banjo.

"Will you and Charlie come too? I could do with your help."

Banjo looked at Charlie and nodded. "Yes, we will come."

The three followed Jarrah to the pickup truck. Harry sat in the front with Jarrah; Banjo and Charlie sat in the back surrounded by more farming utensils.

It took half an hour to reach the end of the plateau and the track down the side of the cliff; it was almost six o'clock. Jarrah stopped the pickup and got out; he looked down the steep slope.

Banjo and Charlie jumped down from the back and joined him. There was more discussion.

"Jarrah says the pickup won't go down, it's too steep."

"That's ok, we can walk down; the chopper should be here soon," said Harry.

Banjo looked at Charlie; Harry sensed resistance. "It's ok if you don't want to come down, I understand. I'll go down and see how they are."

"Yes, that will be best. We will stay here for a short time in case you need anything, then we will go back," said Banjo.

"How will you get back to Darwin?" said Harry.

"We will not return to Darwin; our work here is done," said Banjo.

Harry walked up to Banjo and Charlie and shook their hands and then gave them a hug; then he went to Jarrah.

"Thank you Jarrah for your help; you have saved our lives," Harry said and repeated the farewell gesture. Jarrah lifted a two-litre bottle of water from the back of the truck and handed it to Harry. "It will keep you going until the helicopter comes," he said.

"Thanks," said Harry and he set off down the track to the valley floor; it was much quicker going down and within ten minutes was running towards Marci. She was next to Nate who Harry could see was sat up.

"Harry...! Am I glad to see you," she said. She stood up and greeted Harry with a hug.

"You ok?" said Harry.

"Yeah... I'm ok, better now, though," said Marci.

He looked at Nate. "And how are you, ya old bastard?" said Harry in an Australian accent.

"Sore head and the left leg's crocked but could be worse,"

said Nate. "Thanks for getting me out."

"No worries," said Harry and he laughed; he was picking up the colloquialisms he realised.

"What's happening? Did you manage to get help?" said Marci.

Harry described his journey and the meeting with Jarrah.

"I got through to Den on the radio; asked for a medivac. Should be here in an hour or two," said Harry. "Banjo and Charlie said they would wait for a bit, in case we need anything; they're a bit reluctant to come down here."

"Them and their bloody serpent," said Nate.

"What about Ying?" said Marci.

"Don't know, she's gone," said Harry. "I told Den to get the police."

"Bloody Chink, never trusted her," said Nate. "Leganes said she would be an asset."

Harry handed Marci the water from Jarrah then rummaged around the crash site to see what else he could find; they still had a long wait ahead of them. He found the mosquito nets hanging from a rock and took them back to Marci and Nate. At least they could have some respite from the flies. The sun had dropped behind the escarpment and they were now in shade but it was still very hot. He also managed to retrieve the chocolate bars from the cab and handed them around. They had melted into a gooey mess but would keep them going.

Marci was more concerned at Harry's face and arms. The angry red welts left from the insect bites were now irritating and she applied more cream. He was covered in blotches.

"You need to rest up a bit, Harry," she said. "You've got some serious sunburn there." She found some pain-killers in the medical kit and handed a couple to him. "Not sure if they'll do any good but you never know."

"Thanks," said Harry. "Here, can you give us a hand? We can make a canopy with the nets. It'll keep the mosquitoes off us." So Marci and Harry arrange the nets over the three of them and they hunkered down waiting for rescue.

It was almost seven-thirty before the faint drone of a helicopter could be heard coming up the valley; Harry removed the netting; Nate had drifted off to sleep. "Nate, come on, wake up the chopper's here," said Harry. Then it was in view and he wanted to whoop for joy and relief. Nate groaned as he regained consciousness. Marci and Harry stood up and started waving frantically.

They watched as it started to descend. The group covered their eyes as the rotors stirred up the dust, debris and insects into a huge cloud. Three men got out; one was wearing a paramedic jumpsuit with the word 'Doctor' on the back. The other two Harry recognised were part of the security team.

The doctor ran across to Nate as the pilot shut down the helicopter.

"Doctor Neil Francis. What've we got?" said the medic.

"Broken leg, possible concussion," said Harry. The doctor made an initial check. "Ok, we'll get you in as soon as we can. Good job with the splint, by the way. What about the others? They said something about fatalities."

"Yes, in the truck," said Harry and he led the doctor to the open cab. Francis climbed up and looked inside.

"I think one is dead. Not sure about the other, I thought I could feel a pulse earlier," said Harry.

The doctor popped his head up. "Can I have some help here, please," he said, and the security guys clambered up.

Between them, they man-handled Heinz and Pieter from the cab and placed them on the ground.

"Yes, this one's dead," said Francis, looking at Pieter. "This one has a pulse but it's very weak."

He opened his medical kit, took out a syringe and injected something in Heinz's arm.

"That should help until we can get him to the hospital," said Francis.

They carried the two Germans to the helicopter one-by-one on a stretcher and then returned for Nate.

After a few minutes, everyone was on board. The pilot started up the helicopter and lifted off. He hovered over the plateau edge for a moment and Harry was able to wave to the Aboriginals who were still there. They waved back and got into the pickup.

The sun was setting in the west as they passed over the desolate but beautiful landscape. With the Super Puma's cruising speed it would take nearly two and a half hours to get back to Darwin. It was almost ten o'clock, and quite dark, as the lights of the city came into view. There was little talking on the way, the noise of the rotors precluding any proper discussion. The doctor had injected Nate with morphine to kill the pain in his leg and he was asleep for most of the journey. He had also given Harry some anti-histamine tablets which had eased the itching from the insect bites. They had made him drowsy and he too had snoozed for much of the time. He was thinking again of the Aboriginals and their warning about the Valley of the Serpent; it had been a presage.

The landing pad at the hospital was illuminated in preparation and a few minutes later the pilot gently eased the chopper down. Helicopter arrival was a common occurrence due to the large area it serviced and a team was on standby to attend to the group.

It was the same place where Harry had been treated for the snake bite and Nate was taken to the accident ward while Heinz was rushed to the intensive care facility; Pieter to the morgue.

Harry and Marci stayed with Nate for a while to make sure

he was comfortable. He'd been able to phone his wife to tell her he was ok. "Gonna get some right stick about this," he said after the call.

Eventually, the pair left Nate and walked back to reception.

"So, what do we do now?" said Marci.

"Well, we've got no samples. They're in the Toyota."

He turned to Marci. There was something he had been thinking about all the way back from the valley.

"Look, I've been thinking; I reckon we should call it a day on this project."

"What do you mean?" said Marci.

"Well, I don't know about you, but it just doesn't feel right; you've seen what the area means to the Aboriginals."

"But that's not our decision," replied Marci.

"No, that's true but what if our findings were inconclusive... say, for instance, we didn't find the levels of Uranium oxide to make it viable?"

"Lie, you mean?"

"Hmm, not necessarily," said Harry. "Think about it, without the soil samples there's no firm evidence of the level of Uranium, only our spectrometer readings. I can't really complete my report with any certainty."

"But they were pretty high, Harry... the readings."

"Yeah, but they don't know that."

"Den's probably told them; I did give him the figures."

"Hmm, I'll have to give that some thought."

"Don't forget they could always send us back out again to get some more," said Marci. "There are other sites."

"Yeah but not with the same level of Uranium," said Harry. "And it'll cost... It'll also take time, meaning more delays; I'm not sure how that will go down."

"I don't know," said Marci. "It'll mean I'll be out of a job... and what about Den, and Nate? Can't see him agreeing."

"He might," said Harry. "When we've had a chance to talk to him."

"He was up for a big bonus if this came through, and I mean big. One hundred thousand dollars he told me."

"Hmm, that's a lot of money," said Harry.

"Yeah, and I can't see him giving that up," said Marci.

"We'll chat about it tomorrow. Have you still got your car keys?"

"Yes, thank goodness; still in my pocket," said Marci.

"Me too. What say we get a taxi?" said Harry. "Oh, just had a thought, what about the key to the depot?"

"Yeah, I've got that; Nate gave it to me in the chopper."

Harry and Marci left the hospital and took the first taxi that was waiting outside reception back to the warehouse to collect their cars. Marci was calling her husband to say she was back. Harry wanted to call Becs but would wait until he was in his car. He could feel his face and legs tingling; a mixture of sunburn and insect bites.

The pair exited the warehouse and Marci locked up. Harry headed back to the flat. He tried calling Becs but there was no reply. He would try again later.

He pulled up to the entrance of the tower block and keyed in the passcode for the car park. He pressed the lift call button and waited patiently for it to arrive. He had a thought; he would need to do some shopping to replace his stuff in the Toyota; he was unlikely to see it again. He took the lift to the twelfth floor. Luckily, his key to the apartment was on the same ring as his car keys.

As he reached the door, he checked his watch, ten forty-five; he would try Becs again. He turned on the light and went in; there was an envelope on the floor.

He put his keys on the table and opened it. It was from Becs.
'Dear Harry,

I just wanted to let you know that I've been called back to Sydney. I phoned the editor after our chat on Friday and told her I was being followed and she said it was too dangerous to stay. I've probably got all the information I need from here anyway and there's no reason for me to stay. They want to go with the story as soon as I can finish it. Thanks for your help and company. It's been fun.

Take Care

Becs x'

Harry read it again. He thought about calling her in Sydney but decided it was best to let things go. As she said it had been fun; he was pleased that she was safe.

He rubbed the stubble on his chin, after almost four days without a proper wash he was desperate to have a bath and a shave. He walked into the bathroom and looked in the mirror; his face was swollen and speckled with insect bites; he would never forget his time in the Valley of the Serpent.

Chapter Eighteen

Officer Pascal Calvert of the Brigade Fluviale, was on a night patrol with his colleague Eric Joachim. The Brigade Fluviale, the river police, knew the Seine better than anyone, particularly its dangerous currents which could pin unsuspecting divers to the bottom or sweep them downstream. The elite squad were all expert divers, swimmers and boat handlers as well as armed officers.

They were in a high-speed rigid inflatable and cruising along the dockside area around Quai Marcel Boyer looking for any criminal behaviour in the wharves. They had received a tip-off that a large quantity of drugs was going to be landed. They were in stealth-mode, engines just ticking over and gently gliding along the dark waters watching the bank. Calvert spotted some activity on the quay ahead; he alerted Joachim. Three men appeared to be holding something which they then threw into the water. The men quickly left the scene and Calvert immediately deployed his search beam which lit up the river and adjacent quayside. He spotted something floating in the river. He pushed the boat to full power; the Suzuki 500 engine roared in response and they were alongside it in seconds. They could see it was a woman; she was floating head down in the river.

"Quick, help me get her on board," said Calvert and between them they pulled the woman into the boat.

"Is she breathing?" said Joachim.

"Yes, she's still alive but we must get her to a hospital quickly."

The Clinique de Bercy was just on the opposite side of the Seine from the quay but access from the river was not easy. Joachim called ahead to get an ambulance to the nearest docking point some two hundred yards upstream. Then he started CPR.

It was less than five minutes before Calvert negotiated the craft alongside the wharf. He could see blue lights flashing and then an ambulance pulled up. There were steps leading up from the water to the riverside parkway. With no time to lose, Calvert picked up the woman and put her over his shoulder then climbed the twenty or so steps. Within moments the medics had her. She was wrapped in silver foil and an oxygen mask put over her face.

The crew closed up the ambulance, thanked their police colleagues and sped back to the hospital. The emergency unit was ready for them. She was stretchered into the ward and the doctors went to work. They quickly discovered she was drugged but her vital signs were good and airways clear. They took a sample of blood and within half an hour, had established the drug and dosage and were able to counteract the effects. Twenty minutes later, she started to come round.

"What is your name?" asked the doctor.

"Alette Brenôt," said the woman drowsily.

Monique, despite her condition, had the presence of mind not to use her real name; she had been saved but was not out of danger.

She remained under observation and a gendarme was stood at the entrance to the ward waiting to get the all-clear from the doctor so that she could be interviewed. Monique was desperately trying to clear her head, thinking of a plausible story. If the police started an investigation, word would soon get out that she was alive; at the moment it served her purpose for certain people to think she was dead.

There was a discussion at the doorway between the doctor and the police officer. Monique was starting to feel more alert as the recovery process took effect. The gendarme entered the room and sat down on the chair next to the bed. He took out a notebook.

"Madame Brenôt, my name is Sergeant Bourdelle; I need to ask you a few questions. Can you tell me how you came to be in the river? Do you know what happened to you?"

Monique looked at him. "I am trying to remember... but my mind... it is... all so unclear. I remember walking, a car pulled up and the driver he asked the way... Then there were other men... they pushed me into the back of the car." She paused as if collecting her thoughts. "I don't remember anything else... until I woke up here."

"Can you remember the man... the driver? What did he look like?"

"I cannot remember; it was dark."

"Can you think of any reason why someone would try to kill you?"

"No, no I cannot think... maybe they had the wrong person."

"Do you live in Paris?" said the officer.

"No, I am just visiting here. Why would anyone do this to me?"

"That's what we need to find out," said Bourdelle.

Monique looked at the officer and closed her eyes. "Please, no more questions. Can I do this in the morning? I need to sleep."

"Of course, madame... thank you. Please try and remember what happened, anything to help us find the people who did this. I will call again in the morning."

"Thank you," said Monique and closed her eyes again.

As soon as the officer had left the room, she removed the drips from her arm and tried to get out of bed. She was unsteady but managed to walk to the doorway. Straight away she had a problem; she had no clothes. They had been removed by the medics and she had no idea where they would be. They would also be soaking wet.

She padded along the corridor in her bare feet, dressed only in a hospital gown and followed the exit sign. A couple of nurses walked past her without taking any notice but she felt conspicuous. Then, just before the reception area, she saw a door with a small sign on it; 'Nettoyeur,' – 'Cleaner', it said. She tried the handle; it wasn't locked and she went inside. It was dark as she searched for the switch, then light. It was only a small room with six lockers against the wall. There were a couple of overalls hanging from a peg and she grabbed one and put it on. She turned out the light and pulled the door open a fraction until little by little she could see. Coast clear; she vacated the room and walked into the reception. There was a desk with a nurse attending and a small waiting room. Five people were sat on chairs reading or playing on their phones. Monique ducked down and sat on the back row next to a young man who appeared to be texting.

"Hello, can you help me, please? I need to borrow your phone. Just one call... please. It is very urgent."

He looked at her, dishevelled, speckled with mud and dressed in a cleaner's overall.

"Sure, here you go," he said and passed the phone to her.

She dialled Bernice's number. She was taking a chance; she had no idea whether the men had returned. It rang out. It was eleven-thirty; she hoped Bernice had not gone to bed. "Come on... come on," she whispered under her breath. The call dropped after about twenty seconds; Monique tried again.

"Hello," said a voice on the other end after three rings.

"Bernice...? It's Monique. I'm in trouble; I need your help. I'm at the Clinique de Bercy."

"Monique! Are you alright? I have been worried sick. What has happened?"

Monique didn't have time to give Bernice the full story. "I will tell you when I see you but I need my suitcases, my phone and my purse. You still have them I think. Can you bring them to me now? I will wait outside the hospital on the corner... please hurry."

"Ok, I'll be there as soon as I can. I will have to bring the children; I can't leave them here."

"No, that's ok. Thank you; please be quick."

Monique handed the phone back to the young man. "Thank you, thank you," she said and walked towards the toilets next to the main entrance. Monique entered; she would wait there for as long as was necessary to avoid detection and, more importantly, keep warm, her newly-acquired overall only providing a modicum of covering.

Monique locked herself in one of the cubicles and waited for what seemed to be forever. All the time she kept thinking about Scheck and his cronies, then Edward. It would be his doing; there is no way the security team would have taken this action without his direction.

She tried to estimate the time it would take Bernice to arrive; probably half an hour to reach the hospital from the apartment. She looked at her wrist; her watch had gone, whether lost in the river or removed by the medical staff she didn't know. After what she considered to be an appropriate amount of time, she left the cubicle and headed cautiously into the reception area. There were a couple of patients waiting to be seen by the medical staff; her earlier phone benefactor had gone. She checked the desk, no-one there; so she put her head down and walked out of the main entrance.

Midnight, the area in front of the hospital was deserted except for a lone security guard who appeared to be walking aimlessly around the forecourt. "Merde," she said to herself and ducked behind one of the pillars supporting the entrance canopy. At least it appeared no-one had realised she had left her ward. She could hear an ambulance in the distance heading in her direction. The guard heard it too and walked back into the hospital. Monique took a chance and hurried away, crouching so as not to be seen.

Rue de Port aux Lions, is situated alongside the hospital, ninety degrees from Quai de Bercy which runs parallel to the river. Monique walked to the corner of the road and waited in the shadow of one of the blocks that fronted it. The ambulance rushed passed her and into the hospital entrance. She could see the paramedics open the door and take someone inside on a stretcher, the security guard a bystander.

It was not a cold night but wearing just a hospital gown and a cleaner's overall Monique started shivering; shock was beginning to set in. Despite her survival, she was mentally in a bad way; her hair was still bedraggled and damp from the river and her bare feet were freezing cold.

As vehicles turned the corner and approached she left the confines of the building and walked towards the road. At least two drivers slowed down thinking she was a prostitute.

It was another twenty minutes before Bernice's car headed up the road towards her. Monique could see her sister driving and quickly left her vantage point, went to the curbside and waved. Bernice stopped and Monique got in.

"Hello Auntie Monique," said a very drowsy Sophie; Guy was fast asleep in his car seat.

"Hello Sophie," she replied and turned to Bernice. "Thank you, I'm so sorry you have been caught up in all this."

"That's ok, I'm sorry I took so long... I had to get the children dressed... I have been so worried. I didn't know what to do. I phoned Victor; he's returning early tomorrow. What on earth happened?" said Bernice, as she drove away.

Monique explained the events as best as she could remember them. Bernice was horrified.

"Why would he do that, try to kill you? He's your husband."

"It is the way he is," replied Monique. "Did you bring my things? I will need to change."

"Yes of course, do you want to come back to the apartment?" said Bernice.

"No, it is not possible, just in case. Can you take me to a hotel? Anywhere, it doesn't matter. Tomorrow I will go to one of the airport hotels."

"You are still flying out on Saturday?"

"Yes, I need to get away as soon as I can."

Bernice saw a hotel ahead; they were not far from the Gare de Lyon where Monique had arrived.

"What about here?" said Bernice.

"Yes, anywhere, that will be fine," replied Monique.

"Where are you going, Auntie Monique? You can stay with us," said Sophie sleepily.

"I can't Sophie but I will see you soon, I promise," said Monique.

They were approaching the hotel entrance.

"Can you park somewhere? I will need to change. I can't go into the hotel looking like this," said Monique.

It was a large hotel and there was an access road which went around the side. Bernice followed the road around.

"This will be fine," said Monique.

"All your stuff is in the boot. I wasn't sure what you would need," said Bernice. "Oh, and I brought this as well," and she handed Monique the envelope with the computer discs.

"Thank you, I will keep this," said Monique.

Monique got out of the car; the night air was a shock to the system, she opened the car boot.

Her two suitcases, carry-on baggage and handbag were there. She opened one of the suitcases and took out some underwear, jeans, a top, and a jacket and quickly changed behind the car. She slipped on a pair of trainers and checked her handbag. The phone and charger, passport, flight documents were all there together with her purse and the money she had changed. Her makeup was in her carry-on case. She took one of the suitcases out but left the other; there would be too much to carry. She put the envelope in her handbag and finally threw her hospital clothing into the boot and closed the lid.

Monique pulled her chosen suitcase to the front of the car and Bernice got out and hugged her. Monique put her head in the car to say goodbye to the children but they were both asleep.

"Give them my love," said Monique.

"I will. Please be careful, Monique. Call me when you can."

"I will call you tomorrow... Oh, I nearly forgot, I've left one of the suitcases in the back; it is too much for me to carry. I will be back to collect it as soon as I can... oh, and my hospital clothes."

"No problem, I will see to it." said Bernice.

Bernice watched her sister walk towards the front of the hotel and into the hotel reception; then headed back to the apartment. "Where's Auntie Monique?" said Sophie a little later, then fell back to sleep before Bernice could answer.

The hotel was not busy, just a night porter manning the reception desk. He viewed Monique with suspicion; no makeup, hair a mess, she looked more like a vagrant. His demeanour changed, however, when he saw her expensive luggage and heard the way she spoke. He also noticed the wad of Euros in her purse. She had the presence of mind to consider that someone may be tracking her credit card usage which would give the game away so she paid for the room in cash; so far, so good. She would have to take a chance once she arrived in Australia.

She took the lift to the third floor and found her room; the first thing she needed was to have a bath and wash her hair. She could smell the staleness of the river water on her skin, she was anxious to cleanse herself.

Monique, unsurprisingly, found it difficult to sleep. Apart from the effects of the drugs; there was the trauma of her capture and attempted murder. She had no idea what the future held. Would she have to continue her life under an alias? How could she expose Edward and the company that had almost killed her? If she could just get to Harry, at least he understood. She wanted to call him again but would have to wait; he would not be available.

The following morning she showered again and changed into jeans and tee shirt. Taking no chances, she ordered a room-service breakfast and then watched TV until midday when she was officially required to vacate the hotel. She had called Bernice and the phone was answered by Victor who had returned from Brussels. He wanted to make sure she was ok then passed the phone over to Bernice. They chatted for some time; she also had to speak to Sophie and Guy who had been excused kindergarten and she felt a tinge of sadness that she couldn't stay longer. She would make up for that she vowed.

She packed her bags again, left the room and dropped off her key at reception before taking a taxi to the airport. It would mean another hotel until her flight the following day.

At seven o'clock Saturday morning, Monique was entering the duty-free area of terminal two, Charles de Gaul airport; she had one or two purchases to make before her journey. She needed a new jacket and to replace her watch. She would have to use her credit card but decided it was a risk worth taking. There were several designer outlets catering for her needs in the duty-free area. The retail therapy lifted her spirits, that and the thought of meeting up with Harry again. By nine, having completed her shopping, she was on the plane sat in her business-class seat drinking champagne and waiting for the flight to take off. She felt a sense of relief as the plane headed down the runway; next stop, Hong Kong, to refuel, then Sydney, Australia.

Chateau Jura, Friday

Scheck and his henchmen had driven through the night following their mission to silence Monique on Edward's orders. They were in good humour on the journey back believing, not unreasonably, that their endeavours had led to a satisfactory conclusion. After a brief sleep in his room at the Chateau, Scheck was on the phone to his boss in Hong Kong with the good news.

"Excellent, excellent," said Edward. "We can talk more when I get back. How will you explain her absence?"

"We can say she has gone to Paris to visit her sister," said Scheck. "Which is true, and if she is found, well, it will be a terrible accident. There will be no loose ends," Scheck assured him.

Monday morning, David Leganes was at his desk early. He had been monitoring all calls from Darwin getting updates on the prospecting mission; there was a lot riding on it. He was pleased that initial findings had proved so encouraging and was looking forward to getting the results from the second site. Everything pointed to a positive conclusion. He had done some calculations, his own investment in the project should net him around three million Swiss Francs. In Edward's absence, he was also keeping the Frankfurt syndicate updated; there were smiles all around.

The call that came to his extension at around quarter to eight was not well-received. He listened as Den described the radio call he'd received from Harry.

"What do you mean, sabotage?" he bellowed down the phone at Den who was doing his best not to irritate the Head of Research.

Leganes listened as Den related Harry's radio message. The truck had been sabotaged by Ying, Nate was in a bad way and two of the security team were possibly dead.

"What about the samples?" asked Leganes.

"No news, I'm afraid," said Den.

"What do you mean no news? Didn't you ask?" said Leganes.

"I was more concerned with my colleagues," said Den.

"Well, can you speak to them and find out? This project is vital, you know that, don't you?" said Leganes.

"Yes," said Den.

"Ok, well, call me as soon as you have any more information," said Leganes, and put the phone down. He put his head in his hands in frustration and stress. He wasn't sure how he was going to tell Edward.

He picked the phone up again and dialled another number. "Leonard, can you get up here. I think we may have a problem."

Scheck was also in early and quickly made his way to Leganes' office.

"Come in Leonard, sit down," said Leganes when Scheck knocked on the door.

"I've just had a call from Darwin; there's more trouble out there."

Leganes outlined what had happened. "Sabotage... loosened the wheel nuts on Nate's truck apparently."

Scheck looked at Leganes in dismay. "Yes, I remember the Chinese girl, very quiet," said Scheck. "What do you want me to do?"

"I need you to go out there and sort it out. It seems I can't trust the security team to do their job," said Leganes. "I don't know what I'm going to tell Edward."

"Tell him you're on top of things," said Scheck.

"But I'm not, am I? I thought you had seen to everything; we're paying you enough," said Leganes.

"I'll fly out as soon as I can and see to it personally," said Scheck.

"Well, make sure you do. We can't afford any more slip-ups. Frankfurt is nervous enough as it is. If they pull the plug, there'll be no Australian project, and you know what that means..." Leganes looked at Scheck with a grave expression. "With the amount of money that's tied up out there, it could bring the whole business down."

Scheck went to get up. "Wait... there's something else. There're some samples from the first site which apparently show significant deposits of Uranium. They've been lost. Find me those samples and get them here for analysis. If they confirm the field findings conclusively, we'll be back on track."

Back in Darwin, Tuesday morning eight-thirty, Harry was feeling more refreshed after a relaxing bath and a decent night's sleep. He'd applied more cream and the insect bites were less troublesome; the swelling on his face had also gone down. He decided he would call in at the hospital on his way to the office to see how Nate was progressing.

He reached the ward and Nate was just lying on his back staring at the ceiling. His leg was raised on a pulley in a plaster cast. He looked around when he heard someone approach.

"G'day Harry," he said.

"Hi Nate, how's it going?"

"A bit crock, if I'm honest. Leg's been giving me gip and I've got a headache from hell. Thanks again for getting me out by the way..."

"That's ok," said Harry.

"Bloody Chink; I hope Scheck's lot catch up with her. She'll be sorry, that's for sure... any news where she went?"

"No nothing," said Harry.

"So what's happening?" said Nate, slightly calmer after his outburst.

"I don't know, just going into the office. Not sure what we can do, though. We've lost all the kit... and the samples. Have you spoken to your wife?"

"Yeah, she's giving me a right going over. I can see why the Abbos go walkabout. Wants me to give it all up and leave."

Harry's ears pricked up. "That might not be such a bad thing," said Harry.

"What do you mean?" asked Nate.

"I was chatting to Marci last night, and, well, I've got real doubts about this project."

"Yeah...? Why would you think that?" said Nate.

"I've been doing a lot of thinking and, to put it bluntly, it doesn't feel right. I mean think about it; you're a bushman by heart, I can see that. Don't you feel...I don't know...uneasy?"

"Hadn't crossed my mind if I'm honest; I'm in for a lot of moolah if this comes off. Set me and the wife up for life."

"Yeah, ok but at what cost? I was chatting with Banjo and Charlie and I can see why they're so against it," said Harry.

"Yeah, well what would they know; they're just bloody Abbos? Anyway, why are you against it all of a sudden? I thought you were here to make it happen."

"Yeah, well let's just say I've changed my mind."

"Well, don't let Leganes or Scheck hear you talking like that, they won't be happy."

"But what if we just recommend that it's not worth the investment? I mean we've got no samples so they can't prove anything," said Harry.

"What about the money they've already spent?" said Nate.

"They'll just have to write it off," said Harry.

"They won't do that; there're too many people involved.

They'll want some return, that's for sure."

"But if I do recommend that we don't go ahead and pull out, would I have your backing?" said Harry.

"You leave me out of it. I've got enough trouble with the wife. Only wants me to help her set up a tourist business, you know, show people the sites."

"You'd be good at that and you won't have the hassle."

Nate was deep in thought. "What's Marci say?"

"She'll come round, I think."

Nate continued to be non-committal and Harry decided not to push it further. He changed the subject.

"Any new about Heinz?" said Harry.

"Nah, heard nothing," said Nate.

There was an uncomfortable silence.

"Right, I'll get on. Do you want me to bring any grapes?" said Harry with a broad grin.

"Bugger off, ya Pommie bastard," said Nate. He was on the mend, thought Harry.

Harry arrived at the office and parked up. The car park was practically empty, just Marci's Fiat; no sign of the minibuses. With his work laptop still somewhere in the Toyota, Harry had brought his own and he retrieved it from the back seat.

There was a sombre mood; Marci was at her desk and Winda was making tea. Marci had already brought her up-to-date with the news.

Marci's eyes brighten when he walked towards her pod; Winda poked her head around the kitchen door. "Would you like a coffee, Harry?" she said.

"Yeah, thanks," said Harry.

He told Marci about his conversation with Nate.

"I asked him if I were to recommend we pull the plug would he support it."

"What did he say?" said Marci.

"Didn't want to be involved," said Harry.

"Yeah, I thought that would be the case. He's a wily old customer, always plays the politics," said Marci.

"We can discuss it with Den when he gets in. Get his thoughts," said Harry.

Den arrived a few minutes later and spent some time discussing the trek and what had gone wrong.

"I couldn't believe it was Ying. I mean, she just didn't seem the sort. Just goes to show," he said. "Does anyone know where she went?"

There were blank looks. "I followed the tracks for a while but I think she headed south... Rather her than me, that's all I can say. I wouldn't have tackled it on my own, that's for sure... Where are the security guys? They'll be interested," said Harry.

"Not seen them since Friday," said Den. "Reckon they've left."

"What about the Chateau, have you told them?" asked Harry.

'Yeah, spoke to Leganes... more bothered about the samples," replied Den.

"That doesn't surprise me," said Harry.

Marci joined them. "Any news about Heinz?" she said.

"No," said Harry. "Nothing, I'll make some enquiries next time I visit Nate."

Harry took a drink of his coffee; he needed to say something to Den.

"I was saying to Marci earlier, I've got some real concerns about this project. Forget any emotional or idealistic reasons; having seen the terrain first hand I can't see that the site is going to be viable, irrespective of the uranium oxide content. Do you know how much the Ranger Mine cost to set up?"

Den looked at Harry. "Not off the top of my head but you're

talking billions of dollars."

"The infrastructure alone's gonna cost that, given the remoteness of the area," said Harry.

"It was pretty wild around Ranger when they built it," countered Den.

"Yeah, but the costs have soared since the eighties," said Harry.

"True," said Den.

Marci chipped in. "Yeah, but I think they factored that in... in the original proposal that was put to the Australian Government," she said.

The conversation was interrupted by the sound of Den's phone ringing from his pod. Harry declared a recess for more coffee to enable Den to take the call. Winda who was still in her workstation volunteered to do the honours.

Harry could see Den's face change as he listened to the caller. After five minutes he hung up.

"That was the police, they've found the Toyota. It'd run out of diesel in the bush somewhere about forty miles from the Stuart. They found Ying''s body too. They think she must've been driving round in circles for hours and got lost; looks like she tried to walk her way out of it. The dingoes have been feeding on her, they said."

"Jesus," said Marci.

"They traced us through the leasing agents. They're sending someone out to collect it. Hopefully, we should get it back tomorrow," said Den.

Harry looked at Marci. "The samples," they said in unison.

"That puts a different complexion on things," said Marci.

"Yeah, but it could be the answer to our prayers," said Harry. "We can send them samples, just not the ones they are expecting; if you're up for it."

Marci looked hesitant. "Hmm, not sure about that."

Den had heard. "You can leave me out of it, if anyone finds out we've messed with the samples it won't be just your job on the line, judging by what's been going on around here."

"Yeah, ok Den, I hear you. Don't worry; I'll take the can if it comes down to it," said Harry and went back to his workstation leaving Marci and Den in conversation.

For the remainder of the day, Harry started to map out his report. Unfortunately with most of the technical data on his work laptop he had to check with the team on points of detail. With the possibility it might be returned the following day, he decided to produce an outline only and fill in the gaps later.

Then, at four o'clock, his mobile rang.

"Hello," said Harry.

"Harry, c'est Monique."

"Monique?!" Harry almost shouted but quickly contained his excitement. "How are you?"

"Je suis en Darwin... er, at the airport."

"What?!" Harry was momentarily speechless. "But that's great... wait, I'll come and collect you – twenty minutes, ok?"

"J'attendrai, Harry... er... I will get un café and wait."

Harry walked across to Marci. "I have to go, something's come up. Are you going to see Nate tonight at the hospital?"

"Yeah, I'll try," Marci replied.

"Give him my apologies. I'm going to be tied up. I'll call in the morning," said Harry, and almost ran out of the building leaving Marci perplexed.

He started the Suzuki and headed for the airport. He was there in fifteen minutes and parked in the short-stay car park. He walked to the arrivals gate and there she was waiting, wearing a light-weight beige jacket, smart jeans and a white top. She looked beautiful.

Harry felt a sense of exhilaration and ran across to her. She smiled for the first time in a while.

He wrapped his arms around her and held tight.

"Oh Harry, I have missed you so much." They kissed, a lingering kiss; the kind that lovers do after a long absence.

He took her luggage and wheeled it to his car.

"Have you anywhere to stay?" asked Harry.

"No, I have not arranged anything."

"Good, you can stay with me... if you like," he added.

"Mais oui, of course."

"I've just moved into an apartment. You'll have to excuse the mess."

"It will be wonderful, I am sure," said Monique.

She looked at him. "What has happened to your face?"

"Oh nothing," replied Harry. "Just a few insect bites."

They stowed Monique's luggage and headed to the flat. Monique held Harry's hand when he wasn't holding the steering wheel or changing gear.

"That's where I live," said Harry, pointing to the tower block.

She squeezed his hand and smiled.

Harry parked the car and between them, they took Monique's luggage to the lift.

"We're on the twelfth floor," he said.

They exited the lift; Harry led the way to his apartment and opened the door.

Monique looked around the room.

"It's not very big, I'm afraid," said Harry.

"C'est perfect," said Monique. She took off her jacket and they embraced again.

"Would you like a tea, coffee, or I have some wine if you prefer?" asked Harry.

"Oui du vin, it will be ok, merci. I have had much coffee," she said.

Harry poured two glasses. "Come on, tell me the news."

Monique didn't know where to start but gradually she related the events of her escape and then her capture in Paris. "I was, er; very lucky, the river police they found me otherwise I would be dead."

"Jesus, I can't imagine what you have been through. I'm just sorry I wasn't there for you," said Harry.

"It is ok... er... I understand; it was not possible."

She told Harry about her sister and Monique's concern for her. She would phone her later and let her know she had arrived safely.

Harry contemplated Monique's story and felt a well of sadness.

"Come on, let me show you where to put your things," said Harry, snapping out of his ruminations, and leading her to the bedroom.

Monique started undoing her blouse and jeans and then got into bed. Harry followed her lead and got in next to her. They held each other for a while and then nature took its course.

It was everything Monique had imagined. "C'est merveilleuse... Je t'aime, Harry," she said as they lay there together.

She looked at him closely and started examining the bites, scratches and bruises on Harry's body. "Are you sure you are ok," she said. "You have medicine?"

"Yes, I'll be fine; don't worry."

Harry wasn't used to anyone being concerned about him and realised he was experiencing something special. Ever since the cave incident, he had found it difficult to form any sort of attachment with girls. The physical side wasn't an issue but it was as though the near-death experience had taken away an emotional function; the part that forged a deep bond with another person. With Monique, it was different.

"Are you hungry?" he asked.

"Oui," she whispered.

"Come on, I'll take you out for dinner."

So that night Harry took Monique to an Italian restaurant on the quayside overlooking the harbour. It was a warm evening and they walked along the waterside for a while watching the sunset.

"C'est perfect," said Monique, not for the first time.

Monique slept soundly that night. Although she had cat-napped on the plane, it had been the first proper night's sleep she had had for a while. Harry awoke a few times, thinking about some of Monique's revelations. He thought they would be safe for a while but he knew they couldn't afford to be complacent. He also thought about the longer term. It was unlikely he could stay with Helvetia once his report had been received. He decided he would return to the UK and search for new challenges; he would take Monique with him.

The following morning, Harry left the apartment key with Monique. It meant she could come and go as she pleased and would give her time to acclimatise to the time zone; maybe even do some shopping. As he was about to leave, Monique went to her handbag. She gave him the envelope containing the computer discs.

"You need to see these, I think. I found them in Edward's safe. They may be important."

Harry opened the envelope and looked inside.

"Thank you, I'll look at them at work."

He kissed her goodbye and left for the hospital.

When Harry arrived at the ward, Nate was more like his old self.

"They say I can go home tomorrow," he said. "Not sure I can do much knocking around at home. Thought I might come into the office and annoy one or two folks."

"You'll have no problem in that direction," said Harry and smiled. He decided not to say anything more about the report. "They've found the Toyota, by the way, did you hear?"

"Yeah, Marci told me last night... Do they know where?" said Nate.

"Out in the bush somewhere... Ying's dead."

"Yeah, I heard. Well, she probably got what she deserved, I guess," said Nate.

"Mmm," said Harry. "Police are bringing it back this morning sometime."

"Right, ok, well that's good. There was a lot of kit on board if it's not been destroyed... Let me know the latest tonight if you're coming in."

"Yeah, right," said Harry.

After ten minutes with Nate continuing to complain about his wife's nagging, Harry excused himself; he needed to get back to the office.

"I'll call in again tomorrow. Is there anything you need?"

"A couple of Sheila's with big hooters would do the trick, mate."

"Might struggle there but I'll see what I can do," replied Harry.

He was pleased to see Nate was making a good recovery. He made some enquiries about Heinz and he too was now out of danger and was being flown back to Germany to complete his recuperation.

Harry returned to the office. Only Marci was in and was engrossed in some paperwork. After a quick conflab, Harry went to his workstation and logged onto his laptop. He pressed the button on his CD Rom drive and fed in the first disc. He scanned through the first document.

"Wow," he said to himself. "Now this could really put the cat among the pigeons.

Chapter Nineteen

Harry continued reading the documents on the discs; he was amazed at what he found. Details of payments to politicians, bribes and a list of people considered opposed to their Australian project, which included Professor James Harvey of Queensland University. Harry was trying to work out why Edward would keep such a document; extortion or covering his back crossed his mind. At least one on the list of antagonists was missing, presumed dead.

The question, though, was what was he going to do with the information? A thought immediately came to mind. He called Becs' mobile. It was picked up on the third ring.

"Hi Becs, it's Harry."

"Hi Harry, how are you? How was the trek?"

"Don't ask... a bit of a disaster," he said, without elaborating. "Look, I haven't got long but I've got hold of some information which I think will help your investigation. Can I send it to you?"

"Yeah, of course, let me give you my address."

Becs gave him her contact details.

"Thanks," said Harry. He repeated the address to make sure it was right. "Look, this is extremely damning and sensitive information. I suggest you hold fire on publishing any article until you've had a chance to check it out but I don't think you'll be disappointed. I'll get it posted tonight."

"Thanks, Harry. Look, I'm sorry I had to run out on you. It was all getting a bit spooky up there."

"It's ok, I understand."

"If you're ever down this way, call me up. There'll always be a bed for the night."

"Thanks," said Harry. "I'll bear that in mind... I better go; I'm ringing from the office. Take care, Becs."

"You too, Harry."

He rang off.

Before he packed away the discs, he copied them onto his laptop, and then made a further copy onto a memory stick. He put the discs into a 'Jiffy' bag, sealed it and wrote Becs' address on the front. He put the memory stick in his drawer for the moment.

"Just popping out, won't be long," he said to Marci.

Harry went to the main CBD Post Office and waited in line. He explained to the clerk that he wanted it to go express, secure delivery and she gave him some options. He passed over the package and paid. "That's going to put the cat among the pigeons," he said to himself as he walked back to his car.

Back in the office, Den and Winda had arrived and Harry brought them up to date with Nate's recovery. "Threatening to come in tomorrow," said Harry. "I suggested he stayed at home." There was only muted laughter.

Later that morning there was a call from Tallara in reception. "The car's here," said Marci, relaying the message.

Harry immediately got up and joined her and they walked down to the car park where a police officer was waiting. There were introductions and the officer handed over the keys. "We've finished with it but you might want to put more diesel in; the budget only stretched to five dollars," he said with a grin. "Oh, and we've confiscated the rifle, by the way."

Harry acknowledged and thanked the officer who turned and walked away. They examined the contents. "Nothing missing that I can see," said Marci. "The samples are here... and your laptop by the look of it," holding up his computer bag.

Harry was looking around the vehicle and trying to imagine the desolation Ying must have felt in her last hours. He suddenly felt sorry for her, despite her actions. He stood chatting to Marci for a few minutes.

"Are you up for what we discussed yesterday?"

"What, the samples, you mean?" said Marci.

"Yeah, we can drive out a way, shouldn't take long," said Harry. There was a moment's pause.

"Hmm, I'm not sure," said Marci.

"Look, no-one's going to know," said Harry.

"Can't say I'm happy. What if the security guys find out?" said Marci.

"I'll say it was my idea," said Harry. "I can do it on my own but it will be easier with two."

"Ok, but as long as we're clear this was your idea," said Marci.

"Yeah, of course," said Harry.

Harry went back to the office to let Den know they were going out and would be taking the Toyota. He did not give the details but Den guessed what was happening.

"So, what's the plan?" said Marci

"I thought we could go south until we hit the bush and then find somewhere to stop but first we better put some diesel in," said Harry.

They stopped at the first petrol station they came to and Harry put in fifty dollars worth of diesel. "Remind me to claim that back," said Harry.

He drove off and they headed out of the city on the Stuart Highway; they didn't have long to wait. Just south of Howard Springs the buildings disappeared and trees and scrub-lined the road.

"Anywhere here will do," said Harry as they came to a lay-by.

"Won't they be able to tell when they analyse the samples?" said Marci.

"I wouldn't think so. The mineral makeup's pretty similar to Kakadu, only without the uranium oxide," replied Harry.

They pulled over and got out. "We just need some loose soil," said Harry.

He lifted the box of samples from the first site off the back of the truck. It was heavy with about thirty canisters. He took one of the containers out.

"If we empty out, say, three-quarters, then mix in some from here then it will dilute any uranium to unviable levels. What do you think?"

"Yeah, that should do it," said Marci. "But I'm still not comfortable with this."

"Don't worry," said Harry. "It'll be fine."

So for the next twenty minutes, Harry and Marci emptied out some of the contents from the samples and replaced it with soil from their parking spot. Harry shook the canisters, in turn, to make sure the soil was suitably mixed in; then they headed back to the office.

Harry called Den from reception to help with the unloading. "You can leave me out of it, I'm not getting involved," said Den and put the phone down.

So it was down to Marci and Harry to carry the stuff from the Toyota back upstairs and with his work laptop now recovered, he would now be able to finalise his report.

"Den, can you get the samples back to the Chateau?" Harry said when they had unpacked the gear.

"You do it yourself, mate," Den replied and went back to his computer.

Winda heard the exchanged and intervened. "There's a courier service we use, I'll call them," she said and picked up her phone.

So Harry packed the samples ready for dispatch; it was as though they had become toxic, even Marci had distanced herself from them. They were eventually collected by the courier just after lunch much to everyone's relief.

Meanwhile, Den made another call which he was dreading.

"Leganes," barked the recipient.

"David, it's Den... from Darwin," he said meekly. "We've got the samples back. They're with the courier. You should get them in a few days."

There was an expression of relief on the other end.

Den explained the discovery of the Toyota. "Ying"s dead."

"Well that's no great loss," said Leganes.

Leganes hung up and wondered if he should recall Scheck but then thought it wouldn't do any harm for him to do some digging. He would brief him with the update when he landed in Darwin. He left a message on Scheck's phone to call him when he landed.

Harry returned to the apartment around four-thirty; Monique flung her arms around him in relief as he walked through the door. Despite her escape, she was still anxious that Edward would trace her in some way but with Harry's return, she felt safe again. She had spent the day in the flat until lunch time and then gone for a walk and found the coffee shop by the launderette. She had tied her hair back and wore her sunglasses in an attempt to disguise her appearance.

That evening they went out for a meal again; this time Monique insisted on paying and during the evening Harry raised the question of 'the future'.

"Since the trek, I've been thinking a lot about what I should do." Monique looked at him, her eyes locked on his.

"Once I've got my report away, I'm going to hand in my notice and return home; there's nothing more for me here. You could come too if you want," Harry added and waited for a response.

"Mais oui, yes, I would like that," she said, "but... je m'inquiète... er, I worry about Edward. What if he finds me again?"

"But he thinks you're dead so he won't come looking for you, you'll be safe."

Monique took a sip of her wine, looking far from convinced.

Harry changed the subject.

"There is something else I need to tell you. I've sent those discs you gave me to a newspaper reporter friend who is doing an article on the mining industry here. It could work for us."

"I hope so Harry."

Thursday morning, Harry was at his desk finalising his report; it would not make good reading at the Chateau. Leganes and Edward both thought that Harry would endorse the project, particularly as the spectrometer readings from the initial soil samples had proved so positive. Harry covered this in his report and said that the traces of uranium oxide were of low-grade. He quoted specific technical data to support this. He concluded that, given all the information they had acquired and, taking into consideration the terrain, it was not a viable project. He recommended that it be terminated. He saved it as a draft for the moment.

With everything in limbo, there was not much for the team to do; that changed with the arrival of Nate on a pair of crutches. Harry followed him into his office and brought him up-to-date with events including the discovery of the Toyota and the soil samples.

"We've got them off," said Harry, not mentioning the tampering. "We'll just have to see what they say when they get them."

"Hmm, I guess," said Nate.

"I've also finalised the report, not sent it yet but I'm recommending that the project is pulled."

Nate looked at him. His eyes narrowed and Harry thought

he was about to explode into another round of expletives. Harry decided to get in first.

"Look, irrespective of any environmental issues, I'm convinced this is not a viable project. I just don't see how they're ever going to make it pay. The investment is colossal, and that's without all the opposition because that won't go away."

"But they were only going to sell the rights," said Nate.

"Yeah, I get that but where would they get a buyer? They could be waiting for years... the amount of money needed to get the project off the ground will run into billions. I did some calculations based on the Ranger output and you're talking about a thirty-year return, minimum, most likely much longer. Nobody's going to want that... I think in the long run the company will thank me for being cautious."

"Hmm," said Nate.

He left Harry and immediately announced a team meeting. Winda was back on coffee-making duties. He waited for the depleted team to settle then started his pitch.

"Right, I know things have been a bit tricky over the last week or so but we're back in business now."

"What business would that be, Nate?" said Den. "Cos from here it doesn't look like we've got a job."

"Why do you say that?" said Nate.

"Simple... no project; no job," said Den. Winda nodded.

"We don't know anything for certain. We'll just have to wait and see what they say at the Chateau."

"Well, from what I've heard, Harry here's recommending that it doesn't go ahead, so that's us fucked," said Den.

Marci and Winda looked at each other. Harry looked down. "I can only call it as I see it," said Harry.

"Well, it's alright for you, you don't live here. It's not so easy getting work, you know," said Den.

This was a different side to Den that Harry hadn't seen before.

After a few more minutes of fruitless debate, Nate dismissed the team. Harry stayed back.

"What was that all about from Den?" said Harry.

"Probably getting some stick from his missus. She's a bloody nightmare, only met her once; ya don't wanna be crossing her, that's for sure," said Nate.

Harry went back to his workstation to finish his report. Den was on the phone again.

There was an arrival at Darwin International airport later that afternoon. He checked his phone and picked up his messages while he waited for his baggage at the carousel. "Ring me when you land," said a voice mail.

He rang Switzerland; it was six forty-five a.m. there and the Head of Research was sat at his desk. He picked up the phone.

"David, it's Scheck. You left a message."

The Austrian listened while Leganes brought him up to date.

"So the girl is dead and the samples are found," he summarised. "What am I doing here then?"

Scheck's eyes narrowed as Leganes continued his account.

"Hmm, I see, so it is possible the girl may have had an accomplice. What information?" Scheck had screwed his right hand into a fist.

"What?!" His voiced was raised; one or two passengers were alerted and looked in his direction.

"You think Herr Bentham has interfered with the samples? Why would he do that? Who has told you this? Den Travis... ok, ok, do you have his phone number? Yes, leave it to me... No, I will see to it... No, it won't be a problem..."

Leganes gave Scheck a number which he wrote down on the back of his boarding pass.

Scheck consulted the electronic notice above the carousel. *'Baggage expected 4:20'.* Ten minutes. He phoned the number.

"Herr Travis...? It is Scheck... from security. Herr Leganes says you have some information for me." Scheck listened and then recapped.

"So, Herr Bentham wants the project shut down and is sending a negative report... and, you say, you think he has changed the samples. What do you mean, you think...? Has he or hasn't he? Oh, he has... for certain, I see. Who else was involved? What, no-one...? I see, so Ms Davenport she has helped him...? No, I will deal with her later. Do you know where Herr Bentham lives?"

Den already had the information at hand from Winda.

"Launceston Towers, apartment 1203? Ah, yes I have heard the name. No... but we have had some business there before."

Again, the boarding pass came into use.

"No, I will find it... thank you. We will speak tomorrow... I will mention your help to Herr Leganes; he will be very grateful I am certain. Auf weidersehen."

Scheck picked up his hold-luggage which was now on its second circuit of the carousel and left the airport. He took a taxi to his hotel; he would be going out later.

After a meal and change of clothing, he was ready for his mission. He was a large man, shaved head and, outside the Chateau, had a penchant for wearing hats; he was dressed in a lightweight off-white jacket, matching trousers and deck shoes. He had his favourite Panama; which enhanced his rather sinister appearance. He looked like someone from a 1940's gangster movie.

He took a taxi to a familiar destination; Nate called it 'The Depot'. It was the warehouse where the team had collected their transport for the trek. It had also been used as a base for the security team during their stay in Darwin. With everything much quieter now, Scheck had recalled them back to Switzerland.

In his pocket he had a set of keys; he knew which one would fit. He opened up the pull-down frontage. Inside were the two Duchamp Foundation minibuses. He had the keys to both and went to the nearest one and got in. He opened up the glove compartment; it was still there, the Glock G26 Subcompact revolver, also known as the Baby Glock because of its size and easy concealment capability. He put it in his jacket pocket and started the minibus, drove outside and headed towards the tower block address as provided by Den.

Despite having had meals prepared for her in the Chateau for over six years, Monique enjoyed cooking and to pass the time she had made Harry a special French meal. She was starting to feel more confident in her new surroundings and had been shopping in the local mini-market next to the garage. The dish was simmering in the oven when Harry arrived back from the office. He couldn't remember anyone else, apart from his mother, cooking for him and was taken aback by the aromas emanating from the kitchen as he walked in.

"Mmm, something smells good," he said as Monique went to greet him.

He brought Monique up to date with the news from the office and told her he would be sending his report off the following day with the recommendation that the project should be aborted.

"Edward, he will not be happy. He has spent much money on this, I know."

"Yes, I know that too but I can only say what I believe."

"I think they thought you would just, how you say...? Ratifie?"

"Ratify..? No, I don't work that way. We have done a thorough investigation and that is my opinion and if they don't like it, then that's tough." He didn't mention the tampered soil samples.

"Ah, but you don't know them."

"I'm beginning to," said Harry.

Harry and Monique continued their discussion while they finished their meal with a bottle of wine.

Scheck pulled up outside the tower-block in the minibus and checked the information Den had given him again; apartment 1203.

He took the lift to the twelfth floor and walked down the corridor to the apartment. He clutched the gun in his pocket and knocked on the door.

Harry looked at Monique. "Who's that at this time of night?" he said. "Wait in the kitchen; I'll see who it is."

Harry opened the door; recognition was instant.

"Herr Scheck! What are you doing here?" He shouted loud enough for Monique to hear.

Scheck immediately put his foot in the door so Harry couldn't shut it.

"Herr Bentham, we need to have a discussion," he said with his strong German accent.

He barged in.

"What about?" asked Harry.

"Sit down," said Scheck and took the gun from his pocket.

"You have been... what is the word? Sabotaging, yes, sabotaging the project."

"What do you mean?" said Harry.

"You have been changing the samples, I have heard. Edward will not be happy about that."

Harry sat on the settee. "I have been saving the company money. It's not a viable project."

"That is not your decision to make. What is your connection

with the Chinese girl?" asked Scheck.

"Connection...? What connection? I don't have any connection. She tried to kill us, messed with the wheel nuts on the truck, nearly killed Nate, and then tied me and Marci up. She left us to die."

"Hmm," said Scheck mulling over the last comment. Den had not mentioned this.

"I think we need to go for a walk," said Scheck. "On your feet."

"I'm staying here," said Harry, defiantly.

Scheck unlocked the safety catch of the Glock. "I said get up."

Scheck was stood with his back to the kitchen totally unaware of someone behind him.

Monique was holding a full bottle of Merlot and brought it down on Scheck's head as hard as she could. He dropped like a stone. Harry quickly retrieved the gun. Monique froze, still holding the bottle with her hand over her mouth, shaking like a leaf.

"What are we going to do Harry?" she said, looking at Scheck's prostrate body.

Harry stopped for a moment to think. He bent down and checked the Austrian's pulse; there was none. There was a large dent in the back of his head where it had caved in under the force of Monique's hit.

"I think he's dead," said Harry.

"Oh non! Merde. Qu'est-ce shoud nous faisons?" said Monique. Harry hadn't understood her... "What are we going to do?" translated Monique.

"It's ok, it was in self-defence. He was going to kill me," replied Harry. Monique was starting to become hysterical. Harry stood up and held her.

"Shhh... It's ok... It's going to be ok."

"Nous devrions appeler la police... er... we should call the police," translated Monique after she had regained her composure.

"We can't involve the police; there'll be too many questions... I think we need to dispose of him."

"I do not understand," said Monique.

"Well, he drugged you and put you in the river, yes? You were lucky to be alive; he threatened your family."

"Oui, that is true."

"He would have killed me too if you hadn't had stopped him," said Harry. "If we call the police, Edward will find out where you are and he will send someone else."

"Oui," said Monique.

She was still shaking. Harry went to the bedroom and took a sheet off the bed.

"Here, help me," said Harry, and between them, they managed to roll the deceased Scheck onto it.

"We can drag him to the lift and then to the car."

"But we cannot, they will find out."

"No-one will find out... It's for the best," replied Harry.

Harry went through Scheck's pocket and took his keys and wallet.

"Come on, give me a hand. Check and make sure there's no-one coming... regarde," said Harry to make sure she understood.

Monique opened the apartment door slowly.

"No-one is here," said Monique and between them they managed to pull Scheck's body on the sheet down the corridor to the lift. Harry pressed the call button. It seemed to take forever. Harry was looking around to make sure no-one was about; there was no way he could explain away this situation. Monique wanted to run away but she was blindly obeying Harry, totally in shock.

He looked at Monique; there was an unmistakable noise,

footsteps coming up the stairs, probably two floors below. "Come on, come on," he whispered under his breath. There was no plan B.

Then the lift appeared and the door slowly opened. They dragged Scheck inside on the sheet and pushed the button for the ground floor. The door closed just as the person walked past. Harry exhaled sharply; Monique was just staring at the call buttons watching the lights change as they descended. It was late but people were still around. If anyone else called the lift they were in trouble.

The elevator reached the ground floor and the door opened. Harry could see the minibus parked outside the main entrance about twenty feet away. He was in a quandary; the minibus would be easier to transport the man but it was conspicuous. There was no alternative; they would have to take a chance.

"The minibus," whispered Harry. "Go and open it."

He gave her the set of Scheck's keys and Monique crossed the forecourt to the vehicle. Harry was crouched over the sheet in a forlorn attempt to conceal it in some way.

Monique was stood fiddling with the keys, her fingers couldn't function properly and she fumbled them until they dropped to the floor. Harry looked around anxiously. "Come on, come on," he said under his breath, not for the first time. She picked them up, steadied herself and managed to find the right one. She pulled the door handle towards her; it wouldn't open. Harry could see and made a sliding motion with his hands. She understood and slid the door open sideways; it was heavy. Harry started dragging the sheet backwards across the tarmac, hoping upon hope that no-one was looking.

He reached the side of the vehicle and got inside. The Austrian was sat on the sheet with his head slumped forward against the side of the minibus. It looked like something from a theatre farce. Harry took the end of the sheet next to his head.

"Grab the other end," he said.

Monique lifted it up and Harry pulled hard until Scheck was inside the vehicle. There were two rows of seats behind the driver and the Austrian was laid on the floor immediately in front of the first set.

Harry got in and Monique handed him the keys. They set off.

"Where will we go?" asked Monique.

"I think I know a place," said Harry.

He had the semblance of an idea. Having studied many maps of the area over the last few weeks, he knew the locality pretty well. "Somewhere where he won't be found," said Harry.

To the north of the city, there are several coastal reserves where tourists can watch the wildlife. Buffalo Creek is one of the lesser known and least developed. It would take them about twenty-five minutes to get there. There was a track that led right up to the creek itself, this time of night it would be completely deserted.

After about twenty minutes they eventually left the tarmac and bounced down an unmade road, Monique was getting nervous.

"Are you sure we are doing right, Harry?" she said.

"Yes, it's the only way. He's dead, we can't bring him back. We need to get rid of him. There will be too many questions if we go to the police. Don't forget, Edward did try to have you killed and he will try again if he finds out where you are."

"Mais oui," she said in resignation and stared ahead. The beam of the headlights illuminated the canopy of palms that shrouded the car; it looked like they were travelling through a tunnel.

Five minutes later the track ended; in front of them Buffalo Creek glistened in the reflection from the minibus's headlights; a myriad of starburst patterns. As it was the dry season, the creek was low but there was a swift current heading out into the Timor Sea less than a quarter of a mile away. The track dropped downwards towards the water's edge where there was a small wooden landing stage which would enable boats to be launched. Harry stopped the minibus at the top of the slope and got out.

He slid open the side of the minibus and grabbed the sheet. He tugged it and Scheck dropped unceremoniously to the floor.

"We need to take off his clothes," said Harry.

"I cannot do that," said Monique.

"Ok, I'll do it," and Harry started removing his jacket, shirt, trousers and shoes leaving Scheck in just a pair of shorts. "Quick, help me," said Harry and between them, they dragged the Austrian down the slope to the landing stage and pushed him into the creek.

Harry watched as the luckless Scheck bobbed for a moment before dropping beneath the water; in moments he was being carried out towards the open sea. He thought he could hear other splashes but in the dark couldn't make out the cause. He took the Glock from his pocket and threw it into the middle of the creek.

As he walked back up the slope there was a yellow sign which Harry could just make out in the gloom; *'No Swimming – Crocodiles'*. There was a picture of a cartoon crocodile with its mouth open.

Harry wrapped up Scheck's clothes in the sheet, got into the minibus, and then headed back to town.

On the return journey, Monique sat in silence, staring ahead, still coming to terms with what had happened.

"Don't worry," said Harry. "It's for the best," recognising Monique was still in shock.

There was one problem which Harry was trying to resolve; what to do about the minibus.

"Yes," he said to himself but out loud.

"What?" said Monique, momentarily disturbed from her thoughts.

"I know what we can do with the minibus... I'll drive it to the office and park it there."

Monique didn't really understand but Harry was clear.

He stopped in a back street a couple of blocks away and got out. He took the sheet from the back and rolled it up and shoved it under his shirt. Then he put on Scheck's trousers over the top of his jeans then put on his jacket. Scheck's favourite hat was still in the well of the passenger seat.

"Pass me his hat," said Harry. Monique stretched across the driver's seat and handed it over. He stood there in Scheck's clothes then pulled down the Panama.

"How do I look?" he said.

"Trés bon, mais pourqoi?" said Monique.

"Cameras," said Harry, "in the office car park. If anyone checks it will look like Scheck. The pictures are not very clear, I've seen them. Can you get out and wait here? I'll be back in a few minutes."

Monique complied and Harry drove off. She watched, wondering what was happening. Harry eased the minibus through the entrance to the office car park where, only a few weeks earlier, reporters were amassing. Now it was deserted. He stopped in the far corner and wiped down the steering wheel and the dashboard as best he could, in the hope that he and Monique had not left any usable fingerprints. He then wiped Scheck's wallet and put it in the glove compartment.

He locked it up and walked back to collect Monique. She was stood waiting on the corner. Harry ducked behind a hedge and took off Scheck's clothes then wrapped them in the sheet.

"We can walk back to the flat, it's not that far," he said and they headed back hand-in-hand to the tower block.

On the way, they came to a restaurant which had long since closed and outside was a dumpster waiting to be emptied in the morning. He opened it and pushed Scheck's clothes inside. The keys to the minibus were in the jacket pocket. He pulled a couple of cardboard boxes over them and closed the lid.

They arrived back at the apartment and were confronted with the enormity of what had happened. Harry picked up the wine bottle that Monique had used to kill Scheck. "I need a drink," he said.

It had been a restless night for both of them. Monique was suffering from post-traumatic stress; killing Scheck after coming so close to dying at his hands was weighing heavily on her mind and she had hardly slept. Harry had also spent several hours awake, trying to work out where Scheck had got his information. There was clearly someone in the office who had been talking to him and by a process of elimination, it could only be Den. He was not sure what to do about it, not yet.

He eventually got up and made some tea around six-thirty. Monique did not want him to leave but he had some loose ends to tie up in the office, he explained. "I'll be back soon," he said as he kissed her goodbye.

As he parked the Suzuki, he noticed the minibus was still where he had left it.

Only Marci was in and as he entered the office she walked to him straight away.

"You need to read this," she said before he had time to speak.

It was the morning edition of The Sydney Tribune.

'Greed and corruption in the mining industry; P.M. implicated – exclusive by our reporter Rebecca Connolly', was the headline.

Harry started to read it. It ran the front page and the two next inside pages. It described the bribery of ministers, with evidence, some of which had come from the discs; extortion, putting pressure on opposition groups, the disappearance of the professor and the death of the student. The company at the heart of all this was Helvetia Mining Services of Switzerland. It exposed their operation worldwide, not just in Australia.

It was a thorough piece and with government ministers and even the Prime Minister implicated, other news agencies were eager to pick up the story.

Winda arrived and then Nate, on his crutches, about twenty minutes later. Marci showed them the newspaper.

"Well that's really fucked us up now good and proper," said Nate. "Looks like the missus is gonna get her way. Where's Den, by the way?"

"Not seen him," said Marci.

The conversation was interrupted by a commotion outside the office door.

"Winda, see what's going on will ya," said Nate but before she could investigate the door opened and a number of police officers burst in.

"What the bloody hell's going on?" said Nate as one of the officers approached.

"Inspector James Drummond, Serious Crimes Division, I've got a warrant to search these premises," said the man, flashing his identity badge. He handed Nate a piece of paper. Marci and Harry looked at each other.

"You in charge?"

"Yeah," replied Nate.

"I need you and your staff to move into a separate room and provide us with all keys to desks and passwords for the computers. On no account are you to make any outside calls or contact Switzerland by any means."

"Jeez," said Nate. "Winda, you better see what the officer needs."

Harry and Marci went into the conference room with Nate hobbling after them. Winda escorted the Inspector to the workstations. The police started taking away the computer equipment and filing cabinets on luggage trolleys. The four could only watch the activities. Harry noticed one of the officers pick up his work laptop and place it on one of the trolleys.

"Well, I won't have to worry about my report, that's for sure," said Harry.

"What do we do?" said Marci.

"Start looking for another bloody job," said Nate. "I don't know about you but I'm going for a beer. Anyone wanna join me?"

Nate walked across the office and spoke to the inspector who was directing operations. "Do ya need us to stick around or can we go?" said Nate.

"No, you can go but leave details of where we can contact you. We will need to interview you in due course," said the inspector.

There was still no sign of Den so, having given one of the officers their names and addresses, it was just Marci, Harry and Nate for the bar. Winda just wanted to go home. As the four left the building, the car park was full of police vehicles. Their doors were open and officers were ferrying the files and equipment back and forth. With their cars blocked in, they decided to walk the short distance to the bar. Winda was on the bus. There was a tape across the car park entrance with a police officer on guard. On the other side of the line, there was a group of people and as Harry and crew approached they started yelling questions.

Harry turned to Nate. "Words out."

"Yeah, you can say that again."

Ignoring the group of reporters, the three made their way to the bar, leaving Winda at the bus stop. Harry said goodbye to her; he realised they would probably not meet again.

The mood was sombre as the three sat on bar stools. Nate's crutches were leant forlornly against the bar. The team were in a contemplative mood. Despite everything that had gone on, Harry considered Marci, and Nate, friends; they had shared a lot together.

"Do you think about the trek?" said Marci.

"Yeah," said Harry. Nate didn't comment; he was in a dream.

"It could have ended differently," said Marci.

"Yeah," that's for sure," said Nate.

"Perhaps Banjo had a point," said Harry.

They sat staring into their beers. Nothing more was said on the subject but Harry did wonder whether a greater force had stepped in to help them on that day.

There was some speculation on what would happen next. Nate had a horrible thought that he might not get paid.

"Hadn't thought about that..." said Marci. "What about you, Harry; what will you do?"

"Go back to the UK, I guess. Looks like I'll be out of a job too."

Nate looked at the pair. "Right drink up you woosies, I'm having another. Harry, mate, what're you having?"

"Not for me, thanks, Nate. I think I'll get off," said Harry.

"Yeah, go on," said Marci. "I'll keep you company."

Harry was expecting more Aussie jibes but Nate just held out his hand. "Right you are, Harry, mate. You take care, ya here."

Harry responded; it was an emotional farewell with hugs all round.

Harry walked back to the car park on his own, leaving Nate and Marci with their refills. The reporters had dispersed and there were only two police vans left. A couple of officers were sat drinking coffee from take-out cups.

Harry got in the Suzuki and for some reason checked the foot-well for any intruding reptiles. One of the officers raised the police tape for him to leave and he headed back to the apartment with the news.

Monique was surprised to see Harry back early but was relieved. She had been trying to sleep but was starting to get flashbacks, not just of Scheck but of the Paris incident too. When she closed her eyes she had visions of water and suffocation.

She hugged Harry.

"What are you going to do?" asked Monique.

"Well, my work here's done, and I can't see me getting any more projects, can you? I'm going to return to the UK as soon as I can. I want you to come with me."

"How is that possible?" said Monique.

"We just buy tickets and go," said Harry.

Epilogue

Liaising with their Australian counterparts, at just before midnight, European time, a squad of Swiss Gendarmerie arrived at the outer perimeter of Chateau Jura commanded by Inspector Serge Armand. As they approached the security gate, Armand spoke to the duty guard and showed him his ID. The barrier was raised and three vans of armed officers made their way to the castle.

The vehicles entered the courtyard and the officers dispersed across the Chateau. It was only a skeleton staff on duty, including a night porter on reception and within minutes the entire building was in lock-down. Over the next six hours, boxes of files and computers were taken away. As the day staff arrived, they were interviewed and sent home, except for the senior executives, who were taken into custody for further interrogation. Specialist teams, familiar with organisational crime, were drawn in to examine the many thousands of documents seized in the raid.

Experts briefly examined a number of soil containers which arrived from Australia just after the raid but they were found to contain nothing untoward, just dirt.

More and more damning evidence was found as the investigation picked up pace. Questions were being asked about the weaponry in the Armoury and a further investigation was started in order to look into illegal arms dealing. It was soon established that a terrorist organisation had been involved through third parties based in Frankfurt; a sideline masterminded by Leonard Scheck but financed by Edward Duchamp.

Duchamp was arrested on his arrival at Geneva International Airport when he returned from Hong Kong. He had not been able to make any contact with the Chateau for the last two days of his trip which had caused him concern; he had no idea what was going on. A team of detectives were waiting for him and he was taken into custody for questioning. All senior executives were interviewed over several weeks including David Leganes. With the net closing in, he agreed to a deal and gave the investigators further vital information. He was able to provide the names of contacts in Frankfurt as well as details of bribes, offered as inducements, to politicians in several countries including Australia.

Back in Darwin, the office was closed down. Nate was the only one of the team to be interviewed by the Australian investigators but he had little to give them. The police were satisfied that his role in the organisation was purely operational.

As the investigation continued in Australia, the role of the Duchamp Foundation was starting to unravel following Becs' disclosures. The enquiries lasted many months with different strands. Bribery, corruption and extortion involving politicians were of particular interest to the Australian authorities. Several politicians who had links with Helvetia, resigned after continuing press articles, primarily from Becs Connolly, gave more details of shady dealings. The Prime Minister was forced to answer questions on 'several matters of importance' relating to his re-election campaign. Helvetia, it was discovered, was a significant donor. Becs' reputation as an investigative journalist was enhanced to the degree that the Pulitzer Prize was being suggested for her work. Her editor believed it was on a par with Bob Woodward and Carl Bernstein of Watergate fame.

In Darwin, the death of Sophie Darling and the disappearance of Professor James Harvey were now being linked to Helvetia. Witnesses from the Aboriginal community and opposition groups were coming forward and giving evidence of intimidation and threats. One name kept surfacing in the investigation; Leonard Scheck. Although based at the Chateau,

Scheck had his own security consultancy which was employed by Helvetia. His office in Frankfurt was raided by German police and evidence was obtained, confirming his connection to the arms dealing operation.

Heinz Schröder, the injured bodyguard and the only Scheck employee to be traced, was eventually interviewed by Australian police in a hospital in Hanover. He was able to give detectives more information about the extortion and murder regime exerted by Scheck. He denied any wrongdoing but said he had heard that Scheck had ordered the killing of both the student and the professor to stop the opposition to the mining proposals. When pressed about these rumours, he claimed he had been told that Professor Harvey had been garrotted by one of the security guards and thrown into the sea. He knew nothing else about the girl. There was no evidence to link the bodyguard with the murders. He eventually left the hospital after almost nine months but would be confined to a wheelchair for the rest of his life.

Warrants were issued for the arrest of Leonard Scheck and several other bodyguards employed by the Duchamp Foundation. Scheck had disappeared and none of the others, including those involved with the attempted murder of Monique Duchamp, could be traced. As part of the investigation, police in Darwin had viewed the office CCTV tapes from the Helvetia offices. It was Nate who identified Scheck but no-one could explain why he would drive the minibus to the office car park at midnight and leave it there. There was nothing to show where he went next and there was no record of him leaving the country; he had disappeared.

Eventually, Nate became a tourist guide as his wife had wanted. Winda joined a local law firm specialising in contracts. Den never returned to the office but did find work as an assistant in a local chandlery. Marci got a job as an administrator at the

University.

It was a week before Harry could sort out his affairs in Australia and get a flight for the two of them. Monique insisted on paying so they could travel business class. With the office closed and no-one to sort out any administration, he packed his suitcases and returned the apartment keys to the agent leaving them to sort everything out. He did the same with his hire car. Monique, meanwhile, continued to suffer from her ordeals. She believed that people were still trying to kill her and had developed agoraphobia; she would not leave Harry's side.

Things improved once they arrived back in the UK. They stayed with Harry's parents for a few days but it was a difficult situation despite the warm hospitality. Monique found it hard to settle and, after two weeks, told Harry that she needed to return to Paris to be closer to her family. She had spoken to Bernice regularly since her return from Australia. She wanted Harry to join her there but he decided to stay and look for other opportunities; he, too, was becoming restless.

It was another emotional farewell for both of them. Harry took her to the airport and watched her walk to the departure lounge. He would never forget Monique Duchamp.

Monique had accepted her sister's invitation to stay with her and her family in Paris until she had got back on her feet. She had not mentioned the Scheck incident in Australia to them but it still continued to haunt her.

She was reading the Sunday papers in the kitchen shortly after her arrival back in Paris and an article caught her eye. The Helvetia case had continued to attract media interest, particularly in France and Switzerland.

"Où est Monique Duchamp?" was the headline. It gave some background and there were pictures of her and her husband in glamorous locations; rumours were rife that she had disappeared. She showed it to Bernice.

"What are you going to do?"

She was in a dilemma. It had served her purpose for Edward to believe she was dead; it had kept her safe. It was her assistant, Françoise Fouvert, who had contacted the authorities, worried because she had heard nothing from Monique for several weeks and was concerned for her safety. Edward, when questioned by police, maintained she was in Paris.

With Edward safely in custody, Monique contacted the Swiss Authorities. She was interviewed by the investigating team about the organisation's affairs but not arrested. She divorced Edward soon afterwards. She still owned a substantial holding in Helvetia but sold her shares and eventually fulfilled an ambition to buy a boutique, specialising in upmarket lingerie and nightwear. It included an apartment above the shop, less than a mile from her sister.

At his trial, Edward Duchamp was convicted of numerous offences including money laundering, illegal arms dealing, bribery, extortion, and tax evasion. He was sentenced to thirty years in jail. David Leganes was sentenced to three years but, in light of his contribution to the investigation, it was suspended.

Helvetia Mining Services Ltd, which was still a very profitable company, was later bought out by a Hedge Fund and is still operating around the world but with an entirely different management team. It has moved its headquarters to an anonymous office block in Geneva.

Harry Bentham eventually joined another mining company and moved to the United States in early 2007.

22nd June 2007

It was a hot day in Paris and the pavement cafes were overflowing with customers enjoying the summer sunshine.

It seemed incongruous that in such weather a man in a sports jacket and Panama hat would be shopping on the Rue de Passy. The man checked the piece of paper again; 'La Courtesan, #28 Rue De Passy'. He could see the address numbers ascending as he walked upwards, against the traffic. Then he was there; just a single window with mannequins dressed in exotic underwear. He would not be the first man to stop and glance at the display models. There were no customers inside; the sign said, 'Ouvre'. He pushed open the door and there was a loud 'clang' from the bell above the mantel. Monique was sat behind her serving counter at the back of the shop, checking some recently arrived stock. She looked up at the customer; men were not always easy to deal with; they had little idea what their wives or girlfriends would like. "No, red would not be a wise choice," she would regularly say.

"Puis-je vous aider," she said.

The man took off his glasses. "I have a message from Edward," he said in English but with a Germanic accent.

"Kurt!" said Monique.

The man pulled a gun from his right-hand jacket pocket and calmly removed a silencer from his left. As he screwed the silencer in place, he spoke to Monique who was frozen with fear. "Edward was surprised you were still alive; he has sent me to remedy that."

The shot hit Monique in the temple; she was dead before she hit the floor.

He dropped the latch on the door, switched the sign to 'Fermé' and left; he was soon swallowed up in the early evening jostle.

Post Script

In August 2012 the Reverend Miki Rey donated all the land designated the 'Kakadu Gap' to the Kakadu National Park, ensuring Uranium mining could never be carried out there, ever.

The End

ALAN REYNOLDS

Following a successful career in Banking, Alan established his own training company in 2002 and has successfully managed projects across a wide range of businesses. This experience has led to an interest in psychology and human behaviour through watching interactions, studying responses and extensive research. Leadership has also featured strongly in his training portfolio and knowledge gained has helped build the strong characters in his books.

His interest in writing started as a hobby but after completing his first novel in just three weeks, the favourable reviews he received encouraged him to take up a new career. The inspiration for his stories comes from real life events with which many people can easily identify.

Alan now has a world-wide following with his books selling in the US, Canada, Australia, across Europe and throughout Asia. In 2015 Flying with Kites won a prestigious Wishing Shelf Award for Adult Fiction and in 2015 The Sixth Pillar was a shortlisted finalist.